BACK AT THE SPIKE

BACK AT THE SPIKE

David Constantine

Ryburn Publishing

This collection first published 1994
by Ryburn Publishing,
an imprint of
Keele University Press,
Staffordshire

Composed by KUP Services
and printed by Hartnolls,
Bodmin, England

'The Home Boy' was previously published in Critical Quarterly.
'The Mermaid' was previously published in Critical Quarterly and
reprinted in Best Short Stories 1992 (Heinemann).
'Trains' was previously published in Iron.

Contents

The Home Boy

For Mary-Ann

Your grandmother can remember the home boys. They came from a home in Warwickshire. They were orphans and where they rightly 'belonged' perhaps nobody knew. They were sent out into employment when they were about as old as you are now. Quite a few came to the islands before the scheme was stopped. I daresay most of them were lucky and got in with people who treated them well. Some, I am sure, found a real home for the first time in their lives. Others weren't so lucky.

The islands were very cut off from the world in those days. There were hardly any visitors, even in summer. The steamer was only once a week. When they heard her come in – she sounded her hooter – the men on the off-islands got ready to meet the launch. They went down to the quay with their ponies and traps.

One Saturday in October there was the usual crowd on the quay (what we call Old Quay now). The mail was the first thing to be landed, nothing very much, in a big sack. Then came drums of oil, boxes of groceries, provisions of all kinds for the winter ahead, each package labelled. Everybody helped with the unloading, except Jago. He sat in his cart, watching the others work. It was rare that the launch brought anything for him. They wondered why he had bothered to come down.

The job looked finished and they were already untying the moorings when Matthew, the boatman, called out: 'Hang on, I've got something else for you here.' He went into the bows and drew back an old oilskin. A little boy came to light, asleep. He wore boots, long trousers and a jersey. He had a flat cap clutched

7

in one hand. And pinned to his jersey was a white label. The boatman woke him gently. The boy opened his eyes and looked up at the quay and the men's faces over him. He had no idea where he was. 'Bad crossing,' said Matthew sympathetically. 'Who's he for?' someone asked. Matthew hesitated. 'Me,' said Jago, from behind the group. He got down off his cart. 'He's for me. Says so on him, I should hope.' And indeed the label on the boy's jersey read: 'Benson. For Jago.'

Matthew lifted the boy up. Jago reached down two great hands and took him. And like that, as though he were any other parcel, Benson was carried to the cart and put behind the seat, not rough-ly, but indifferently. 'Cast off, Sam,' Matthew said. The launch manoeuvred away. The men dispersed without any of the usual fun. Jago was last. A girl, turning her father's pony round, tried to smile at Benson, but the sight of Jago frightened her off.

Jago lived alone at the far end of the island, over by the deep sound. He drove past the others who had called at the post office for any letters. He went on home. It took half an hour and in that time he did not address one word to the boy huddled on the board behind him.

Jago's house was beautifully situated. It looked west over unin-habited islets and black rocks to the open sea and the finest sky for sunsets imaginable. And it had a garden, sheltered by a dense flowering hedge against the southwesterly gales and tilted up to receive the island's long, long hours of sunshine. Jago did nothing to it – he grew a few beans and potatoes for himself – but the garden flourished like a paradise. In season one bank was purple-red, orange and creamy-white with mesembryanthemum; there was a rattling palm-tree, a white-flowering yucca, a line of red-hot pokers and a cascade, a wilderness of geraniums, such as gardeners on the mainland would have paid the earth to have one cutting of. Out of the very walls of the house grew enormous jutting ice-plants, there were trails of aubrietia, alyssum and hon-eysuckle everywhere; not a ledge, not any crack or cornice was untenanted by flowers.

Jago had no liking for the place. He crushed things under foot whenever he moved, he ripped things out for another row of cabbage. He tipped cans and bottles in a heap without any thought. He was big, overweight, all his movements were clumsy.

Now Benson, one of the home boys, was to work for him. Jago gave the boy a room upstairs, quite unfurnished, with a mattress along one wall under the window. Benson knelt there when Jago had gone, and looked out. He could see the beach and the deep sound and the little boats, some pulled up, some agitated at their moorings. The tide was setting fast. The sky that way was very red. Benson felt sick again, thinking of the steamer. The wind was getting up. The window was ill-fitting and he felt a draught. He saw men go down with ponies and ropes and haul in their boats far up the beach. The year was closing down and Benson was on the island as distant as possible from the middle of England where the big institution stood which until then he had thought of as home.

Night fell and a storm began. Jago came in with a blanket and a tin bowl half full of soup. Still he said nothing to the boy. The window rattled, rain hit it as though flung in fistfuls. Jago closed the door, Benson heard the key turn. He tried to eat the soup but couldn't. Then he lay shivering under the blanket. He had never heard such noises as the wind was making. It was thrashing the waves of the sound, flailing them and ripping at every upright and crouching thing, coming from over the whole extent of the Atlantic sea, as from the far end of the universe. Later he would grow used to the wind; he grew to like it better than the noises Jago made. He could distinguish its tones and notes and how they were formed – whether sieving through the hedge, whipping round angles of stone or thwacking at the roofs of houses and sheds. In the dark he became able to see with the mind's eye what things the wind was hitting, how hard and to what effect. And the blows of the wind were preferable to the blows dealt him by Jago.

That first night the storm blew itself out in the small hours. Perhaps Benson slept, for it seemed to him suddenly that he had been transported yet again. The house was wrapped in a damp silence. A sea-fog writhed slowly at the glass. Then through that silence, regularly but always as a terrible shock to his heart, came

the groan and lingering reverberation of the fog-horn and a weak
red light flickered across his room. Those were the experiences of
the little boy called Benson who had come from the very inland
heart of the country for the first time to the sea. Those were the
clearest things, the wind, the tormented waves, the fog-horn and
the light, and they were things he got used to and even grew to
like. But there was more besides in that first night, and worse, the
voice of a man somewhere below him, a man singing or groan-
ing, a sound he could not understand and one he wished the
hurtling, frightening wind would cover.

They were asking why Jago wanted a work-boy anyway. He
wasn't a worker himself, half his land was unused. Profits didn't
interest him. 'Perhaps he's lonely,' said Gibson, a man whom
profits did interest. And they all laughed. There wasn't a policeman
on the off-islands. Nor is there now, for that matter. But there
wasn't even one on Cressa in those days. Not much wrongdoing
is expected in small communities. Everybody knows everybody
else. The community sees to all its members, like a family. Jago
wasn't the only odd person on the island by any means; but some
of the other eccentrics were odd in a sociable sort of way. Jago
was very unsociable, he lived as far away from the ordinary people
as it was possible to live. Not that he could be blamed for where
he lived. He had the house from his father, who had also been
odd and also in an unsociable sort of way.

After the storm the islanders went down with their carts for
seaweed. Jago went too, Benson riding behind. The smell of it
made the boy retch. Jago pitchforked huge loads of the heavy stuff
on to the cart. Benson saw the little sea-creatures wriggling desperately in it. He walked back up the sandy lane from the beach
holding the mare's reins. He liked the mare. Suddenly he remembered the girl who had wanted to smile at him, how she had
turned her father's horse gently to the slope. That was the one
nice thing about yesterday, he thought. But he was in such a
confusion that he couldn't have said for certain whether she was
on his island or not.

Jago's fields were not so isolated as his house. They adjoined
others, where men were also working. Benson led the horse slowly

up and down while Jago forked the weed on to the earth, to fertilize it. They made several trips. It came on to rain. Jago gave the boy an oilskin to wear – his hands vanished in the sleeves, he tripped in the folds – and they continued working. When they had a break they sat together against the wheel of the cart. The wet streamed off Jago; the boy looked clownish and minute beside the man. He ate the mouthful of dry cake that was offered him. The rain came on heavier and they packed up for the day. While Jago unharnessed the mare and rubbed her down Benson stood in the yard, not knowing what to do. Jago turned and bumped into him. 'God damn you,' he said, 'get out of my way.' Those were the first words he said to Benson and saying them he lashed out with his hand and smacked the boy over the face, so that he fell down in the puddles. Benson crawled up against the house wall, as much out of the rain as he could get. The plants stuck out of the stones high above him. They looked like limbs, their appearance frightened him.

Jago had gone indoors. Benson sat where he was. He heard the mare snuffle and shake herself in the dry stable. He thought he would go in there with her, but half way across the yard he was halted by Jago's voice calling horrible words at him. He withdrew to the wall.

In the late afternoon the rain stopped and a mild, warm light slanted from under the sagging clouds into the garden, full on the wall where Benson sat. He watched the drenched flowers steaming in the late warmth. The vapour seemed their visible scent. And one blackbird began singing, in a pure and confident voice. Benson had nobody to miss. He had not been taken from a mother and father to this place. There was nobody in the home he remembered with particular affection.

From indoors, from the room above him, came a sickening noise, the sounds he had half-heard under the wind the night before. He could not call it sad or angry, he could give no name to it. Then the window opened, so that the noise was louder; there were words to it, but he could not make them out and did not want to. A bottle flew through the air and smashed among others in a heap by the hollyhocks. Benson stayed out till dark.

Then the door opened and Jago motioned him inside. He expected to be hit but instead he was given the tin bowl half full of soup
and this time he ate. He lay on his mattress in the empty room.
He dreaded that he would hear the noise again. He hoped the
wind would rise deafeningly. But the night remained very silent.
Benson slept. He was woken either minutes or hours later by a
crash so heavy it rattled the window above him. After that the house
was silent, like something struck unconscious. Benson slept. The
next thing he heard was the pure birdsong at first light. He lay looking at the sky which became clear blue. But it was late morning
before the key turned in the lock and he was let out for the day.

The islands are not called the Fortunate Isles for nothing. After
the bad gales in October and November, when for days at a time
nobody stirs abroad, and after days on end of unmoving dense
fog, when the land seems dissolved in damp air, then comes a
mildness before Christmas and the earliest of the flowers are ready
to be picked. The islanders did not entirely forget about Benson,
the home boy, but when they did think of him, when they were
cooped up indoors and even the most harmonious families were
getting on each other's nerves, it was with bad consciences. He
was something they remembered unwillingly. They did not like
to think of him in Jago's care. They shuddered to think what his
life must be like in that house whose door nobody passed. Had he
lived nearer, they said, they might have called, in a casual way, to
see how he was managing. As it was, they had no business at that
end of the island; or rather, what business they had they saw to
quickly, with a guilty look at Jago's uncurtained windows. James
Goddard went to see to his boat one day and confessed to his
neighbours afterwards that he had heard the boy crying out 'don't
hit me, mister, don't 'ee hit me like that' – and the neighbours
made it their business to tell the Minister when he came over the
following Sunday. But the Minister was on circuit from the mainland and the best he could do was tell the police and six or seven
weeks later all that happened was that Goddard himself, who was
an island councillor and an elder in the community, was asked to
keep an eye on things, if he could. Then he felt he had been a
fool for interfering in the first place.

Adjoining fields were separated by very high windbreak hedges, so dense they were impossible to see through. They made up a maze of squares and oblongs and only the islanders knew their way about, through narrow gaps from one field to the next. They were very still, sunless days when the picking began. Jago had a couple of small fields of early sols, on the rising sandy ground just above the beach. He showed Benson the knack of picking. The boy looked in horror at the man's great finger and thumb, at the tufts of black hair on the backs of his hands. He snapped the flowers off callously and tucked them back in his fist so that the heads wagged as though the necks might break. Benson was given four rows nearest the hedge to do, he was to lay down the flowers in bunches whenever his fist could not hold any more. He worked uphill. Jago moved away to the other side and lumbered hideously up the rows, laying down bunch after bunch as though they were birds or animals whose necks his hands had wrung.

At first Benson was bad at the work. He could neither snap the stems quickly nor hold the picked flowers in his grasp. He expected Jago to come over and punish him. He was sobbing in fear. Since he was too small to reach over the rows as a grown man would he edged along in the narrow space immediately under the hedge, which meant, of course, that he was wrong side on for picking. But he was afraid to go in among the rows for fear of treading down the flowers.

Most of the islanders were busy picking. Benson could hear some of them in the next field; there was a remark every now and then, and laughter. The voices were distinct and pleasant in the stillness. At a greater distance he heard two men shouting a conversation with one another over an intervening hedge. It seemed to Benson that they must be throwing their voices high, to clear the hedge-top. He looked up: the hedge was three or four times his size.

It was then that he heard the whistling. He could tell neither who nor what was making it, nor exactly where it was coming from. He thought it the loveliest sound he had ever heard, and he was afraid that Jago would beat him for listening to it. He dropped the flowers and covered up his ears. 'Shh!' he said to himself, 'oh please do hush.' But the whistling went on, it was inventive, like a blackbird's singing. Jago was coming over. The whistling ceased. He picked up the few bunches Benson had already laid down: grasped in his fist they looked nothing. There was a strange look on his face, not just the anger Benson expected, but a sort of misery too. He stood looking down at Benson, the boy cowered away, shielding his head. Through his raised hands he saw the man squeeze with all his strength on the flowers, until their juices ran out in a trickle from his closed fist. Then they were useless and Jago tossed them on the ground. 'God damn you, get on with it,' he muttered, and turned to go. When he was only a few yards distant the whistling, that was really to be called a singing such as birds make, began again. Jago halted in his tracks, and there was an innocent silence. When he continued the beautiful voice resumed. Jago bent over his work like one trying not to listen; or perhaps at that distance he really could not hear.

In fact there was soon no such sound to be heard and Benson crept up the hill picking in silence. But next came a voice whispering his name. Or not his name proper, but what he might naturally be called by someone who liked him: 'Ben, Ben, can you hear me?' He did not dare reply, but nor did he want the voice to go away. He looked across at Jago. 'Aye,' he whispered, not daring to move his lips, 'aye, I can that.' He stood up with a fistful of flowers ready. Before the hedges had been planted there were only stone walls between the fields. These survived, though overgrown and concealed by the greenery. Where Ben stood the wall was very low, there was only the dense thickness of branches and glossy leaves between him and the voice. 'Listen for me when we move up,' it said. Ben went on picking and the voice kept exact pace with him. Mostly it was the whistling, threading the hedge alongside him like an underground stream, but sometimes, in clear tones, he was asked: 'Can you hear me, Ben?' and he answered through clenched teeth, as loud as he dared: 'Aye, I can that.'

Then Jago went out of the field. 'Quick, Ben, feel,' said the voice, and the hedge rustled exactly where he was. He put in his hand, in among the dense leaves, and with eyes on the gap at which Jago would reappear he felt desperately to find the hand searching for him. And his hand touched the girl's before Jago came back, her hand was as small and warm as Benson's was. He carried on working and the girl whistled through the stones of the wall and through the foliage of the hedge, in pure merriment at having outwitted Jago, all the way to the top of the field. There Jago called him away and made him load up the bunches that were already picked and together, either side the mare's head, they went back to the packing-house.

Benson knew she was the girl he had seen on the quay. He had not once been there again since his arrival on the island. Jago had only gone down a couple of times himself and had left Benson locked up indoors. But now they had two dozen boxes of flowers to send off. The launch was due. Benson loaded the cart. There wouldn't be room for him anyway since he couldn't very well sit on the cardboard boxes. He was expecting to be locked in his room. Why then did Jago let him go and even make a place for him on the driver's seat where he had never been allowed to sit before on all their trips down to the beach or the fields? Benson did not know. He sat by the man who was worse than an ogre to him, saw the reins in his great ugly hands, looked up in fascination and terror at the black unshaven face. The smell of Jago's clothes, the muttering of his lips, the dirt on his boots – everything was a horror to the boy. But he was going down to the quay. James Goddard saw them pass the post office and said that perhaps things weren't so bad after all.

She was there on the quay with her father and her brother. They had four dozen boxes to send off. She watched for a moment to meet his eyes. When Jago seemed preoccupied she pursed out her lips, to show him that she was the one who could whistle like a blackbird. Then the launch drew alongside and Ben worked in the line of men handing down the boxes. Everyone wished him well but he kept his eyes lowered. He had the feeling that he would suffer for every kind look he answered. He dared not even wave to Matthew, the boatman, as the launch, laden with flowers for the big cities, headed away. He turned back. He still wore his home clothes, he had no others, they were dirty and getting ragged. The cap would have suited an old man better. Passing to Jago's cart he dared to look at her once more. She was leaning against the tailboard of her father's cart. As Ben passed she stood quickly aside: she had chalked her name there in clear letters. Ben shook his head miserably. He couldn't read. She covered her name up again. Jago was behind him and perhaps he saw.

As soon as they got home Jago took a rope's end to the boy. He hit him without mercy. Then he tied him by the leg to a tethering ring in the yard and left him there for the night. In the night Benson, his body stiff with cold and pain, heard Jago in his room howling to himself. The boy stopped his ears, but he heard the great heavy man, drunk and in misery, cry out to God to strike him dead, to make an example of him and strike him down dead with fire. But it did not happen that night. Instead the sky rained pitilessly on Benson.

It was time to be making the pots ready and seeing to the boats. There were some mild sunny days early in the year before anyone on the mainland dared think of spring, and although the commercial flowers were picked in bud, so that only the families in the cities saw them opened, still the island, and her sister islands, flowered abundantly. There were old fields left unpicked where the bulbs thrived on their own and put forth year after year in white, orange and yellow. There were mild moist days when the ground stirred with things growing. Jago took the boy down to the deep sound, unlocked a shed on the headland and set him to checking and making good the lobster pots.

'It's deep out there, boy,' he said. 'Aye, mister,' said Benson. 'There's a hole out there as 'ud swallow a fleet. The *Olaf* went down there and only one come ashore of all her crew and 'twere my father found him – just below here – and d'you know, boy, he hadn't a stitch on him when he come ashore and his own mother wouldn't have knowed him, for he'd been in that great hole, see.' 'Aye, mister,' said Benson, trembling.

When the boat was caulked and painted Jago took Benson out in it, on a flat calm day. Before they shoved off he took a large stone from the beach, as heavy almost as he could lift, and set it between his feet while he rowed. Benson sat in the stern, the man never shifted his eyes from off his face. Soon they were out in the deep sound. There was a coolness, of the open sea. Then Jago shipped his oars and the boat rocked gently and almost noiselessly.

Slowly the bows turned until they were pointing to the small headland where Jago kept his pots. 'Be about here, I reckon,' said the man, watching the boy's face. 'Just about here.' He lifted the stone, held it overboard at the extent of his arms, held it until they trembled with the weight, then lowered it gently, leaning until the boat tilted, until the stone was touching the surface of the sea. Then he let go. The stone vanished instantly and without a sound, breathing up a few bubbles. Jago looked at Benson: 'D'you take my meaning, boy?' 'Aye, mister,' said Ben, white in the face. 'Well then, we'll go homealong.' And he began rowing again. Ben sat feeling sick, but as they neared the shore, over Jago's shoulder, he noticed the girl. She was standing on the headland waving to him, behind the man's back. There she stayed until they were very close in, and Ben watched her furtively.

Thereafter when they went potting together the same fear was in Ben's mind, though Jago made no more insinuations and it was into much shallower water than the great hole that the pots, with their bait of dried gurnard, went bubbling down. There was no money in crabs; none, at least, in the smallish ones Jago caught. He ripped off their claws and tossed them back and boiled up the bits for his supper in a saucepan at home. But when he got a lobster he took the trouble to sell it to Stevens near the post office who dealt with a retailer's on the mainland.

In spring, when Ben had endured with Jago for a quarter of a year, he began thinking how he might escape. He woke early and knelt at the window. In the sound he saw the small boats moored again. Supposing he could cross at least that stretch of water? One island after another stepped down in diminishing sizes further and further out to sea. They were all uninhabited. Was he to hide there, with the colonies of rats? Sometimes ocean-going ships passed within sight, occasionally they even anchored in the deeper water off Treseal. One day a warship came and rode overnight at anchor in the deep sound, where Jago said the *Olaf* had gone down. Benson never thought very much of the mainland, it was so distant. Besides, there was nothing for him in England.

Jago drank himself into a stupor most afternoons. Beforehand he took the precaution of locking Benson up or tethering him like an animal in the yard. Curiously enough, he was never cruel when he was drunk. When he beat the boy he was in sober mind. But drunk he was very miserable and it was then, late in the afternoons, that he called on Almighty God to punish him. He never made amends there and then by releasing the boy and showing him some kindness. Instead he inflicted his misery on the boy's ears. When the brandy bottle was empty he flung it through the window on to the pile by the hollyhocks. Soon after that he fell asleep; often, quite literally, he fell to the floor. Then there was an hour or so of peace and quiet. Ben lay nursing his sore places and wishing he could die or escape. The birds came out of the garden close to him, rabbits ventured through the hedge and fed on the vegetables and more often than not the sun shone and the garden bloomed and scented as though in joy and relief that Jago was absent for a time.

Then one day when he had been so maltreated that his wish to die was greater than his wish to escape Ben distinguished among the variety of birdsong in the garden the imitative whistling of the girl, and before he could raise himself up she had slipped through a gap in the hedge and was lying next to him on the dusty ground under the iron ring to which he was attached. She brushed the hair out of his eyes. Her cleanness and prettiness and charity were like qualities of another world to Ben; and his fear of what would happen to her and to him spoiled his joy and the beginnings of pity for himself and love and gratitude for her. 'He'll lather you,' he said, 'go back quick to your mam and dad.' 'He's sleeping,' she said, 'like a porky pig.' Ben lay with his eyes on the window. 'What's your name?' he asked, 'tell me quick, 'fore he wakes and lams into me.' 'Anna,' she said. 'Write it quick in letters.' She wetted a finger and wrote the name in capitals, in the dust where they both lay. Then he took his eyes off the window: how simple and beautiful the name looked. 'Anna,' he said, 'one way an' t'other.' 'You do it,' she said. 'Can't,' Benson replied. She took his hand in hers, pointed his finger and drew the name with it, below her own letters, in the dust. 'You can write,' she said. 'Listen: I'll help you escape.' But then Jago stirred in the room across the yard. His manner of waking was to give a howl of loathing. The rabbits fled, the robin flew from the yard. Anna, in all her haste to be gone, was yet held for a moment by that sound. She wrinkled her brows, as though it were more puzzling to her than terrible. But Ben pushed her away, and rubbed out the letters with his hand. Rising to her feet, already leaving the garden, she whispered to him: 'my dad goes out to the crabbers.' Then she had disappeared and Ben lay against the wall under the ring, like a bundle of rags, his heart pounding against the dirty ground in fear and love.

For a week he did not see her again. He knelt on his mattress in the early morning, wondering about the crabbers. When he and Jago went out with the pots he wondered all the more. Would they come in on land and punish Jago for ripping the claws off their brood? – and then take him, Benson, away to somewhere safe? In the serene weather Jago's mood was worsening. He addressed the boy with nothing but blows; he ducked him in the horse-trough and left him gasping in the sun for breath. Then, a week after Anna had been, he took Ben coldly out into the yard, tied him to the ring and lifted not a rope's end but a stick against him. He had struck the boy once, with all the force of his arm, and was preparing to strike again, when something hardly to be called self-control halted him, some trick of the sun, so that it struck him in the eyes and there, cold sober, he was put in mind of his wish to be dealt with by God and he dropped the stick and ran indoors and in a short time two bottles had smashed into the hollyhocks. With the silence, with the birds and the rabbits, Anna came, carrying a great clasp-knife and cut Benson free. The stick had ripped open his jersey and the weal across his back was horrible for the girl to see. He could hardly stand, she had to lead him through the garden and tug him bodily after her through the hedge. But when Jago woke with his yell of disgust and staggered to the window to see what harm he had done only a length of rope remained, dangling from the ring – and at that Jago roared like a mad thing and clutched at his head and at his heart and toppled from the window in to a dense deep bed of burning bright flowers and lay among them, stupid, until dusk.

But then he roused himself, swilled his face at the horse-trough, picked up his stick and went in search of Benson. He checked first that the boat wasn't missing and looked in the shed where the pots were kept. Then he followed the coast path round the western end of the island. He climbed, cursing, to the outcrop known as Bishop Rocks and came back over the headland to within sight of his own house. The boy might be anywhere. Somebody would have taken him in. By now it was almost dark. He fetched a lantern from home and knocked on the nearest doors with his stick. Nobody had seen the boy. He stamped from their thresholds in fury and disbelief. He trudged the length of the island, all along the southern shore, as far as the quay. A few men sat there in the dark against the wall, smoking. They already knew. 'Lost the boy, have you?' said one voice. 'Shouldn't have treated him so rough,' said another. Jago swung round in a rage, the lantern light dashed on to their faces. They ducked in alarm. 'You sure you lost him?' asked Jenkins, one of the bolder men. 'Sure it wasn't a accident on purpose?' Jago might have struck him but at that moment, against what light was left in the western sky, a couple of small boats were seen putting slowly out, crossing the deep sound. 'Who's that?' Jago asked, his voice hampered with anger and agitation. 'Who's that?' 'Reg and Clarence, for your brandy,' said Jenkins sardonically. Jago began running hopelessly along the beach. The men behind him laughed. He tripped, and the lantern smashed. He ran on in the dark. Midway along he raised his voice in a great cry. Safe in her bed Anna heard him and shuddered, and again wrinkled her brows in puzzlement at a certain note she detected in that cry.

Benson was gone. He was in one of the boats with Clarence, Anna's father. They were making their monthly trip to meet the Breton crabbers, out of the way, behind Treseal. They had sides of pork on board, and woollen and cotton goods from the mainland, to trade with the Bretons for brandy. And that night Benson was traded too. In the morning Clarence left an extra bottle with Jago's quota, as a joke.

So much for Ben's escape. But that is not the end of the story. Very few people ever knew the truth. It was soon put about, even by those who knew better, that Jago had taken the boy out and drowned him in the deep sound, where the *Olaf* went down. Jago himself could not be sure either. He remembered hitting the boy with a stick, fit to kill him. After that he couldn't say. But when a policeman came, almost a year after Ben's disappearance, Jago denied having drowned him and since nobody on the island had anything to say, the matter was dropped. Ben was, after all, only a home boy.

Anna knew where he was. He was on the Breton boats that hove to behind Treseal once a month. For two years she wrote him simple messages in capital letters and her father passed them on when he swapped his goods for brandy. She hoped that somehow he would be learning to read. Then she was sent to school on Cressa and couldn't communicate with him, except in the holidays. His first message back to her was written in neat capitals, in French. She couldn't understand it. After the holidays she took her note to school, stole the dictionary and translated her message from Benson word by word. He asked her could she whistle still like a blackbird. When she was next home she squeezed through the gap into Jago's beautiful garden and crouched hidden among the flowers and listened to him howling and calling on God to strike him dead with a bolt from the skies. She crept forward until she could see the tethering ring in the yard. The length of rope still hung from it. Then, in hiding, she pursed up her mouth and sang and whistled like a blackbird. Soon Jago fell silent.

Anna became outstandingly good at French. She read everything the school had. She did her set work in no time, did some more for good measure, and then composed letters to Ben. In the holidays first her father, later her brother, traded them for Ben's replies.

When she was eighteen her parents sent her to college on the mainland. Now she enclosed her letters for Ben in her letters home. She had every intention of going to France and there would have been no need to abscond, her parents had nothing against it. She was home over the summer helping her father with the bulb-planting, She was to have gone in September, before the new college term. But then war was declared. She stayed home and listened on the wireless to the news that France was overrun. Then Ben wrote to her, still in French, from Brighton. He had been with his fishing-boat at Dunkirk. Now he was with the Free French.

The islands did very well during the war. The flower-farmers made money hand over fist. Flowers were in demand, for funerals. Jago worked his two or three fields as before. When asked by Gibson why he didn't bestir himself and join in the gold-rush he replied that he didn't want to make profits on corpses.

Nothing much happened to the Fortunate Isles during the war. There was nothing to bomb. Almost the only incident occurred at Christmas time in 1940, when the the cities on the mainland were being systematically flattened. Jago had picked the field Benson had helped him with years before, and had loaded up the cart with bunches of early sols. He was leading the mare out on to the sandy coast path home. By chance Anna met him there. She was bringing the men their snack. She had never in her life exchanged one word with him; nor, of course, since she was grown up, had she ever been again into his garden. Now they met, full on the path – the beach and the sea to one side, hedges and the sandy flower-fields to the other. She need not have stopped, but she did. She was thinking of Ben and she thought she saw in Jago's ugly, havocked face that he, on seeing her, was thinking of him too. Never having exchanged a word before they both now began together, without any formalities of good-day or how are you, and speaking together neither heard what the other said, and both halted in embarrassment. Anna motioned Jago to speak first but he did not succeed in saying anything, for at that moment the island suffered its one attack from the air. One sole fighter plane came in very low and very fast from the south, over Cressa, and for the merest, idlest pleasure its pilot strafed the beach and the fields where Anna and Jago stood. She saw the plane first in his eyes, she saw his mouth say 'God', then he fell on her and knocked all the breath from her body.

The plane had gone. There was some shouting. The men ran out of the fields on to the path that goes so leisurely and sweetly through the rushes along the dunes. Anna's father was calling her name. He was the first to come upon Jago lying inert, a dreadful deadweight. His jacket was ripped across. Anna was discovered beneath him, with blood on her face from Jago's mouth. As soon as she could speak she said that old man Jago had saved her life. But in general this was not believed.

Jago did not die, not for several years. He came back, badly crippled and unable to enunciate his words clearly, from the hospital on Cressa. He lived in one room, the one giving on to the garden, and Anna made it her business to look after him. She cut the remaining rope from the iron ring. For most of the day he stared dully down at his hands. He drank a little in the afternoons. Anna got to know what his words were. She would bend to listen. He was saying that God had struck him dead.

Ben came to the island on leave. He and Anna conversed in French. His English made her laugh. They came into Jago's garden together. Anna pursed her lips, cupped her hands and whistled so like a blackbird, with such confidence, purity of tone, abundance and joy, that Jago looked up. He saw Ben standing with her – and at first it was almost worse than the fire from the skies.

Under the Bridge

Meg was discharged from the hospital but her next-of-kin did not come for her. Nobody did. She sat among the outpatients, then in the tea-room with the visitors. When visiting time was over she was noticed by a nurse, who said she should be on her way. She joined the other poor people in the bus shelter. The wind blew in through its broken panes. The wind came over the flat country on which the hospital was set like a camp. The verges along the dead straight road were black. The bus did not come. A mother and her daughter began to walk, the daughter tottering on modish heavy shoes that gave her the appearance of a cripple. They clutched one another and tried to keep straight on the black grass. But the road continued perpetually. Others also began to walk.

The bus came. Meg was taken into town and those by the roadside between stops were not, though they waved and cursed. In town she waited for another bus. She thought she might as well go home.

She had asked for the chapel, but where the bus stopped there was no chapel. The conductress watched her hesitate, but did not offer any explanation. Then she snapped: 'D'you want this stop or don't you?' and rang the bell. Meg stepped down as the bus began to move. There was no chapel. There was a flat wasteland of broken bricks. One building stood: The Loves, but nothing else in the vicinity, and even the lines of the streets had been obliterated. Meg picked up her suitcase and walked to where the houses began again. Her own street was the first, it adjoined the wasteland now. Had she been gone so long? There were not even any bulldozers in sight. The work was finished, they were going to leave it like that. The wind came over the new space.

At home – she walked in the back way without knocking – Meg found she had been replaced. A woman she did not know was preparing a meal, her husband was dozing by the fire. They said they were not expecting her so soon. The woman made her a cup of tea. Meg looked round: most of the things were still as they had been, there were no new photographs. 'I see the chapel's gone,' she said. 'Aye,' said the woman, 'the Club's gone too. Now he has to walk to Crook.' Meg stood up and went out the way she had come in. She walked in a straight line to The Loves, over the flattened bricks; and from there diagonally to the bus shelter, which was the only upright in her view. The bus came after half an hour with its lights on. It was the same conductress.

Meg thought the town might be warmer than what remained of Springwell was. She wanted more upright buildings around her. The flat land worried her. She sat with her suitcase on her knees. Remembering her pills, she took the bottle out of her coat pocket and swallowed two. Everybody looked. Her eyes were becoming peculiar again, the faces of the other passengers stretched and shrank. She would have left her case on the bus, but the conductress shouted after her.

Meg moved to a bus stand where there was nobody waiting. But still a bus came. She moved away and joined a long queue. When a bus came she stood aside and the people passed her – one, two, three, four, and so on into the twenties. She moved once more. A queue formed behind her, a bus came. She ran into the café. She had money enough for a cup of tea. She laid all the coins on the counter and the woman took what it cost. Meg was able to hide her case under the table and nobody called after her when she left. Nor was it raining.

Later she was walking by the river. The flood had only gone down that afternoon. The paths were muddy and under the bridges there was a smell not of piss but of the river. She stood close to the edge, the water slid past with great rapidity, level with the path. The place smelled like the grave and was as dark. Meg became aware that somebody else was with her in the vault. She heard him move. She thought of stepping into the river to avoid him. Instead, she turned. He had come out of hiding against the wall. She saw white hands and a white face, otherwise nothing. Taking her by the shoulders he drew her away from the water and forced her against the wall. His left hand came over her mouth: she felt it to be very cold, but soft and nerveless. She bit into the skin, but then began to weep in pity for them both, and had he relaxed his force a little she would have kissed his hand. He tore at her clothing, she heard him begin to sob. He found her blouse, the belt and buttons of her skirt. She would almost have helped him, he was so maladroit. He sobbed, she heard how close and high the river ran behind his back. Then all conviction left him and he lapsed. For pity she would have held him. Indeed, something like hope revived in her, seeing one so helpless. But in his loathing he raised his hands away from her and covered his white face. Meg saw that they had some common ground and in excitement said to him: 'I love you.' But at that he opened his hands and ran off with a cry. Meg was left. There had been no embrace, neither was any the warmer.

In the night she was found by the police, who supposed from the disarray of her clothing that she must have suffered an assault. But she would not make any statement, nor give any details about herself except that she was ill. There were some telephone calls on her behalf. Then she was taken from the police station to the town psychiatric hospital and given a clean nightdress and pills to make her sleep.

They soon knew who she was and where she was from. To her disgust they recovered her suitcase from the café at the bus station. She said she was homeless, but they said she had an address to go to. She said the house had been pulled down. She was perhaps mistaken but it seemed to her from the doctor's tone of voice that they were not prepared to let her stay. She asked for her clothes. The buttons of her coat were all ripped off. The bottle was still in the pocket. Meg turned her back on the nurse and swallowed the pills remaining. They were not sufficient to harm her much, but she hoped the nurse would not know that.

The stratagem worked, she was allowed to stay. But there was some resentment against her – she had forced their hand – and she was not treated kindly. In anger one day a nurse shouted that everybody knew about her dealings with men. They knew what she had been doing the night the police brought her in. Thereafter Meg felt she had the name of a bad woman. Thinking about the event, she felt a rush of excitement. The blood surged from her heart, her lips were dry as though in fear, and before she could control herself or dissemble she was laughing and weeping ecstatically. She was given a sedative and put to bed. She scolded herself: she must be more secretive in future. The memory was a very potent one. It possessed her body and soul. The poor boy, what pity she had felt. She, Meg, had felt pity. She wept silently, in pure compassion.

When she woke she felt she had only dreamed. There remained the usual dullness in the head. She felt cheated, but of what she could not be sure. She had dreamed a happiness, and lost it again on waking. Meg went carefully through her belongings. The nurses had been stealing from her. She looked them full in the face when they brought her meals. She ate the food defiantly, knowing it was poisoned.

She was at liberty to walk about the female wards, and into the day-room where the chairs were set around the walls. She would sit there for a time and stare, with the other women, at the space left in the centre. It seemed intended for a spectacle, but nothing happened; or rather any occurrence there, the passage of any patient or attendant, seemed itself a spectacle. One afternoon a couple of women fought, and those seated around the walls applauded and jeered. The two women were taken away to the locked ward.

Soon Meg's status was that of a voluntary patient. She could go when she liked, they were not obliged to keep her; indeed, they could discharge her when they liked. She told herself that in fact she was incarcerated. They would arrest her at the gates. But also she was afraid of being expelled. She believed them capable of any wickedness. The best energies of her mind were spent on fathoming their ways. She watched intently, for long periods her mind was never vacant, she took note of every movement, word and tone. At the same time she applied herself to concealing what her preoccupations were. She forced herself to appear unconcerned;

she strove to answer civilly and to seem unafraid. She spent entire
days in these obsessions.

Then she would wake and find the drama had ended. There
was nothing after all. Her existence was not threatened by anything so definite as other people. They were indifferent to her and
she to them. She was left to herself. She feared nothing so much
as these collapses of her drama. When there were no ostensible
reasons within her grasp she was left without any reason for her
condition. Then she knew they would not arrest her at the gate.
She could leave when she liked.

When asked about her next-of-kin she said she had none. But
they were able to discover that she was married. They also told
her that she had two children, but she insisted that she was
childless. Then some called her a liar; others said it was a mark of
her illness. She was a bad woman and a liar. Or she was ill. At
times she was deeply affected by their opinions. She wept at the
injustice they did her; or took the censure to heart, and wept over
her own badness. Then she was strict with herself, believing that
severity, even if unjust, would do her more good than would
understanding and condonement. But again she became indifferent. What they thought and what she thought herself was of no
consequence. She knew there was more hope in anxiety than in
indifference. But nothing could prevent indifference when it
chose to come. And in that state they might thrust needles into
her, she would feel nothing.

Waking early she heard the rain. She was frightened, but
nobody came to mind whom she might call. There was a bluish
light at the end of the ward, where two nurses sat talking. Meg
was afraid they would know she had woken early. She hid her
face. Of those sleeping none breathed easily and quietly. Under
sedation they still suffered their dreams. Waking early, hearing the
rain, Meg would have liked to hold somebody, to be held by
somebody, even by such as the sleepers were who lay under their
own nightmares. The rain vertical, the rain slanting, while the
river flowed from under it, increasing. Over the open spaces, of
black fields, of flattened brick – the rain horizontal, into the faces
of people walking to the bus-stop or to The Loves. 'Where

should you like to die, Meg?' she asked herself, if it could not be
at home in her own bed with the family around her. She was not
ill enough to die. It was not an illness patients died of. It would
be years before she died in the natural way, as many years as she
had already lived. When she heard the rain she did not want to
die out of doors. She asked herself was she afraid of dying. She
answered that it was the cold she was afraid of and the wet.
Further, that it was not dying she was afraid of but living. She was
not one of those who die or want to die because they have nothing to live for. She had nothing to live for, but that of itself would
not cause her to want to die. She was one who would die or wish
to die because she was frightened by the life she had. She was an
incapable person. She could not see to a man's needs, she had not
brought up her children successfully, she had nothing to say that
would ever affect anyone. And left to herself, giving nothing
to anybody, still she could not be nothing and no trouble to
anybody, but must ask for assistance and attention. Because her
own single self – no good to anyone – was more than she was
capable of looking after by herself. She could not take a room and
manage week by week; she could not cook, not even for herself;
or do the washing, even only her own; or keep house, even alone.
And why not? She answered that it frightened her. Life did not
have to assume any unusual forms, but as it appeared day by day
it frightened her.

There were patients who at the least occasion said: 'I'll kill
myself.' Soon this gage of seriousness amounted to very little. 'I
mean it,' they added, 'I really mean it.' But it was not in its being
disbelieved that the threat they made amounted to very little.
When the others – the patients and the staff – 'did not take such
a person seriously' it was not that they did not believe he would
one day do what he said, but that they did not care whether he
did it or not. Meg saw a youth in Therapy one morning goaded
into opening his veins with a pair of scissors. He said: 'I'll fucking
kill myself.' 'Go on then,' said a voice. 'I fucking will,' he said,
'I fucking mean it.' 'Go on then,' said another voice, itself wearied
to death. And the boy dug into his wrist with the steel points. Then
he sat weeping with pain and shame until he was taken away

angrily by a charge nurse. 'I fucking shown 'em,' he said, holding up his wrist. But he knew he and his life-blood did not matter.

Meg did not believe the assurances of the Chaplain that she, like all God's children, was able to be loved. She saw that he, the Chaplain, did not love her. Or she did not see that he did. He was busy, and whilst he was speaking to her his eyes were wandering down a list. He was speaking of the love shown her by the doctors and nurses. But Meg did not believe they loved her. She believed herself to be the material of their employment. Sometimes they said to a difficult patient: 'Our job would be a lot easier without people like you.' Certainly, some patients strove to be as exasperating as possible. Confined to bed they would foul the sheets. Or they provoked what punishments the hospital had it in its power to inflict: the loss of voluntary status (so that they might be confined against their will), or the loss of compulsory status (so that they might be evicted against their will), or confinement in the locked ward with the violent and the malcontents. Then there remained only the threat, and finally the act, of suicide. This, if it followed closely on one or another of the hospital's punishments, was an effective insult or embarrassment, and might seem worth a life at the time.

In desperation or out of cruelty a nurse would occasionally threaten a patient with ECT. The conditions of this therapy were so like those of torture that merely to mention it excited terror. A terrorised patient would soon believe that all who were not patients – the lowest orderly, the meanest visitor – had it in their power to prescribe a course of ECT. One effect of the treatment was loss or distortion of memory. For that reason it was not given to professional people, whose memories were important in their work. But to the poor, the unskilled, the unemployed it was given very readily. The effects were in any case said not to be permanent. However, for their duration the patient was left without much foothold anywhere.

In the long hours Meg turned a good deal to her past. Finding no attachment outside herself she turned instead to the person she once had been. She thought of herself then as a younger sister. But in that endeavour the effects of her treatment were a fatal interference. Above all else she wanted clarity of picture; and around the picture – say, of herself playing quietly while the adults talked – she wanted a crystallization of feelings, of such feelings as are necessary for life. Though she had no hopes of actually recovering them she did seek the assurance that once they had been hers. She wanted to see clearly what it was she had lost. But now even that was denied her. She did not have the power to direct her memory. Meg was to be seen staring fixedly at the ceiling, or sitting against the wall in the day-room, eyes closed, fists clenched, face streaming with tears. All names eluded her, all places and people. No clue she took up conducted her anywhere. She never did see clearly what it was she had lost. When she described her condition she was told it was due either to her illness or to her treatment. She was told that out of her derangement a sane person would emerge. But it was in the nature of her condition that she should doubt whether a sane person ever would emerge. She found nothing in herself on which to ground such a faith. She had no memory of wellbeing. Unable to see what she had lost she came to believe that she had not lost anything; that she was a person who had never had anything to lose. Against this persuasion she only had the word of the doctors and the nurses, of people whose professional case she was. And they could not persuade her. Meg could not be filled with conviction. She was a bottomless pit.

Meg's husband visited her. She was not expecting any visit and it was half an hour before she could be found. He was waiting impatiently in the tea-room. He began at once. She had no right to keep him waiting among all the nutters. Meg looked around. They were all poor, visitors and patients alike, in ugly clothing. She herself did not know the nutters from the sane. She looked dispassionately at her husband, as at any stranger, and saw that he was in fact afraid. They did not even have a table to themselves, but shared it with a girl and her mother. The girl was talking rapidly about some emotional trouble; the mother looked blankly over her daughter's shoulder at the yellow wall, perhaps at the clock. Meg interrupted her husband and asked after the children: one was in a home, she gathered, and the other was in trouble

again. She was going to ask after the woman in her kitchen, but
not knowing her name she got no further than 'How's…', and
this beginning her husband overwhelmed in a rush of complaints
about his back and about a delay there had been in the payment
of his social security benefits. Meg became terribly tired. She
cleared a space among the ash-trays and the tea-cups and laid
down her head on her arms. She caught the stare of hatred and
embarrassment on her husband's face, then forgot him entirely.
When she next looked up another man was sitting there muttering to himself. She left the tea-rooms and walked back across the
grounds towards the wing she was accommodated in. It had
stopped raining. The big yellow chestnut leaves were printed out
flat on the black paths. She saw two men in white pacing up and
down in conversation. She imagined they were discussing her
case. The visitors were beginning to trail away, down the paths
under the autumn trees. The wet smell reminded her of the river.
She felt an excitement around the heart and low in her belly.

Whenever she could Meg watched the rain. In the day-room
she knelt on a chair and pressed her face against the window.
Showing her back she was odd in the line of patients. At night she
listened to the rain. She deceived the staff and avoided taking her
sleeping tablets. She wanted to be able to hear the rain. In fact she
slept well, in a sort of conscious sleep, hearing the rain. The rain,
the river, the boy. She gave up all other thoughts. The staff eyed
her curiously. Meg knew they knew she had a secret. But they
would never guess it. She saw a picture in the newspaper of the
river flooding. Slyly she tore it out. It showed an entire tree
lodged in an entanglement on the weir. On the bank a crowd of
people stood watching. She hid the picture. She felt certain the
boy was drowned. It seemed to her now that he had stepped
backwards off the path into the water. She saw him throwing up
his arms, then turning like a log, slowly, in the rapid flood. The
bridge she remembered as the tomb itself. The boy's assault was
all she could remember in her life of any moment. She blushed,
she cooled her face against the pane. At night she thrust her hands
where he had touched her, and trembled. She pitied him for the
guilt and shame he had endured. Gladly she forgave him his haste

and his intention. She wished he could have known he was forgiven. For some days she held her mind to the rain, the increasing river and the boy. She put all her feelings into them. Her fear ran together, from all quarters, into a concentration in the river. There she could hold it steady. If her fear was inexhaustible the river was too. It came and came. Meg lay awake trembling. Or she knelt in the day-room, gripping the back of the chair. She was shaken through and through, they would see from her shoulders how she felt. She prayed they would let her be. She did not want them to sedate her. She was seeing things her own way at last. When she thought of certain flat places, from which the rain would never run, she was overwhelmed with horror. The flat road, the flattened village. To be got into the river was what she wished. Her nightmare was a straight flat road. What animated her was a hillside, a steep side-street, steps, gutters. 'I will go in the river,' she said to herself, in secret and in triumph. But one day she was seen to be weeping in the day room. A fellow patient reported her. They turned her face from the window to look in on the ward, and her tears, her burning eyes, being then apparent, she was taken back to her bedside and sedated. That night they watched her carefully, there was no avoiding the tablets, and she did not hear the rain. But she dreamed of the dead boy. He had reached the estuary. He turned once more, his arm came up stiffly out of the water like a branch, his face was shown to be washed almost clean away. 'Hurry,' she said to herself.

There was no evidence in Meg's face of her condition. There was no disfigurement. The eyes, though their vision was often strange, did not bulge or squint. She had sometimes imagined her face to be suffused with a hideous colour, but the mirror always showed her pale and not abnormal. There were very few definite signs, even weeping was equivocal. One woman had bitten her bottom lip through, but Meg bore no such marks. On the day of her death she was glad to be capable of appearing normal. She put on a dress of her own, an old fashioned dress she believed she looked well in. She contemplated her face: she was thirty-nine, there was grey in her hair. The only freedom left her was to take her own life in her own way, to affect nobody, for reasons not manifest in her face.

All along it had been an element in her horror of life that nothing fully realized what she felt. She was not in pain, it was not excessive pain she could not bear. It was not her husband, he could not make her want to die. Nor could her village and its obliterated streets. For periods she might lay the onus on these things, and they would bear it, for a time, but then release themselves and leave her again without an image or an explanation of her state. But the river and the boy were enduring well. The boy desperate for love and whom she might have loved. Why, he was a thing she might die *for*, and not because of. Nobody stopped her at the gates, and it was no great distance from the hospital to the river. Meg prayed she would uphold her reason as far as the river. Once in the water her ideas would be drowned. For this reason or that or for no reason at all – the act was the same. But in a little space before the act she would exalt herself.

The Mermaid

Jack woke, Ev was snoring, but above that sound he could hear
the sea, the wind had got up, there was a big sea, the sound of it
made his heart beat faster. Gently, gently, he slid out from beside
her, crept to the window, parted the curtains a fraction, enough
for one eye: no rain, only the wind, a sliver of draught, the sash
was trembling and across the street, across the field, there was the
sea coming nearer and higher, the white sea. He thought: There'll
be some wreck, the breakers coming in like friendly hounds with
timbers in their mouths. Glancing down Jack saw that his John
Thomas was out, up and out, sticking its head out of his pyjamas
into the cold room, stiff as a chairleg. Always the same when a
man wakes, especially in the middle of the night if he wakes then,
he mentioned it to Stan one day when they were sitting in the
Folly Field watching the visitors, and Stan said his was the same
whenever he woke, especially if he woke in the night, like a
tableleg, so that you wondered what was going on down there
when you were sleeping, all night long, something must be going
on, in the mind at least, but you never remembered it, worse
luck. Gently, gently Jack slid in again. The sea. He might get a
nice piece of wood. What time was it? Ev had the clock on her
side and her teeth, in a glass of water, guarded it, she knew the
time and what time to get up and when the alarm went off Jack
went downstairs and made the tea, at a quarter to eight. Ev wore
a mob-cap in her sleep, lay on her back and snored, her sharp
little fingers gripping the eiderdown. Jack did the trick he had
learned from Stan (it seemed to work): lifted and let fall back his

head six times on to the pillow, to wake at six and be on the beach
before anyone else, after the wood. Funny how the brain works.
Jack was listening to the sea and going down nicely to where the
mind whatever it thinks is not to blame, when Ev hit him suddenly on the nose with her hard elbow. The shock was frightful,
his eyes wept, he felt at his upper lip whether blood were coming
out. Ev snored, the clock was smiling faintly. Marvellous how a
woman knows, deep down, even in her sleep, she always knows
what's going on in her loved ones.

Jack went out the back way, down the garden, past his shed,
into the back lane and round. It was still dark, there was nobody
about. A car came by very slowly. He stood on the little street like
a malefactor; then crossed, entered the field, hurried to the beach.
The sea had withdrawn, the waves were milky white in a dozen
layers where they spilled and ended, the widening beach was
empty. Jack got to the tideline and struck along it into the wind,
shingle and dunes on his right hand, the lights of town far ahead
of him on the bay's long curve. The sky, lightening, was enough
to see by, and new wood always showed up. He soon spotted a
nice length of six by four, tugged it out of the slippy deadweight
of thong and wrack, dragged it into hiding in the dunes. So he
went on – a fishbox, a wicker chair, a useful pole – making caches
in the dunes. Nothing like it, nothing else in his life was like
getting up early after a wind in the night and scouring along a
mile or so for what the sea had left. Everything pleased him, even
the plastic bottles and tubes, the women's things in different
languages. You never know. He had found a bed once, without its
bedding, of course, but a bed all the same, thick with barnacles
and weed, he couldn't budge it, there it stayed, for weeks, he felt
sorry for it in the daylight and was glad when a gale took it away
again, a bed on the sea, all rough and slippery and stinking.

At the seawall, that would have taken him as far as the railway
station, Jack turned back. Ev would be waking and wanting her
cup of tea. It was light. The first masters and mistresses were coming along the wall, out of town, and along the beach, out of the
village, with their dogs. Jack took up his best piece, a plank, and
shouldered it. Later he would get Stan to come down with the car

and fetch the rest. The wet plank under his steadying hand, its rasping sand, its smell of brine and tar, he nestled it into his neck. He would have liked to find some wood he could carve, but mostly it was cheap timber used for packing, or it had been in the water too long. Once he had found a log he thought he might do something with, four or five feet long and about nine inches thick, very smooth, he carried it home, it was surprisingly light. The worms were in it, shipworm, he split it and all the naked creatures, as squelchy as oysters, were brought to light in their honeycomb. Soon the two lengths, leaning against the wall, began to stink, and Ev made him take them back to the beach. He went to the trouble of throwing them back into the water at high tide, but by then, needless to say, the worms in their wooden cells were dead.

Stan said he would get Jack a nice piece of wood to carve. His neighbour had cut down a cherry tree, it was blocking the light. He cut it down one Sunday while it was flowering. Stan said the neighbour's wife was heartbroken. She was a very handsome woman, he visited her sometimes with little presents from the garden, her husband was away, driving around up country on financial business. Stan and Jack met in the Folly Field and sat on a bench watching the visitors. In summer they liked to watch the girls going into the sea and coming out again. Stan had a word for the very short skirts they wore: he called them fanny-pelmets. Jack said the word to himself as he walked home and while he was doing woodwork in the shed. The next time he came into the Folly Field Stan was already sitting there with a fat log of cherry wood between his knees. Mrs Wilberforce's compliments, he said. Most of the visitors had gone, there was nobody much to look at. Here, said Stan, take a look at this. And slid a pair of nutcrackers from his inside pocket, a carved black woman, naked, as a pair of nutcrackers. The nut goes in between her legs and when you squeeze, it cracks. Ethel won 'em at the Chapel ladies' whistdrive.

Jack came in the back way but Ev was at the kitchen window looking out. Jack had the log on his shoulder. It was a weight. He smiled, and pointed at it. Ev came into the garden, wiping her hands. That friend of yours, she said. He had it off a neighbour, Jack replied. They chopped it down, it was taking up too much

light. Ev liked the look of the cherry wood. Make a nice something, she said. Take that filthy coat off before you come in. Jack
laid the log on his workbench in the shed. Its bark was red and
smooth. Such a beautiful length of tree. Jack stroked it, sniffed it,
laid his cheek on it. Time you finished me that stool, said Ev when
he came in. Nearly done, he said, one of the legs was wrong.

Next day Jack went out early picking mushrooms. They grew
in the field across the street. Must have been horses in there years
ago, he said to Stan. Funny to think of them nearly on the beach.
Jack had a secretive way of picking mushrooms. He was sure he
was the only one who knew they were growing in that field. He
was out early, but other people might be out as well walking their
dogs. He held a plastic bag under his old raincoat. He held on to
it with his left hand through a big hole in the pocket. That way
he could slip the mushrooms in and nobody noticed. Sometimes
he had to stand over one and pretend to be looking out to sea.
The Minister's wife was passing with her alsatian. She said: Good
morning, Mr Little. Good morning, Mrs Blunt, said Jack. He
picked a good lot and sorted out the best of them in his shed.
They were for Mrs Wilberforce. The rest he took in for himself
and Ev, to breakfast on. Not so many this morning, he said,
I dunno why. Your eyesight's going, I shouldn't wonder, said Ev.
She was partial to mushrooms with a bit of crispy bacon. When
the tea was made and they sat down in the little kitchen by the
fire she would become quite jovial and holding up a mouthful of
mushroom on her fork would say, for a joke, that she hoped he
wasn't poisoning her. How black the morsel looked when she
held it up. No danger of that, said Jack, eating his own with relish.
He was so fond of the feel and smell of mushrooms when he was
picking them and of their taste when he was eating them that he
could scarcely believe they were not forbidden him. And what a
strange thing to come of horse-piss! It was a miracle you could eat
one and not die.

After breakfast Jack went out into his shed. To finish that stool,
I hope, said Ev. Later he slipped out to the Folly Field with the
mushrooms for Mrs Wilberforce in a little wicker basket. Give
her these, he said to Stan. And thank her very much. She can keep

the basket too. I found it on the beach. Stan set off at once. Always glad of an excuse to call on Mrs Wilberforce, he said.

Jack came in at dinner time with the stool. It was a four-legged one, quite low. I put a bit of decoration on it, he said, to brighten it up. Yes, he had carved the seat into the likeness of a smiling face. It's the sun, he said. Uncomfortable to sit on, I should think, said Ev. Still, I can always cover it with a cushion, and it will be handy for standing on, to reach the Christmas pudding down.

There was not much doing in the Folly Field, most of the visitors had gone. The little fair had shut, all but the roundabout. She's having her morning, said Jack. The house is full. I can tell you what they'll be talking about, said Stan. You heard the news? Jack hadn't. Councillor Rabbit exposing himself in Chapel. Jack shook his head. There's something wrong with us, he said. They were singing 'Love divine, all loves excelling' when Betty Creeble looked across the aisle and there he was with it out. Of course, when she'd seen it he hung his hat on it. But by then she was hysterical. He'd just been round for the collection too. Jack shook his head. Whatever's wrong with us? The Minister's having a word with him, said Stan. Stan's daughter was coming across the Folly Field with her boy and girl. Down for a week or so, said Stan. She got a husband yet? Jack asked. She was eating an ice cream cornet. Seems not, said Stan, doesn't seem to want one either. The children ran to the roundabout and climbed into a fire engine together. They were the only customers. The girl began ringing the bell. Then they were off. Stan kept up with them and did the circuit several times, prancing and neighing like a little horse. Jack was glad their mother was not wearing a very short skirt, but her jacket was open on a pretty blouse. Dad'll give himself a heart attack, she said. Your ice cream's coming out the bottom, said Jack, if you don't mind my saying so. He felt for a handkerchief to wipe her blouse, but dared not bring it out. Never mind, she said, and put her mouth under the cone where it was leaking. Jack paid for the children to have another ride. Stan went on hands and knees in the opposite direction. The boy looked as dark as a southern Italian, the girl was as blonde as corn.

Then the owner gave them a ride for nothing. Jack tugged his
beret and said he'd better be off. Not going in, are you? said Stan.
You must be mad. I'll be in my shed, said Jack, doing my carving.
Tell Mrs W. I'm doing a mermaid.

When he was carving Jack always thought of school. It was in
the country, the boys came in from the farms. They were slow at
words and figures, but it had happened every year that a boy in one
or other of Jack's classes discovered he could use his hands. Never
knew I had it in me, they used to say. They did some lovely work,
Jack had some in the attic still, it was better than his own, and when
they outdid him he was proud of them, he had shown them they
could do it, that was his part and he was proud of that. They made
serviceable things, he guessed there must be hundreds of useful
household things still being used in that region of the country in
the homes and perhaps taken elsewhere by now as families moved,
perhaps even abroad. And if a boy ever asked him specially and they
could get the wood he let him carve whatever he liked, a bird or
an animal, for a present. During the war there was a camp near the
school, for prisoners of war, Italians, they were marvellously good
with their hands. Jack slipped them pieces of wood whenever he
dared and they gave him back what they had made of it with their
clasp knives, in exchange for cigarettes. Once he had a crib given
him at Christmas: an ox, an ass, the manger, the baby Jesus, Mother
Mary and Joseph and a couple of shepherds, all simple, warm and
true, they were lovely to feel in the hands. They must be still in
the house somewhere, Ev had never liked them much, he thought
every Christmas of giving them to somebody with children.

Jack knew that his own hands were not especially skilful. Mrs
Wilberforce's log of cherry was too good for him. But he had an
idea, he knew what he was trying to do. It was common knowledge what a mermaid looked like. She must have long hair and a
fishy lower half and be carrying a comb and mirror. Jack thought
he could do the fish scales pretty well, like leaves, like a low long
skirt, and it was there that he had begun, below the waist, and she
was taking shape. Time passed him quietly by. When Ev called
him in for dinner he started like a guilty man and hid his carving
under a pile of potato sacks.

I hear the illegits are down again, said Ev as they ate their cod. Jack admitted that he had seen them on the Folly Field. The man gave 'em a free ride, he said. I wonder she shows her face down here, said Ev. I wonder Ethel gives 'em house room. Seem nice enough to me, said Jack. They would to you, said Ev. But it's the mother I blame. Poor illegits, how'll they ever manage, I'd like to know. I wonder Ethel can look me in the face. Jack finished up his cod. He was thinking of the children on the roundabout, one blonde, one dark, and of the young woman's blouse and how she had stood next to him and given him a friendly smile. Then he wondered what Mrs Wilberforce would have to say about the illegits, and whether she was really interested in his carving. I see you put a cushion on my sun, he said. Looks better, said Ev. Behind her, on the wall, was a piece of marquetry he had done when they were married. It showed the church they were married in. He felt a crumpling sadness at the sight of it, and a sort of pity for them both. He rose. I'll see to these, he said, taking the plates, which were green and in the shape of obese fish. You'll want a nap after your morning with the ladies. There's pudding, said Ev. You know very well I always do a pudding. When she came in again – it was spotted dick – Jack said, wishing to smooth her: Bad business at the Chapel, so I hear. No woman's safe, said Ev, not even when she's singing hymns. Who told you anyway? That Stan, I suppose. I'll see to these, said Jack, as soon as he could. You'll be wanting a nap after your ladies.

Jack sent another gift of mushrooms to Mrs Wilberforce. Tell her she can keep the little box, he said. I found it on the beach. She says thank you very much, said Stan, and how's the mermaid coming on? Tell her she's coming on very well, said Jack. Her tail was done, he had even managed to give a flourish to the extremity. Then he dug out a little hole for her belly-button and that was it, all of the bottom half of her was done. Now for the rest. He admitted to Stan that he was going to find the upper half more difficult. I mean, he said, everyone knows what a fish looks like. He knew as soon as he came up to her hips and when he was making the hole and the little bulge (like half a cherry) for her belly-button that the rest of her was going to be difficult. The sea

was quiet, the roundabout and every other amusement in the Folly
Field had closed, on the beach the Minister's wife was unleashing
her alsatian. No wreck, said Stan. Nothing, said Jack. What's Ethel
say about you visiting Mrs W.? Nothing, said Stan. I go in through
the garden, behind the bonfire, she never misses me. You mean
you do your visiting in your gardening coat? Doesn't bother her,
said Stan. And what d'you do up there? Stan had the face of a
childish devil when he grinned, and his hands, when he rubbed
them together, sounded as though they felt like bark. Have a chat,
he said, have a cup of tea. Nothing else besides? A saffron bun
maybe, if I touch lucky. Jack did not know where Mrs Wilberforce
lived exactly. Some days he might have gone that far and called on
Stan, but his usual walk was along the beach as far as the seawall
or along the front as far as the Folly Field. That way Ev knew
where he was. What's she like? he asked. I've maybe seen her on
Thursdays in the post office. Fullish, said Stan, and blonde.

The ladies Ev had when it was her turn to entertain were
mostly grey, grey or white, but not an old colour, more like a frost
and snow scene on a Christmas card. They came in talking and
when they were in they began to shout. When it was over they
shouted at the door, and went away again talking. They often
wore blue, and jewellery, their mouths were done in red, and
certainly one or two of them were fullish. Sometimes the noise
they were making suddenly grew louder and Jack was worried in
his shed that they might be coming out to visit him, to do him a
serious mischief in a friendly sort of way. Mrs Blunt had a face
which was massive and immensely powerful around the jaws, her
tongue was like a steak. Betty Creeble (the lady whom Councillor
Rabbit had offended) seemed to have fractured as a flint does,
rather than to have worn as will, for example, chalk. Jack thought
Ev's ladies fiercer than buffalo. Must be very nice, he said, at Mrs
W.'s, I mean. Some conversation with a well-spoken woman must
be very nice. Stan offered to take him along next time he went –
Come up the ditch, he said, and meet me by the bonfire – or next
time Ev had her ladies, to be on the safe side; but Jack declined.
He was gazing at his hands. Using the chisels and the hammer so
much had made them sore.

Half way. Jack decided to start at the top and work down to her middle. He gave her a round face, like the moon, but left it blank for the time being and did her hair, which he imagined a golden blonde, he took it right down her back to where her fishy half began. She was lying face down, her front was unspoiled trunk of cherry tree, and he did her hair, spreading it so that her bare back was covered, streams of hair, plaited, in long knots, a semblance of wrack and thong, as was fitting. Then he hid her under the sacks and went in to wash his hands.

By the way, said Ev, as they ate their haddock, I've thought what you can do me with that nice piece of wood. The haddock was yellower than usual. Funny how very unlike a fish it looked. I'll have a lighthouse that lights up. That would be very unusual, don't you think? You mean with a flashing light? Jack asked. Yes, flashing, said Ev. And if we stand it in the corner no one'll see the wires. And do some waves around the bottom to make it look more real. I see what you mean, said Jack. But I think you'll need a longer piece, and not so fat. It's long enough, said Ev, and you can shave it if it's fat.

The bare lightbulb, the steam of his tea, the smells of wood and of the seashore. Jack lifted the mermaid out in her sacks and uncovered her. She was face up, a blank round face, her arms were still encased in the unquarried wood. He had decided she would be empty-handed after all. He had decided she would be hugging herself as though she were cold. The hair came down her shoulders as far as her waist like a cloak, but open, entirely open, at the front, so she was cold. Used to the sea, and cold? The air was colder. He gave her an open face, her smile was innocent and broad, but her eyes were so wide open it was shock her looks expressed. He roughed out her arms the way he wanted them. It was time to begin dividing and shaping her breasts. Happy valley, as Stan said. But the time was a quarter to eight and Ev had woken and would be expecting her cup of tea. Mushrooms, she said when he came in with the tray and wished her good morning. You haven't been out, I don't suppose. Just off, he said. But they're getting to the end, you know.

Soon there were no more mushrooms, neither for Ev nor for Mrs Wilberforce, the nights drew in, the mornings were darker.

Jack walked on the beach as far as the seawall or sat with Stan in the deserted Folly Field. I'm doing her bust, he said. Get me some oil, will you, next time you're in town. And he gave him the money out of the pocket without a hole. Ev wants a lighthouse, he added, one that flashes.

Her bust, her breasts. Jack was doing them after an idea he had of a woman's breasts in perfection in his head. By her slim arms, vertical and horizontal, they were enclosed and given a lovely and entirely natural prominence. Day after day, in the early mornings as it grew light and in the late afternoons as it grew dark, Jack was working on the mermaid's breasts with a love and patience that were a wonder to him afterwards. He was glad to have finished with the necessary chisels and the knives. Now he eased the finer and finer sandpapers with oil to induce the wood to become as smooth as skin. Her hair was rough, as it should be, and all of her fishy half, and even her face he was happy to leave like a doll's with broad features, but on her huddled shoulders, her hugging arms, and on her breasts that were like young creatures in a nest or fold, he worked, in the sweet wood, for the perfect smoothness of a human and living form. He was in a trance of work, under the bare bulb, his mug of tea absent-mindedly to hand, the sky outside either lightening or darkening. It put him in mind of the best work ever done by the most gifted boys (surprising themselves) in all his years at school, and of the animals reached out through the wire by the prisoners of war in exchange for a couple of Woodbines or a twist of tea. The memory – the association – filled him with pride.

After such work he came into his own house like a stranger.

There was a big sea. Jack lay awake, listening. He would wake himself early, but not to go looking for wood. His time before Ev woke was for the mermaid. He lay awake in the night, thinking. The sea came nearer. Jack was thinking of the illegits, and of their mother, Stan's daughter, who had stood beside him carelessly in the Folly Field.

Next morning after breakfast Jack climbed into the loft and found the nativity carvings. They were in a shoebox wrapped in brown paper. When he unwrapped them on the dining-room table they gave him a shock, it was years since he had had them out, and when he took the animals and the human figures one by one into his sore hands he felt a joy and a grief that bewildered him. He fitted the baby into the crib, set father and mother at the head, and crowded the shepherds and the ox and the ass around as though their curiosity were greater even than their reverence. The carving was rough, but every figure had its own liveliness, its dignity and an almost comical manifest good nature. Jack was entranced, like a child, he sat at the table staring, reached now and then for the ox or for Joseph or for the mother herself, as though by pressing them in his grip he could get a little way further into the feelings that were troubling him. He felt regret, but also a sort of gladness and gratitude that he was coming nearer to the source of his regret. Then Ev's voice said: What d'you want getting them out for? She startled him, she stood facing him across the table and her face had slipped, he had never seen such a look on her before, she looked momentarily disfigured as though a stroke had halted her and set her oddly in relation to the world. Well? she said. Well? Her voice had gone strange. Jack was balancing Joseph and Mary in either hand. Thought I'd give 'em to the illegits, he said. Thought they'd look nice where there's a Christmas tree. Ev screamed, once, then again, it was a sound that seemed to have in it nothing at all of personal volition, as though she were ripped. Then she sat at the table and began to weep. Jack put the figures back into the shoebox and the brown paper around it easily resumed its folds. It was paper of a kind no longer ever seen, thick and with an oily texture. Written on it in Ev's big capitals, in purple copy pencil, was the one word NATIVITY. I'll have to get some more string, said Jack.

As he stood up with the box in his hands Ev uncovered her face. And where's my lighthouse? she asked. That would have been nice for Christmas in the corner. It was an ordinary morning in November, a Thursday. Shan't I be going to the post office? said Jack. Don't change the subject, Ev replied. I want my lighthouse. Jack set down the nativity box again, went down the garden to his shed, took up the mermaid in her sacks and carried her thus into the living room. There he unwrapped her on the table, turned on the standard lamp and set her upright on the orange floral chair. I made this instead, he said. Ev stared, said nothing, only stared at the mermaid standing on her fishy tail and smiling foolishly and hugging her breasts as though she were very cold. Ev said: So that's what you've been down there doing. Yes, said Jack. What do you think? Nice, said Ev, very nice. A mermaid will be very unusual. Her voice was quiet, Jack was beginning to smile. So you don't mind then? Stan says he'll get me another log. He tells me Mrs W.'s got one left. Mrs W., eh? said Ev. So that's where you get your pieces of wood from, is it? Just the one, said Jack. But she'll very likely give me another, for your lighthouse.

Very nice, Ev said again. She was standing in the lamplight next to the floral chair on which the mermaid was standing. Only one little thing, she said: Her tits will have to come off. Pardon me? said Jack. Cut 'em off, said Ev. I have my ladies round. They can't be expected to look at things like that. It isn't fit. You'll cut 'em off. Then she'll be very nice. Quite unusual really. Jack was looking at his hands. They were calloused and sore from the work he had done on the mermaid. Ev, he said. Her face was remarkable for its infinite creases and wrinkles, but her hair was newly permed. She was smiling, she seemed on the verge of a sort of hilarity. It wouldn't be natural, said Jack. Who ever saw a mermaid without a bust? That's not the point, said Ev. You'll do as I say. Jack got to his feet. He found that his hands were trembling. He took up the mermaid and was wrapping her safely in the potato sacks. Ev said: And don't think I'm having her down there in your shed. She belongs in my front room. I'm having her on show. Jack backed away, hugging his burden.

When he came in again the table was laid for dinner. The nativity box was lying on the hearth empty. The fire was burning very fiercely. Ev set before him the pale-green fish-shaped plate. I've done you a nice piece of sole, she said.

Jack sat in the Folly Field with Stan. He was cold. She wants me to cut her bust off, he said. Hell hath no fury, said Stan. I don't follow, said Jack. I told her it wouldn't look natural, but she's adamant. He did not tell Stan about the nativity figures. He was ashamed. Stan finished his cigarette and tossed it away towards the empty beach. I'll tell you what, he said. Why don't you give her to Mrs Wilberforce? She's always asking how you're getting on. Jack was tempted, he was very tempted. His heart raced at the proposal. Though he could not be certain that he had ever seen Mrs Wilberforce, the idea of her, the idea in his head, which came not only when he sat with Stan in the Folly Field, was luminous and detailed. In spirit at least he often sat alongside Stan on the comfortable sofa in her parlour drinking tea and, on the luckiest days, eating one of her buns whilst the winter evening drew in. She lit the lamp, but left the big curtains open to watch the starlings hurtle past on a livid sky. And she might ask Stan would he mind throwing another log on the fire, and there they sat, making conversation without any difficulty, and she was indeed, as Stan had often said, a handsome woman. No doubt about it, the mermaid would look very well in that room. The sea was not *so* far distant (you could hear it when the wind was right), and the noise the big trees made when there was a wind in them was very like the sea. And didn't the mermaid belong there after all, to make up for the flowering cherry tree which Mrs W. had been so sorry to lose? She'd murder me, he said. She'd never know, said Stan. She would, said Jack. She finds out everything when her ladies come. Pity, said Stan. Would have made a nice present. Jack wondered whether his friend were deceiving him. Perhaps Mrs Wilberforce never asked after him, perhaps she had never heard he was making a mermaid, perhaps Stan would present it to her one evening as the work of his own hands. Suddenly Jack even doubted whether he had been given any credit for the mushrooms. Stan could be very sly. Jack recalled numerous instances of his slyness in the course of their long friendship. Jack had become very downhearted by the time he said good-bye.

Jack switched the light on and unwrapped the mermaid. She lay on her back, her face as round as the moon, a helpless smile, hugging herself for cold. He was amazed at his achievement; or call it luck, a once in a lifetime abundance of good luck. The way her breasts were was exactly how the idea of them was in his head. He laid his cheek on them, closed his eyes, took into the blood of his heart her scent of oil and wood. Then he left her uncovered on the workbench, under the bare bulb.

Ev was getting the tea ready, a nice salad. Well? she said, chopping a cucumber. What if I made 'em a bit smaller? said Jack.

Ev put a hardboiled egg in the egg slicer. Cut 'em off, she said.

Next day, in the afternoon, Ev had her ladies. Jack took an unusual walk, away from the Folly Field. He walked through the village to the cemetery, and sat there for an hour or so looking out to sea. When it got dark he came home again, though he knew that the ladies would only just be having their tea. He could hear them from the kitchen, they were in the front room and the door was closed, their noise seemed greater than he had ever heard it. Were they more numerous? Had every lady in the Chapel come? He went a little way into the hall. The ladies were in the highest spirits. They beat at one another with their voices. Jack went a little nearer, applied his ear. But nothing very distinct was audible. He bowed himself, he knelt, he applied his eye. He saw his mermaid. She had been brought out of the corner and was standing on her tail in an easy chair. She smiled her smile, without any hope of pleasing. It seemed to Jack that the space within her arms was cavernous. Then she was obscured by a welter of blue and silver and gold. The hairdos of the ladies fitted their heads like shining helmets, their mouths, open for an enormous hilarity, were as red as jam. Jack rose very slowly and out of habit made towards the back door and the garden – but bethought himself and turned and climbed the stairs to bed.

Jack woke in the night, there was a high wind, Ev was snoring by his side, but above that sound he could hear the sound of the sea, the sea had risen, he imagined it foaming white and slung across the bay from point to point. There'll be some wreck, he thought, and did the trick with his head he had learned from Stan. Rose secretly before first light and taking his old coat from the garden shed was soon on the beach along the high water mark. The tide had turned and was beginning to withdraw, it dragged down the shingle like a death rattle. The weed was a yard high, packed solid. The wind had scarcely lessened and there was rain on it. Jack's small exaltation left him at once. He could see no wood, nor anything else worth picking up. The lights of the railway station and the town looked infinitely beyond his strength, even the seawall was too far, he skidded and stumbled in the weed and on the pebbles. Then it was enough, and he halted. Rolled in weed there was a dead thing at his feet, a seal, and for no good reason he began to tug at the slippery stuff, to free it. He got the head clear and the flippers, then desisted. One eye had gone, the other was beaten in, the head, so shapely on a living beast in water, was monstrous. And all below was deadweight in a stinking winding sheet.

A wet light eastwards over home. Jack stood. In the narrow strip between the shingle and the surf a man and his dog were making their way. Jack moved from the cadaver as though he were guilty. The walker was Councillor Rabbit and his dog, a dachshund, trotted beside him on a lead. Meeting Jack, he cast down his eyes and halted to let him pass. But Jack addressed him. Wet, he said, I'm turning back. Councillor Rabbit was a big man in a trilby, which he had to clutch hold of or the wind would have taken it. He wore a very large herringbone overcoat and polished Oxford shoes. His face, when he allowed Jack to look into it, was as sorrowful as a bloodhound's. It had slipped, it had collapsed. Though Jack had hardly exchanged a word with him in all the years he grasped him now almost familiarly by the elbow and turned him towards home. He did not want the dog to go sniffing at the seal.

Councillor Rabbit was easily led. There was enough room for the two men and the dachshund to walk side by side between the pebbles and the waves. You never let him off? said Jack, nodding down at the adipose dog. Safer the way he is, said the Councillor. Besides, he's going blind. From under the brim of his trilby he was glancing fearfully at Jack. They made their way, exchanging remarks about this and that. What's he called? Jack asked. Billy, said the Councillor. The little dog's belly left a trail on the wet sand. He's not much of a runner, said the Councillor. As they neared the dunes and the wider beach below the Folly Field other dogs and their masters and mistresses appeared. I generally come out early, said the Councillor. You'll maybe want to go ahead. No, no, said Jack. I'm in no hurry. And again he touched the Councillor amicably on the elbow. First came the Minister's wife, Mrs Blunt, and her alsatian. It was bounding free, in and out of the retreating tide, and others were advancing after her, more or less frolicsome and fierce. The Councillor was inclined to halt, it seemed he might have stared into the dunes until the trade and chapel people had all passed, but Jack with gentle touches to the elbow kept him going. So they shuffled forwards, Jack and Councillor Rabbit and between them, on a tight lead, Billy the little wheezing dog.

Trains

The approach of a train. Above their heads it whistles and the pretty glasses shiver. In the silence then they listen to the clank of trucks. The Widow's bosom heaves. I can't bear hearing 'em, she says. I was born and brought up under the railway line but since that young feller went and did what he did I can't hear a train without getting palpitations. There's hardly a night I don't start up in bed. Hook-nosed, white-powdered Mrs Clack. Her podgy fingers fidget on the bar. Him with his wisp of beard and frightened eyes. He lay in bed. She thinks of him lying there listening to the trains, the north and the south bound, the goods trains full and empty with their different beats. Who knew the trains and where they were coming from and where they were heading, and chose himself one, and having chosen it he chose a bit of track and went and watched his train go by. How many times? He turned away, back down the embankment and through the allotments where fathers of families were tending their leeks and dahlias. Kept turning away, until his courage was adequate, or his despair. The Widow remembers him coming for a room as though it were yesterday. Would you have a room? he asked, head on one side, standing in the gloaming in his thin clothes. They said you might have a room. How long for? she asked. He shrugged: For the foreseeable future. Those were his words, she says, I'll never forget those words. Well, she had a room in Holly Street, just round the corner from her public house, in her dead father's house, last one on the left, at the dead end, where the embankment blocks the street and where the trains go, fast or slow, after they've come over the viaduct or before they stretch themselves across it. Suited him fine, with his no possessions but a few funny books, under the trains, the windows rattling many times a day, many times also in the night. Whistle, and steadily approaching leap of devouring noise.

There was a girl in that house under the railway line, in Lilian's father's house in Holly Street where the lad lived with the wisp of beard and the collection of funny books, there was a girl in there, Louise by name, but it did no good. The trains went to and fro, they shook the house, and one of them one morning, the 6.05 London to Edinburgh that doesn't stop here but goes for the viaduct like a beast leaping, the 6.05, running ten minutes late and angry no doubt, went over his funny head. Nothing Louise could do. In Lilian's view men ask too much of womankind. To hear you talk, she says, a woman's to blame every time a man gives up the ghost. We need a lot of looking after, Mrs Clack, says Joe. You can say that again, she says, from the cradle to the grave it never stops, you're always round our skirts wanting your noses wiped. A woman never has time to do anything else. That's in the nature of things, says Bowles. Men have all the worries, they have to answer the big questions of life. It's only right and proper that women should get their tea and try and cheer 'em up a bit. He shoves his pot across. Dumbly the men watch Lilian work the handle of the pump. Down and down and down she depresses it.

Of Louise it was widely known that she loved nothing better than to synchronize the climax of her sexual pleasure with the coming of an express train. She was a dab hand at this, she didn't mind admitting it. Her young men got used to the idea, and only the stupidest among them took offence. Some, of course, after the conceited nature of the male, imagined her shudders were due to them themselves; but they were at best a vessel the god locomotive briefly filled. She loved all the trains, even the ancient puffing billies that pottered by in slack periods, trundling a few empty wagons; also the local couple of carriages that never got up steam; and the long, sometimes as it seemed never-ending march of clanking coal-trucks. But she loved the through trains best, the terrific expresses hurtling north or south, and they were the ones she rode into her finale. It was said she could hear them crossing the Tees or the Tyne, that she was attuned to the first vibration of the miles and miles of track and could feel it beginning to throb and could hear the iron beginning to sing long before anyone else could. But that is very likely lies.

Louise often came knocking on our friend's door. Often? Well, if she had no company or if she woke up too late to get to work. His room was upstairs at the back of the house, over the yard. You're nearer the trains than I am, Louise said. Lucky you. The worst room in the house in every other respect: never any sunshine, distemper flaking off, a rattling sash that wouldn't shut, a cracked pane, a boarded-up hearth and soot coming down behind it and bits of brick and birds. But it's true about the trains. The first thing to start and the last to finish was a big glass lampshade dead in the middle of the ceiling. It started like a tickling under the belly-button. Nothing wrong with that room, says Lilian, nor with any other room in Father's house, and no sense throwing away money on decorations when people aren't stopping. She dabs her diamante eyes: the one for Father who drank himself to death, the other for the waif who laid down his head and died. She can't forget the day he turned up on her doorstep asking did she have a room to let for the foreseeable future.

Louise cried when she heard what had happened, and she broke her heart crying when she saw our friend's funny books. She moved out next day and married a signalman. Now she travels where she pleases on his special pass.

But what was she like, this Louise? What were her chief qualities? A creamy white skin; a triangle of maidenhair of an astonishing blackness and copiousness; a kind heart. Plump? She was rounded, her curves were firm. She was said to be very careless in her dress. The postman and the milkman always knocked, Jehovah's Witnesses and men selling encyclopaedias called there oftener than elsewhere and once a quarter when they left home to visit 39 Holly Street officials of the Gas Board and the Electricity Board whistled and sang and polished the peaks of their caps. Some say she never noticed what she had on and what she didn't have on. Lilian: Don't give me that. She's answered the door stark naked to my certain knowledge. Still half asleep, Mrs Clack, it could happen to anyone. Rat-a-tat-tat, here comes the postman, she's nearest the door, she stands there rubbing her eyes and yawning in his face.

Late in the evening if there was nobody with her or late in the morning if she had overslept she might come up and pay our friend a visit. Either time he'd be in bed. The door was never locked, she knocked, he never answered, she opened it and said can I come in? He never answered, he'd be sitting propped up against the greasy wall with his hands outside the covers, flat, he had lovely hands, she said, except his nails were dirty. Their conversations, such as they were, took place mostly across the gap from the door to the bed. I'm out of sugar, she began, or have you got a slice of bread? It was remarkable, she observed, how little he seemed to occupy the room. Apart from the few books there was little sign that anybody lived there. He had a kettle and a cup and a few other bits and pieces for catering, and perhaps there was another shirt or something in the wardrobe. She was comparing the place with her own room, where human occupation was obvious in a big way.

It was Slim who said that about the whiteness of her skin and the blackness of her burning bush. He knew a man in town called Peg who knew a lad called Ike who had known Louise. Slim said it as though he had known Louise himself. She leaned in the open doorway with her dressing gown coming undone and asked our unhappy friend for the loan of a spoonful of sugar or a slice of bread and when he said help yourself, she still stood there and after a silence tried something else. It seems she had none of the ordinary womanly designs on him, but the thought of him up there all on his own in the back room overlooking the dustbins preyed on her mind or at least it occurred to her and gave her a funny feeling if she woke up with nobody to have breakfast with or if it was late in the evening and there was going to be nobody in her bed. None of the other lodgers interested her, though she interested them; anyway, it is not known that she ever went knocking at their doors on the scrounge.

How you feeling today then? she asked, and a conversation might follow on from that. He had a posh voice, slightly squeaky;

the sight of his lips moving in their bits of beard gave her the creeps. Certainly there was something of the insect about him. Stetson, for instance, was of the opinion that squashing was what he wanted. He said this at the bar, whenever the subject came up. Louise thought otherwise, she was not appalled by spiders (fortunately in that house) and would go to some trouble to save them from drowning in her bath. Those lodgers who were interested in Louise but in whom she was not interested opened their doors a crack when she went for a bath, since it was always on the cards that she might walk past a minute later naked and carrying a spider in her gently clenched fist. Our friend smiled a lot, but always in a sneering way or as if his lips were being pulled by a spasm. His teeth, alas, were in a poor condition. He wore spectacles – Jesus, says Joe, do we have to think of these things? – which he often removed as he spoke or as she spoke, and rubbed his eyes, the lids of which were sometimes as red as cockscombs. His hair was like his beard, nothing much.

To her enquiry after his health he replied: Better, thank you, how kind of you to ask. If it were evening and she enquired what sort of a day he'd spent he raised his hands and let them fall and said words failed him, he must be very blessed, he doubted whether many people ever had days like his. He had sat under the broken statue of Apollo, he said, in Wharton Park, and had watched the trains, it was an excellent place to watch them from, you could see them coming, out of the north and out of the south, at a great distance.

When he mentioned the trains she glanced at him searchingly to see if he knew her open secret, and there was indeed a look of insinuation in his eyes; but what he was alluding to was his own business, of course, and he was darting her glances to see if she had guessed it. Finally, since one insinuating look looks much like another, she could not be sure, but said in an even and friendly voice: I'll come along with you one of these days, I like trains too, you know. The motioning of his hands was courtesy itself, but his lips twitched like a devil's and what he emitted was a high giggle which soon faltered and broke.

Do you know, he said, you are the only person I have spoken to since a week last Friday. Louise was horrified. But in the shop?

she said. He served himself, there was no need to speak, the woman told him what it cost and he gave her the money. The Chinkies do the same, they never speak, I've been observing them. And at the NAB? I nod my head, he said, or shake it, as the case may be. I sign on the dotted line and go away again. I shouldn't come bothering you, says Louise. You mebbe like not talking. Once in a while, he says, can't do much harm. And listening? You'd mebbe rather not listen to human speech? Mostly I don't, he says, I overhear a few things, but on your average day no one addresses me.

The next step, obviously, was to ask him what he thought about all day then, sitting up there under the statue of Apollo or down in the square under Lord Londonderry and not speaking to anybody and not listening and never being spoken to, and our friend had maybe hoped she'd go that far; but her instinct warned her off. If Louise wasn't afraid of spiders she was terrified by the thought of a spider swirling down the plughole and drowning in the drains, and the thought of what he filled his skull with day after day seemed to her very like a plughole and a long long fall and a drowning in the dark.

There must have been a silence then, our suicidal friend a trifle peeved perhaps that Louise had not asked to be shown the contents of his head, and Louise herself backing away in her thoughts from the horror of him and moving on to the safer ground of a general pity for the lonely and the beginnings of an uneasiness on her own account. Then, in the silence, she felt the first still very distant vibrations of an approaching train, one from the south, an express certainly. She looked towards the bed again, and for perhaps ten seconds was able to study its occupant's face without his knowing. The features had lapsed into an expression of complete sadness, without sarcasm. Then he too, still before the lampshade on the ceiling, picked up the tremor of the train, and his eyes turned to hers. They frightened her, there was a gleam of wicked hope in them. She continued to stare at him, ever more fixedly, as the train approached and as her famous sensations intensified she set them against his.

Hard to quite locate the agonies a shivering lampshade causes in a man. Sometimes it seems to start in the core of the heart and go down through into his cock and not come out of there but course up and down the lengthening innermost capillary with shock after shock; and sometimes from the back of the head and down the spine with a terrible quick tickling into his vestigial tail; and always under the belly there's an itch that can't be scratched. If that were the only noise the room would have been unliveable in and a man in bed there would have expired if it had gone on for very long; but pretty soon it was lost in the general din. Louise, no doubt, could hear that lampshade, or some similar thrilling and tickling, under all the ensuing racket, running through it like an exquisitely thin reed. The sash started rattling, the gasfire buzzed; the noise came on at a steady gallop, its wheels pounding the track, which whined like ice. The whole room shook, you felt it seized and battered by the noise, you lay in bed and felt broken apart.

When the train came overhead they both closed their eyes. When they re-opened them, when the long tail of carriages had been drawn away and the room little by little and each part after its particular tone (the lampshade last, lingering and lingering) had ceased to tremble, when they opened their eyes, our friend the first to, only Louise was smiling. It's good in here, she said, you're lucky. Sometimes they hoot, I like it when they hoot. His hair was damp, his face was the colour of the wall, he was biting on bits of his Fu Man Chu moustache.

Louise began to talk. He nodded for her to continue, so she did, but his eyes were away on the far wall, staring and desperate. He wore a white shirt in bed with a filthy collar, down which he pushed a finger from time to time. He was damp throughout. Louise talked, not looking at him. She wondered aloud whether she shouldn't just chuck up her job – if she missed many more days they would sack her anyway – and go down to London for a few months. She had a friend down there she thought would let her stay. She wondered sometimes why anyone stuck around in this dump. What she liked about the trains, she said, was that they were always going somewhere, even the slow ones, even the little local ones, and if you got one you could change and catch another, the lines went everywhere, like veins, so she believed, like the veins and arteries that went all over your body.

Slim had it from Peg who had it from Ike that Louise if ever she went rambling on and nobody was paying much attention would absentmindedly start feeling herself through the gaps where buttons were undone (or missing more like) in her slatternly dressing gown. That is, she liked the feel of her own skin, for which nobody can blame her, so while she talked she gently rubbed with the flat of her hand or searched over herself with her finger-tips or scratched with her nails and pushed down naturally off her creamy tummy into her abundant curly private hair and went on talking about getting out of this place and moved her hand up feelingly over her ribs and tickled herself in the armpit and felt the heartside of her lovely bosom and stood in the open doorway leaning back on the doorpost, one foot in a shoddy slipper and with the other, bare, feeling the length of her leg from the knee to the ankle.

On the late evening before the day in question she came up after closing-time with a bottle of Bull's Blood and her Micky Mouse mug. Sunny Jim was in bed, sitting upright. Mind if I come in? she asked. He didn't say no. For once she shut the door. Mind if I light the fire? she asked. I've had a bath. He didn't say no. She had: the skin under her open dressing gown was rosy and damp, blotched here and there with talc. Her black hair, where it lay on her neck, was wet. She knelt and lit the fire. Mind if I open my bottle? she asked. It's my birthday. He didn't say no. He said: There's a knife in there with a thing on it. In the drawer under his books. The knife was the sort a jolly old scoutmaster might wear, dangling from a leather belt on a clip on his hip, a big black jack knife, rough to clasp and having for parts: one blade, one gouge, one corkscrew, sprung like sharks. You do it, she said.

Fastidious fingers with dirty nails – he picked the spiral out – handed the knife back with the tool protrudent. You do it, he said. Louise sat down on the bedside chair, she bored the cork, she screwed, she gripped the bottle between her slippered feet, oh lovely view of her rosy breasts, the folds of her tum, her hairy lair, intensely foreshortened. Our friend had closed his eyes.

The cork coming out made her laugh. You got a cup? she asked. Never mind, we'll share. Glug, glug, glug, glug – you first, say Happy Birthday. When he smiled it occurred to her that perhaps there was something wrong with his mouth, perhaps there always had been and he had tried to hide it with his bits of hair. When he smiled his mouth looked like something a surgeon had made for him. He smiled and smiled and toasted her with the Bull's Blood, cocking his funny head to the right. He handed her the cup and she drank from the other side.

I'm going away, she said, I've made my mind up, no sense rotting in this hole anymore. Did you get any presents? he asked, did you get any birthday cards? That's usual, isn't it? People send things, the postman comes. I was still in bed, Louise replied, I had to get up and answer him. Our friend reached for the mug and drank it off. Thin throat, she thought. He took off his glasses whilst she poured some more. Her nipples, both on show, were pink as rosebuds; his eyes looked like bits of old foreskin. He looked eyeless when he sat there with his eyelids down, as though he were left with two red holes. How have you been? she asked. Oh better, he cried, oh better and better – isn't it obvious? And what have you done all day? I watched the trains. From up on the hill? No, from another place, close to.

She drank. You're a funny boy, she said, I've not met many like you. I'd be surprised if there were any, he said. She shrugged. A train, a slow one. They sat and watched one another through the noise. It's behind his eyes, she thought, behind his red eyelids and somewhere at the back of his eyeballs. The train was interminable, a laborious clanking. I quite like the slow ones, Louise said. I don't, he said and nor would you if you were me. If you were me you couldn't imagine anything worse than a slow train, and the slower the worse.

They drank in turns, passing the cup. Soon she was careless of which side she drank from. She sat on the chair by his bed, her breasts came out, she covered them when it occurred to her to, her knees poked through, the length of her leg showed as far as the black shadow. It's as though you're poorly sick, she said, and I'm here visiting you. I'm incurable, he said, I'm beyond the reach of medical science. You look like Jesus, Louise said, at least you do when you take your glasses off. He took them off, he lolled his head against the dirty wall. It's the beard, I suppose, she said.

But if it's your *birthday*, he said, and you're giving me this Bull's Blood to encourage me, I ought to give you something, oughtn't I? What's he got in this den he could give a girl? she wondered. Not his horrible knife, I hope. In here, he said, patting the breast pocket of his dirty white shirt. Do you want it now? Yes please, she said.

He slid in two fingers, the middle one and the one nearest the thumb, to be exact, and brought out, gripped between them, a flattened ha'penny, held it, turned it this way and that. Have it, he said, my dearest possession, have it and Happy Birthday. Louise took his present in the palm of her hand. It was very thin, no longer quite round, rather pear-shaped. Thanks, she said, are you sure? Wear it there, he said, extending his dirty pointing finger close to her bosom, on a chain if you can get one fine enough, or in a pocket on the left side. I will, she said, copper's supposed to be good for you. The eye of faith, he said, peering very closely, can still discern one of our kings, the bald one, this way up, and tails is a galleon, a ship of hope. But they are flattened and ghostly. It's been under a train, she said. It has indeed, he said, it's been under a great black locomotive of the Duchess class, 46229 the Duchess of Hamilton, weight one hundred and five tons. I've had it since I was ten, I kept it for good luck.

There's a place not very far from here, the kids get down the embankment. One way, south, the line is clear, but from the north it comes suddenly out of a tunnel. He was on his own when he did it, of course. He watched the others doing it from the bridge, then when they'd gone he went down himself with his ha'penny in his hand. He watched them listening on the line, they kneeled in a row and all put their ears down. When they'd gone he went and did the same. It was late afternoon, winter. At the age of ten he had no idea why things were like they were and why he was like he was. At the age of twenty he had none either. At the age of ten he was already beginning to doubt whether things would ever get much better. He got down on his knees, bare knees, took off his glasses, laid his ear on the cold rail. There was nothing but silence, the stones dug into his knees, the cold went into his cheek and the side of his head. It was some time before he heard the singing in the track. Ever since then he has heard it coming nearer, the thing that is between a feeling and a sound, a certain terrible frequency, like a lightbulb before it goes. He withdrew in good time, as soon as the singing had acquired the definite undertone of wheels, as soon as the track had begun to yelp and whang. He placed his ha'penny and climbed to safety up the bank. The train burst out of the tunnel, he was thrown back by the noise, but clutched with his eyes at the name and number and saw the fire. Then he went down, searched for the coin, and was lucky to find it in the growing dark. Thereafter he wore that copper wafer nearest his heart.

Right, said Louise, I'll be off then and thank you very much. The gas had gone out, there was no point asking him for a shilling. Wait, he said, and touched his watch that lay on the counterpane. Do me a favour will you and wait seven minutes. The sleeper's due and it's generally on time. She didn't say no. She took the mug off him, took up the empty bottle from the floor, put the knife away. Alright, she said, and then I'll go. When she was seated again, facing our poor friend, she clasped her hands in her exposed lap and waited. She heard it first, and seeing her face he saw that her apprehension of the trains was finer then his. It came on steadily, she did not close her eyes. She lay back in the chair, the room began to sway. She opened her hands and pressed them outwards between her thighs, she rocked and swayed as though she were travelling. She stared at him, she fixed him, she held him to her eyes and would not let him look away, she watched him through, his eyes never closed, they fixed hers like an insect's, he was seeing the visored head of Death approaching but she held on and smiled her smile and he smiled his and over them both together the noise of iron went and after that, in one long plume, a scream.

That was lucky, she said, he hooted. And now I'm off. Sweet dreams.

Louise had a bad name, no doubt. Very good of the signalman to marry her, Lilian says. If he has seen the tear-shaped ha'penny, and surely he must have, he'll have read her the riot act about the foolishness of children and how he hopes to God none of theirs'll

ever do anything of the sort. He'd be bound to come down heavy
on such larks. Ike said, according to Peg according to Slim, that
the sight of Louise with her tits coming out revolted him. He said
she was only fit to honk on, nothing more. You men are all alike,
says Lilian, and a woman has no defence but her good name. You
have your way and treat us common as dirt. Mind you, some ask
for it. She hopes no daughter of hers would carry on like that.
If she'd had one, that is, which she hasn't. But why they think that
girl might have done any good is beyond her. Anyone could see
he was too far gone and it would take more than a chit of a girl
to bring him back. An experienced woman might have managed
it, of course, but not that little slut. Still, it is very sad. She'll never
forget him standing there asking if she had a room for the foreseeable future, by any chance. An educated voice. What is the
point of education if that's what it does to you? The Marquis
agrees. Besides, it's not at all certain she made any effort to save
him. Her and her Bull's Blood. I don't recollect, says Lilian, you
ever saying she pleaded with him. Any normal girl would have
pleaded with him. There's some might say she even drove him to
it, by flaunting herself, I mean. I mean if he was religious. You
said she said he looked like Jesus when he took his glasses off.
Touch me not, says the Marquis, in an educated voice. He is
about to say he will have another of the same but everyone has
paused, everyone falls silent, nobody moves, the Widow clasps
her hands on her lurex bosom and above her the tremor starts,
among the fairy lights, along the row of pretty glasses, a shiver, a
subtle tune, it finds the frequency of everybody's fears, the men at
the bar and Lilian who serves them, they bow their heads,
wishing the noise itself would come, come quickly, the real noise,
come quickly over them while they are silent and thinking only
of their terrors.

Silver Wedding

Roger was making the necessary arrangements. He phoned his daughter. 'Saturday,' he said, 'you won't forget?' 'You didn't need to remind me,' she replied. She sounded cross. Roger began to get into a tangle. 'Not for me I don't mean. For your mother.' He was making things worse. Alice said: 'You mean it's her day not yours?' 'Of course not,' said Roger. 'It's both. Only women...' 'I see,' said Alice, and put the phone down.

Roger was upset but he kept going. 'I don't want anybody faulting me on this one,' he said. He had no idea why Alice was turning against him lately. He chewed his beard, a trick of his when he was nervous. Then he phoned his son. A voice said: 'Yes?' 'Can I speak to Fred, please?' There was a thudding noise, steadily. The voice shouted: 'Fred!' Then: 'Not in.' 'Could I leave a message, please?' No answer, but Roger said: 'Would you tell him, please, that it's his mother's silver wedding on Saturday and we'd like him to come home.' 'Jesus,' said the voice. Roger's own voice sounded posher than he liked it to sound when talking to young people.

It was a relief to phone the florist's. They were polite to him. He decided, on impulse, to spend exactly twenty-five pounds. 'One for each year,' he said to the florist. 'Very nice,' she said. When that was done he felt pleased with himself, but also like weeping. Nobody could say he wasn't doing everything he should. He decided that rather than go out for a meal they would stay in, as a family. With the flowers that would be nicer. Then he cycled home.

When he told Pat he thought they might stay in, as a family, rather than go out for a meal he thought she looked a bit disappointed, so he said not to worry, there'd be a surprise or two, and on impulse then, excelling himself, surprising himself, putting himself beyond any possibility of reproach, he added: 'And we'll ask your mother.'

That was that then. The day before, Roger sat down at his wordprocessor, retrieved the file he called NEWS and wrote a couple of paragraphs about the silver wedding. Events of that sort he usually wrote up before they happened. Some events, obviously, you couldn't do that with, because they happened unexpectedly. For example, when Sam, the spaniel, went after a rabbit and got his nose bitten by a badger, that had to be written up afterwards, and very funny Roger made it too. But things like a silver wedding, once the planning was done, mostly went off as expected, and Roger found it better to do them beforehand, almost as part of the planning, because afterwards, to be honest, he never felt like it. Besides, as everybody said, it was very easy to make alterations on a wordprocessor, so he always could, if necessary, if things turned out very different after all, he always could make changes either then, after the event, or at Christmas, at the editing stage, when he did the final version of the Newsletter and sent it out to all their relatives and friends.

Roger wrote up the silver wedding day: the children coming home, their presents (he put a question mark inside a pair of brackets), mother coming, her present (another question mark), the family all together for a nice evening meal, his little speech, memories, bed. Then he went downstairs and put his arm round Pat. 'Big day tomorrow,' he said. 'Lucky it's Saturday,' she said. 'We can lie in.'

2

Pat woke first. She was lying there thinking, tears in her eyes. A sunny day. The children would come. She knew they would side with her, against their father. She loved them, she would let them side with her, and her mother would be against him too, and she would not like to see him so on his own, he looked betrayed. She dreaded their anniversaries. The room was light. Roger lay on his back, asleep apparently. People, people of that age at least, should never be looked at asleep. Best to wake in the dark and put on a face before the daylight comes. Roger lay there visible. On his back, with his beard, his arms outside the covers, he looked as though he were lying in state. Pat turned on her side, to face the window, and in that moment he slid out and made for the door. She saw that he reached for his dressing gown hurriedly and that he looked her way, she saw that he looked like Adam when God called after him in the paradise garden, but more than that she could not see without her glasses.

In Roger's absence Pat took off her nightdress and sat up. When he came back it was with her tea and biscuits. 'Happy anniversary,' he said, and kissed her hair. Drew the curtains, let in the sun. 'Where's yours?' she asked. His tea. 'Downstairs,' he said, and added, as though he had a secret: 'Things to do.' Pat covered her breasts and sipped her tea. 'We could have had a lie in,' she said. But Roger was gone. She dipped a biscuit in her tea. She heard the post come, an immense amount. Seemed it would never stop.

Roger said he had to go into the Department for an hour or so, to sort things out. He thought Pat looked a bit disappointed when he said that, but thought she would be happy again when she saw what he was bringing back. She watched him through the kitchen window putting on all his gear: helmet, clips, luminous bands. 'He'll be hot,' she thought, and added: 'With that beard.' He rode off. He had left her all the cards to open. There were dozens. Everybody who got a Newsletter at Christmas had sent them a card, and a few more besides. Such a lot of friends they had, and even more relations, as it seemed. There was one bit of bad news among all the congratulations: Paula had written to say that Mike's remission was over and they didn't hold out much hope. Pat halted there, at the little scribble on the white and silver card. Sadness all around, like the sea, and as though you were living below sea-level and anywhere, at any moment, a drowning sea of sadness might break in. Pat was still sitting there, half the cards unopened, when Alice arrived. 'Where's Dad?' she asked, having kissed her mother and hugged her tight. 'He's had to go in to work for an hour or two,' said Pat, 'to sort things out.'

Pat thought Alice so beautiful she could hardly believe her to be their child. 'It makes me think we must have been different then,' she said aloud. Alice made some coffee and took it out into the garden. 'Bring the cards,' she said. 'I want to see.'

Roger was in his room. There were no messages on his answer-phone, none at all. He stood at the window. He had a view of the car park. He stood chewing his beard and clasping and unclasping his hands. Really, he did not intend to struggle for very long. He intended to give in to the temptation, but guessed he would have more pain from it than pleasure. In effect, he was screwing up his courage to bear a pain, not struggling to deny himself a pleasure. He lifted the phone. 'She'll be out,' he said. She was. 'Gwynedd?' he said, his voice absurd. Then came her voice, recorded, briskly inviting him to leave a message. He put the phone down; lifted it again at once, dialled, held his breath for the duration of her cool recorded couple of sentences, and burst over the tone into the free space she allowed him: 'Gwynedd, it's me. I love you, I love you, I love you, do you hear? I love you.' Put the phone down, sweating, shaking, full of horror. Since a moment ago he had had no intention of saying any such thing, he was suddenly frightened of himself, as though it were not for him to say what he might do next.

He opened his post. Nothing much, the usual offers of more life insurance. One from Texas looked important. He thought for a moment that he might be being head-hunted and that he might perhaps make a new beginning in the New World, but it was only an invitation, addressed to him personally, to purchase a Texas Fruit Cake and have it sent to arrive for any special occasion. There was a card from a former student. She was in Haiti, helping to organize a co-operative. She sent love.

There was nothing else for him to do, or nothing he could bring himself to do. He covered his eyes and thought of Gwynedd's body. He wished he could wipe her tape clean of his hectic message; but there it sat, she would come in, press a button, suddenly hear it. He had said he would be an hour or so. He lay on the sofa, thinking, until it was time. Rose, took two bottles of champagne out of the fridge, put on his gear, cycled home.

Pat and Alice were still in the garden. Roger saw them before they saw him. Pat's face was quite different now. Alice's style, which could be hard (perhaps her very difficult work demanded it), had relaxed, softened, she was gentle, attentive, they were equal. He paused, at a great distance, until they noticed him. He was embarrassed walking the thirty yards across the lawn. 'Take your helmet off at least,' said Alice. 'There's nowhere to kiss you.' 'You haven't been long,' said Pat. He took the two bottles of champagne out of his haversack. 'And see what I've brought you,' he said.

Standing there, he began to sort through the cards. He seemed to be checking them against a list. Every now and then there was a little surprise. 'Nice to be loved,' said Alice. He came to Paula's and halted. Pat, on edge for him to reach that one, leaned forward, as though to help. In her own feeling over the sad little note she put out her hand to her husband, but he drew away. 'Yes, it is very sad,' he said, 'but there's a time and a place for everything. You don't put a thing like that on a silver wedding card.' He turned away, he calculated that the day had another ten hours to run and he did not see how he would be able to bear it.

After lunch he said he thought he might lie down for half an hour. Mother and daughter urged him to do so. He lay down in the sunny bedroom and thought about Gwynedd's body. He made his heart pound and his mouth dry up in desire and fear of her. Her gaiety, her tricks. She would come and go, she pleased herself, he never knew how he stood with her. He counted himself lucky ever to have seen a body like Gwynedd's, let alone to have had the kissing, caressing and entering of it. He dozed and dreamed. Dreams in a doze are often of a frightful kind. Nearer the surface it is almost the waking mind that suffers them, almost the waking ordinary daytime person who sees himself there in his own house and home completely vulnerable, there for the taking whenever a catastrophe chooses to occur. He heard a shouting and laughter that seemed to him demonic, and sat bolt upright, his heart going like a rabbit's. It was only Fred. Fred had arrived, they were welcoming him. Roger doused his face and went down.

Again the walk across the lawn. This time there were three of them at the table, looking his way. His bad dreams were still on him, perhaps they were visible in a swarm around his head. Certainly there must be something the matter with him, the way his family were staring across the space. But he shook hands with Fred. He liked to grip hard, as his own father had always told him a man should do. Fred let him, suffered it. 'You got the message then?' Roger asked. 'Didn't need it,' Fred said. 'Knew anyway.' Fred's fingers were stained with paints and inks. He had working hands, and never tried to get them clean. 'Well here we all are,' said Roger. 'Yup,' said Fred. 'I'll go for your mother,' Roger said to Pat. 'No, no,' said Pat, in haste, in an anxious haste, 'I'll go, you talk to the children.' 'When you come back we'll have presents,' Alice said. 'Will we, Fred?' 'Yup,' said Fred.

Roger asked a few questions. Though the children were friendly they both held back. He knew, as if a good angel had suddenly given him a chance, that he should sit down and strive to take a real interest in their lives, get Alice to explain one woman's case to him in every detail, get Fred to describe one typical class from beginning to end, but he failed, it seemed too late, and he said he thought he might do a bit of gardening. 'Good thing on a day like this,' said Fred.

Roger got changed and was soon on his knees the other side of the rockery and the rustic. He chose the most doltish job and went at it mechanically. He kept hearing his own voice telling Gwynedd, on an answerphone, that he loved her, again and again. Truly, it seemed to him that having done that he might do anything. He feared exposure, brought on him by himself. Everyone would laugh. Even if he committed suicide they would laugh.

Glancing up, through the rustic and across the rockery, he saw the children at the white table. The sight seized hold of him. Fred was telling some tale, leaning forward, telling it rapidly, Alice was listening with her sharpest attention, and frequently laughing, always on the verge of laughing again, and whenever the amusement broke out of her she gripped Fred's hand in delight. Roger stared at his son. He had seen it in a lot of young people, but never so much as now, in his own son, a carelessness, a boldness. The way his hair was razored back, so that the skull showed, so that his ears were revealed, his features were entirely exposed, sharp,

not handsome, without the least concern to be thought handsome, only bold, open, quick, his lips and eyes especially were
quick. Rooting out weeds where they might just as well have
been allowed to flourish, Roger did not see how he could ever
have fathered a child like Fred. What if he were suddenly offered
the chance to start again? In America say, or somewhere even
further off. He knew that he would not have the nerve.

Pat arrived, with her mother. 'You've been a long time,' said
Roger. He kissed his mother-in-law. She had shaved her lip, but
not well. She was a little taller than Roger, bony, dressed in a
sheer blue. 'See what Mother has given us,' said Pat. It was a
bulbous wine-jar set on a silver pedestal, fitted with a silver
handle, stoppered with a silver cork. 'Listen,' said Pat. She raised
the gift, as though to drink, and a tune came out of it, out of the
base in which was the mechanism of a musical box. Mother was
tickled. 'Bottoms up,' she said, 'and out comes a tune.' 'Very
original,' said Roger. 'What tune is it?' '"Over the Rainbow"',
said Pat, 'a teeny bit slow.' Then Fred fetched his. It was a mural,
on hessian. He unrolled it across the lawn, about forty feet. 'My
kids did it,' he said, 'so it's multi-cultural. Since most of 'em don't
know what a silver wedding is I told 'em to work on Mum and
Dad, or Mum or Dad, or failing that on what they think heaven's
like.' Alice was on her knees. 'Fred, it's wonderful,' she said. Roger
and Pat were pacing the length of it, like royalty. 'Here's you two
here,' said Fred. 'Olly did you big and in the middle. His Dad's in
jail for killing his Mum.' They were coming down a stairway
hand in hand, smiling like new moons, behind them were
rockets, coloured fountains and shooting stars. To right and left of
them stretched a suite of scenes. Pat detached herself, went along
slowly, peering closely, and began to sob. Fred shrugged. 'All in
all it's positive,' he said. 'Art always is.' 'My turn,' said Alice. Went
in, came out holding a silver bowl, which she had filled with
fruit. 'It's old,' she said. 'I cleaned it up.' It was dented here and
there, but the lines of work on it looked infinitely rich. You
might dwell on them for hours. Roger began to take the first
photographs: one of Alice proffering the bowl and of Pat receiv-
ing it. There was something solemn and admonishing in the girl's

stance and expression, something shy and almost fearful in the woman's. When the photo was taken they turned and faced him.

Later, the champagne. Then, right on cue, Pat taking off her apron, the flowers arrived, by a special delivery. They were sensational: white and silver, white carnations, lilies, roses, freesias, camellias, simple marguerites, and at the heart of them a dense clot of the most vivid red. Naturally, Roger could not reveal the symbolism of their cost. He wondered if there was any discreet way of putting it in the Newsletter. More champagne. He had begun a little speech when the phone rang. Alice answered, came in and said: 'It's for you, Dad. Some woman.'

Gwynedd. 'Three things,' she said: 'One, I got the job. They mentioned you. Whatever you wrote about me must have helped. So thanks. Two –' Roger tried to interrupt. She would move: when? Could he travel that far? How often? Would she welcome him? Again the conviction that his life was unravelling. Even his voice would not serve him. 'Two,' said Gwynedd: 'Congratulations.' What on? Roger really did not know what on. 'And three: Best not to leave anything personal on the answerphone. I'm not the only one who plays it back.'

The family were round the table, waiting, looking his way. As he came in Mother took a photograph of him with her polaroid. She loved to see the picture rising into being at once. But it was very dark, Roger seemed to be groping his way out of an abyss. 'Sit down, Lazarus,' said Alice. 'You need the flash, Mother,' said Roger. 'Let me do one of you.' Flash! Out came Pat's mother, upright, long, blue. 'It's very good,' said Pat. 'Apart from the eyes.' The eyes had come out red. Mother, seated opposite Roger, seemed to be emitting fire from her eye-holes. 'Mind if I have it?' Fred asked. 'I could use it.' So the evening wore on. 'Your mother must stay the night,' said Roger.

3

Roger undressed and stood in front of the mirror. He was better naked than clothed. There was no belly on him, he kept himself fit by cycling and jogging, and his head, which during the daytime often looked baffled and cumbersome, taken with the whole length of him lost most of its disproportion. Then he forgot where he was, stared, and dwelled on the fact that he was losing Gwynedd. His wife came in silently from her bath, the front of her body covered with her bundled clothes. She addressed him in the mirror. Quickly he covered himself with his hands. 'Who phoned?' she asked. 'Only a woman from work,' he said. 'She phoned to say thank-you. I helped her get a job.' He slipped away and found his pyjamas. Pat walked to and fro in the room naked but for her glasses, stood at the dressing table, stood at the open window.

In the dark, lying by him, she said: 'Did you take your pills?' 'Yes,' he said, 'but they don't seem to be doing me any good.' After a silence Pat said: 'Shall we try?' 'Try if you like,' said Roger. Pat began, with one hand, with two, and then, drawing back the sheet, with her breasts, her cheek, her mouth, for several minutes. Roger lay still, his mind blank. 'I'll go again,' he said when she desisted, 'and ask for something stronger.' Nobody should say he wasn't doing his best. Silence a while. Roger was thinking that his life had perhaps another thirty years still to run and he did not quite see how he would get through it. Then Pat said: 'You know the one that happens in the mornings sometimes...' She waited. 'I've told you before,' he said, 'that one doesn't mean what you think it means. It's only physiological.' 'Mother said what's it matter what it means,' said Pat. 'I beg your pardon?' 'Mother said...' 'You told your mother? You tell your mother things like that?' 'I have to, Roger. I have to tell somebody. Mother made me nag you to go to the doctor's, to be honest.' 'I see,' said Roger, 'it's all coming out now. No wonder she looks at me the way she does.' Pat was crying. 'Sex isn't everything,' Roger said. 'Haven't you just had a lovely day?'

Naturally Roger was angry that his wife had betrayed him to her mother, but not so angry as they might think he was. In fact he smiled. They only knew half, one half, they didn't know the other half. 'I'm furious,' he said. 'Don't be,' said Pat. 'I know it's my fault and it makes me so unhappy.' 'You'd better tell me what else your mother says,' said Roger in his sternest voice. 'She says

why don't you try thinking about someone else.' Roger blushed,
unseen under his beard and in the dark. 'I don't understand,' he
said. 'Like a film star, she means,' said Pat, 'whether you've tried
thinking about a woman film star who might be more attractive
than me. That was what she said. Whether that might do the
trick.' 'I couldn't do that,' said Roger. 'I wouldn't feel right doing
that.' 'But if it worked,' said Pat, 'it might get us back into practice.
And I wouldn't mind for once.' 'Well I would,' said Roger. He
kept his mind blank. Pat, still in tears, persisted. 'That one in the
morning, how long has it been there?' she asked. 'How should I
know?' Roger answered. 'I'm asleep.' 'Well perhaps it's been there
quite some time,' said Pat. 'Perhaps we could use that while you
are asleep. As Mother says, if it's there, it's there.' 'Try if you like,'
said Roger, 'but I'll be asleep.' 'And if you wake it will vanish,
I suppose?' 'I suppose it will,' said Roger. Then he said again that
sex wasn't everything.

In the dark, lying apart from Roger, Pat began to think of
Paula's Mike.' When she last saw him it was the beginning of his
illness. Strangely, he looked younger. He complimented her on a
new dress she was wearing. She remembered blushing. They had
just told him what his illness was, and in a rush, in a sort of
licence, which she encouraged, he took her hand and began
reminding her of this and that. Paula was there, watching and
listening without any jealousy, only with a desperate sadness lit
intermittently by the light on the faces of Mike and Pat as they
remembered things. There was a clarity about his face, an uplift-
edness. He said he knew it was going to be hard and he was
certain he would lapse and lapse again but at the present moment
it was his determination not to lose or spoil any single moment of
love, and those in the past he would fetch into the present, and
Paula agreed. He began to recall a particular night, it was soon
after he and Pat had met, they were walking home, there was a
green sky and a new moon and one star near the moon… Then
Paula stopped him, gently, and not out of jealousy but because he
was flushed and starting to tremble, and the two women were at
once in an alliance to soothe him down. Pat thought hard about
him, recalling more and more. Then the pity of going out of life

at his age, at her age, overwhelmed her. Paula had not had anywhere near twenty-five years. Their children were very young.

Roger was doing as his mother-in-law had suggested, thinking
of someone else, he felt licensed to, it was his revenge, and not of
a film star but of Gwynedd, of how firm she was where his wife
had gone slack, how tight, how she took what she liked, did what
excited him because it excited her to have that power, bestrode
him while he lay there, fitted him in, pinned his arms down,
moved, observed his face, smiled. 'My compliments,' she said.
She often said that, and also: 'I shall miss this, you know.'

Roger became aware that his wife beside him in the darkness
was weeping quietly. He took her hand. Then in pity perhaps,
perhaps in pity for both of them, certainly in a rising fear at his
own future life, at the blank ahead of him, he was about to turn
to her, much as her mother had said he should, just as he might
have on many previous nights and never had, he was about to
turn to her with the power which had been lent him by thinking
about Gwynedd's body, when she said: 'I was thinking about
Mike, about Mike and Paula. It's so sad.'

Then Roger was indeed angry. He turned away. 'If you'd
married him,' he said, 'you wouldn't have had this problem,
I suppose you think.' 'He's dying, Roger,' said Pat. 'I know that,'
said Roger, 'and it's very sad. But there's a time and a place for
everything. I don't want to have to think about your old boy-
friends on my silver wedding day.'

4

Roger was in his room. He had two minutes before the day
began. He often thought about suicide, but rather as though one
day it might happen to him and not that he might ever do it. He
lifted the phone, dialled, she wasn't in, her cool voice invited him
to leave a message. 'Gwynedd,' he said, 'it's me. I'm coming with
you. I can't live without you. Will you marry me?' Stood holding
the phone then until the knock came at the door.

When the day ended, he was in his gear, helmet and all, ready
for home, he played through the messages on his answerphone.

This and that, nothing much. Then suddenly: her laughter. No words, only her laughter, on and on. She sounded nearly hysterical, he guessed she must be weeping with laughter, she could hardly get her breath. When it was over he pressed the buttons and listened to it again. For the rest of his life he would always be able to listen to it, whenever he was alone and had a couple of minutes.

The Special Hand

'Donald!' 'Sunny!' 'How very nice to see you!' They shook hands, Cholmondeley-style, the elderly man with a force that crushed any hand unprepared for it, but Donald, accustomed, gave in heartfelt vehemence as good as he got. Sunny beamed on him. 'How did you do, old chap? Any news yet?' 'This week, alas,' said Donald. 'Are you hopeful?' 'I've a chance.' 'I'm sure you have. And whatever the good Lord sends it won't spoil being here again, eh?'

The Officers were assembling, as they arrived, for tea in the Head's room. Sunny was eyeing the door. Whenever it opened, the company shouted with delight. Nobody was not an old friend. 'Must say hello to the others,' said Sunny. 'Did you have a good trip?' 'Fine. Only one sick.' 'There's always one.' 'Always,' said Donald, waving to Jukes in the corner with two or three from Bristol. 'Where's Pater?' But Sunny had gone to the threshold and was welcoming Anthony. 'Tony will know already,' Donald thought, and taking his tea into the window he stood looking out. Frank, from Birmingham, came up and squeezed his arm. 'Alright, Don?' Donald nodded and smiled. Nobody could object to Frank. 'You know, Frank,' Donald said, 'I suppose there must have been times when we've come here and it's rained, but somehow one always thinks of Cholmondeley in the sun.' Frank agreed. 'Very nice to be back,' he said. He had the appearance of a sergeant-major, a kindly one. Having Anthony on his mind and Anthony's results, Donald became warm, almost effusive, towards Frank who, though much the older man, had attended far fewer parties. Indeed, with his contingent of four lads from a boys' club Frank was a novelty still, in a sense an experiment, still being monitored at meetings of inner groups which Donald had recently been invited to join. 'Do you know, Frank,' Donald said, 'this is my twentieth party.' 'Crikey!' said Frank, 'they'll be giving you a gold watch and chain.' Donald smiled. 'Twenty's nothing. Gerry over there's been thirty times at least.' 'But this one's his last,' said Frank, and added quickly 'so I hear.' 'Really?' said Donald. He did not like to learn anything new from Frank. Frank became confidential, Donald shrank from him, but learned nonetheless that Gerry had decided to become a monk. 'That's why he looks so miserable, I reckon,' said Frank. 'What does Pater say?' said Donald, more to himself than to Frank. 'Where is he, by the way?' Frank shook his head. 'He was here not long since. Now you see him, now you don't. Business, I expect.'

There was no light on earth like that at Cholmondeley, over the grounds in the late afternoon in summer. The Head had a private garden, whose scents came in upon the company now through the large open windows. Beyond the garden were elms and beeches and the light in them was like a realization of ideal peace of mind and sunniness of spirit.

'Listen, chaps, I say, listen everybody,' Sunny was calling them all to attend. They turned. Donald knew at once what the good news was, old Sunny's face was radiant with it and Anthony, dark-haired, six foot tall, was abashed. When Sunny announced 'Do you know what? Tony's got his First!' and the clapping started up, loud and generous, Donald, to his shame, had a little spasm of spite. But he went over immediately, shook hands, and his words to Sunny – 'They give 'em away in Modern Languages' – were, he was sure, said in a tone of raillery without bitter springs. Sunny was delighted. All the wrinkles of his face, all the creases, were shown to be those of smiles, for not one remained to be activated by a grimace or a frown. It was a face that to be seen at its best had to be seen smiling, and it nearly always was. 'Does Pater know yet?' Donald asked. 'Haven't seen him,' said Anthony. 'Where is he, I wonder? I had the viva this morning, the list went up after lunch, I've come straight over.'

The rest meanwhile, the younger boys and those among the older boys who had never been asked to be Officers, changed out of school uniforms into shorts or slacks, into cricket shirts or rugger shirts, gym-shoes or sandals, into the free costumes of Cholmondeley, took tea and biscuits hastily in the dining-hall, and then dispersed around the house and grounds, into dormitories, the common room, the games room, to Lords, the Oval, Eden Field, the Copse or to the swimming pool, searching for old chums and, having found them, revelling in their company. That first excitement was nearly unbearable. One could never know for certain who would be there and who would not. Some expectations were cruelly disappointed. For accidents intervened, and even betrayals despite assurances given in letters in the months between, and a boy might look for his particular friend in vain and learn from some third person of his prevention or defection. The chagrin he felt then was overwhelming, he loathed the week ahead. But Cholmondeley had a way of curing such griefs, and by chapel-time on the first evening when the party was entire and one knew one's partners in the tournaments, by then or certainly soon after then, certainly by Sing Song, there were no sad faces.

Baby changed slowly, letting the others leave him. He was in the Beak's dormitory, and the Beak had not arrived and nobody knew when or even whether he would. Baby was thinking that if the Beak stayed away his own vague disinclination for the party would become disgust. Glancing through the window – he was in the Tower – he saw several hurrying to Lords clutching walking sticks for golf; and he ascertained, with the tragic satisfaction that was becoming his manner lately, that he had no wish to join them. He might just sit where he was until the Beak arrived. Or he might write to Sally. That thought came to him with a little shock of pleasure and wickedness. Half-dressed, half-undressed, he sat on the bed and took out her photograph, and being alone in the remote dormitory he soon felt his sensations grow to peculiar power. The girl's face, then the whole room, misted before his eyes. The feeling wavered in its direction, but at last, with a rush, ran along lines of a pure and general love. Baby pulled on his shorts and rugger shirt, but instead of going out immediately among the others, to see who had arrived and who had not, he bethought himself charitably of Goda, and went off to look for him, in Anthony's dormitory.

Goda was in bed with the blankets drawn up to his chin, eyes wide open behind his spectacles. 'You no better?' Baby asked. 'I thought you'd be alright by now.' Goda didn't speak, only shook his head. 'You should come out,' Baby said, 'the air will do you good.' He noticed a smell. Looking down, he saw that his feet, bare in sandals, were touching a heap of Goda's soiled clothes. 'We'll have to get these washed,' he said. 'Anyway, you'll not be needing them now. Put your other things on and come down.' 'Got no other things,' Goda said. 'What d'you mean you've got no other things? I gave you a list, didn't I? I told you what to bring.' Baby's charity was giving out, he was beginning to feel only impatience with this little boy who had very suddenly vomited all over himself on the bus from Cheltenham. 'What Mam put in is awful. I look really daft. I'm staying here till them dry.' 'You'll do as I say,' said Baby, 'and get up and jolly well join in. I'll take these down to Mrs B. You get yourself dressed and I'll meet you in the hall in five minutes.' Goda began to cry. Baby, stifling his disgust, bundled up the stinking jacket, shirt and trousers and hurried away, shouting 'look sharp about it!'

He was running across the first landing when the door of a room, properly a housemaster's, opened, and there stood Pater, one arm around the shoulders of a boy. The sun, shining through a gothic window, caught the couple full on. Pater was beaming and blinking, his head shone like a saint's, his spectacles flashed back the light. Perhaps he ought to have been the more off-balanced, stepping thus into a steady shaft of sun; but he was quite composed, so was the boy with him, as though they had been waiting their moment to step out and surprise Baby. 'Here he is,' said Pater, 'our Baby Smithy, the one we have been keeping you for.'

Baby, very conscious of the bundle in his hands, did not approach. 'This is your new chum Michael,' Pater was saying, 'and he is from Somerset, whence all good things proceed, and I warn you, he knows an awful lot more about you than you do about him.' Michael did not seem embarrassed by Pater. He looked straight into Baby's face. He was sun-tanned, in a way that town boys never are. Short sleeves, bare legs, blond down on his cheeks and lip; and his eyes were of a startling blue. Baby, facing Michael's cleanness, felt ever more keenly his own accidental impurity and he backed away, as he would have before a pretty girl, blushing, and ill-wishing the nuisance Goda. 'I'll get rid of these,' he mumbled. 'What's the matter?' Pater asked. 'Baby wasn't sick, was he?' 'No, not me,' said Baby with a look at Michael, 'a new boy.' 'Alright is he now?' Pater was asking, 'you've seen to him, have you?' 'I'll get rid of these,' Baby said, 'then I'll see you in the hall, Michael, shall I?' – and he sidled by, keeping his distance, as though, through Goda's vomit, he were leprous. Pater and Michael, as one, turned to watch him downstairs. 'Yes, that's right,' Pater was saying, beaming out the sun in an arc from his spectacles, 'see Michael in the hall. I've told him how much you will like one another.'

Some for months, since the last party, had longed not only or not so much for the company of a particular friend as for engagement again in a particular game. In daydreams they had seen themselves at Lords with a walking stick or on the Oval with a puddox bat or leaping in the front line of a volley ball team on the Eden Field or seated at a green baize table for tiddlywinks or mah-jongg. Now they were already back in their obsessions, and Baby heard, with a little thrill of recognition (though it was not his especial passion) the click of the shot and the clatter of the first wink landing in the empty pot, as he and Michael went out together, taking sticks and balls in case they felt like golf.

Enough had assembled for a scratch game on the Eden Field. Michael and Baby stood to watch, Baby greeting old friends. Such was the Cholmondeley spirit that had they stood on the sidelines for more than five minutes some player, however intense his own enjoyment, would have ceded his place to one of them with a friendly excuse, and his example would have been quickly followed. To avoid this they walked on, to Lords.

Their sympathy was already an accomplished fact. To be sure of their own company they began a round of golf, following other pairs and foursomes. The field was golden with the summer evening light. Beyond the hedges the county stretched to all horizons, purely rural. One could not imagine that it harboured any ugliness. Michael was used to this, it affected Baby more. The hay had been taken off not long since, the after-scent lingered, and this, with the light, excited in the townboy a rush of memories and aspirations. He tried to tell Michael what it was like; then, the way becoming clear, inverted his walking stick and struck off carelessly for the first hole. It wasn't a bad shot, but Michael's was better, though even more nonchalantly done.

They walked across, getting wisps of hay between their toes. The field still showed its ancient strips, in gently rounded ridges under the grass, and playing this lie of the land was one of the skills acquired by golfers at Cholmondeley. Around the flags Pater had an area mown short, but outside these circles there was a lot of rough. Michael hit the post in three, Baby in four. A party immediately ahead of them was taking an age. 'They ought to wave us on,' said Baby. Michael was forever glancing at him. 'What did Pater tell you about me?' Baby asked. 'Nothing awful, I hope.' 'He likes you very much,' Michael said. 'He doesn't know my bad side, that's why. He only knows me how I am when I'm here.' 'Are you different when you're somewhere else?' Michael asked. 'Surely you're not.' 'Nobody's his usual self at Cholmondeley,' Baby replied. 'You've come on your own, I know, but when you come with a group you see the others changing once they're here and they'd see you changing too if they cared to look.' 'You're one who looks,' Michael said. 'I can see that already.' Baby was flattered. 'Besides,' he said, 'I've got a girl now and that makes a difference. Have you got a girl?' Michael shook his head. 'No, I haven't,' he said. 'Not now, you mean?' 'Never have.' 'Then you can't have tried. You wouldn't have much trouble if you tried.' 'What's it like?' Michael asked, his voice going deeper, more local and hampered, 'what's it like having a girl?' Nothing loath, the evening inclining him to confidences, Baby would have talked there and then out of the fullness of his heart about Sally, but the foursome ahead at last succeeded or gave up and moved on, leaving the second hole free.

Goda had done as he was told and stood now waiting where Michael had waited for Baby, under the trophies and under the gilt list of Cholmondeley's past headboys. He was wearing the proper togs his anxious mother had bought him. And now the Officers were coming down, eager to get in a game of something before Chapel. The tournament lists, overlooked by Baby and Michael, were posted on a board where Goda waited. 'Let's see who I'm with,' said Donald. The golf was alright. 'You're with Perkins,' said Gerry beside him in the quiet sad tones he never departed from, 'he's one of ours, a nice lad.' It was customary to partner an old hand with a new boy. Winning was not the thing, the game was and the good of the party. 'Well, he'll help me along a bit,' said Donald correctly, 'perhaps I'll reach the second round this time.' And he turned to the tiddlywinks. Tiddles was what he cared about. Missing the game too much in the long intervals between Cholmondeley parties he had set up a league at school in his year as Vice-Captain and persuading other schools to follow suit had organized matches throughout the counties of Lancashire and Cheshire. Lately, having got the thing going at Oxford, he had appeared on local television potting six in a row from the base-line. 'Oh blast!' he said, so that Gerry, and Anthony approaching on his left, looked at him in shock. 'I'm with Goda.' Coming on top of the announcement of Anthony's First this was very trying. 'I thought we weren't supposed to be with our own people.' 'I expect they thought you'd help him along a bit,' said Gerry mildly, 'or perhaps it's a mistake.' Donald knew he was wrong and began putting a brave face on it. 'A man like you can carry anyone,' said Anthony encouragingly. 'You could even carry me.' They chose sticks and went out.

Goda waited, having heard everything. Sunny was last down and smiled at him. 'Alright, old chap?' 'Yes thank you, sir,' Goda replied. Mrs B's dachshund Virginia came out and snuffled at him. Its coat was of a repulsive sleekness, its dugs trailed on the carpet. Goda looked away. Everyone was out, except those in the games-room across the hall at tiddlywinks. Goda hung in the doorway but did not dare go in. His own presence, the consciousness of it as ridiculous and offensive, worked on him and for relief from himself at last he went out on to the forecourt where, as he reasoned, Baby would easily find him.

On the gravel, full in the declining sun, four third- or fourth-timers, fairly sure of themselves, had set up a table and were playing mah-jongg. They had gone some way over towards the east wing of the house, and in that position, a solitary group, they were very conspicuous. Behind them was a deep and vivid flower-bed; the stone of the house, where it showed above the wisteria and through clearings in the creeper, was as warm and homely and grateful a substance as set honey. All was mild and peaceful, and Goda was drawn.

The boys were quite engrossed, playing quickly as they had been taught to at Cholmondeley, deftly and with concentration. Goda had never seen the game before. The tiles were beautiful and fascinating: those in the wall showing only their backs, deep honey-coloured; those discarded and in the players' racks showing their mellowed ivory incised in green and blue and red. The few spoken words, as each in turn declared the tile he was discarding or claimed, by some right mysterious to the onlooker, a tile he wanted, deepened the feeling of silence and thought. Approaching nearer, since he was ignored, Goda dared to look over a shoulder at the hand of tiles being assembled on a rack. He forgot his long shorts, his stiff sports shirt, his exceedingly white pumps, in the excitement of beginning to discern, without being told, the pattern the boy was working towards among the suits. He shared the satisfaction when, with a click, a third was added to two there waiting of its kind. Searching along the rows of discarded tiles he began already, for himself, to see what other orders might be sought. He forgot that he had been waiting in vain for Baby, and that he had overheard what Donald Blower had said. He would have given the world to feel the tiles, they looked both warm and cool. As they were named, being put down, so Goda learned them, and began to understand the players' risks and chances. He would have watched the whole game to the end, in a deep and self-forgetting concentration, but when he had stood for some time, he would not have been able to say for how long, Pater came out and advanced upon them playing in the corner.

'Oh curse, oh curse,' they muttered. He put a stop to it, as they knew he would. 'Not the time, you abominable boys,' he said, 'mah-jongg begins tomorrow, as you well know. Disperse at once. Pack them neatly, Big Ears, across not down.' One took the box and the four wooden racks, another the table, the two others two chairs each, and trailed away, under his eye. 'That leaves you, little boy,' said Pater presently, turning on Goda. 'Who are you?' 'Goda, sir.' 'I'm not a sir, child, don't call me sir. Of what school, of what team, in the golf, in the tiddles with whom?' 'I'm with Donald Blower in the tiddlywinks,' Goda replied. 'Lucky man, he's the master. Practise, practise – finger and thumb –' Pater demonstrated – 'strengthens 'em for the long shots.'

They were not unalike in appearance, Goda and Pater, in squatness of figure, roundness of head, and in their manner of blinking behind their spectacles. 'What are you good at, little boy?' Pater asked. 'Rugger?' Goda shook his head. 'The sprint?' Goda looked at his feet. 'Perhaps you are good at mathematics' Pater suggested, that having been his own relief in a world of loneliness. 'I'm no good at anything much,' said Goda, but added in a rush 'I should like to play that game though, I might get good at that.' 'We *sometimes* let the babies play,' Pater said very slowly, 'if they promise not to snivel when they lose.' '*I* wouldn't snivel, sir, not me I wouldn't, and I think I've got the hang of it already, just from watching.' 'H'm', said Pater, 'we shall have to see. There's a waiting list, of course. Where are you going now?' 'I'm waiting for Baby Smith, he said to meet him the hall.' 'This isn't the hall.' 'No, sir.' 'Don't call me sir. You may look for Mr Smith on Lords. Thattaway.' He pointed through the Copse. 'But shake hands first.' Goda held out his hand. 'All wrong,' said Pater crossly. 'The little finger comes down *so*, and fits with mine. That's how it's done at Cholmondeley, and don't you forget it. And grip properly, I want a hand in mine not one of those tulips. Now be off. Chapel's in ten minutes. You'll hear the bell.' Pater watched him out of sight.

When Goda emerged from the Copse they were already leaving the Eden Field, at a trot, tossing the volley-ball between them. They overwhelmed the small boy and passed on. The golfers were coming in too, some practising shots along the path (though there was a rule forbidding it). Goda hesitated, he was all contrary. The chapel bell began, and a fear that he would do something wrong during the service possessed him. He stood in the path, looking from Lords to the Copse and back again. Then came Michael and Baby walking together and so deep in their own sympathy that they almost passed him by. He wished they would, he had stepped aside, not wanting to be noticed, when Baby glanced up. Not for anything would Goda have wanted to cause the older boy such shame. Baby blushed. 'Oh Michael, I forgot Goda,' he said.

They sat together in Chapel, the three of them in a line, Goda in the middle. Baby, whose religion at home was falling off week by week, experienced now a strong emotional condition in which love for Sally and Michael and shame at his neglect of Goda were confused. Gerry took the service. His sad voice touched the tone of Baby's feelings exactly. Sunny, at the organ, combined with the Cotswold evening light to produce an atmosphere, a state, in which all the boys, together again, more or less entirely dissolved. In a space for private prayer the song of a blackbird, like the liquid harmonies of grace, was heard by all, with a communal joy, through the open door. Goda prayed that he might play mah-jongg. In the front pew, facing him across the aisle, Pater, hands clasped in an even more than Cholmondeley interlockingness, pitied him. How many boys he had watched at prayer and how few of them had not gone under in the flood tide of piety. Sing, blackbird; play with a mellow sadness, Sunny; shine, westering light – that deeper and deeper God, through his agent whom they called Pater, might stir in the hearts of another clutch of young-sters before they aged and the cities hardened them for ever.

They trooped out, to Sunny's musings. The good intentions, even of the worst of them, were at least as palpable as the scented evening air. They went head down, the older ones with hands clasped behind their backs, turning over Gerry's words; and when they looked up again and addressed one another it was with a sigh. Elsewhere perhaps the transition would have been impossible, but on the spirit of Cholmondeley they were carried from Chapel into dinner and out of dinner into Sing-Song in easeful undulations.

Sing-Song indeed repeated Chapel in secular form and brought the company to bedtime. The songs were community, folk-traditional, national, Boy Scouts and of other brotherhoods, but they worked like hymns, and the singers swayed together to old favourites that brought tears to the eyes of some seniors and rooted in the hearts of the little first-timers for ever more. Friend-liness was the air they breathed. Pater and Sunny sat in leather armchairs of honour on the front row, a couple of current pets on either hand, and enjoyed the performances enormously, Sunny with a childish unadjusted mirth, Pater with an admixture of nostalgia, loneliness and theological pessimism. Donald, as Master of Ceremonies, kept the first evening short. The younger boys would be tired after their journeys. Simon Pickering, from Bristol, did birdsong imitations; Twigs, from Wolverhampton, played a seal song from the Western Isles, on his flute; and Donald himself, to fill in, as he put it, recited the whole of 'Sam, Sam, pick up tha musket', flawlessly. A few of the Officers joined Pater and Sunny for cocoa. Having seen Goda safely back to Anthony's dormitory Michael and Baby said goodnight on the landing. They shook hands, Cholmondeley-style, and, on impulse, Baby touched Michael's cheek.

The Beak had arrived, late and unnoticed. Baby had forgotten that he was missing him, but their reunion was nonetheless warm. He was unpacking. 'I'm in green this year, dear boy, everything green.' He had sandy hair, the colour ought to have suited him. 'What team am I in, did you notice?' 'Blue, you're in blue.' 'Am I boss?' 'Of course you're not, Anthony is. He got his First, by the way.' 'His first what? Ought to be past his first by now.' The Beak was undressing, everything green. He was all angles; chin, elbows, knees, all jutted. The light green shirt was dark under the armpits with great spheres of sweat. 'Like a pig,' he muttered, 'all them mucking stairs. The doctor says I should lie still, at room tem-perature.' In green pyjamas he stood in the middle of the small dormitory, put palms together, stuck out his elbows, squeezed tight shut his eyes and bawled: 'Sleep my babes no ill betide youse

all through the night guardian angels watch beside youse amen.'
Then put out the light and ordered them all to keep their gobs
shut until 9am unless there was a fire. He crawled into the lower
bunk, below Baby. Baby heard him sighing and scratching. Himself he was almost asleep when in very clear tones the Beak asked:
'Is that filthy dog dead yet?' 'No,' said Baby, 'it bit one of Frank's
boys as soon as they arrived.' 'I'll have it this time,' the Beak said,
'so help me God.'

   Baby woke early in an intense happiness and longing which
he first ascribed to Sally but a moment later, with a shudder of
memory, to Michael. It was light, the doves in the big trees had
begun their repetitions. He dressed quickly, to go swimming.
Though they had made no arrangement he felt sure that Michael
would follow the same thought. He crossed the quiet landings,
left the house, went out through the shrubbery along the wall of
the headmaster's garden, to the pool. His sandals were black with
dew, it was copious on the grass above his bare ankles, running
cold through his toes. The morning was silver-grey with dew and
mist. There was nobody at the pool which was not a very grand
affair, only an oblong of still cold water with a few leaves and seeds
and beetles on the surface. There was an open shed to change in.
Baby hesitated and watched the path. Only when he saw Michael
coming, alone, did he realize what disappointment he would have
felt had it not been exactly so. He waved, and looked away, his
heart thumping, his face flushed with shyness. 'You here already,'
Michael said, 'and nobody else.' And he stared at his friend as
though that were the only wonder. He was naive, the openness of
his face made one turn from seeing it, his accent was gentle. 'You
alright, are you? I couldn't sleep for thinking about you.' Baby
nodded. 'Are you going in? It looks freezing.' Michael turned
abruptly and pulled off his shirt. To change they faced away from
one another. Michael took three steps to the pool and without
any hesitation flung himself in. His characteristic grace was a total
nonchalance. His body, his looks, his natural skills were something he gave no thought to – and especially not now that he was
preoccupied, in a fashion quite new to him, with someone else.
Baby stood on the edge watching Michael swim. He admired

him without any envy or restraint. He stood watching until he
heard shouts and saw Jukes and a crowd running already changed
towards the pool. He was in the water with Michael, at the far
end, when they came leaping or diving in, one after another, half
a dozen of them, making a huge noise and splash. Then nobody
stayed in long.

Not looking at Michael Baby found himself drawn irresistibly
to look at the others when they were towelling themselves dry.
The smell of cold water came off their bodies. The sexual place
drew his eyes despite himself. How dark it was on Jukes, and even
on Anthony, how very dark, the flesh itself seemed almost black.
Michael was behind him somewhere and the feeling of his own
nakedness passed down his spine like fear. He dressed in haste.
The others chattered casually, two had seized each other by the
wrists and were wrestling naked on the edge of the pool. There
were cheers and jeers when they both went in, one clumsily, one
with a graceful cartwheel. Baby glanced round secretly. Michael
was dressed and was watching him, not the wrestlers. They set off
back to the house together.

Donald came to Goda's dormitory immediately after Quiet
Time and took him down to the games room, to practise. He
hoped they might put off the first round for a day, but their
opponents, happening to be present and seeing how things stood,
challenged them on the spot. Donald was trapped. As an Officer
he was forever chivvying others to get on with their first rounds.
He played his heart out, to no avail. He put in all six of his own
from the base-line, as he had done on television. He asked of
Goda only that he, as feebly as he liked, should get his little winks
into play. But even this was more than the chap could manage.
Understanding nothing of levers and aerodynamics he flicked
them high and backwards off the table to the floor. No encour-
agement or example could correct his mistakes in time. The
opponents, playing steadily, took three games in a row. Donald
was out of the tiddles in the first round, which had never been
known before. Several people watched the game. They agreed that
Goda had played as badly as it is possible for a human being to play;
but some also commented that Blower had not taken it very well.

Goda's partner in the golf was the Beak. Goda, unacquainted with him, supposed he would be like Donald, and waited in a dumb terror to be summoned. The Beak, however, was going into town; he was anxious to see if the same girls were still serving in Ann's Pantry. Baby pointed Goda out to him and he came across, in green, winking and grimacing. 'Practise missing,' he hissed. 'Get us through the first round and you're dead.' And he slipped the child half a crown.

Goda went and stood on the forecourt where the tables for mah-jongg would be set up. It was easier than he had dared hope, as though prayer were indeed effective. Pater came out like Toad, two boys in attendance carrying with difficulty everything necessary. He nodded to Goda, in greeting, and struck the ground with his stick where he wanted the table set. Goda beseeched him with looks, and again Pater nodded, this time in assent. A moment later he was seated at the table, he Goda, the worm, and under nothing worse than Pater's heavy banter was pushing his fingers blissfully through the ivory tiles. 'Form your walls,' said Pater, two eighteens and the trick is this –' he ran a forefinger along and smartly brought the double row exactly flush. 'Form the City.' Each pushed forward his rack, shunting the four built walls until their corners met. 'No cracks, mind. Keep the devils out.' Then the dice: 'Throw for East Wind.' It came to Goda. In that capacity he threw a nine. The forefinger counted anti-clockwise. 'Your wall, little boy. Throw again.' He threw a twelve. Twelve tiles along, counting from the right, the wall was breached by that same forefinger with care, Goda moving back his rack, and the pair pushed out were laid one over each preceding crack. 'Now take.' And by turns they took: a four, a four, another four, and a one, except East Wind who, beginning the game, takes two.

Goda learned the ritual there and then, once and for all, with an exactness unprecedented in all his studies. And to distinguish the One of Bamboo from the Seasons and the Flowers; to place the Green Dragon correctly tails down; to know his blank brother; to chow, to pung, to pung for a kong – he felt these things were coming back to him, as though elsewhere in some happier existence he had played to his heart's content in a friendly company with the cool and clicking tiles. Nothing was kept from him. He was given his little ivory tally sticks, a hoard of them, to settle his debts. He was told of the major values of the Ones and Nines and of the Winds and Dragons. He was shown ways to enhance an ordinary hand, and the sheet his fellows consulted so solemnly they passed him as a matter of course when he asked for it, and his mind then was pleased by the simple beauty of the Seven Pairs and by the neat intricacy of Crochet and Knitting, but by the Thirteen Unique Wonders and the Nine Chances or the Wriggling Snake and by the lovely Jade Hand the eyes of his imagination were flung open wide and he felt the tears start and he felt a trembling through his body. Unnoticing he took into his memory for ever all the contingent details of that first afternoon – the dull conversation of the doves, the frenzied reverberations of trapped bees, boys shouting in the distance at the pool, scents, a sunny light, the warm stone – they entered the feeling of mah-jongg, they were woven into it and any one of them thereafter was a crystal potent with all the rest. Goda opened his heart naively to a future of hopeless longing.

Pater watched him knowingly. Such passions are not good when they come with a rush on a life unused to gratification. But Pater let it run. Curiously indulgent he let them have more than the customary number of games. He knew very well the intensity of everything at Cholmondeley and often would intervene to curb it. Sometimes his boys looked up from their games with an expression nearer to despair than joy and he knew they wanted an adequate object for their surmounting feelings. Their feelings exceeded the game, they exceeded their companions; and every-thing around, the pleasant details of God's summer world, these did not meet and calm the feelings but excited them further, higher, up and beyond, over and away. The boys might run and shout and weep (he had watched them weep) and not know where to turn with their intensity. Pater watched, teasing and smiling, until by the unfolding purpose of the day his boys were got into Chapel. And there he put a name – the love of Christ – on their various loves, he marshalled their passions towards thanksgiving, humility and service.

That night Jukes, declining Sunny's invitation to cocoa (he was fagged, he said) went over the wall after lights-out for an assignation at the back door of the Lamb and Flag. Those in his charge in his absence amused themselves with Wilcox, a third-timer from London, who was possessed of or by an extraordinary faculty for talking, walking and doing whatever he was bid in his sleep. They soon had him sitting up grinning (eyes tight shut) on the bed edge, his sex uncovered and alert. Michael was the only one in the dormitory to whom the fun was no fun, but he watched from his bunk despite himself. They were telling young Wilcox all sorts, getting him to confess and at once realize his wildest dreams. He turned his blind face this way and that, he answered and addressed them in a strange flat voice like that of the deaf, he pleaded, he groped, and at last grasped into his arms one very young one offered him giggling as a surrogate, and him he covered with kisses and squeezed between his clutching thighs. The rest shone torches on the pair. The little cries the dreamer made troubled Michael profoundly. It was the publicness and the deludedness of Wilcox's pleasure, but also: its sharp intensity. The cries were of surprise; what he felt surpassed what he had been able to imagine. When Wilcox lay down a torchlight on his face revealed that he was weeping quietly and that his smile was of beatitude.

'What's it like with girls?' Michael asked. They were in the Copse, shortly before Chapel, walking up and down. Baby was embarrassed to answer. It depended what Michael meant. If he meant what was it like loving someone as he loved Sally then, he was discovering, it was much like feeling what he felt for Michael. That itself was not describable, and he did not think that Michael was expecting him to try. As for the rest, or the other, that Michael perhaps meant, it was not so much shyness as ignorance that kept Baby from answering. Kissing, any boy could surely imagine, and walking hand in hand, but the rest for Baby too was all hearsay. What he had heard said he would be reluctant to pass on. It disturbed him too much. Had he glimpsed more than Michael in the accidents that come everybody's way? Girls stooping carelessly, girls sitting as they shouldn't. Of the peculiar fascination of girls, of their scents, clothes, talk, perhaps he knew more, but in things like that, even to please Michael, he was lost for words. 'I don't know,' he said, head down. But he felt that Michael would have thanked him for anything, for any little scrap, for any nothing, and not so much to learn by it as to be having a talk on that subject. So he knew he was disappointing him when he asked 'How did you get to know Pater?' Michael started, and replied quickly, to get that diversion over: 'He knows my schoolmaster.' 'And he recommended you?' Michael shrugged. 'I don't know how it was.' 'I'll bet I do,' said Baby, taking his arm. 'Sally's lucky,' Michael said, 'all the girls you've had are really lucky.' 'I haven't had that many.' 'Liar.' It depended what he meant by had. 'Aren't there any girls in Somerset?' 'Not ones I like, not ones I can get to know. Show me her photo, will you? Tonight?' Baby grinned. 'You'd better come up and meet her. She'd like you better than me, and I wouldn't care if she did.' Michael gripped his hand and unlocked all his fingers. 'Like that, is it? Do you walk along like that?' 'More like this.' Baby showed him.

The chapel bell began. They came out of the Copse together. Goda was waiting in the chapel porch. He was scared of going into the place alone. So they sat in line again, facing Pater across the aisle, but Michael was the middle one of the three, and when they knelt for their own prayers, whilst Sunny on the organ worked them all into the mood, quite deliberately and with perfect understanding Michael and Baby knelt with their bare legs touching from the ankle to the thigh, and prayers coursed through them like a common bloodstream. Rising, neither looked at the other nor blushed, but Pater, bowed and praying fiercely through splayed fingers saw their faces illumined, and between their beauty and his loneliness and his ascetic God he surfaced and sank among his thoughts and prayers like a man in a maelstrom. Before Sing-Song Baby ran upstairs for Sally's photograph and slipped it to Michael where they sat with Goda and the Beak towards the back. Blower was reciting the whole of 'Albert and the Lion'. Then Wilcox sang 'Bread of Heaven'. He had a crew-cut and his ears were like pot-handles; his voice, though, climbed effortlessly to a place beyond longing, to somewhere one could imagine as the highest Alpine meadow, and there it pastured, with sheep and angels. In the silence afterwards the Beak's voice came as a shock. It was as if a gargoyle had spoken. 'Pity there's no Shakespeare this year,' he said. Michael meanwhile was doting on Sally's face, and looking from her to Baby and back again.

Goda, humiliated in the morning's team-games, found three to play mah-jongg with in the afternoon. Who they were was a matter of indifference to him, he did not even learn their names. They wanted to play, that was sufficient, they made a game possible. They were all courteous to him. Somehow the serious and beautiful game imposed it. He had set his heart on the Seven Pairs, the least of the Special Hands, and on the slightest promise he went resolutely for this, ignoring his opponents' speedier progress to smaller achievements, resisting the call of a discarded third for the two of a kind concealed in his own rack. He was unsuccessful, and overall did badly. But the afternoon was instructive. There has to be some basis, some gift to begin with. It is of no use storming at circumstances with inappropriate demands. He had patience and resoluteness, but he needed adaptability too. And he needed luck.

In the volley-ball one lens of his spectacles got cracked. It was a classic case of somebody taller and better able stepping in from behind to do what he himself was obviously incapable of doing, and at a moment in the game when to return the ball with speed mattered supremely. Goda was knocked to the ground and, play continuing vigorously, soon got under everyone's feet. When the point was decided they helped him up. 'I don't think it will fall out at least,' said Frank kindly, 'but if it works loose you'll have to put some sticky tape across it.' Goda's vision thereafter, since he did not have a spare pair of spectacles, was less than imperfect. Half of reality had a fault through it, and the sun danced continuously on his left in a merry rainbow. He was an eyesore. Better favoured people, ashamed of the feelings he provoked in them, would say of him: 'Well, he doesn't make the best of it, in some ways it's his own fault.'

The Beak came out for the golf. He had one arm around Goda's shoulders and was grimacing horribly. 'I've changed my mind,' he said, 'I'm playing to win. Gimme that half-crown back.'

A crowd was following, since anything the Beak did attracted attention. Their opponents – Gerry and a youngster from Birmingham, one of Frank's boys, called Alec – were waiting for them on Lords. Pater was there too, sitting on a shooting-stick. 'Come along, little boy,' he called, 'this is your chance.' The Beak was winding both his arms, like the wings of a plucked chicken they looked, and the green sports shirt was black with sweat below them. His thin legs were quite densely haired, in a faint blond; he wore suspenders to his green socks.

Alec drove off, with a clean, dead serious, absolutely trustworthy smack. Frank had told him that the game was the thing at Cholmondeley and that winning didn't matter. Alec nodded, but in his heart he wanted to do very well. He took his dad's view: that in some unclear way this Cholmondeley business was a leg-up, out of the mire. But when he had done a thing well and he was sure they couldn't fault him then he was candid and charitable and not in the least boastful. So he stepped aside now for Goda, who had to follow him.

Perhaps three dozen people were watching. Goda missed. He missed again. He went to the left and to the right of the ball and above it. The Beak nodded. 'That's fine, old chap. That's fine.' Goda hit the ground under the ball, causing it to start with the shock and roll forward an inch or so. 'Beautiful,' said the Beak, 'now we're moving. You've lined me up nicely.' Gerry, for his shot, was fifty yards down the field. With a mournful grace he landed the ball a stick's length from the post. The Beak took a run-up and flailed in a way Pater thought dangerous; missed and fell. Alec hit the post. For the second hole it was Goda to drive off. He shut his eyes – his vision was too poor to be of any help – and on the fourth stroke made contact. The ball went some way towards the flag, not a great way and not directly, but Goda smiled and the crowd cheered.

'There are different kinds of ridiculousness,' Pater was thinking. He was beginning to dislike the Beak and to wonder whether future parties might not manage without him. 'There is Goda who is a laughing stock and who makes no reprisal, and there is this Beak chap to whom nothing is holy' (following Alec's shot he was prone on the grass, potting the ball feebly onwards with his stick as a cue). 'Goda is more blessed than the Beak. It was unwise to pair them off. Goda suffers, and the Beak is merely heartless.' It occurred to Pater to wonder who had invited Goda and for what reason. Blower's contingent was normally very reliable. At the third hole the Beak drove off in classic style, a full dead-straight drive that landed the ball on the green within easy putting distance. Gerry's looked amateurish by comparison. Of course, Goda fluffed it, his shot went wide and into the rough. The crowd groaned and he was close to weeping. Alec finished from twenty yards. The Beak's fine drive had enraged Pater: it was no fluke, the man could play perfectly well when he wanted to, and there he was now hacking and swinging like a lunatic. Goda, confused, did his level best, but the game was soon lost, five and four. They all shook hands. Neither Gerry nor Alec quite enjoyed their victory. 'Bad luck, partner,' the Beak said, 'a bit more top spin and we'd have had 'em.' A few of the spectators stayed on to watch Blower and Perkins versus Frank and Wilcox, but most had only come to see the Beak.

He performed every day on four or five occasions. That morning he had bent his fork into a fish-hook, dangled it on an old school tie and trailed it, baited with sausage, under the table for the waddling dachshund to take. He could make the young boys double up and roll on the ground with laughter, he could halt a match of volley-ball when he liked, laughing both teams helpless. Only occasionally did the Master of Ceremonies ask him for a turn at Sing-Song. It was impossible to follow him. Once, when he was still an Officer, he had taken the chapel service. His sermon had the congregation in fits, boys hung weakly into the aisle, waves of laughter went to and fro through their private prayers. And never the ghost of a smile on the Beak's face. He jutted out his chin, he brushed to one side the quiff of sandy hair, gripped the pulpit and leaned down over them. Nobody knew what his text was, nobody could recollect any one thing of what he had said. He had bizarre knowledge, he worked it like a bran tub, he surprised himself sometimes by what he came up with. Sunny laughed like a horse, he was a spectacle of mirth, there at the organ he turned his streaming face this way and that for all to see. Pater laughed like a man won over by the devil to a delicious sin.

Returning from Lords and the golf tournament the Beak walked fully clothed into the swimming pool. He walked in as though he had to, it was on his route. Sticking out his arms and legs he was then towed backwards to the far end by Jukes. Others heaved him out and he resumed his conversation with Goda, who had gone round. 'Make them tell you what the Dinner Hand is,' he was saying. 'They won't tell me. 'Fraid I'll win, of course.' The water was causing his shorts to come down.

About the mid-week, actually during Quiet Time, Pater sent for Baby. 'Watch yourself,' the Beak said, 'I've known men disappear in there.' On the landing Baby waited for the messenger to go out of sight. Then he knocked, the door was already ajar. 'Come in,' said Pater, the words were quite clear. Baby however, pushing open the door, halted in embarrassment. Pater was sitting on the bed facing away and bending over, so that Baby at first thought he must have taken ill or be praying. His flannel trousers hung with their braces over a chair. How wide they looked. Baby stepped back, pulling the door to. 'I said come in, didn't I?' said Pater, still bowed forward and grunting with the effort of his occupation with something else. 'Come in and shut the door.' But for the trousers everything was tidy. A bible lay open on the bedside table. 'Come and sit by me.' One hand was freed from its work for a moment and patted the bed. Still Pater had not looked round.

Baby did as he was told and edging past the chair saw that Pater was engaged in winding an elastic bandage around the calf of his right leg. The left was done already. He wore his woollen socks, their suspenders hanging loose, flannel drawers and a striped shirt whose flap lay in a large bib on his thighs. He finished the bandaging and pinned it tight. Then he turned to Baby sitting uncomfortably beside him on the bed. 'You and Michael,' he said. Baby blushed and looked at the carpet. 'Too much of a twosome. That's no good for Cholmondeley. Share and share alike. Do you understand?' Baby nodded and was rising to leave, but Pater held him back. 'The power of friendship is very great. You can charge many lives with it, lives by nature and through misfortune less

luminous than yours.' Baby nodded, thinking of Goda. But he
knew in his heart that when he was with Michael he wanted
other company as little as when he was with Sally. Michael, he
knew, had become quite innocently indifferent to anything else.
And after Cholmondeley and outside Cholmondeley when and
where would they ever see one another again? Lost in the bitterness of this thought he sat there dumbly, forgetting Pater.

'The child is transparent,' Pater was thinking. 'The thought of
having less than absolutely all of Michael's company brings him
close to tears.' And he wondered again, as he always did, each year
with a further overlay of nostalgia and envy, at the openness and
power of the love his boys felt for one another. His fingers
gripped into Baby's shoulder. The boy's slimness, the purity of
the boy's skin, the lightness of his hair, his innocence worked on
the senses and the conscience of the elderly clergyman until he
trembled. He had no hope of pleasing, he had never had any such
hope; he had become as indifferent to his own portliness, baldness, elderliness, oddity, as the first of his boys were to their good
looks and skills. He was a poor vehicle, like all flesh, through
which feelings, like a Pentecost, stormed. He thought of the
senses as so many menials, fetching and carrying for him in love.
With the backs of his fingers he stroked the boy's cheek. The
softness of the skin was sweeter than any fruit. And one curl of
fair hair, towards the nape, below the ear, was it not something
like the rose or the lily or all that order of 'dappled things' for
whose beauty Hopkins had praised God? All form, all things the
senses seized, they were the work of God, and what they excited
was love. For pure sensation, the better to realize the boy's softness, Pater laid his own cheek against Baby's and stroked it gently
to and fro. It rasped like sandpaper and the spectacles bumped
clumsily. The boy had stiffened and was all contained revulsion.
Pater knew as though the feelings were his own that by dint of all
the willpower he had Baby was holding down an instinctive
disgust under respect, affection and charity. And that knowledge
goaded him. He rubbed the harder, knowing his bristles hurt; he
made noises like an old dove, and nuzzled with his lips upon the
boy's eyebrows and into his hair. Gently Baby put him away and

rose to leave, but Pater rose too and took him forcibly into his embrace. He seemed immensely strong, he pressed the boy against himself. 'Remember what I said,' he murmured, 'share yourselves out. I shall be watching you.' His hands played over Baby's back, under the thin shirt, down the lovely sensation of the spine and in a fierce thrust down some little distance under the belt. 'I love my Baby, we all do, doesn't he know that? We all want a share in him.' The boy would not resist, he was trying above all else not to let Pater see his face. He wanted to be gone, to see Michael, but he could not quite refuse the man whose little noises of affection now resembled the snuffling of Mrs B's dachshund. It was Pater himself who suddenly sat down, head bowed, and bade him go and by way of good-bye drew him in between his knees and bowed and pressed his face against the hidden sex.

Blower got word of his Second. He was preaching in Chapel that evening and in his bitterness came near to railing against God. He had written a sermon on 'Let your light so shine before men…', as his contribution to a discussion continuing day by day among the Officers on the subject of talents and leadership. Blower, after his bad news, stressed more than he had intended the need to shine forth in the teeth of unrecognition. For the first time Michael and Baby were sitting apart, facing each other across the aisle. Pater saw Michael's eyes fixed on Baby with wide open pleasure. He prayed hard: 'Let me not be spiteful, Lord. Let me never be jealous.' Michael was following the service mechanically, rising, kneeling, sitting, singing, without in the least being distracted from his passion. Sunny, to whom Donald had admitted his disappointment and sense of grievance, prayed for words to console him with; Pater, to whom Sunny had felt duty-bound to pass on Donald's confidences, cared much less.

In Sing-Song, unbilled, uninvited, the Beak came forward and did an amalgam of the Balcony Scene from *Romeo and Juliet*, Henry V to his men at Agincourt, and the loves of Perdita and Florizel at sheep-shearing. In all the laughter Michael suddenly found himself weeping at something either Florizel or Juliet had said. The Beak played Henry as though he were Richard III, hunching one shoulder, slavering at the mouth, and shuffling closer and

closer to the chairs of honour in the front row. Then he
straightened up, nodded politely and said in a voice not his own
but which not everyone present could place: 'Thought the boys
shouldn't miss their Shakespeare, sir.' It was then that Pater
resolved not to have the Beak again. Frank, glancing Gerry's way,
raised his eyebrows; Gerry shook his head sadly. Blower did his
best after that, dividing the audience into two halves for the Frog
and the Steamroller; but all those who had ever been through the
performance before thought it inane or, in its conclusion, when,
conducted by Blower's two approaching fingers, the rumble-
rumble-psst and the flip-flop-flip-flop met in a loud squelch,
disgusting. Sunny spoke to him privately afterwards, and revealed
that he had himself come down from Balliol with a Fourth,
having worked 'jolly hard' for three years. Donald nodded, hating
Sunny. 'I don't think it matters in the least,' he said. 'That's the
spirit, old chap,' said Sunny, beaming.

   Michael read Sally's letters as they came. In the third there was
a friendly paragraph about himself, and a photograph inscribed
'For Michael with love from Sally.' He was breathless with surprise and delight. 'Did you ask her for that?' 'Yes, I did,' Baby
admitted. 'It's nice, isn't it? It's not the same as mine.' 'Oh, she's
lovely, Baby, you are lucky, but so is she lucky. Have you been
telling her about me? What have you been saying?' Baby only
grinned. Michael went on: 'I wonder if we'll ever meet, all of us.'
Sally was a pretty girl, to judge by the photograph, with short,
almost boyish hair, large eyes, and the friendliest smile. 'Is that a
gap in her teeth?' Michael asked. 'Yes,' Baby said, 'you can only
see it when she smiles.' And he added, on a rush of memory, 'You
can feel it when you kiss her.' Michael was amazed. 'What do you
mean?' he asked. 'I don't understand you. How can you feel a gap
in her teeth when you kiss somebody?' 'You feel it with your
tongue, when you put your tongue in her mouth.' Michael stared.
He had no words to express his astonishment and excitement.
Baby did not in the least want to seem either knowledgeable or
condescending, so he said in the simplest tones he could find:
'Girls like being kissed like that.' And he added: 'They like you
sucking their tongues as well.' 'And do they do that to you?'

'Of course they do, Sally's a genius at it.' Michael put the photograph away in his shirt pocket. 'You can give me the other one back now,' said Baby, teasing him.

Afternoon. The Beak had gone to Ann's Pantry. Sunny had taken a party looking for fossils in a quarry at Leer. Michael and Baby were lying, as they ought not to have been, alone in the Copse. They both had tournaments to play. Baby lay back, staring into the tree-tops. For the excitement of the feelings there was nowhere like Cholmondeley. He was debating with himself whether his few confidences were a betrayal of Sally. He decided they were not, and imagined so passionately an equal love between the three of them in some blessed place apart that he raised himself up on one elbow and looking down into Michael's face and occasionally teasing his parted lips with a finger Baby divulged still more from his little hoard of privacies.

The white clouds sailed over Cholmondeley, remote and lovely. Mrs B had brought her chair into the sun and was sitting with all her bulk agreeably spread, the sausage dog in her lap and Mr Chapman standing by in case she should want anything. Those who loved mah-jongg were at mah-jongg. On Lords there were groans, and shouts of triumph and friendly derision; in the pool there was splashing and horseplay; on the Oval there was five-a-side soccer, boys from the Midlands stripped to the waist. The Beak sat in Ann's Pantry, a waitress malleable with laughter on either arm.

Goda, expertly packing the tiles away, asked casually what the Dinner Hand was. 'The Thirteen Unique Wonders,' said Anthony, 'it's been that for years, nobody can get it. Who's for a dip before tea?' Goda knew the hands by heart. In bed, in the dark, he reviewed them under his mind's eye. None was so rare and beautiful as the Thirteen Unique Wonders. He was out of the tournaments, so was his team. He would not be asked to do anything at Sing-Song, nor to read in Chapel. Cholmondeley had dropped its demands. He had made no passionate friends. He lived for the afternoons, when there was always somebody with whom he could play mah-jongg. If Pater ever wanted a player he saw no objection to taking on Goda. His banter was less, he saw no reason why the child should not enjoy the game while he could, since he enjoyed nothing else. Noticing that he rarely hesitated in his play Pater observed: 'The Chinese discard the tiles face down. Poor old Perkins couldn't sit there looking to see what has gone.' After that Goda trained himself rigorously to remember the discarded tiles. He often won, and tried to show no emotion. But it was clear to Pater, who loved to contemplate the various passions in his boys, that in Goda he had found or made a player of an extraordinarily pure intensity. When Goda was close to the completion of a hand his yellowish complexion paled to a nauseous shade; when he called mah-jongg his voice was strange, pitched too high, or unsteady or choked; and when he displayed his tiles his joy embarrassed him, so that he mumbled and hid his face and smiled to himself. It frequently happened that some ambitious enterprise of his was scotched by an opponent finishing as cheaply as possible. Then Goda quickly dispersed the fragments of his hand, muttering that he had no score, and not willing that anyone should see what he had gone for and failed to achieve. So Pater watched, and admired the boy in that single respect. It was his private boast that no boy, however below par he might prove to be, ever went from Cholmondeley untouched. In some, he knew, it was Chapel that rooted ineradicably; in others it was a team game, or the golf or the tiddlywinks; in others it was Sing-Song or the camaraderie of the dormitories; in most it was all these things in one intense allegiance which Pater saw no reason not to call religious.

Prayer came easily to boys who woke every morning hearing the doves and who, every evening, were tired after games and the friendly competition with one another. Prayer, directed beyond, was the only expression for feelings which did indeed seem to transcend all those things and people and occurrences by which they were in the first place excited. What a greedy sacrament tea was day after day at Cholmondeley! The appetite had a peculiar edge and its satisfaction every day seemed like a miracle. Even some of the youngest boys felt they must look beyond Mrs B and Mr Chapman when they wanted to give thanks. It seemed to Pater sometimes and to Sunny constantly that such love and joy and gratitude as came into being unfailingly at Cholmondeley ought, if properly directed, to be able to be the salvation of mankind. The boys themselves were only waiting to be told where to turn with their fervent energy. One felt it in Chapel, in the force of prayer or in the singing that filled out the verses (by Pater) and the music (by Sunny) of the Cholmondeley Hymn. Most never knew anywhere else anything of that order in their lives. When the Officers talked about leadership their question was really how to conserve and turn to good ends the Cholmondeley spirit in the long months of everyday life that lay between one party and the next. They arranged local meetings and conferences, they met like masons, knowing one another by the handshake. But there were no local parties, that was impossible. The formula for success – for the heightening of youthful feelings into the sacramental – would only work at Cholmondeley, and there it worked infallibly. What separate and singular intensities Pater had brought to bear, like rays from a burning-glass, on God. What strings of feelings he held in his hand, like a puppeteer. Their distinct loves came to one point, came from one source Pater would have said, went home to one goal, passing through the poor differentiated media of their lives.

'Has he asked you to Rhydwen yet?' the Beak asked. 'What's Rhydwen?' 'His hideaway, in darkest Wales. Only his sweeties go there.' Baby wasn't much interested. 'He never asked me, of course,' the Beak went on, 'but I know all about it from my spies. You climb mountains all day, play mah-jongg all evening, and go to bed by candle-light. And there's a lady called Olwen who sees to your every need.' 'Well he hasn't asked me,' Baby said. 'Thought he might of,' the Beak said, 'when he had you in the other day.' Baby blushed. 'He told me off,' he said. The Beak was intrigued. 'Told me not to go around with Michael all the time.' 'Oh I see. Michael's a love, that's true enough. You know who got him here?' 'No, who? Yes, I do: his schoolmaster.' 'And you know who that is?' 'Who?' 'Old "Is this a puddox bat I see before me?"' 'The Shakespeare chap?' 'In sooth.' 'He came last year.' 'But not this year, my sonny.' 'And why not?' 'He's in jail.' 'Oh I see, that's what you were getting at the other night. And what's he in

jail for?' 'The usual, my dear, the usual.' Baby shook his head.
'You know too much,' he said. 'Have to,' said the Beak, 'for the sake
of my act. What if I don't come again? Will you still come?' 'I'm
glad you came this time.' 'That's not what I asked. Would you still
come here without your Uncle Beakey?' 'If Michael does I will.'

After breakfast the Officers met in the Head's room. They
prayed, and began their business, which was to review the current
party and plan the next. The names of all the first-timers were
read out and the Officers were asked to say how they had shaped
up. Blower wondered about Goda, Cholmondeley was not quite
his cup of tea perhaps. He certainly hadn't done very well in any
of the games. 'But has he enjoyed himself?' Anthony asked, 'that's
surely the point isn't it?' Blower replied that it wasn't the whole
point. Anyway, it was obvious that the child hadn't enjoyed
himself. 'There was that accident with his glasses,' Frank observed.
Donald Blower said he very much disliked having to play devil's
advocate but, if pushed, he would say that a misfortune was an
opportunity to display one's strength of character, and Goda had
not done so. 'What's he like in the dorm?' Sunny asked. 'Very
quiet,' said Anthony, 'he seems to like sleeping.' 'It's not strictly
true to say he hasn't enjoyed himself,' Pater remarked, 'he has
played at mah-jongg with the most evident enjoyment.' Blower
said there was always something, it was not possible to come to
Cholmondeley and not enjoy something. Three or four Officers,
when consulted for their opinions, had to admit that they did not
know exactly who Goda was, which in itself rather told against
him, some new boys being known to *everyone* before Lights Out
on the first day.

There was a silence, nobody quite liked to say the final word.
They looked to Pater, but he would not speak. His eyes, behind
their spectacles, were twinkling at the Officers with a faintly
bitter mockery. He knew better than any of them what a Goda
was like. In the end it was Sunny, to everyone's relief, who found
a form of words. 'I think,' he said slowly, as though the words
were being given him one by one, by God, 'that Goda is the sort
of little boy we here at Cholmondeley are training ourselves to
help. I rather doubt if he himself will ever become one of Life's

Helpers. I rather see him remaining among the Helped.' This accorded nicely with the trend and spirit of the week's discussions and sermons, and found general approbation. Pater grinned broadly and Sunny blushed as though, contrary to form, he had potted one from the base-line. They were passing on to Hawkins from Wolverhampton, an incontrovertible success, when Pater held them up: 'Might I enquire who invited the little boy Goda and in what intention?' Everyone looked at Donald. 'Yes, it was Baby,' he said. 'I gather he's Goda's form prefect. So far as I understand it, he wanted to bring somebody from unfortunate circumstances.' 'Exactly what we've been discussing,' Sunny murmured. 'And since we all like Baby,' Blower went on, 'and this was his first year for extending invitations we let him have his way. To be honest, I had my doubts all along – about the principle, I mean, I didn't know the child myself.' '*Are* Goda's circumstances unfortunate?' Anthony asked. 'I gather they are,' Donald replied. 'Might we know in what way?' 'I don't think they should influence us here,' said Donald. 'And nor do I,' said Jukes, wearying of this discussion of a boy he could not place. 'What Sunny said stands.' 'No, but look, it *is* a tricky one,' Robert put in. 'You don't think we'll lose Baby, do you, if this little chap doesn't come again? I mean if it's his first year for inviting someone and we shoot him down.' 'Not so long as Michael comes,' said Pater, and there was general laughter. 'A propos of Baby,' he went on, 'I was thinking he should be an Officer next year, and I thought of having him at Rhydwen for a week to see how he makes out.' 'Have we finished with Goda then?' Blower asked. 'Can we move on?' Everybody thought so. 'I'm so glad he has enjoyed mah-jongg,' said Sunny. 'We have been able to give him that at least.'

Goda sat in the grass watching the volley-ball finals, the Beak sat next to him. Baby and Michael were playing, on opposite sides. It was warm, many of the boys had taken off their shirts. Goda was happier than he had been all week. He was happy to be a spectator, and the Beak kept up a facetious commentary. Under their limp hair, where the sun had touched him, the Beak's arms were of a boiled pink. He had drawn up his knees and was peering between them, hunched like a vulture, his head swivelling left and right with the play. Next to him sat Goda, dark and ugly, with the cracked lens across his left eye, grinning and chortling, sometimes rolling over helpless with mirth and sometimes applauding loudly when Baby or Baby's team did well. He was at ease, the frightful requirement to participate had passed from him. Though that pitch was the scene of his being trampled under foot he viewed it without fear or resentment.

The ball went up against the blue sky, and those to whom it descended received it bravely, crouching and fending it back again with both hands or cleverly angling it over to brush the net or leaping to smash it down from a height unreturnably. In the longer rallies it was marvellous to see the total concentration of all the boys, the anticipation on every face that his turn to act might be next. The team having played together for a week there was some understanding among them, so that the least good members were allowed and compensated for and the best were served and exploited. They were very sweet these matches in the sun on a background of elms, oaks and beeches. Playing next to or against a particular friend one loved him exceedingly, admired and emulated him with an edge of passionate wish to outdo him too. The older boys, heroes to the younger, increased their command. But the game at its most intense, for crucial points, was like a dance and a chorus. Again and again poses of grace and power were struck and lost, as through that corporate body the principle of youth passed like the breeze through trees and played like light on water, and one or another unremarkable boy was touched, in the self-forgetting co-operation of the game, by a redeeming beauty. The Beak, with his commentary, salted the performance, he discerned ridiculousness, he called it forth. Had he chosen to he could have put a mad laughter among them, as Pan does fear, and caused them to fall to their knees or cling to the posts or lie prone, the ball rolling away neglected.

Goda's wellbeing increased. He wished it were not too late to write once more to his mother, with a better report. Of course, his heart was set on the afternoon's mah-jongg; but at last, a slow learn-er, he was beginning to comprehend that spirit of Cholmondeley

which, Sunny said, should be a 'Light of the World'. There in
Cholmondeley's grounds he was beginning to see scattered bits
of paradise through his cracked glasses.

Pater sat opposite him in a short-sleeved shirt, a canvas cap on
his bald head and his stick crooked over the back of the chair.
Wilcox, with cropped hair and ears like a marmoset, was on
Goda's right; and on Goda's left was Gerry. Three other groups,
at their tables nearby, were playing quietly. The presence of Pater
commanded decorum for the game. There was some chatter and
relaxation when a game had ended and the scores were totted up
and the tally sticks went to and fro and the hands were over-
turned, but with the building of the City silence was reimposed.
One heard most clearly then the sleepy doves. Mrs B came out
with her chair, the dog yapped and dozed off in her lap, Mr
Chapman tiptoed away. The tiles, being shuffled, being sorted in
their racks, clattered quietly. The players' voices were low, what
they said was necessary. Hilarity from the pool, but very faint.
Indoors, in a dormitory by an open window, somebody was practising the flute. Soon the assiduous efforts and repetitions went
over into a deliciously self-indulgent rendering of those pieces
the player was entirely master of.
    Goda's luck was in. He met her more than half way, he was
disposed to be lucky. He won the first two games with hands that
were enhancements of the ordinary, one all concealed and rich in
Winds and Dragons, the second all Bamboo, green and red, and
in both hands there was the careless bonus of a Season or a
Flower. He scored well, but scarcely noticed, the hands were so
pleasing to look at he was loath to part with them. But what he
had made up, the order he had assembled, went back face down
into anonymity and chaos. Wilcox in a self-important manner
consulted the sheet of Special Hands. Pater teased him for
delusions of grandeur. Gerry, more reserved than ever, seeming
on the brink of some terrible loss or absence, smiled. Pater, off
Wilcox, chowed repeatedly and showed, in victory, a hand
of supreme cheapness. But he became East Wind. There he
remained, winning three times with hands not unlike Goda's, the

normal gilded, and, as his privilege, doubled in the payment due
to them. Goda, during those three, tried Crochet and Knitting,
and came near. Whilst they were shuffling Pater stretched his legs
in strolling to the other tables to see whether anything very
extraordinary were being done there. Perkins had just gone out
with the Seven Pairs, his best hand ever. The victory seemed to
him a substantial gift, that he could pack and take home. But
Pater, doing his rounds, saw nothing higher, there was nothing
assembling in any of the racks that would finish like Himalayan
peaks above all the rest.

Gerry won with the last possible tile (when the hand for the
absent player had been separated off) and became East Wind.
Pater was richest, Goda was low in funds, having aimed high and
missed too often. Gerry, winning as East, reluctantly extorted a
payment that almost broke him; but he replied at once with a win
of extraordinary speed and simplicity, the tiles falling to him turn
by turn, and East Wind's risks and privileges passed to him. He
was afloat again, though not rich; he indulged himself with
Dragons and the lovely One of Bamboo, then, discerning a cheap
haste in Wilcox's play, chowed twice and won. 'One more game,'
said Pater. Goda started. The flute had long since ceased. There
came an ugly snore from Mrs B's lap, like a death-rattle. Gerry
smiled with infinite understanding upon Goda's shock at being so
curtailed. 'There'll be other games, old chap,' he said. Wilcox
grinned: 'He'll be first here next Easter, he'll be sitting here with
his table ready when the rest of us arrive.' Wilcox breached the
wall, clumsily. Pater glared at him and snapped: 'Keep your mind
on what you are doing.'

They drew their tiles, four and four and four and Goda's two.
The sudden thought that his first Cholmondeley party was all but
over had brought tears to his eyes and he looked dumbly and
unclearly at the tiles coming together in his rack. 'You to start,
old boy,' said Pater in such kind tones that Gerry, who could
remember the ending of his own first party, loved him intensely.
Goda put down, to be replaced with a playing tile, the Season of
Spring. 'Number 1,' said Gerry, 'that's a very good start.' Still
miserable, Goda discarded something. Play passed to Wilcox, and

only then did Goda blink the tears from his eyes and discern among his tiles the making of a supreme beauty. His imagination and his calculating mind came to bear on it at once. He was like a poet, when they seize with gratitude and wonder on their given lines. Of Bamboo he had the Nine, of Circles the One and the Nine, of Characters also. He had two winds, the South and the North; also the blank White Dragon and the Red that is like a dagger. Through the encumbrance of unwanted tiles he *saw* the finished hand. Then it vanished, and he was left with the fixed determination to restore it. What luck that in his dejection at the outset he had not thrown away anything he needed. Now he set aside to be discarded three Three of Circles whose beauty and value might have deflected him from his ambition. Play came to him and he drew the East Wind. That confirmed him in his faith. What he discarded Gerry claimed, so play came again to Goda and he drew the West. Then he was into the doldrums and for four turns of the game drew nothing constructive but discarded quickly and each of his opponents took up something; each, harmfully to Goda's purpose, was settling for the ordinary. He drew the Summer Season and declared it. In replacement he took up the twin to his East Wind. What he discarded Wilcox chowed, *his* hand was beggarly. Wilcox put down the Bird of Bamboo, and Goda could do nothing, watched it fly. He tried not to hope, but in wave after wave the wish for this one thing above all else in life passed over him and he shuddered under it. Pater threw away a Green Dragon, and Goda stood by; Gerry another, and he was helpless; but then he drew a third. What he put down Wilcox chowed. Glancing at his rack Goda deduced from the transparent arrangement there that Wilcox was wanting only two. Pater and Gerry were deeper, it was not possible to say, but both had two finished trios exposed. Play came to Goda and he drew the Autumn. Wilcox whistled through his teeth, for which he was rebuked. Gerry glanced at Goda with some understanding of his luck. The thread suspending Goda's chances was drawn out thinner and thinner. He feared there could scarcely be another round of turns, but in a marvellous unbearable pause four tiles were taken up and four discarded and not one interruption for any claim was made. Goda drew the Winter. A set was rare, he had already the aura of an extraordinary fortune, so that all three looked at him curiously. But what he replaced the Winter with he had no use for and as he set it down there was Wilcox, like the very cynic and underminer of greatness, claiming it for a miserable run. Like Goda now he wanted one tile. Pater raised a finger, then gravely set apart the Dead Fourteen. Goda began to hear his own knell tolling. Sweet bird, Bird of Bamboo, oddest among the tiles, hardest to learn, easiest misnamed, unique. Her mate, the Nine, was solitary in Goda's rack. What Pater played Wilcox called for, to win. Goda closed his eyes. But Wilcox, red as a turkey cock, was admitting he was mistaken, he had muddled his needs. 'Penalties, penalties,' Pater murmured, 'men in Peking have been stoned to death for less.' Gerry discarded. Everybody looked at Wilcox, who was wriggling in his seat and seemed scarcely able to restrain his grabbing hand. Then Goda, asking nothing, taking nothing from anybody, having claimed nothing from all that all three had thrown away, drew the green bird, and paused. They all waited, he was never slow to discard. He had gone an ugly white. 'Well, child?' Pater said. Goda swallowed. 'I've got the Dinner Hand,' he said.

By tea-time nobody at Cholmondeley did not know that Goda had got the Dinner Hand. It was everybody's talk. Spectators at the finals of the golf and the tiddlywinks exchanged further details. His score had been such that not his three opponents together could pay him what was due. The hand itself was set at the limit, his four Seasons doubled it three times, and being East Wind he asked that total twice. Pater in thirty years had never seen such a score. Preaching in Chapel, as it was his tradition to do on the last night, he spoke of God's grace, how we can get it neither by force not by stealth, but how it comes, when it is given, in circumstances apparently unpropitious, upon people apparently unsuited, and how all we can do is be disposed, lay ourselves open, strive to be always not unworthy of its being given, should it ever come. As always, he moved many of the boys to tears. Michael saw grace in Baby's love, Goda in the Thirteen Unique Wonders, and the gratitude of both was boundless. Pater urged them all to preserve as well as they could whatever had been best in the week gone by, and to bear it with them like a lamp among others less fortunate than themselves. More than one boy at the right age, and the moment inclining, opening and lifting him, had felt Pater's words to be the Holy Spirit and had received into his heart a sense, as tangible as a crystal, of election, love and purpose. Gerry, on the threshold of his monastery, felt confirmed in his vocation, and wept for joy quite openly. Less even than usual was lost of this heightened mood during the slow walk from Chapel through the warm evening grounds to the common room and the refectory. That night the boys swayed together in the Cholmondeley Song. The Beak was mysteriously absent, but few noticed. 'One of the best ever,' Sunny said to those Officers who had no more pressing engagements and had joined him for a last cup of cocoa.

Baby was at the pool first, bleak with approaching absence. The morning, indifferent, ascended to its usual beauty. Then Michael came running. They swam quickly and got out. Nobody else would come, it was not sensible, in fact there was a rule against bathing on the last morning. In miserable love they stood looking at one another. Michael's helplessness touched Baby to the heart. Neither had anything to say. They had said they would write, they would both come again, they would try to meet in the meantime. Neither had said the word love, each gazed with an infatuated seriousness on the other's face. They turned aside, to dress, and in that moment sexual passion entered the vagueness of Baby's feelings like the white sun coming through, and he turned, naked himself, and stepped the necessary paces to Michael who had his back to him and was towelling one foot dry raised on the bench. He touched him on the shoulder and felt the same shock and they faced each other naked for the first time and saw with their own eyes, each in the other's body, what sex was like in its urgency, single-mindedness and beauty. Baby touched his friend's soft cheeks, stroked them with the backs of his fingers, then kissed him on the mouth.

After breakfast there were the customary speeches. A small boy in school uniform carried an envelope to Mrs B, who feigned surprise. Three cheers followed. The Beak, in the general roar and cheering with the best, kicked the dachshund sharply on the snout. Pater and Sunny were cheered. Then the first school groups began to make ready to leave. How strange all the boys were to one another in their uniforms. What a show of badges and mottos: Sapere Aude, Lampada Trado, Fluctuat Nec Mergitur. There was much exchanging of addresses. In uniform, in their university, city or service clothes, the older boys, the heroes, were terribly overawing to the youngest, who wondered how they had ever dared be at all familiar during the week. They took photographs, asking permission.

Pater took Michael and Baby on one side and invited them to spend a week with him at Rhydwen, at the end of August. Neither dared look at the other. Their thoughts came in a rush choking their throats and clouding their eyes. Pater squeezed their arms with a force that bruised them. Then he said good-bye to Goda. The little fool got the handshake wrong again. 'Never forget your moment of triumph,' Pater said. Goda felt haloed around with it, for all eternity. He could not begin to voice his gratitude to Pater and the paradise Pater governed. 'You'll be hearing from me, of course, about the dinner,' Pater said. 'What do you like to eat?' Goda mumbled and shook his head. Pater was thinking the dinner would be very difficult, what with Goda being the way he was and Gerry taking himself off to a monastery. Perhaps he would send the little boy some money instead.

Walking into town to catch the bus Goda dared to ask Anthony whether the dinner would be a very posh affair. 'Black tie,' said Blower, overhearing the question. Anthony looked at Blower with dislike, and for all his answer to Goda patted him sadly on the shoulder. Goda felt the beginnings of an anxiety he could not name. He consoled himself with his victory, which nothing could tarnish. 'I shan't mind if I never win at the game again,' he thought. But then a longing to play, to feel the tiles, to build the City walls, to begin the making of a beautiful hand, the desire for this took hold of him.

In the bus to Cheltenham Goda was sick. Seeing Blower staring at him with intense disapproval he felt another access of fear. 'I say,' he whispered to Baby who was looking after him, 'you don't think he'll not let me come again, do you, on account of me being sick like this?' Baby smiled at him. He was turning over in his mind, in a condition of intense happiness and excitement, the advantages, the licence, which Michael's being a boy gave him over Sally. At Rhydwen they would surely share a room at nights. In his own deep and benevolent joy he smiled at Goda who, anxious, repeated his question. 'Of course you'll come again,' said Baby. 'We'll see to that.' And he hugged the evil-smelling child close.

Purity

Eva came home, and soon she knew she was pregnant. Her first feeling was joy, and thereafter, in all the worse and worse that followed, she was glad that her first feeling, when she knew she was carrying his child, was brave and heedless joy. She wrote to Paris, but got no answer. The weeks passed, the months. She wrote again, happy still, making no demands, only reminding him, as though nothing had changed, of what they had agreed. But he never replied.

The birth was difficult, and she was much torn. No one was with her before or after. Then, pestered by the hospital, her parents took her in. She became ill, her milk ceased. Grudgingly they saw to the baby boy. But they stilled him at nights, when he cried and cried, with brandy on a spoon. Sick, body and soul all asunder, Eva had to be content that they did no worse.

The snow came, the farm was cut off for weeks. The whiteness was her own blank misery, the cold her loneliness. She could not stand without support, the room tilted when she walked a few steps. When the deer came out of the forest for food her brother took a shot gun and fired at them. They fled, leaving one wounded. From her window Eva saw the creature drag itself back into the trees. At nights she imagined it dying.

As soon as the ways were clear she left home with her baby and found a room in town. She called him Philip. She wrote once more, but there was no answer. In the warmer weather she took the baby out, but dumb and lonely. Her days were long, her nights bitter. She fretted, her love for the child would not come right since his father did not want to know her. She looked at herself in the glass and wept to see a face so much altered.

In the town there was a French Society. She saw a notice of its meetings and for some time dwelled on the idea that she might attend. She ought not to lose the language, even if she never went to the country again. So she told herself. Besides, she needed to go out, the solitary life was bad for her; and when her landlady, on the floor below, offered to look after Philip once a week she took the chance.

They met in a back room of the Municipal Museum, a building that had once been a private house, in a stately park. The steps, the portico, overawed Eva. She was poor, her clothes had mostly been given her. She stood hesitant. Nobody invited her to come in, they stared at her through the open door, they were all old, all women, sitting round a large polished table. But when one rose to shut the door Eva stepped forward, with something of the boldness that had first brought her to the notice of the man in Paris.

The meetings were nothing, she made no progress, her language would not come back. Still she went, her landlady was kind and said the evening out did her good, so she walked each Thursday throughout the wet spring, and attended, as though it were a connection still, if not any hope.

One Thursday, it was in late April, a foreigner came. She looked up from the magazine she was puzzling over and saw him standing on the threshold as she herself had done. But he was prepossessing, the ladies welcomed him in. Eva heard him say that he wished to borrow books. There were high shelves full of books on two walls of the room, but none of the Society ever looked at them. He was asked if he would like to participate in the customary proceedings first. Politely he agreed. Though his foreignness was obvious, his language was word-perfect. Sitting down opposite Eva he appraised her oddness in that place so coolly and exactly that she blushed. The macabre absurdity of her one evening out became evident to her. They began the reading. A magazine was circulated and each in turn read aloud from it. The French was old, from the era of its being spoken before the servants, and only dimly remembered. The women spoke it thickly, and through various handicaps of speech, sight and the brain. Each read until she was exhausted, or until the page was snatched from her by a jealous neighbour. But the foreigner, when it passed to him, read with a purity of accent which, for the memories, brought tears to Eva's eyes. He read a paragraph from an article about the English Royal Family. Then, bowing politely, he gave way to the lady on his left. When the turn came to Eva she read with care, her finger following the words. She excited some envy and did not read for long. Looking up she saw him studying her with an open curiosity.

They came out together. 'What a morgue,' he said, 'what a necropolis.' He seemed to assume that she was not really one of the company. Eva smiled, not fully understanding. He held up his book. 'They won't let me take more than one at a time. I'll have to keep coming. There are fourteen volumes. What do you come for?' 'To keep up my French,' Eva replied. 'Then I'll see you next week,' he said, and ran down the steps and away through the park. She felt gaiety in him, and mockery.

After April, but for the foreigner, she might not have attended anymore. Perhaps she was almost ready to let France go, since no word came from there. The language was crumbling away, the absence eroded it. And what did she need with French in her daily life? Then the foreigner said, with a careless generosity: 'I'll give you lessons if you like. Truly, you'll never learn anything in there.' Eva stared at him, and shook her head. 'Why not?' he asked. For answer she thrust her hands into her coat pockets and began to walk quickly towards the street. At the gates they halted. 'Think about it,' he said. 'I'll be back next week for Volume Three.' And he added: 'My name is Paul.' 'My name is Eva,' she replied.

She could do nothing much about her clothes. In the brighter weather they looked worse, they were drab and shapeless. She looked at herself without them, her figure had gone slack.

'Why do you say no?' he asked. 'That room is a place of death, and their French is unintelligible.' 'I can't pay you, that's why.' She looked at the ground. 'I see,' said Paul, 'I thought it might be that. Well I don't want paying. I don't need the money.' 'Still I should have to do something for you in return.' She glanced at him. He was looking up and away from her, to locate a blackbird whose

pure singing had accompanied and now interrupted their conversation. 'Hear that bird,' he said, 'and look at him. He's in the last
of the sun. You don't need to do anything for me. I don't need
anything doing for me. Shall I meet you in a café?' Eva blushed.
A white scar became very visible on her lip. 'Come to my room,'
she said, avoiding his eyes, 'then I can cook you a meal in return
for the lesson.' Paul shrugged. 'Alright,' he said, 'if you like. But
really you don't need to. When?' Thursday would be best, she
thought, the landlady might still look after Philip. 'Good,' he said,
'I'll collect my book from here and come to you.'

He arrived, carrying the next volume and a couple of texts of
his own for her to read from. The room was small, at the back
of the house, overlooking a garden where there was an apple tree
full of blossom. He sat on the bed, Eva on the one chair opposite
him. Then he began speaking to her in French. He phrased
everything simply and clearly. It seemed to her that she had never
heard the language in such clarity before. She understood his
questions. Where had she learned French? In school, in France?
Did she have friends in France? And he helped her to form her
replies. She watched his mouth, she watched his lips and tongue
and teeth pronounce the words. It began to come back to her. To
conclude, he handed her a book and made her read aloud, a
poem. Leaning back comfortably against the wall he corrected
her pronunciation and repeated each line in turn, for her to imitate.
She saw him, slim and dark, in simple close-fitting clothes, leaning back quite at home and reciting a poem by heart for her to
follow. Her room seemed to light up. Her happiness in Paris
returned to her. She had been brighter then, prettier, more sure.
Paul said that was enough for one day. Flushed and smiling and
more pleased with herself than she had been for many months she
went on in her own language to tell him in a rush about her time
in Paris. It had been her one chance, the opportunity had come
like a miracle. He ate his meal nearly in silence, listening, so that
afterwards she was ashamed and had she had his address she would
have written him a note of apology for her self-centredness.

He arrived punctually and for an hour spoke only French. Very
soon she understood all he said. He began with news of 'les

vieilles dames dans leur musée'; then induced her to talk about herself. How the foreign language opened her! Soon she told him how she had fallen in love. He rephrased the story for her, and she repeated it. She loved her story in the phrases he lent it. She seemed a brave and passionate young woman. Certainly she had been able to affect a man, one older than herself, quite an emi-nent man, she thought, and very gifted. He was her teacher in the art class she attended. Paul listened, and reworded things for her with an indifferent even sympathy. She read aloud: 'Mon enfant, ma soeur, songe à la douceur...' Soon, in her little room with its window open on another early summer, she laughed more freely when he described, with a pure facility, the old ladies around their polished table, some dead, some comatose, some only sleep-ing, droning, snoring, whilst the dead who lived, the poets, the masters of language, looked down upon them from the walls.

She had been an art student in Paris, only for a term. On the evening when Paul took back the last volume of *A l'ombre des jeunes filles en fleurs* and borrowed the first of *Le côté de Guermantes*, Eva, after the lesson, gave him a folder of her work to look through whilst she prepared his meal. They were water colours of flowers and pencil and charcoal drawings of people. 'You did a lot of anemones,' he commented. 'Those were for myself,' she replied, 'I had them in my room. In the class we drew from life.' Paul turned from the colours, from a delight in colour, to the sparse lines and the shadows of the studies and the portraits. Some were the worst faces off the streets, their eyes cavernous with apathy after suffering. 'I suppose such faces are more interesting than normal ones,' said Paul, 'for an artist, I mean.' 'All faces are interesting when you study them,' she answered, 'and lovely too, in a way.' She had bethought herself of something and was glancing rather anxiously from the stove to see how far he had got in his leafing through the folder. At last she crossed over quickly and took it from his hands. 'You needn't be shy,' he said to her in French. 'Are there some of your teacher?' Not hesitating for long she took out a sketch and handed it to him. 'Was that in your room too, like the flowers?' Paul asked. 'Non, dans son chambre.' 'Dans *sa* chambre,' said Paul, 'dans sa chambre à lui.' It was the face of a man about forty. 'The eyes are particularly good,' said Paul. 'He looks a clever man, a little cruel perhaps. Or perhaps I only say that because I know he was unkind to you.' 'Was he kind to me when I first loved him?' Eva wondered, 'or was he always cruel?' She looked at the picture with as much interest as Paul was showing. 'Did he do one of you?' Paul asked. 'I'm sure he did.' 'I can't show you that,' Eva said quickly, and went back to the stove. Serving his meal she said: 'I'd like to draw your portrait one day. Will you let me?' Paul shrugged, and said he did not see why not.

She never reflected on the fact that neither language was his own. His facility made her forget. In either he seemed quite transparent. He replied with an apparent total candour. 'Are you engaged?' she asked. 'Not formally,' he replied. 'I mean we never announced it. But we shall marry when I go back.' 'You are agreed on that?' 'Oh yes,' said Paul, 'though I don't remember that we ever discussed it.' 'And whilst you're away will she go with anyone else?' 'Oh no.' 'But if she did?' 'If she did I should suffer but it wouldn't make any essential difference.' 'And if you did?' 'If I did she would suffer, but less, I think, and it would make no difference.' 'And she would tell you if she did, and you would tell her if you did?' 'Of course. But we shan't.' To Eva they seemed radiant people.

When he next came he said: 'I've brought you a present. Victoria sent it for you.' It was a headscarf, light as air but bright with the colours of many different flowers. 'It's beautiful,' said Eva, looking at herself. 'How kind of her.' Paul shrugged. 'So you told her about me?' 'Of course I did.' 'And she doesn't mind you coming here every week?' 'Of course she doesn't.' Looking at herself in the glass Eva knew that to be sent such a bright and happy gift she must have been depicted to the foreign girl as sad and dowdy. But what could she do? It was so. 'I can't send her anything in return,' she said. 'She doesn't want anything,' said Paul. Eva's poverty came over her again. Then suddenly her face in the mirror lit up with an idea. 'I know,' she said, and for a moment she was pretty, 'I know what I can do. I'll send her your picture. She would like to have your picture.'

Paul took off his shoes and sat on the bed, removing the pillow and leaning back against the wall. Eva placed her chair. 'Can I read?' he asked. 'Alright if you must. I suppose she is used to seeing you reading.' Paul opened the third volume of *Guermantes*, and for the first time since leaving Paris Eva began to draw. 'Dessiner, c'est connaître.' She could hear him saying it. He walked from pupil to pupil. At first his looking over her shoulder had made her nervous and clumsy. He took the pencil from her stiff fingers and with a few strokes brought the pain of a model's face to life. 'This is the line,' he said. 'Look at the mouth. See, it has become thin and tight with worry.' They never once had a model like Paul, it was not in her teacher's nature to let them contemplate such faces. The men he hired were defeated creatures, and the women, at best, were ordinary. He showed his class the swollen feet and veins of a shopgirl, and the slackness in the flesh of a frequent mother. He pointed these things out. After such teaching she had drawn her teacher, become her lover, with an honesty he approved of. Paul, through two clear languages, seemed known to her already. She saw the fineness of his features, the neatness of his hair combed forward and lying on his forehead in dark curls. He was self-possessed, wanting nothing from anybody. His skin was clearer than hers, his hands holding the book were still and small, the nails obviously cared for, whilst hers, holding the pencil, were bitten to the quick.

He was reading, she was drawing, each in a deep concentration, when there came a gentle knock at the door. Paul looked up without the least embarrassment, although they had never been interrupted before. It was the landlady, apologising, she had to go out, could Eva take the baby? He was asleep, he would be no trouble. Eva laid him in the cot at the foot of the bed. She would have resumed her work, but Paul said he must leave. The landlady, when she next met Eva, apologised again for disturbing them. She meant well. 'He looks a nice boy,' she said. 'If only you could get one like him to take you on.'

There are two volumes of *Sodome et Gomorrhe*. Paul fetched the first. 'The ladies are cross with me,' he said, 'because I never stay.' 'If they knew where you were they'd be more than cross with me,' said Eva. She had learned a poem during the week. Eyes on his face she recited the lines nearly perfectly. 'You are getting better and better,' Paul said. 'All thanks to you,' she replied. 'I was thinking perhaps I could try a novel on my own soon. Would I like what you're reading?' 'No, I don't think so. Not yet anyway.' 'I daren't go back there to borrow one.' 'I'll see what I've got at home,' Paul said, 'or I'll buy you something. You might like Maupassant to start with.'

After the lesson Eva went downstairs for Philip. 'She's very sorry. She says in future we can have all the evening to ourselves, but tonight she's going out again.' 'It doesn't matter,' Paul said. The baby was awake, but heavy and dull. There was nothing of the father in his looks. Eva made up his bottle. 'Don't you feed him yourself?' Paul asked. 'Is it because I'm here?' 'I can't,' she said. She moved the cot as far from the bed as possible and laid the baby down. He slept at once. Then she prepared Paul's meal. She had bought some beer. The window was open on a close evening; the room had become warm from the cooking and the air that entered was no cooler. The blackbird started up, but soon fell silent, as though overweighed. 'I don't want you to read tonight,' Eva said. 'I want to be able to see your eyes.' Paul, already comfortable on the bed, his legs stretched out, his back against the wall above her pillow, put down *Sodome et Gomorrhe*. She poured him another glass of beer. 'You drink some too,' he said.

Now, as she drew, his eyes were on her. When she looked up to study him their eyes met. Again under the eyes of a teacher Eva worked with her old intentness. Quickly she finished the drawing already begun and handed it to him. 'Stay though,' she said, flushed in the cheeks, the scar on her lip more than usually evident, 'I want to do another one, it's different tonight.' He saw himself as she had drawn him, composed, in a thin black jersey, innocent, almost feminine. 'Quel petit abbé!' he said. 'Am I really like that?' She smiled, she was pleased with the picture, his for-eignness was in it, his politeness, his slight formality, his peculiar childish candour. 'Show me how he drew you,' Paul said. 'I want to see the picture he did of you. Je veux voir s'il t'a comprise ou non.' 'Il m'a très bien comprise,' she replied, and shook her head. 'If it's because you're naked you needn't mind. They way you've drawn me I'm as good as naked, spiritually at least.' He flattered

her, so she rose and fetched out the picture from its folder.
'There,' she said, 'see what he did and what I'm like.'

The man's cruelty was apparent at a glance. The shock of it
passed over Paul's face. He had got her to pose in such a fashion
as to indicate that she would always do whatever he cared to ask
of her. The indecency was not in her character, that was obvious.
The power of the picture lay in his having conveyed exactly her
gaucheness and suppressed distaste. Under the smile her mouth
was set in a determined obedience. 'Where did you get that scar,
by the way?' Paul asked. 'My father hit me when I was small.'
'What with?' 'With his hand. His wedding ring cut me.' Paul
looked again at the picture, then laid it aside and drank off his
beer. 'You have been abused,' he said. 'I know,' she said. 'He
wasn't the first.' 'Who wasn't, your father?' 'No, him in Paris.
Perhaps my father was the first. Be still now, I want to finish.'

Paul leaned back his head against the wall. Soon Eva finished
the drawing and sat looking at it. What had she made of him?
Something had come into the second portrait which she could
not name but which disturbed her. She knew she had done
something which would have won her teacher's praise. He would
have much preferred the second version to the first. It pleased and
shocked her to realize this. She glanced at Paul. He had closed his
eyes. It entered her mind that his eyes were closed knowingly, that
he was exposing himself to her contemplation. The baby was
asleep, the landlady was out. Ascribing disingenuousness to Paul
Eva now thought bitterly, almost maliciously, of service, of neither
Paul nor Victoria wanting anything of her. But she wanted
nothing for herself, unless to affect, to impinge, to create a want,
of herself. She put aside the drawing and went on her knees by
the bed. The movement did not cause him to open his eyes. The
silence of the room, the silence of the garden droned in her ears,
her heart thumped and she weighed her intention for and against,
the good in it and the bad. Then she leaned forward and began.
Glancing up bitch-like from what she was doing she saw him
open his eyes and shut them again at once. He made some effort,
not to stop her but to engage her, feeling for her breasts, pulling
at her skirt, but she put him away. Her breasts were flat and the

place between her legs had been made ugly by the birth so that she was ashamed. When he desisted immediately she felt how uninviting to the touch her dull clothes were and that he must be glad not to have to go on. She exulted all the more then in what she was good at.

Eva ran the tap and spat into the sink. Turning she faced him with a smile but his look shrivelled her and she wiped the back of her hand across her mouth. She dreaded that he might have seen some triumph in her smile. 'What's the matter?' she asked. He sat on the edge of the bed and covered his face with his hands. She knelt by him. When she saw the tears well through his fingers she cried 'my love, my little boy, what *is* the matter?' He wept, his body shook with sobs. She pulled at his wrists, to see his face. For very pity she wanted to kiss his eyes. But when she touched him he shuddered as though stricken, his hands came away and she saw a face hideous with shame and hate. He said some words which she did not understand. 'What are you saying?' she asked, 'what is so terrible?' 'Filth,' he said in her language for her, 'you loathsome filthy bitch.' Each word was spat into her face. Then came his hands, seizing her by the throat. 'Why did you muck me up? I was alright, you dirty slut, I didn't want mucking up.' He squeezed her throat and shook her where she knelt. She screamed, choking. His thumbs pressed. Then the baby woke and cried. Paul, in loathing, pushed her away, picked up his book and left the room. Eva ran to lock the door. Then lay on the bed stupid with fear. The baby whimpered to sleep again.

She woke in the night, breathless, choking. She saw his face, twisted with sin. And so it was for two or three nights: nightmare or sleeplessness, one constant preoccupation with his revulsion and assault. She spoke to no one, she averted her eyes. Was she leprous to look at? She saw his hands coming together on her throat. Food choked her, no water was pure enough to swallow. There was an equal war for two or three days, between him and her, around the unalterable fact of his disgust. Then it was settled, against her. She had abused him, the wrong was all hers. She thought of the girl, she saw her grieving, abused. The scarf, the one light pretty article in all her wardrobe, now she would never

wear it. By the mid-week, knowing that he would not come, Eva
thought only of what she had forfeited, and the weeks and the
months and the years of her life extended into the future desperately. She was all penitence, she was all self-abasement.

She went early and stood in the path where he must pass to
return the ninth volume and borrow the tenth. Arriving for their
evening the ladies sneered at her. Then Paul came. 'Wait,' he said.
'I'll change my book first before they start their silly reading.'
They walked up and down under the lime trees. He was quite
composed and gentle. 'It's not you,' he said, 'it's not your fault,
I let you. I'm sorry if I hurt you afterwards.' 'You'll come again
then?' she said. 'Come now.' He shook his head. 'No, I'm not coming ever again.' How bleak, how uniformly bleak the life ahead of
her would be. 'Please,' she said, 'forgive me, come again.' 'I do
forgive you. Besides, as I said, it's not you, it's me, I loathe myself.'
'It was a mistake,' she said, 'it was my mistake, I'm very sorry. But
don't leave me alone now, I beg you not to.' He was inflexible, he
said he did not trust himself. 'Who minds?' Eva said. 'You said
yourself that Victoria would not mind.' 'I mind,' said Paul. She
saw the revulsion in his eyes again. He turned and walked away.

She held off for two weeks. Loss seemed a compound state,
never lessening, always increasing. One evening she remembered
the Quai des Fleurs. There was dust, the banks of flowers had
been wetted. Was that not good? Such love that one wept for
joy over it. She wept in desolation. She went again and stood in
the park but seeing her he only shook his head. The ladies – the
fossils, the skeletons – knew what was happening and jeered. *La
Prisonnière, Albertine disparue, Le temps retrouvé*. When he came to
return the last volume she was there once more and stood in his
path. 'I shan't go again now,' he said. 'I've finished it. They were
getting very cross that I never stayed.' 'You'll be going home
soon,' Eva said. He nodded. 'I could have had a few more weeks
of you, Victoria wouldn't have minded, you said yourself she
wouldn't.' He shrugged. Then he added: 'Don't let your French
fall off again, will you? The language is a skill, it's got nothing to
do with particular people, and you were good at it. Can you still
remember your poem?' 'Yes,' she said, 'I can: "Quand vous serez

bien vieille, au soir, à la chandelle…" You forgot the drawings. Don't you want them?' Paul blushed. 'Perhaps I should take one, but you must keep the other.' 'Which one then?' She took them both out from under her ugly winter coat and unrolled them for him to choose. He chose the first in which, so she believed, she had caught his purity.

The Starlings

She has looked forward to the short days, but now they have come what have they brought him but a fearful restlessness? In the long evenings, she thought, in the dark early mornings, he will get on with his work. The short days will be undemanding, he will save his strength. He is writing a little book, part autobiography, part history of the parish he was born in. He has made all the necessary notes, collected all the references. He has unearthed letters from old friends and articles he wrote for the newspaper many years ago; volumes are open on his writing table, others close to hand are stuck full of markers. In winter there are fewer distractions. He will rise at his usual summer hour and instead of going out into the garden he will make himself a cup of tea, switch on the lamp, and begin. By four in the afternoon they will have drawn the curtains, and before supper and after all the time he could want will be his. Instead, this terrible agitation. His wife is in tears over him.

He sleeps like a man knocked out by drugs, misses the early time, wakes when the tardy light begins, wakes with a guilty start, he cannot tell where he is, his heart is racing and pounding. When he dresses he is all fingers and thumbs. He must be in the marsh before the light is established, or he will miss the starlings taking off. Crazy! And when he returns, wet through as like as not, he has no intention of stopping, he sits in his coat, he breakfasts impatiently, then he's gone again, out the door, in his old shoes and his mac, bare-headed, the fool, at his age, to walk to the north coast. He will come back with the starlings, at dusk, at the end of a short day, exhausted. And his writing? He has the long evening. But the fire defeats him. He falls back on the sofa, nose in the air, one leg stretched out, the other touching the carpet. Mad old man. His wife has to wake him at bedtime.

She is growing to hate the birds. At four, when they return, she draws the curtains against them with an angry swish. Makes the tea, he will be in soon, worn out. In the mornings, emptying the teapot, she sees them, hears them, whizzing overhead. He will be in soon, briefly. She makes his breakfast. Once she asked should she clear away his books and papers off the table, since he didn't seem to be doing anything with them. Just you dare, he said, just you dare. She does not dare. She tries to reason, but if it is morning he stamps out of the house and if it is evening he falls asleep.

Returning from the north coast he passes his house (already lighted) as though it were a stranger's. He passes towards the marshes, the swift birds overtaking him. Handfuls of birds, pelting showers of birds. How many heads? Scores, hundreds, thousands. Their intentness, their rapidity. But flocks further off and higher can be seen to have a pulse, a rhythm, almost leisurely, like one animal loping through the sky. Low down, however, close to his own head, they dispirit him with their purposefulness. In the marshes, between the sea and the reeds, he positions himself. There is a moat between him and the reeds, but he has found a little promontory of firm ground and on the extreme end of that, the scummy water on three sides, he is as near as he can get. The sea at his back and a strong wind off the sea, the starlings home into the wind. He knows (he has seen them) that towards the north coast, where they forage in the fields, they enjoy quite a degree of separateness, they walk apart, pecking at the earth; but in the sky above the marsh, when they come home for the night, they clot, they cake, and out of the vast white sky they drop abruptly, you might say they were seized, they add themselves to what of their corporate body is already in place, they extend and thicken the slick of them through the reeds.

The event might be imagined in total silence. The birds come over and fall out of the sky. But really there is no silence. There is the sea, fetched in its noise nearer and nearer by a steady wind;

and the birds, when they have fallen, mutter and fidget. That is what has got into him: the marsh itself, every burdened reed, its audible, tangible fidgeting. Not just the starlings, every other bird in there fidgets and cries. He would not like to be the mother of a marsh like that, trying to hush it. If it were one beast you would say it was tormented. The sea like the condition of tinnitus. The creaking, squawking, harassed restlessness of the marsh has entered his heart and his blood. He hurries from the place, his fatigue is terrible, he has wounded his feet trekking after the starlings all day long.

For much of the night his sleep is no better than the marsh's. He seems near the surface, muttering, crying out, unable to keep still. There is a noise in his head as though a man were riddling shingle. He has sharp clarities, like the moonlit bright interstices of open water in the marsh. They flash in his head like fragments of a migraine. For most of the night that is his sleep. Only towards morning, when he should be rising into the scholar's cool lamp-light, clear-headed, determined, refreshed, his soul full of its project, at that hour he has been slugged unconscious, at the hour of the scholar and the writer he is lying stupid and obliterated in a sleep as black and as deep as the mud in which the laden reeds are rooted.

The coat he wears, only an old raincoat, will hang over the Aga during the night and be warm and dry for him next morning. His wife will stuff his shoes with newspaper and put them near the singing kettle, to recover. He looks a tramp, she says, he looks like a scarecrow. Bur who sees him? Nobody. Or if they do he never notices.

Once or twice, after tea, he has felt he might start some writing after all. He goes in there, switches on the lamp, the room is chill, better that way, but he puts on the electric, just one bar, faces the television, sees himself reflected in the empty screen. Opens his notebook, to begin. The references, the memories, the bits and pieces in his scrapbooks, only want collecting together, into sentences and paragraphs – letters into words, words into sentences, sentences into paragraphs, paragraphs into chapters, chapters into the book. What an infinite number of letters go to make up the chapters of a book! He must collect them in.

But where to begin? With his own birth, or his father's, or as far back as he can go on his father's or his mother's side? Or with Doomsday? Or with the etymologies of all the villages, hamlets, farms in the parish? He has materials for all these. On a map the area that concerns him is a circle not more than six or eight inches across. Everything is in there. And the book, when it is done, will not be a very large book, not more than a dozen Woolworth's exercise books. But how many facts and memories in that small compass, how many thousands of letters and words, a lifetime's, a headful, night after night after night of dreaming full. So where shall he begin? He sees his enquiring eyes in the television screen. After an hour his wife plucks up her courage, comes in with a flushed face from the fireside, finds him asleep, his head on the white pages, a dribble of saliva wetting them.

Those blessed birds. They are a famous phenomenon in the neighbourhood, every year. Once he wrote a paragraph about them for the local newspaper. They fell on the road, perhaps by mistake, and stopped the traffic. That was many years ago. But never has he spent his days chasing after them to the north coast and standing in the marsh at the two twilights in all weathers. Why now? He won't answer. He was never reasonable. It is also possible that he does not know. They have no conversation anymore. All she can do is see that his clothes dry overnight, make his breakfast and tea, thrust a sandwich into his pocket when he hurries away. Will he not start his autobiography and history of the little parish? Will he ever get as far as recounting how they fell in love?

His desperate worry every morning is to be in the marsh before the light is well established and the starlings leave. Since he fell into this crazy passion he has never missed the appointment, though every day he fears he will. When he reviews the event it brings tears to his eyes. You would think he were somebody else's favourite child and he had been spared an unbearable disappointment. His relief, his gratitude now, standing on his spit of land between the reeds and the sea! Now once again he is assured that the spectacle of the starlings will not be denied him. Now he thinks lovingly of his wife and of their first meetings.

Soon he will begin to write the story of their life. She will share it all with him again.

Daybreak over the marsh is a busy time. Though he knows what the night has been like – perpetual restlessness and cries – that is behind him and all the noise now is of beginning again. The light climbs hesitantly. Its degrees are scarcely measurable. Only after ten minutes, if you had closed your eyes, you might notice a difference, a rise, an increase, when you opened them. But he will never close his eyes. There is so much to see: the effort of a heron to rise against the wind, its toil, its slow veering away; a purposeful arrow of mallards; the fussing of coots; on a stretch of clear water the triumphant take-off of two swans. Then the starlings start.

They roost through the marsh in a long seam, a dense black stratum, and when the light comes, when it first tickles them, when it gets into them, this layer of birds at its eastern end begins to fray, to unravel, and clusters come loose and hurtle low over the reed-tops where the mass of them still adheres, and settle again on the extreme west. The light is bringing them to the boil. The solid body of birds is beginning to vaporize, but as it leaves go it seeks to reclaim itself, in a flat loop. The birds twitter in the constant anticipation that next it will be their turn to undo. The seam is stationary, but shifting along. So for several minutes there is a continual leaving go and returning. The old man could not bear this perpetual verging on departure but for the certainty that they will all be harried away at last. In the marsh, on his bit of terra firma, the sea in his ears, his shoes leaking, his bare head battered, he watches. How many single birds in one handful torn off? How many in a run of ten yards? Speckles on a starling's coat, cells in its make-up? Infinitesimal dust.

Then suddenly, for no reason that the man in an old coat can detect, the mass explodes, is flung against the wind, lifts, swoops down again. His mind is still grappling with that image of a swarm, a tourbillon, a djinn, when it has been sucked back into the reeds, into the fluttering, twittering, agitated matrix in the marsh. Then again: an explosion, like a tree losing every leaf at one gasp, like a cloudburst. And this time there is no pause: the figure of birds, whirlwind-shaped, swoops to ingest more of its waiting body in the reeds, swoops and ingests, sews itself larger and larger, swoops and sews, against the roaring sea and the wind, with a whirring like flung hail, dips and eats and rises swollen and, full, having swallowed itself entirely, explodes once more and over the man in the marsh bears like a shadow, like a dense ghost, overspreads him, covers him, then swings on the wind and makes away north-wards towards the coast. It buffets his head, every morning his blood prickles with the agitation of the entire marsh, and the eruption of the birds at last almost batters him flat. And with a gasp, with a wrenching of the heart, he sees that the immediate phenomenon is only a part, only a small part, of the whole. Everywhere in the marsh, far beyond the reach of his hearing and almost beyond his sight, there are such swoops and devourings and outbursts, and over the reeds now bereft of their blackness the birds conglomerate, they trail like a sleeve, they make large wings, they flap like one giant bird. Then they pelt away, dust upon dust upon dust, and the sky clears and he is left with the wind at his back, tears in his eyes and shivering in the cold and the damp.

Stiffly then, on feet still hurting from yesterday, in shoes letting in the wet, he makes for home, to get some breakfast and pick up his sandwiches. He stinks of the birds. His wife will view his spattered head and shoulders with disgust. But she will sponge him clean. Then he will set off towards the north coast, athwart the country, across the railway line and the new road, through several parishes by lane and stile and muddy track, to meet the starlings walking on the fields, each separately, with a good space between them. By the time he gets there the day will be half over and it will seem to him that nearly all his strength has gone. No sooner there however, and seeing the busy birds in the fields, he will have to turn round and come home again. For the short day will be thinking of ending and, mechanically, with the alteration of the light, with the sensation, perhaps akin to fear, of approach-ing dusk, the birds will be driven to the south coast and the marshes, and he will limp in after them, to witness the last of their number, those who have travelled farthest, bedded down.

Stone

Emma Kolben had been told so often that her father was a capitalist swine that she had long since ceased to give the matter any thought. Certainly she believed it. In the circles in which she moved it was taken as read. Bert never mentioned him without the title. 'That capitalist swine, your father...' he would begin. His father was another, but in insurance, not property. Still Emma kissed hers when she met him, called him Daddy and generally paid him very little attention. She had a room of her own in the family's spacious flat, came and went as she liked, stayed at Bert's when he wanted her to. Her mother worried but Kolben could not be induced to put his mind to her. He did not believe a daughter could do much harm.

Bert was anxious. After some years at university reading economics he had begun a teaching diploma. This was in accordance with the view that the way to change lay through the institutions, violence having failed (having produced its own fascism, as they said). But to subvert the schools one had first to get in; and for radicals, or even ex-radicals, getting in was no longer a straightforward business. He was anxious because he faced an interview, in which he would be examined for soundness in democratic principles. 'The swine,' he said, 'they'll have something on me somewhere.' What exactly? His elder brother, in the heyday of '68, had gone to Paris, in solidarity, and, safe in banking now, had tales to tell of police brutality and the *communard* spirit. Bert had missed that. The movement had turned sour by the time his time had come. He had met a girl once who had slept with a friend of Baader's; by chance he had got to hear of a 'safe address' in Stuttgart, and nothing would expunge the street and number from his memory. Worst – still not very bad, but worst – he had been among the mourners at the martyrs' funeral, again by chance more than by design (he was in a car when the driver changed his mind and took the passengers along). Though Bert did not raise a clenched fist, nor join in the singing, still he was in the company of those he did. The police photographed thousands system-atically. Emma, unclear, rather thought that Bert was chiefly concerned about unemployment, his own, after so long a prepa-ration in relative poverty. Bert corrected her. The swine were keeping him out, him and his fellows, knowing the risk.

The house was a very big one – worth a million, Kolben said – built at the turn of the century when few voices were raised against the creation of wealth. It had turrets and crenellations, in a playfully military style. All the houses on that broad and leafy street were uniformly enormous, they differed only in their archi-tectural extras. Emma's room had a little alcove, actually in a turret. There she could sit and survey the street, or read. The house was all let out, but for the floor the Kolbens occupied.

Emma's mother owned a laundry. She was proprietress, and employed only one young girl; so that she worked long hours and came home tired, her feet and legs swollen from standing all day. Kolben let her keep the money she made, for clothes and women's things. Himself he worked irregular hours. His wife left him in bed and he would make no appointments before mid-day. In the afternoons he drove long distances to one city or another. Much of his life was spent on the motorway, he complained. The car was accordingly big and comfortable. He came home very late, or stayed away for the night. His wife never quite knew where he was. He had an office, but he was rarely to be found there. Business, business. He was away on business, travelling. He had appointments, meetings, conferences. Work, work. 'You must try to take it easy,' his wife said, with a vague concern. He smiled and sighed. How did she suppose commitments like his could be met by taking it easy? She nodded. They were grateful to him. Times were uncertain and they at least had some security. She was a woman possessed of a seemingly ineradicable innocence and grace. Though her looks had all but gone – in a period of nervous exhaustion her hair had thinned and had never recovered – yet, everyone agreed, she had radiant qualities. Mother and daughter were close, in a respectful alliance sometimes against the household's head.

Perhaps Emma's mother really did expect very little of men. Daily she made up as best she could for things he did. When he took tenants to court, always successfully, she gave them gifts behind his back. When he took in the desperate on terms which broke them she so prepared the room beforehand – working into the night, exhausted – that their feeling on arrival was that they had come as honoured guests. On the table she set a rose, and the traditional gifts of bread and salt. On a shelf she placed some of her own preserves. But if they begged her to intercede in the matter of the rent she apologised and said there she was powerless. She did not know what her husband demanded, nor did she wish to know. But he knew very well that she gilded his arrangements with the grace of charity and welcome, and he thought it no bad thing. Grace was the woman's province. She herself, seeing what he left undone, supposed that men did not think of these things; and seeing what he did, she supposed a woman was generally shortsighted in these matters and could not see all the whys and wherefores. When Emma remarked quite casually that her father was a capitalist swine, her mother was shocked and hurt. 'He works hard for us,' she said, 'we owe him everything.'

Kolben was a jowelled and balding man, with suspicious eyes. Altogether his face was remarkable for its look of injured innocence. So much was said unjustly against him and men like him. On the least occasion he would begin to protest that he was maligned. What he did he had to do, his commitments obliged him to; what he left undone he was powerless to do, there was a limit to the good one could do in the world. He was quick to prosecute; he reached for the Law as for a cudgel. On youth, the arts and immigrant workers he had decided views; all conspired against him, against them he pitted himself. His view of life had a coherence which expressed itself in his clothes and in the furnishings of his rooms. For though he was a big and a heavy man his suits and his casual wear fitted him elegantly and com- fortably. He never sweated, or if he did he changed his shirt at once; he wore nothing constraining. His colour was brown, but nothing muddy or excremental, all the subtle shades. One's sense of his flesh, of the rolls at the belly, of the hairy parts, was reduced almost to nothing. About the house, furnished in matching browns, with much leather and many deep rugs, he moved in soft shoes quite soundlessly. He rarely drank beer; brandy or whisky was his drink. Since he almost never exerted himself physically, travelling even very short distances by car, he kept the blood out of his face. Until he dropped dead he would be presentable.

Though his wife saw to the furnishings nothing among them was of her choice. Or rather, she had for years so accommodated herself to Kolben's taste that the appropriate choices came quite naturally to her. She liked the tenants' rooms. Returning the laundry to one of the girls she found herself enjoying, with a vague regret, a certain carelessness, colour and light. For the house had fine windows and the poorest of its rooms was open to the sun. Kolben had darkened his lounge with heavy curtains, and table lamps made little zones of light in corners. Emma's room was quite her own. She seemed to live on the floor, on large cushions, she went barefoot in there, she sprawled around. Not many of her friends ever came. Bert called her room a liberal bourgeois idyll in a fortress of blood and iron, it made him throw up, he said. But Emma's mother liked to be there. To step off her shoes and curl up on a cushion in the turret window made her feel like a child with a free spirit. Out shopping she had to restrain herself from buying things she thought would be suitable for Emma's room.

Emma was doing a secretarial course, but through Bert, whom she had met at a wedding, she was accepted into at least the outer ring of radical student company. They met in a dark bar opposite the Commercial Bank, drank beer, ate meat balls and, rendered nearly insensate by unremitting heavy rock, commented on the political scene under the slogans and posters of '68. They teased Emma for her destiny of a lackey. Bert never defended her, on the contrary he often took her as a point of departure in his arguments. She was never upset, she believed what they said but it did not touch her. Even the harshest, Klett or Raspe, with their hard language and dirty finger nails, looked at her curiously when the talk passed to Bert, and wondered if he were the best she could do. He was thinning already, but bushy in blond beard, his lips moving like newborn mice in the nest of hair; he had bad breath. Lately, his nervousness had increased and alone with Emma he inclined to the querulous monologue. He had known her three or four years, and was almost proprietorial. She, for her part, was almost persuaded that Bert was her responsibility. She had inherited low expectations from her mother. She loved riding her bicycle, and pedalling from Bert's place in the early morning, leaving him in bed, that was when she felt freest. On those occasions she sometimes met her mother and they kissed with affection. Emma's cold cheeks and bright eyes filled the mother with love and happiness to last the day.

Bert got his teaching diploma, Emma her qualification as a bilingual shorthand typist. Then they were to go on holiday together, to Scotland, but Bert's summons came. 'Ask for another date,' Emma said, 'I can't see the hurry.' Bert was white and sweating. 'I want to get it over with,' he replied. 'The shit-arses, they'll do me down, you'll see.' Emma was puzzled. It would have been simple to get a postponement for a few weeks. 'You go,' he said, 'go with somebody else. I've got to see this thing through. I'll have to talk it over with the boys.' It occurred to Emma that her place might be at Bert's side. In fact the idea of self-sacrifice was forming quite strongly, and had Bert not *urged* her to go, in tones she recognised as sincere, she would certainly have begun her adult life of acquiescence and resignation there and then. Instead, she thought of a girlfriend who might like to take his place. Emma's mother was enthusiastic. 'It might be your last chance,' she said. 'Bert will be all sorted out by the time you get back.' It crossed Emma's mind that perhaps it was generally supposed she would marry Bert.

On the boat the girls fell in with two compatriots and travelled to London together. There the friend, Annette, liked the company and could see no point in carrying on. Emma liked none of the boys especially and in a day or two, weighing the risks and disregarding advice, she took the train to Edinburgh alone. Writing home she concealed the fact that she had left her friend. Poste restante in Edinburgh was an affectionate letter from her mother; nothing from Bert.

Still Edinburgh was not quite what Emma had come for. As the days passed she realised, through its absence, that she had somewhere or something else in mind. She went once more to the post office and there was a letter from Bert. Reading it she seemed to catch the whiff of his unpleasant breath and to see his wet lips wriggling in the beard, his eyes staring with emphasis. Nothing in the letter enquired after her. He seemed to be sweating with fear. Emma folded it thoughtfully. Next morning she began taking buses north and west.

Nobody pestered her. She sat staring out of the window thinking her own thoughts, which were sometimes deep and consistent and sometimes only a vague reflection on the landscape. Towards evening she asked where she might find a bed and breakfast place, and got off the bus as directed.

So she proceeded for three or four days, taking local buses as they came and putting up at night wherever she was advised to. She entered into no long conversations, but the few common courtesies gave her great pleasure. In observation and reflection her days passed. There was never any hurry. When she slept it was always before the strange quivering twilight had become darkness; voices and occasional laughter from the public rooms below soon seemed familiar and reassuring. She was glad that Bert was not sharing her bed. She felt something like gratitude to him for his absence. Just below full consciousness she was aware of taking a deep pleasure in her sleep. She always left the curtains open to enjoy the very last and the very first of the light. The hills imbibed the dark, into the dark purple went all the subtleties of yellow and blue, into the black went the purple. But the streams splashed white still and in a silent rush the stars gathered to whiteness in the broad river of heaven. Age and distance. The infinite sequence, the stepping back, from the little habitations and places

of worship, to the vast eroded hills, to the stars and their enormously spaced proximities. Her sleep welled up from the black
midnight, between the two twilights in their lovely quickness.
She would never again, never and nowhere in her life, be a
solitary stranger courteously received. The curiosity of the people
amused her, she thought their courtesy a supreme and peculiar
grace. They let her be. With many people, young and old, whom
she would never meet again, she exchanged a few words, received
with a smile and a slightly formal bow their good wishes, and
remembered their faces, their kind interest, their tact, for days.

Instinctively she halted before the sea was reached. From a
height she saw a flash of silver water and was told that was an arm
of the sea reaching in, far into the land. Then the bus went down
to a village at the very hub of a wheel of hills and there she got
out to spend her furthest night, in a small private house to which
the driver directed her. The woman's daughter was in Australia.
Emma listened sympathetically. She felt her own attractiveness, in
humility. Then she walked out before bed, beyond the few houses
a little way up the road the bus had gone.

She became possessed with thoughts of her own mother. She felt
her love and its foundation of sadness. She saw her hair, which was
still black in colour but with all its abundance gone. She saw her
fallen asleep exhausted in a deep leather chair, her ankles swollen.
Her face never wore any expression of complaint, only of sorrow,
and when she smiled it was as though an unexpected kindness had
been done to her mouth and to her eyes. Emma paused at a small
stone bridge and looked into the stream, which came down the
purple scented hill in leaps and bounds. She saw harebells agitated
by the splashing, tall foxgloves standing back, the clutches of ferns,
the moss, the blotches of orange lichen, the yellow stars of tormen-
til. And she wished that something of that near perfect realisation
of joy and contentment could be given her mother. Kneeling on
the bank she looked into a still pool and saw the pebbles lying on
the bottom, shimmering. They were flat, more or less oval worn
pieces of schist, greenish. When she took one out its sparkle of
water soon vanished. But she kept it, since it fitted the hand very
satisfyingly, and put it away in the pocket of her faded skirt.

In the morning the woman made her some sandwiches, for free, and kissed her good-bye. Emma took the bus back again, towards Edinburgh, intending not to dawdle. At its first stop, nowhere in particular, a working boy got on. Catching sight of Emma he blushed, and faltered in his words with the driver. Then, quite naively, he came and sat where he would be able to look at her. His admiration was quite open, it filled her with humility. It was no more importuning than the sun, but as straightforward. She glanced at him once, he was in overalls, between his knees he dangled a khaki bag. His hair was thick and tousled, his face weathered, his eyes of an intense darkness. His look was absolutely solemn. For a few seconds she returned it, with a like solemnity, until her heart thumped and she thrust her hands into her skirt, between her knees. When he stood up to get off, the bus halting, the driver calling out to him, the boy made a slight bow of the head to her, in acknowledgement. Then he was by the roadside, vast hills behind him, staring through the glass. Only when the bus moved did Emma smile, only when it was under way and he was being left did she raise her fingers and kiss them to him. He waved, a light came into his face, he waved and grinned, and slinging the bag on his shoulder turned about and went down off the road at a run, down and down, sure-footed, running down and away. Emma took out the flat oval pebble of schist, the light was in it, the light flaked and glimmered on its smooth surface. She decided to give her mother no other present.

In Edinburgh, poste restante, there was a heavy letter from Bert. He had been found unfit to teach, his radical past had been held against him, his protestations of a change of heart had not been believed. The voice of the letter was twofold and contradictory: that of the martyr, that of the reject, the latter becoming dominant towards the end. Emma sighed, it oppressed her. Again she was merely the recipient, and not asked after or in herself addressed. She did not want to stay in Edinburgh, she bought a bottle of whisky for her father and a tartan scarf for her lover, and took the London train. The journey became tiresome, she knew that her holiday was done with.

She arrived home late and, letting herself in quietly, went to bed. In the morning her mother woke her, ready for work. She had been anxious, Annette was back long since without any news of Emma. Her mother sat on the bed, looking down at her. Emma reached for her skirt, which was lying by the bed where she had stepped out of it, and gave her mother the stone. 'I didn't bring you anything else,' she said. 'I knew you would like this.' Her mother smoothed and turned the stone between her fingers. In the light room the scales of mica glimmered. Emma began to tell her about the bus journey. 'You can't imagine the hills,' she said, 'they're like nothing we've ever seen. And the streams, so clear, not like in these parts. That's where your stone is from, out of a stream.' Her mother rose to leave. 'Go back to sleep,' she said. 'Poor Bert,' said Emma, 'what will he do now? He told you, I suppose.' Emma's mother blushed. 'You needn't worry about him,' she said, as though ashamed. 'He's been to see your father. He'll be alright.' Emma was left wondering, but soon fell asleep.

In the evening Bert came, and Kolben was home too. Emma gave them their presents. Kolben was in excellent spirits. He liked the stone, he liked that simplicity, it was a charming idea, he said. Emma's mother came in with a tray of sandwiches and a bottle of wine. Kolben said that Emma would surely remember her time in Scotland for the rest of her life. Such memories gave one the courage to go on, he said. Every marriage needed them. And reaching over he embraced his wife. Then they all drank, to Emma's return, and to the other cause for celebration, which was the setting of Bert's foot on the first rung of the ladder of success. Emma looked to him for enlightenment, but he avoided her eyes. However, she gathered that in some capacity or other he had been taken on by Kolben. 'The fathers got together,' said Kolben with a wink. 'And quite right too, for what is the point of a father who does not give a helping hand?' As to Bert's radical past, it was nothing to be ashamed of. If the State would not take him on, that was their loss. And if one was not to be a bit of a revolutionary when one was young when was one to be one he would like to know? He surprised everybody by admitting that his own youth had not been blameless in that respect. Only, with the years, one saw that more good could be done through the system than outside it. Emma felt a new degree of embarrassment. Her mother smiled in a quick, unhappy way. Then Kolben raised his glass again and toasted Emma and Bert together: 'Future happiness,' he said.

For a pleasant surprise to both his wife and his daughter Kolben took the pebble of schist and had it mounted in a silver casing and suspended from a silver chain. He made a little ceremony of adorning his wife with it one evening when Bert had again been invited. Kolben was exceedingly genial. As a family they ought to be more together, he said. His wife fingered the stone as it lay on her breast, handsomely framed. Kolben took her downcast eyes for embarrassment at his generosity. He kissed her thin hair. 'Let's say nothing about it,' he said. Emma turned away. When Bert, taking her on one side, began rapidly telling her how he saw the future, she felt disgust. 'I'll get freedom to move,' he was saying. 'Without a job you're nothing. But property's where the power lies, he's been telling me a thing or two, your sphere of influence is enormous, it's a better leverage than the schools, that's where change will come from when it comes, from the holders of property, and from insurance too...' 'That capitalist swine, your father, do you mean?' Emma asked. Bert's eyes bulged with the vehemence of the just. 'That's right,' he said, 'there'll be some working together, so I understand, it really is staggering the influence you can exert.' 'What does Klett say?' Emma asked. Bert's lips writhed: 'He can't see it himself, but he will. They're all talk down there, all theory. I'll be the one who's doing something.'

Emma Kolben's mother came into her room to say goodnight. Emma had left the curtains open but there was no late twilight and when her mother came in she switched on the reading lamp. They sat on cushions together. 'Do you like my stone now?' her mother asked. 'No I don't,' said Emma. Her mother hid it in her hand. 'Let's say nothing about it,' she said. 'Your father means well. It was sweet of him really, I'm sure it cost him a lot.' Emma said nothing. Mother and daughter looked at one another. 'Never mind, my love,' the mother said, 'tell me some more about Scotland. Your father's quite right when he says that everyone needs such memories, I hadn't realised that he understood these things. Tell me about the little villages you stayed in, the people must be very different from us, I suppose. And tell me about the streams again. I can't stop thinking about how clear you said the water was.'

The Oxford Story

1

Bernard began to feel bad again. The words were running together in his mouth. The source of his words was inexhaustible, he let them come, but in his mouth they curdled, thickened and began to set. He ended the tutorial without any of the usual instructions and courtesies. 'That book will be the death of me,' he said. The student stared.

Bernard fell asleep.

The trumpet blew for dinner. It was a longish summons, more regretful than urgent. It blew again. Bernard came up in terror, and for quite a gap of time had no idea who he was or where or why. He had wet his beard with dribble and the heat of the gasfire had suffused his face. He panicked. He knew there was some requirement upon him, perhaps to save his life. Bit by bit then everything fell into place. He said aloud: 'It shouldn't be like this. I'm not an old man yet.' He found his gown where Arthur had hung it up.

They were already in, grace had been said, they were already at their food and drink. Bernard must walk the length of the hall, down the aisle between the undergraduate tables, in the candle-light, through the din it makes when people go at their nourishment with gusto and talk at one another across their plates and to either side. On High Table the only space was last on the far right facing the end wall. Bernard got in there, with a nod to the Master. How red the Master looked! His face seemed to roar with blood. For Bernard wine came, and a late Coquille Saint Jacques. Slowly he composed himself – and saw that his opposite was the table's only woman. 'Hi,' she said. 'Now I can talk to someone.' Bernard blushed: 'It's only me, I'm afraid.' 'You'll do,' said Kate. Behind her on the wall were the portraits of the bishops. 'Queer,' Bernard thought. 'Have I ever noticed them before? Kate in front of them is very queer.' He gouged the shell nearly clean and drank off the first wine. 'I'm seeing things queerly tonight,' he said aloud.

Crane sat on Kate's right hand. He was a bald old man, as strong as a bull. The holes of his nose were deeply blackened with snuff. On Bernard's left sat Cruickshank, turning away. He was badly stained. 'It's not always our fault,' said Bernard to himself. 'The servants tip the soup and the gravies over us.' 'I saw your book,' said Kate. 'Well, your translation. It's on display. I nearly bought a copy.' 'Don't,' said Bernard. 'I'll give you one. Will you let me give you one?' He was spinning the dirty shell with his middle finger and a line of verse came back to him. 'Give me my scallop shell of quiet,' he said. The occurrence elated him, and he spoke in a rush about the book and now, on the cold white wine perhaps, the words kept their identity, they arrived in proper formation and meant what they were supposed to mean. For a while he seemed to hold the young woman's attention wholly. 'Anyway,' he concluded, 'it's the best thing I've ever done.' Kate said she looked forward to reading it. The scallop was removed, Bernard licked his finger. Kate said: 'I'd rather sit this side.' 'You mean you can ogle the young,' said Bernard. And he added, boldly: 'They are very attractive in the candles.' He did not dare say how beautiful Kate looked with candlelight on her face, but her interest in his book, her listening to him talk, had opened his eyes and his heart. When Crane engaged her, overbearing her massively, Bernard stared at her face in profile and ignored an effort by Cruickshank to take him up. He chewed bread and stared.

The red meat was brought, and Kate's vegetarian dish. There and then Bernard decided to eat as she did henceforth. The men's plates were swimming with blood. It was scarcely a gravy at all, it was straight blood, and in it the meat stretched. He held up a palm against his serving, and took only greens and potato on to his clean plate. Now the eaten scallops seemed to him very dirty things. He thought of scallop shells at the seaside where he and his mother spent their holidays. How clean he found them on the sparkling sands when he walked alone out there after the tide. It seemed to him that his distress earlier, the bad time in the tutorial, might after all be part of a productive working in his soul. He drank his red wine and signalled confidently for more. Crane, to whom Kate did seem to be listening, caused Bernard no jealousy, for he recognized his attentions, even if Kate did not, as ironic and insulting. He drank, and admired the young woman's face. He remembered she was Italian, and said so a moment later when he saw an opening. 'I was,' she said, 'a generation ago. I've never been home. It was far away in the south. I grew up in the Bronx. My father had a flower shop in there.' Now came Devils on Horseback. Bernard refused them. She was telling him about the flowers, how proud her big Italian father was of them, and what respect he and her mother had in the Bronx, and Bernard was imagining the old couple, very dignified and decent people, in black on a background of white lilies and furious red hibiscus, when Chapman leaned over by the Master's right hand and banged with the gavel hard for silence. The rucking back of the chairs sounded like demolition. The benediction was two words. The trooping out began.

Bernard did a bold thing. Seeing that Kate left her napkin lying he flung down his as well. Chapman came after him with it. 'Dessert, sir,' he said. 'I can't,' said Bernard. 'Something has come up.' The butler was furious. His table in the common room would have a gap. Outside the hall, as the others crossed the flagstones to the warm stairs, Bernard stooped slightly towards Kate's face and invited her to have coffee with him in his rooms. She gave him a look he could not interpret, and accepted. He led her away.

To Bernard there was still a feeling of distress in his rooms, and his hold on the situation weakened; but Kate appraised the place and liked it. 'A fire,' she said. Bernard blushed. 'It's not real,' he said. 'It's one you turn on.' 'Never mind,' said Kate. 'It looks real enough.' She crossed to the window and parted the curtains. He heard her intake of breath. 'That's real,' she said. The great lanterns of the libraries were lit up in the cobbled square. 'I'd love a room like this,' she said, still looking out. 'Maybe you will have,' he said. Then she turned quickly, he saw how moved she was, her eyes were so shining it seemed there might be tears in them. 'Can you *do* anything?' she asked. Bernard was uncomfortable. 'Speak,' he said. 'Speak up. Of course, I'll do that much.' Kate came over and touched the sleeve of his jacket. She *felt* at it, between finger and thumb, all the while looking him full in the face. 'Thanks,' she said. 'That would be friendly. Now tell me more about your book.'

But first Bernard made the coffee. 'I like to have my own coffee,' he said. 'I get it myself on the market.' He went into the kitchen. When he came back with the coffee made and every-thing nicely on a tray Kate was moving along his bookshelves. 'How many rooms do you have?' she asked. 'This,' he said, 'kitchen, bathroom, the usual.' Then he added, and felt the courage go out of him: 'It used to be my tutor's set. I was like you are now. I was in somewhere else for a while, not permanent. Then the job came up here and I moved back. I called to see him when I got the job, just for the courtesy, you understand. But he had no idea who I was or why I had come. He was over by the window, I remember. His front was stained. And on this table was the one thing he had ever done, the one book, I mean, open on this table. All the other books he owned had gone. They were already clearing him out, you see. But the one book he ever wrote was lying open on this very table, and he stood over there and looked at me and didn't know who I was or what I wanted calling. And he was my tutor.' 'Is he dead?' Kate asked. 'No, he's not,' Bernard answered. 'I don't believe he is dead, quite. He's in some sort of a home, but still not dead, so far as I know. All these years.' 'How sad,' said Kate. 'Indeed,' said Bernard. 'And it's worse than that. It's sadder still. You see, it was all wrong what he wrote. He never read anything but that novel, and never wrote anything but his book on it, and what he wrote was wrong.' 'How was he wrong?' Kate asked. 'He believed in an after life,' said Bernard. 'He believed Ottilie pointed the way into an after life. He called her a saint. But she's not a saint. She's a vampire. I ask you, what the devil would Goethe want with a saint? She's a vampire and she sucks the life out of him. It's as easy as that. Poor Wallace! All he

saw was saints and the after life. He told us that when we were
undergraduates, but I never believed it even then, and now I've
answered him back at last, in black and white, in my translation
and in my introduction, after all these years.' He had risen, his
face was flushed, the words had come out of him in haste but in
good order. 'I look forward to reading it,' said Kate. 'Then I'll be
able to offer an opinion.' 'I'm sorry,' said Bernard. 'I was forgetting. Remind me to give you a copy before you leave.'

Bernard sat down again, with the low table between them, and
from thirty years away a boy's face came back to him. He said the
name aloud, in tones of astonishment, as though the boy had
really materialized: 'Andy Jones'. Kate was watching him. 'Forgive
me,' he said. 'I've been feeling rather odd lately. The book, I
suppose. Seeing it out, I mean, after all this time.' 'Who is Andy
Jones?' she asked. 'My friend,' he replied, 'he was my friend. He
was in college where you are now, but he came here for his
literature and we both had Wallace. And he's dead, long since, and
Wallace is still alive. I find that very odd all of a sudden.'

The face was young, almost childish. The black hair went back
off the forehead with a stylishness that seemed too old for the face.
When it wasn't smiling the mouth looked rather weak. The eyes
sometimes affected a hard look. 'He was my friend,' Bernard said.
'Really, I think you would have to say I loved him. He asked a lot
of life, and when it was settled that Wallace would be his tutor all
three years I don't say that threw him off the rails but certainly it
didn't help keep him on them. Four or five of us were friends
together, then he began to drift away. There was a bad crowd,
with people from London and from the town, they sat under the
Camera, just below this window, and he got in with them. When
he came to us it was only to borrow money, and he never paid it
back. But he never asked me for money, he would never have
borrowed money off me and not paid it back. And when he got
the money they bought what they wanted with it and hung
around all day against the Camera and into the night. Now, as for
Wallace, they told us he was ill, but we knew it was the drink, and
though I can't very well distinguish what I knew then and what I
only found out later when I joined the Fellowship I'm sure we

already knew it wasn't illness but the drink, or if an illness then one caused by drink. He slept in the afternoons and set his alarm to wake him for the tutorials at five, but often when we knocked he hadn't come round and he didn't know who we were or what we wanted bothering him. I read out essays in this very room and on that book and all the while he wasn't listening but only trying the best he could to clear his head and look intelligent, and when I'd finished all he said was 'Hm', and poured us both a drink. I never minded much, but Andy did. Soon he stopped coming, and because it was only Wallace there were no reports on him and so the College let him drift. It couldn't happen now, of course. I mean, we don't let anybody drift. But in those days it happened and Andy drifted off, and whenever we saw him he was drunk or stoned, and always needing money. Wallace gave his lectures still, he gave them sitting down, but all he did was read out chapters of his book. I always went, I don't know why, I disagreed with every-thing he said, but it's only now I've set out my arguments against him for everyone to read. That stuff about saints and transcen-dental values when he was too ill to stand, too ill with the drink! Andy despised us. Well, not me he didn't. I wouldn't say he ever despised me. He never asked me for money and I took that for a sign. Then I was going abroad for a year and he was expecting to be sent down. We were in his room, after midnight, he was drunk as usual, but not very. He tried to persuade me to give it up and go away together. We were lying on his rug in the dark and he was talking up at the ceiling. He said he'd be going to Morocco, and see where the fancy took him after that. But I wasn't drunk and I said no, of course. Then he held on to my hand for a long time and was perfectly silent. It was nearly light again before I left. I climbed over the wall and dropped into the square. I'll never forget the sight of the libraries coming out of the dark that summer morning. And that was the last time I saw Andy Jones. We never wrote. When I came back for my final year I heard he was dead. They said he had got sent down and died soon after. He was on heroin by then. I never knew whether he got to Morocco or not.'

The phone rang. Bernard was so startled he slopped the coffee from his cup. 'God forgive me,' he said, 'I forgot the time.' He went into the bedroom to answer it, closing the door behind him. His mother spoke, peevish and anxious. Bernard was curt with her. 'I have a guest,' he said. 'I can't be held always to the precise minute.' He hung up, and hurried back to Kate.

She was standing, to leave. He was distressed, he had more to say. 'Your voice is different when you speak about such things,' said Kate. 'I've no ear for British accents, but something comes up in you, I should say. And another thing,' she said, already stand-ing in the open door: 'Has anyone ever told you you look like D. H. Lawrence?' Bernard was confused. 'There's a photo,' Kate said, 'just about the last, I think. So intelligent and passionate and sad.' Then she was gone.

Bernard crossed to the window. The spire, the chapel and the two great libraries were all illuminated. In the shadows against the Camera there was a little huddle of faceless people. Soon Kate appeared, coming round from the right. Under his window she looked up and waved; turned left then into the lane between the two colleges and went out of sight. Bernard stood at the window. The wall-tie was still there, a large multiplication cross on the wall of Andy's college. You lowered yourself on to it from the coping, and from it then to the ground. In the old days you did, when it was necessary, after midnight, to climb out. He was in turmoil. He stood there hoping for some direction or resolu-tion, but none came. His clearest sentiment was guilt at having cut his mother off. Soon that began to press him and he went to make amends.

She cried quietly for a couple of minutes, but allowed herself to be soothed. She said she thought it was time to write to Mrs Pugh and confirm their usual fortnight in August. Bernard agreed. To conclude, she asked was his visitor a lady. 'Yes,' said Bernard, becoming curt again. Putting down the phone he noticed the com-plimentary copies of his translation on the bedside table, and cursed himself that Kate had gone without hers. He signed one there and then: 'For Kate, with every good wish, Bernard', and took it down to the lodge in a brown envelope. He might have delivered it himself, the distance was trivial, but suddenly he feared losing everything by too much haste and vehemence.

Bernard Marlow's week was very regular. He caught the bus to London every Friday, soon after lunch, to avoid the traffic; and every Monday, after the rush-hour, he caught one back again, in time for lunch. For the rest, he did what his job required of him. He lectured on late Nietzsche, early Goethe, and *Elective Affinities*, the novel of Goethe's early old age; and keeping this last work as something indivisible and invariable he got from the other subjects more than enough material to fulfil his stint in a three-year cycle.

He came out of College at the main gate, kept to the strips of paving stone (he disliked the feel of cobbles under his feet), cut through Bodley's courtyard to the Sheldonian and emerged, having avoided the traffic for as long as possible, through the little arch by the Science Museum on to the Broad. He crossed to the Trinity side immediately and kept to the wall, rounding Balliol into St Giles. That corner had become unpleasant lately, because of the tourists decanted there from coaches. Likewise the Martyrs' Memorial: it was sometimes hard to avoid being jostled. But after that, after two sets of traffic lights, he was soon in the Institute. He followed the same route back.

His second route was to the market. He came out of College at the main gate, turned left along the side of the square under his own windows, left again into the lane between his college and Kate's, and so on in a straight line, crossing the Turl, to the indoor market. Cardew's, where he bought his coffee, was the first shop in. Occasionally he went in further, as far as Palm's, to buy his mother a special sort of biscuit.

He caught the bus to London outside Queen's. To get there he let himself out of College at a secret door. He had the key, and the suddenness of access it gave on to the High still excited him. Then he hurried the couple of hundred yards to Queen's in the din and stink of traffic.

Those were Bernard's three trails from College.

It was Wednesday of Fifth Week in a Hilary Term, two days after his fiftieth birthday, that Bernard flung down his napkin and invited Kate back to his rooms for coffee. Nobody knew he was fifty except his mother, but his translation went on display that very morning.

He heard from Kate on Friday. She sent a card. It was quite a large stiff postcard of the photo of Lawrence, and on the back she had scribbled: 'Well, are you like him or aren't you? Thanks for coffee, thanks for the book. Love Kate.' Then, since there was space, she had drawn two cartoons. In the first he appeared as a bearded pilgrim, an outsized scallop on his hat, making for a range of mountains, with a rapt look. In the second she had depicted herself as Venus, wearing only an academic cap and gown, riding to land on a scallop through the foam. The pilgrim had his back to her, and was heading away. He set up the portrait on his mantelpiece. It looked very out of place, and he felt with a sudden elation that the rest of the room must change to suit this single item. He ate lunch among his colleagues with a secret smile on his face.

On the bus to London, being borne along rapidly through a landscape he was dead to, he had pleasure in the thought that Kate was reading Goethe's novel in his translation. In his own language, on sentences of his own making, its radical injunction would strike into her heart: that if we inhabit dead forms the only honesty is to smash them. The thought excited him. He loosened his tie and felt under his jacket for the thumping of his heart. It seemed to him that more was beginning in his life than he might ever be able to comprehend. He had only given her the bare facts about Andy Jones, nothing about his feelings, scarcely anything at all about Wallace, not about the feelings, and they were what mattered. He wanted her to see and feel what the coming together of Wallace and Andy Jones was like. He remembered with a shock that he had read the essays his friend had written and Wallace had never listened to, and he admitted: 'In those days Andy was ahead of me. He had insights, and a style.' Such a criminal waste. Could one ever do anything worse then betray the young? And sitting there too stupid to take in a young man's thoughts and feelings when he brought them to paper with passion and innocence, that was betrayal. Bernard felt a powerful wish to confide in Kate. He felt there was nothing he would not confess to her. She might, for example, ask him exactly what his feelings were when he lay on the rug with Andy that last night. He swore to be exact and truthful. Suddenly he could imagine leaning against his mantelpiece looking down at her and telling her in a forthright way that she was the cause of this excitement in his life. He would say what he had not dared to say at the time: that her looks in the candlelight, her black hair, her huge dark eyes, her un-English skin, her lips, were astonishing, unprecedented in all his experience of the phenomenal world. Thus agitated and abstracted he passed the journey as though it were a gap in time; and took the Central Line as far as Theydon Bois.

On Monday the traffic was exceptionally bad. Bernard missed his lunch, but seized on a letter from Kate among the brown envelopes in his pigeon hole. She had read it, she had not been able to put it down, her weekend had gone in reading it. She congratulated him, it read like Jane Austen. But what he had written on the text was wrong, all wrong. Wallace was wrong, but so was Bernard, they were both about as wrong as it was possible to be. They misinterpreted Ottilie. Of course she was not a saint, but neither was she a vampire. She was a hero. Her heroism resided in a pitiless withholding, even unto death, to spite mere conventionality and the usual phallic demands. Eduard was a jerk, the Captain a spare wank, Charlotte, though nothing beside Ottilie, deserved some admiration nonetheless. But Wallace with his eyes on heaven and Bernard in his blind approval of a clapped-out Storm and Stress might read the thing till kingdom come and never get it right.

She had seized the book. Bernard was pushed aside. He stood in his set of rooms with his outdoor coat on, and let the day go out of his grasp. Her contempt for Eduard hurt him in his own person. 'But he loves unconditionally!' he said aloud. 'He has that in his favour. Goethe says so himself. Did I not say that in my introduction? Of course I did. And the novella? She is ignoring the novella.' He hurried to the phone. He got her answering machine. Hung up. Dialled again and said, after the tone: 'You can't read it like that. What about the novella? She flings herself in the water. She forces his hand. He brings her back to life by the act of love. They force the issue in favour of love and life, against convention and mere decency. You must see that.'

There was nothing to eat, there was not even any coffee. Should he phone for a sandwich from the buttery? No, he would go without his lunch for once. As to coffee, he could buy his own, and he hurried from College to do so. He wished he might meet her, he wished he had the nerve to seek her out and settle the question of Eduard and Ottilie in his favour. In the lane between the two colleges, walking fast, he was accosted by a beggarwoman with a child. It startled him. Her face was coarse, its veins were broken, the child was snotty and miserable. The woman's belly bulged through her opening coat. 'I've no change,' said Bernard. The woman cursed him. He went ahead. On the left at the far end, leaning back against the vents, another one lay, in the warm gasps of the kitchens. His hat was waiting for change to drop into it. Bernard had never noticed the warmth there before. He felt it on his cheek and on his bare hand. The food smells were disgusting.

At Cardew's he bought his usual, finely ground. Then did what he rarely did: went further in through the slung-up naked carcasses of animals and the bloody-headed birds. The stench of meat sickened him, who had eaten tons of it in his fifty years. Further still, he stood in a queue for a square of pizza and ate with other people over a litter bin. And suddenly he savoured his life, he liked himself, he wished a colleague could see him on this adventure. He cut through to the High, and hurried as though to catch the bus again; but let himself suddenly into his college by the secret door. Slowly then he settled, she would be bound to phone or write.

She did neither. But Wednesday was her teaching day in Bernard's college. He signed on for dinner and added in brackets: veg. He signed off dessert, as she had done. They met again face to face at the far end. They contrived it. 'Well?' he asked. 'The novella is overridden by the context,' she replied. 'It's a romance, the rest of the novel annuls it. If the Captain was her lover then we see their marriage has come to nothing. Or why would he be hanging round Charlotte in his middle age?' 'The Captain was the bridegroom,' said Bernard with some passion. 'A *fainéant*. And the lover takes her from him. He rescues her out of the merely nominal, into the life in truth.' He drank his wine, and signalled Chapman almost imperiously for more. He ate without knowing what, and held forth. He felt he was defeating her, and nothing discouraged him until he caught her smiling at a person behind him in the body of the hall. 'Only a pupil,' she said. 'Go on.' But at once he faltered, the necessary faith was quitting him. He heard the undergraduates leaving the hall and all their hilarity dying away. Never before had he been so aware of the emptying of the hall. And at High Table, as on a dreadful raft, he and his colleagues would end their days together. He saw Kate engaged on her right, and discerned for certain now a desire to please in her manner and in the attention she was demonstrating. When the Master dismissed them, Bernard hurried out alone, feeling her taken up behind him by others whose spirits were higher at that critical moment.

He stood at his window looking out through a gap in the curtains at the illumination and the shadows in the square. Nothing would happen in his evening until he telephoned his mother at 9.30. He wished he had somewhere to go; but there was nowhere except London, on Fridays. He wished he had work to do, of a kind that would fill him up entirely and leave no room for any longing or regret; and it seemed to him that he would never again be as happy as he had been a few months earlier when he was proofreading his text and defending himself against the interferences of a self-important copy-editor. His introduction wanted amplifying, and its arguments strengthening for the specialists; doubtless he would make a book of it, a conclusive anti-Wallace; but now he had no relish for this responsibility. And if Kate was right, even the least bit right, then really he was already superseded, like poor senile Wallace in his home.

Kate came in without knocking. She was halfway across the room before he sensed or heard her. 'I think you wanted to invite me to coffee,' she said, 'but couldn't see a chance.' She stood by him at the window and opened the curtains wider. 'So beautiful,' she said. 'Where else in the world is there a window with a view like this? See how these buildings fit, how they belong. And I like to think of the readers at their desks, especially now, working late and developing ideas that one day the world will have to adjust to. What were you thinking when I came in on you?'

Bernard was not quite honest in his reply. He saw a chance to articulate his trouble in terms perhaps more interesting than those of a disagreement over somebody else's book. 'I was envying Andy Jones,' he said. 'I was wishing I'd had his boldness all those years ago.' 'Bullshit,' said Kate. 'Just like your view of Eduard. Being alive and where the power is, is what matters. Typical of a man to throw it all away before women have seen whether they might like it or not. Charlotte holds on, the men push towards chaos.' Bernard shrugged. He was following the drift of his own melancholy with satisfaction. 'I used to see him down there sometimes,' he said. 'Andy, I mean. I'd be going into Bodley or coming out and he'd be there on a ledge against the Camera with people I never knew. He gave me a wave, and sometimes they all laughed. I took my work into Bodley whenever I could. I love that sunny upper room. I love being there under the portraits of the poets. Then when I came out Andy was with his friends against the Camera. He grew his hair very long, his appearance was filthy, he had a white face, dirty hands, a white childish face.' 'Like Rimbaud, I shouldn't wonder,' said Kate. 'Or Kurt Cobain.' Bernard nodded at the one name and let the other pass. A young man crossed the square and went into the darkness up against the building. A minute later he came out again, and turned into the lane, briskly. 'Dealing,' said Kate. 'He delivers and passes on. You see the world from this window. If you want to, that is.' Bernard nodded, but said: 'Andy thought the same as I did about that book, you know. We lay on the floor in his room or in my room and talked about it. We were like Eduard and the Captain, so much in one another's debt we could never have decided who owed what to whom. But *he* called Ottilie a vampire, I don't mind admitting that. Sex turns to killing when she denies it its proper due. I had that from Andy first. It was in an essay he wrote for poor old Wallace, and if Wallace never appreciated it at least I did. Saint Ottilie! I ask you!' 'The real saint Ottilie was a healer of eyes,' said Kate in tones so gentle Bernard was startled. 'Yes,' he said. 'Goethe says of his Ottilie that she was surely meant to be a kindness on the eye.' 'And so she would have been,' said Kate, 'if men had anything in their eyes but rape.'

Bernard made coffee and they stood either side the real enough fire with it. 'What have you done in my cause?' Kate asked. Bernard blushed. 'I'm not very good at lobbying,' he said. 'But I'll be there, of course. I'll speak up for you.' 'I want this more than anything,' she said. 'I don't mind telling you.' Bernard minded hearing it. 'Please,' she said. Then she said his name, said it for the first time looking at him fully, and took his hand. Confusion overwhelmed him. He was glad of the covering his beard gave to his face. 'Forget it,' she said. 'I'm teasing.' Then she closed her eyes, approached her mouth, and paused at the little distance and on the moment when it would have been his right and almost his duty to kiss her, but the phone rang.

Bernard went into the bedroom to answer it. It was his mother. Why had he not telephoned? She was there worrying. He had a visitor, she supposed, but surely that didn't mean he couldn't telephone his mother. Mrs Pugh had been in touch. She had had a cancellation. She could offer them an extra week. Would Bernard like an extra week at Swanage? They had always said they would like an extra week. Bernard was brutally curt with her, but when he went back into his living room Kate had gone.

In a lecture the following day, scarcely halfway through, Bernard ran into difficulties and had to halt. He was speaking of the term itself: how it had been carried from our world of feelings into the world of science, there to humanize the mechanical separations and couplings of chemical compounds; how Goethe then had returned it to our human world in a troubled meditation on volition and responsibility. He asked what sense was left in the word 'elective'? For once they were in, the lovers seemed to have no choice. But this compulsion, which the women regarded as a monstrous fate, how could one think of it thus when its manifestations were so sweetly persuasive? And he cited the familiar instances: their sympathetic headaches, Ottilie's complete accommodation of her piano-playing to Eduard's wayward flute, the disappearance of her handwriting into his. But when he got beyond the catastrophe and reached the lovers' inability to stay apart, their being drawn together from the far ends of the house, their stillness then in speechless not-quite-touching proximity, Bernard could suddenly not see his text for tears.

There was a pause. It seemed to Bernard that quite a gap in time occurred before anyone noticed that anything was amiss. Then one by one the faces were raised to him. It was a small room – he never had many takers for such a difficult book – but none of the faces, not even the closest, was distinct to him. They were pale lights, nothing more. His eyes had failed him, he could not read his script; but his mouth was useless too, and would not have served him even had he found the words anew out of his own invention. The silence extended, all the vague faces were tilted up to him. He felt a dread and sickness exceeding the real occasion. He made to run from the room, but understood on the instant that there was nowhere he could run to. Then he blinked his eyes clear, worked up some spittle in his mouth, and read the text, or a decent amount of it, in the flat tone of man at a remove from himself and his fellow men because he is drugged or deaf or because a crack has run through his life and he knows for certain that it cannot be mended.

Leaving the Institute he sank at once into a passionate fixation on Kate's lips, proffered him, on her closed eyes, on her hair and complexion like the beloved's in the Canticles, and he held two thoughts in tandem that cancelled each other out: one, that he might be ill, finally, conclusively, ill in the head and in the soul, cut off beyond hope, damned for the rest of his days to look at people as though they were faceless moons; and two, that he would invite her to tea and that he had no tea because he only ever bought coffee on his little sorties to the market. He acted on the second, and departed from his usual route, turning into Turl Street off the Broad. This novelty, and more still the novelty of buying tea at Cardew's, strengthened him. In the alley between his college and Kate's he donated his change to a beggar dressed fantastically in Turkish pantaloons and a wide felt hat. The beggar-man bowed and began to dance a jig. He had all the gaiety of a corpse in the Dance of Death. Now the ugliness of this alleyway struck Bernard more than it ever had before. Grilles, bars, spikes and wire made up the exterior the colleges showed on to a public route, and the exhalations of their cooking and refuse were tepid and foul. But it was a dank sort of day, and the noble trees, a lime, a plane, a horsechestnut, overhanging out of the high garden, merely dripped. The beggars further down, whom he fended off, were sullen and hateful. Bernard's voice, when he used it against them, came out high, posh and cracked.

Bernard wrote to Kate, inviting her to tea, and delivered the note himself straight after lunch. But he had no answer from her and she did not come. Next day he wrote again, wishing her luck, and caught his usual bus to London.

Monday was the day of the interviews in College, Monday afternoon. Bernard rose early in Theydon Bois and made a few notes. He had been thinking how he might best support Kate when it came to the discussion. He was sure she would show up well when he asked her his question about the Joint School and the teaching of the European Novel; but she needed an advocate in the conclave afterwards. Soon he had written a little speech – the best thing he had ever done in that line, he said to himself. In it, of course, he had made no use of the strongest argument of all: that the College needed a woman in the Fellowship. Knowing his colleagues, he knew that argument would be counter-productive.

He took Mother her tea, and said he must leave earlier than usual, the traffic had been very bad lately. She began to whimper. She had passed the most awful night, her heart was racing, her pills had done nothing for her. Bernard experienced a seizure of panic, then saw the moment as perhaps the most critical in his life. It seemed to him that he must choose between Kate and his mother. His mother begged him to sit with her until her condition had become more bearable; but Bernard was firm. In haste and full of resentment he brought her a makeshift breakfast on a tray. She changed her strategy: begged him to put himself first for once, not to mind her, she had no wish to be a burden, doubtless she would manage, she had the doctor's number if it got much worse and Mrs Winterbottom might look in. Bernard kissed her forehead, and promised to phone at 9.30 as usual.

He ran for the tube. One came at once. Moving away he realized he had left his little speech on the kitchen table. No matter, he would do it again. In the dark, just outside Liverpool Street, the train halted. Nothing happened, no word came, everybody sat, hung, sweated. Soon Bernard was suffering disproportionately. It lasted perhaps an hour. Released then Bernard did a bold thing. Mindful of how bad the traffic had been lately he took the Circle to Paddington, for a train, instead of to Victoria for his usual bus. He missed the 10.15, but the next would get him there in time. He boarded it early, and wrote out his little speech. They pulled away punctually, and halted outside Ealing. Nothing happened for two hours. Then they were returned to Paddington. It was a scare, nothing real, services would resume. But Bernard tried a taxi to Marble Arch. Nothing worked, nothing fell out his way. The first bus came by full. Then the traffic was bad, worse after the scares perhaps, or only ordinarily so; but by then it was too late anyway.

Entering College soon after six Bernard met a colleague whose name, after many many years, still always eluded him when he needed it. This elderly man in a crumpled sports jacket said the job had gone to the forty-five year-old from Cambridge with a very solid reputation. Asked about Kate he said she was never in the running after the morning's interviews in the Faculty; the Faculty had vetoed her. Bernard's little speech would have done no good. The colleague in the sports jacket added that, to everybody's surprise, Crane had spoken up very forcibly for her, saying that the College, after six hundred and fifty years, desperately needed a woman in the Fellowship; but everybody supposed him to be being contrary and in any case his arguments were idle with respect to Kate, since the College could not appoint a person the Faculty had vetoed.

Bernard phoned Kate. She was out, and his courage deserted him after the tone. He left two minutes silence on her machine. He phoned his mother. She thanked him for phoning early. Yes, she was better. She was surprised to hear how long his journey had taken. Mrs Winterbottom's son, so Mrs Winterbottom had told her, had got through as usual. If Bernard had not been in such a hurry to leave her when she was feeling poorly he would have got to his important meeting on time. Should she post him the writing he had left on the kitchen table – it seemed to be a little speech or something – or would it keep till Friday? Bernard replied that it could be thrown away.

3

Trinity is sweet in Oxford, as everybody knows. People fall in love and go headlong towards their separations. There is so much water and greenery and over the formal orders life runs as unmanageably as honeysuckle. Some nights the craving in the ancient gardens is so intense a person will try anything to be rid of it.

There was a sad instance of this at the end of Fifth Week. Bernard had been kept from visiting his mother by some business in College. Being in his rooms for the weekend made him uneasy. He heard the sirens, slept badly, thought unhappily of Kate. Since the interviews he had only had one word from her: the bitter word 'Thanks' on a postcard from Los Angeles at Easter. She never came over to teach or to dine; she sent her apologies to meetings. Bernard lay half awake among bad dreams, heard hateful music and the sirens of police and ambulances. On Sunday he woke to a clear and absolutely silent morning and looked through his side window into the lane.

Something had happened. It was all over – finished, done with, silent – but something bad had happened. There under the huge overhanging horsechestnut tree, close by the wall-tie, a chalk outline had been drawn on the concrete, a human shape, like a sleeper face down, the left leg bent at the knee, the right straight out, the arms making a pillow. Next to the shape stood a police notice which Bernard could not read. He dressed and went down. The police wanted witnesses. A student was dead. He had fallen out of the tree at two in the morning. Bernard looked up first at his own bedroom window; then, from the chalk figure itself, directly up into the enormous height, fullness, triumphant greenery of the tree. The flowers were done, the spikes of fruit were forming, there was no limit to the branching, bulk and abundance of the tree, it eclipsed the sky.

Bernard went back in. The porter had the details. The student, a boy at the end of his second year, had climbed as high as it is possible to climb, and fallen; or he had jumped; or, having taken drugs, he had thought he could fly. Anyway, he was dead. The porter had seen him carried off.

The student's outline, the shape of him as he had lain on the ungiving ground, was distinct for a week; got fainter in the dust and under showers of rain; but never quite vanished. A beggar accustomed to sitting precisely there moved along a few yards and leaned back against the wall. Often he seemed asleep and all in all made very little effort. Others further up, in the shadow of the plane tree and in the kitchen smells, said a phrase at least, and the Irishwoman was usually on patrol with one or more of her infants, and came at the public brashly and contemptuously. First thing in the morning the alley was a soiled and littered place, until the sweeper passed.

Bernard had another route by now, not very new, a connection of two of the old ones. He toured the outside of Kate's college in the hope of seeing her; clockwise, down the lane under the chestnut tree, right down the Turl, right again down the Broad, back through Bodley; anti-clockwise sometimes. There was a beggar girl there on the Broad. She was extraordinarily pretty, had braided hair, a silver ring in her nose, her hands and face were filthy, she played a penny whistle as though to herself and kept a dog, an itchy mongrel, curled asleep on the ground between her raised-up knees. After lunch and in the terrible vacancy of the long afternoons Bernard might do the tour, one way or the other, six or seven times. He carried some change in the pockets of his sports jacket and gave here and there. He never saw Kate. On Friday, going for the London bus, when he stepped out of his secret door on to the High, he fell over an old man on the doorstep who had fouled himself.

The rest happened in Eighth Week, with a coda at the end of Ninth. During the last tutorial on Tuesday, in the hour before dinner, all Bernard's words were vacated of sense again and felt like slurry in his mouth. It began well enough. 'You were writing on Unrestraint,' said Bernard. 'Yes,' said the student, a young man at the end of his second year, 'on Restriction and Unrestraint.' 'And did I give you a quotation to think about?' 'Yes,' said the student:

'"Charlotte became more and more confirmed in the illusion that a return to an earlier and more restricted condition would be possible, that a thing once violently released could be brought back into confinement."' 'Good,' said Bernard, he settled himself, the student began to read. There was a gap in time. After it Bernard became aware of silence, and of a young man's face expressing hurt and disappointment. No remedy occurred to Bernard except to begin to speak. And soon his words were as meaningless as they were plentiful. He silted up. His pupil backed out of the room. A minute later the Lodge rang to ask if he was ill. 'No,' he said, and fell asleep until the trumpet.

At dinner he drank as much as he could, truanted from dessert and set off walking. He walked to a place of locks, weirs and sluices. The sky was green by the time he got there, becoming starry, the air scented, soft. But he stood over the weir, and smelled and heard nothing but the water that came from behind him in a dense and savagely rapid mass and emerged and fell away below his face. He wished he were dead, he wished he had died with Andy Jones, he wished he had access to some substance that would make him blithe and kill him quickly. Then the battering of the water obliterated all his thinking, not a word came to mind nor anything that could be called a thought. He vomited his dinner up, and hung there sweating. Couples passed. A woman's full dress brushed him. 'Don't do it,' her companion said, and slung a bottle into the race. Bernard crossed to the pub and drank some brandy. When he came out the big river was moonlit, lovers were on it fearlessly, singing, laughing, some boats carried paper lanterns, a girl in white was leaning over and launching candles downstream one after the other, careless of how soon or late they sank. Music, somebody was playing who knew how, the swans moved in among the boats as into a fit company. Bernard walked the length to Folly Bridge, and drank again, more. Slowly he began to believe he must force the issue in favour of love and life, and when the landlord closed the door on him he hurried to Kate's college and got past the lodge in a rush of drunken students. He had no idea where her room was, and went from staircase to staircase vaguely. The only room he could find in the place was

Andy's. Peering in there, it was on the ground floor, he surprised a naked girl, who screamed. Bernard hid himself in the far garden, and fell asleep. Waking as it got light he had no option but to climb out. This ended badly, but not as badly as it might have done. He leaned over the coping and saw the multiplication cross half way down. He was level with his own room, on the other side of the lane. The vast buildings were assuming their daytime shapes in the mist and the lightening darkness. Bernard lowered himself over the wall and got a foothold on the iron cross. The trick then was to reach down and get a handhold; but for this balance was essential. Bernard fell, and lay on his back in pain, looking up into the chestnut tree. Figures came out of the dark from against the Camera and stood over him. They were hairy, dirty, they stank, they had the gentlest faces he had ever seen. Their dogs sniffed at him. Bernard pointed up at the wall, then laid a finger on his lips. They understood, and bowed their heads. He took a £10 note out of his wallet. They lifted him and held him almost tenderly while he vomited. He was sick until his stomach clenched and heaved on nothing. Then they carried him to the lodge. The porter called an ambulance, the gentle crusty children helped him in. 'Least you're not dead, sir,' the porter said.

That was Wednesday, very early. Arthur served him the evening meal in his rooms, all the courses. Coquille Saint Jacques had come round again, and the College steak. An ankle was broken, but nothing much else; the ankle rested on a cushion; a shoulder hurt, but not very badly. As Arthur was clearing away there was a knock at the door and Kate came in. Arthur asked with his eyes whether he should withdraw or not, and Bernard indicated that he should. Kate said she had heard about the accident, but no details. Bernard gave her none. He began to say that he had done his level best to be at the interview, but she interrupted him. 'Forget it,' she said. 'I've got a job in Buffalo.' He felt her behind him at the window. 'And to be honest,' she said, 'I'll be damn glad to be out of this place. I want to be in the real world, not on a film-set.' Bernard came close to telling her that she was never in the running, that his presence at the interview would have made no difference, that the Faculty thought her not up to the job, but he forbore to. 'And by the way,' she added, 'I've been doing some research.' 'What on?' he asked, though he was not interested. 'On Andrew William Jones,' she answered. 'He died,' said Bernard, 'in 1966 or 67. He had the courage of his convictions and took himself off.' She came and stood in front of him and read from a card. 'Matriculated 1962, took a Pass Degree in 1965. 1972 wrote to the Senior Tutor for a reference. 1992 sent a large donation to the College Appeal and enquired about dining rights for Old Members. It's all on the file. Anyone would have told you. Can't think why you never asked. Present address – shall I read it out, and the phone number? He lives in Essex. You ought to look him up. He's probably a Captain of Industry. And we took his son to read Modern Languages apparently. Who knows, he might have the odd tutorial with you.'

She desisted. He saw in her look of pity how his face must look. Kate stood in the door. 'Forgive me,' she said. 'And forgive me one thing more: this week's *TLS*. It's nothing you don't know already, but I wish I hadn't written it.'

Bernard sent Arthur out to buy the *TLS*. Kate had gathered together four or five new editions and translations of the major European novels of adulterous love; but a good two thirds of her review article was given over to Bernard and Goethe; or, more exactly, to Goethe, Bernard and his old tutor Wallace. For finding these latter two much of a muchness in the wrongness of their interpretations of Goethe's intentions (though all she knew of Wallace, as she freely admitted, was what Bernard said of him), she shifted between them rather casually and finished by conflating them into one, whom she called Wallow. Her arguments Bernard knew already, from her letter and from their conversations; but she had sharpened them and edged them with satire against the Oxford patriarchy who, in rooms with views, celebrated present passion or the after life turn and turn about. To their massive phallic or ersatz-phallic dominion Ottilie said her 'No!', and meant it, and proved it on her body.

In the week's post, which Arthur brought up to him, were several letters of condolence on the review. Through his translation – which Kate had referred to in passing as 'merest pastiche'

– he had 'opened up a debate'; and for that the world owed him thanks not ridicule.

By the end of Ninth Week, though still not fit to travel to his mother's, Bernard was beginning to move around his rooms with the help of a stick. His left shoulder seemed to have slumped a little, but the pain was less. His face, where the beard left it exposed, seemed pinched; but, as Arthur said, a long hot summer would see him right.

That Sunday Bernard woke very early. A noise had woken him, the noise of a steady blowing or roaring. His stick was handy, he got from his bedroom to the living room and drew back the curtains of his windows on to the square. The panes were being subjected to a steady pattering; and below, on the cobbles and on the green in front of the Camera and over most of the square, were people in the costumes of the early nineteenth century all muffled against an intense cold. The roaring came from a generator of artificial snow. Snow lay on the ledges of Bernard's windows and wherever else it could lodge on the facade of his college, and on the pavements underneath. Then the venting machinery ceased and was towed away, and a coach and four drew up under Bernard's windows, the coachman beating his gloved hands and emitting the proper ghostly vapour at his mouth. Next came people in rags, some crippled, many with sores, and entered the lane between Andy's college and Bernard's. Snow lay there too, and another machine was backing towards the market, leaving behind it a likeness of horse dung. The beggars and cripples followed and took up their positions. Then a full crowd scene ensued, wonderfully picturesque, and through it suddenly came a chase, a boy running and after him a pompous old gentleman, there was a very lifelike hullaballoo. Bernard watched. St Mary's clock struck five. He watched till he was sleepy. Then he lay down and lifted his plaster on to the bed.

When Arthur came in with breakfast and the papers it was all over. Arthur, standing at the window, said they were clearing up. He said it was another classic they were doing, but he couldn't be sure which one.

After breakfast Bernard's mother phoned, to see how he was mending. She said not to worry about making the journey to

London. His Uncle Bob had offered to fetch him in a day or two. He had offered to run them to Swanage when the time came, and perhaps stay on with them and run them around a bit. But it was weeks till then. She was sure Bernard would be mobile enough to go out on the sands looking for shells as she knew he liked to do. Meanwhile, she had looked out his father's old stick, the one he had in the Alps when he was young, the one with the little tin shields on of all the places he had visited. 'It's been snowing here too, mother,' Bernard said. 'Quite a blizzard really. Seems to be melting now though.' He stood at his side window holding the telephone. The tramp in pantaloons was passing. He had cut his lips but did not otherwise seem much worse. A beggarchild came in, pushing a baby or a doll in a wobbly pushchair. By now the sweepers had cleared away the artificial snow and the horsedroppings, and there very faintly still was the real outline of a dead boy.

Back at the Spike

For S. G., who cannot read

1

The talk that morning was all of topping yourself. Pat on his hands and knees on the kitchen floor, laying down sheets of a daily on the disinfected floor, had seen a photograph of a man from Barnsley who had done it from the flagpole in that camp in Walkden. Slim asked was it anyone they knew. Luck, said Pat, a man called Freddy Luck. I knew a Luck before the War, said Slim, but he'd be dead by now. Pat wrung the drops out of his nose, splashing the page. It seems the man was up there with his tongue out when the Commandant assembled them for morning prayers. The sun had not risen, they saw him by the light of the Commandant's powerful torch when they were running up the Union Jack. Marvellous really how he managed it. He worked for the Post Office, said Pat, in his early life. He was always climbing poles. Dawn in November is often a bloody business, the sky in a rage, the birds squawking in torment; but had he bided his time, might not a view of the road beyond the Camp, of the famous open road, have given him new heart? Had he bided his time, said Walter, the Commandant would have caught him in the act, and fed him to the dogs.

Ape was furious that the man from Barnsley had made it into the nationals, and with a photograph too. I never even made the fucking Chron, he said. But you're not dead, said Walter. Not that you would have even if you were. I try, said Ape. You never tried. Ape wept. You seen my arms? Have I ever shown you disbelieving pigs my arms? They had, he had. His many wounds. He bade them feel the white and jagged weals among his hairs.

Razor, knife and broken glass. A mercy he could not show them his insides. Aspirin, bleach and paraquat. We were under the bridge once, Stetson recalled, by the old lock-up with a carry-out, when Fatty here came floating by. Some fishermen fished him out. They thought they'd have the five quid body-money, they were all for throwing him back when they found he wasn't dead, but he escaped and threw himself under a bus.

You'll not mind my saying so, Ape, said Norman quietly – and the little wafer of a peppermint was visible in his mouth – but it's not fair on the bus-drivers when you do that. And even leaving yourself to be found by a passer-by, who might be a kiddie or a female bad with her nerves, that isn't right either, in my opinion. Very sorry, said Ape, very sorry for all of them, I'm sure. But it's time I started looking after Number One. No other fucker will.

Let's face it, said Bassett, what you want to do when you do away with yourself is upset someone. In my view anyway. I'd like her to find me curled up in the fridge when she comes home and goes to get her tripe. And I'd like to be there watching her, I'd like to see her face. His lady in her butterfly spectacles, plucked eyebrows, sweptback peroxide hair, aghast, remorseful, too late now, see what you made me do, love Sidney. But it can't be done.

Well, said Norman, that's keeping it in the family at least, and perhaps Mrs Bassett deserves such a shock, it's not for me to say. But I was meaning the General Public. What's it got to do with them? They don't know you from Adam, Ape. I can't see why they should have to clear away your mess. Then Walter intervened. There's people paid to do the job, he said. Any man feeling the urge to top himself should get where he'll be found by an Official. Well that's all you know about it, Mister Walter Clever Dick, said the Ape, jabbing with a forefinger. The paid ones won't let me anywhere near them. They see me coming and they shut the door. Casualty won't touch me with a bargepole, and they've told me in the City Mortuary not to come bothering them. There's only the General Public left. The coppers won't, the firebrigade won't, even the fucking Little Sisters of Mercy won't. You know what Mother Bridie said to me last time I tried it there, and her a Catholic? She opened the door, he was lying on the step, clutching his belly and his eyes all gone. And what did Mother Bridie say? Oh, bloody hell, Ape, not you again. And shut the door. It's alright you saying, he said, not to go throwing himself at total strangers, and to keep it in the family at least or address himself to the proper authorities – what family? his only family is his mother's grave in Langley Moor, and not a paid servant within a hundred miles will give him dying space. I'm barred, he said, no room at the inn. Cack asked him had he tried the tip. I should think you'd get in there alright. Come in the back way where Dougie and me get in with the barrow. Ape said he'd like to know who'd see him if he did it on the Council tip. Dougie and me, said Cack, Boney perhaps. Bone in his cloud of flies. Dear Jesus Christ, said the Ape, you think I want him watching me when I pass away? I want somebody in white. I want a bit of human interest.

Ape wept. He took off his skull cap and laid down his massive head. He had a head of hair like Big Chief Sitting Bull's, the crown coming through it like a developing blister.

There was silence then. There was only the creaking and cracking of Pat's bones as he rose from the floor, fitted himself into the company at the long table and clawed with his crippled hands for a mug of tea. Cack munched on nothing, he had eaten everything, everyone else's remains, there was nothing left, the Grampus beamed at nothing through his broken specs. Ten in the morning of another interminable day. Film on the standing tea. Don't speak of the sadness after coition. It is nothing compared with the sadness after breakfast.

Nelson entered. Entered the silence with a springy step, his sleeves too short, his eyes too bright. Ape lifted up his countenance, all black and red. Come here, son, he said, extending half a hug, come and sit next to your Uncle Jim. But Nelson sat by the one they call Ben Gunn, facing the Ape, and between them on the table for a table cloth lay sheets of the week-old daily news: slaughter, money, tits. His right leg, poised on the toe as though for flight, trembled against Ben's left, and his fingers, which were bitten raw, ceaselessly clenched, unclenched and interlocked. Hands still on a table-top, either clasped or lying companionably

side by side, are a very restful sight, the mind in the head above
either thinking quietly to itself or attending without anxiety to
some conversation. Nelson's eyes went to and fro in a constant
scared appraisal. He wore a gypsy ear-ring and the sky-blue jacket
of a hussar. His jeans were inscribed on either thigh with love-
hearts. He was unshaven, softly. Neither on his hands nor on his
chest, so far as it was visible, lightly hairy, in the manly gap of
his collarless shirt, was he tattooed. Nor, to be honest, was he on
the rest of him. Nowhere, said Ben, on his white body did Nelson
wear a Mam or a Dad, a Love or a Hate, a dagger, a busty wench,
a muscle man, a vampire bat, a sacred head, or even a number, but
only an innocent birthmark, somewhat dove-shaped, below his
heart, and down his arm there had been lettering in biro. His love-
bites were all gone, also his early bruises and contusions.

Kid, said the put-out Ape, these lads wants telling till I'm blue
in the face. How many times I done it since you knowed me?
Nelson: Don't ask me. He meant it too. He meant don't put me
back in mind of your bloody blood, your white eyes (their pin-
head pupils), your gurglings, your puke, please not again. Dunno,
he said, half a dozen. Don't ask me. His eyes were away, his knee
against Ben's knee was going like the shakes. Leave me be. But the
Ape blew up. Half a dozen!? he roared. My fanny! he bellowed.
I done it three times three nights running and you was there.
Item: the opening of the veins on a hearth-rug in a little bedsit
in Pity Me. Item: on the same hearth-rug, before the gore had
dried, the writhing on a previous resident's pills. Item: the last
bus. And when you was gone...

When he had gone, having had enough, with his bedroll on
his back and his dog, a mongrel, trotting to keep up on a long
string, and had tried the life of bridges, garden-sheds and vacant
buildings for a while... the anxiety every evening, the search for
somewhere to get his head down, the before-sleep fear of the
place, the sleeping cold, the sudden starts in real nightmares,
the waking always too early, the day again, cadging, the café,
boredom, fear... when he had stuck it about as long as he could
he went to the place that is the last resort, and knocked at the
gate, requesting admission. Can't you read? bawled Little Hitler.

No animals allowed (except such as are necessary for the main-tenance of law and order, Blood namely, and his colleague, Hammer). Can't you read? No he can't. But he got the message and returned an hour or so later with his wet bedroll and no doggie on the end of his ten-foot piece of string.

So there, said the Ape, that's thirteen for starters. I'm going, said Nelson. I've had enough. He rose. But the paw of the Ape reached out and seized him by the wrist. You're staying, son. There's things I got to say. You'll sit and listen…

His wrist, Nelson's wrist, never well hidden and now yanked into the gaslight, was hurt across the veins and arteries where they are busiest. There was a pause, a dumbness. Ape sat, Nelson sat, the wrist upturned on the newspapers, thin, white, a weak point, too narrow and endangered for the lifeblood to flow there, lay on its back under all their eyes, and whoever had ever had anything helpless at the mercy of his roughness remembered it then and suffered the old mixed feelings and even the worst among them in that respect averted his eyes. But Nelson sat staring at his laid-out wrist, and even when the Ape's black hand had slipped away, still he displayed his wrist and sat there looking at it. His coat was too short in the sleeves, frayed at the cuffs, always rucking up, tight under the armpits, and a desperate costume at the best of times. Nelson stared in pity at his wrist, at the unclean, jagged, stitched-up cuts.

2

Ape left, and the one they call Ben Gunn at once took up again his questioning of Nelson. It was a mild day, though the year was setting inexorably into winter. They had brought McGrury in. His feet were worse. He said he was losing bits every time he took his boots off. Best to stay put, said Ben, hosing him down. Through the wire Ape pleaded with Nelson to accompany him. A new life, kid, he said. No use rotting in here. But Nelson refused. He was afraid of the nights. Besides, he said, a Romany never leaves his dog. That's it then, said the Ape, I'm going in the river, and he set off at a run across a field of sprouts. He'll be back,

said Ben. You'll see. And what's it matter anyway? But the boy
had tears in his eyes and the angry striations across his wrist, as he
hung there on the mesh, were very visible. Ape was diminishing
towards the bloody sun. He seemed to be chasing it.

There and then Ben Gunn began to question Nelson concern-
ing his early life. For whom, he asked him, did he wear a love-
heart on his trouser leg? Surely not for an Ape? For Jo. They
walked up and down along the western fence, Ben laying a hand
on the youngster's shoulder whenever they turned about. The
light was remarkable, Ben never forgot it. Departures worked him
up, even the Ape's across a field of little shrivelling green skulls.
He walked with Nelson, asking, listening and holding forth.
Until the klaxon sounded they met nobody, nobody except the
Grampus who had been sent with rat poison to treat the far
latrines. With a pail in either hand and the nearly level orange sun
blinding his poorly eyes he greeted them amiably. Then Ben's
heart overflowed and with it the words of his mouth.

She was away with him, away in the head, away with the
fairies, cuckoo, starry-eyed. They ran down the corridors hand in
hand, peering through spy-holes into the locked wards, scamper-
ing like mice among the geriatrics, walking the long walks under
the autumnal trees. Palm on palm and bowing to touch foreheads
they saw the big horsechestnut leaves plastered on the asphalt.
And the rain: kept from each other's bed by discipline they heard
their separate rains. Rushed into breakfast down the tunnels of
happy music. Sniggered in the workshop over the foolish little
artefacts. It was their intention to abscond and make towards
Mexico. Ben asked where was the dog and Nelson told him: at a
friend's. Ben asked who was this friend and Nelson told him:
Alfie. And once they were shown the dog, by Alfie, at a hole in a
back gate in the perimeter wall. Patted it, both their hands
coming back together licked. Running away then in tears to hear
him whining. The grounds were very large. Through the red
trees and the yellow trees there was the house itself at a great
distance, and there were the whitecoats walking gravely in con-
sultation or for recreation along the macadamed paths. And the
girl and Nelson heads together, walking. No visitors, they never

had any visitors, but in the intervals between the periods of discipline and even during the disciplines they kept one another company by eyeing and giggling across a room and by coming together to pass through a door and touching. Blue days, the leaves dancing, Jo catching leaves, a wish for every single one withheld from the ground. Wishes like birds, the piles of leaves, the pyres.

Ben asked what were the features by which he would know her anywhere. Her eyes, Nelson replied, they seemed to have been smirched in by sooty thumbs, and her hair, jet black and cropped, her hips, very slim and boyish, and her small breasts. Her conversation was all of running away, of not ever coming back, of going over the wall at nightfall or at dawn and running down a road and finding a hiding place in a wood. But her lips when she talked so quickly were lovely to stop with a kiss, and to purse upon gently then and suck into silence her agile talking tongue, this was better even than listening and, the eyes being closed, the heads together continued their intercourse of crazy promises. Grubby fingers, bitten nails. Ben asked after her wrists, whether they were ripped and stitched. They still were innocent of any wrongdoing. Neither blade not broken glass had ever traversed them, nor had any of the veins ever suffered the entry of a needle. And what of her family, or perhaps she had none? Was she a foundling? She was a lostling. She frequently said so. What she had of history was medical. She was in papers, she said, on forms in cabinets, in little handwriting, and wherever she went her bundle of jottings followed her and appeared miraculously on the desk before her in the clean hands of another professional, under another lightbulb. Could she read and write as well as you, Nelson? Ben asked. Better, he said. And she had a lovely singing voice. What did she sing, the old songs? The new ones, in a funny chant, in a muddle, grinning; and sometimes newest, of her own making. It was forbidden to sing during the disciplines, of course; but she was never properly quiet, any more than a stream is, and if you stood close when she was at a silent task you could hear her quietly soodling. She kept her head down but glanced at you and giggled when she knew you were listening. You must have been a pretty couple, said Ben, and a wonder and a joy to the other inmates.

They did get out once, so the story goes, over the wall as she had promised, and there was the dog, as per the arrangement, tied to a sycamore tree and idiotic with happiness. They were quite without funds. Perhaps they hoped to find a crooked sixpence on the way. It was early morning and they had not eaten. They scampered away down a long straight lane, dragged by the dog and hand in hand. The hedgerows and quiet fields were perhaps abundant in wild fruits and fungi, but they hurried by screaming with laughter and never stopped to look. He wore a sheepskin and she a hooded duffle coat of navy blue serge. The morning was rawky. After an hour when they were hot in the face and weak from laughing and when a clear blue sky was rising out of the mists, they halted, and the big-tongued dog, of breed inde-terminate and of meagre stature, sat in the road between them hiccuping with glee. So far so good. But if they were going to reach a seaboard and stowaway to Mexico, which they knew to be pretty far distant, they must, as they had seen it done in films, hole up for the day in a wood to elude their pursuers. When they thought of the alarm bells at that moment ringing and of the manhunt busily organising, their merriment doubled them up. A wood was an easy thing to find. There was a nice one, red and yellow in its crowns and loud with circling rooks, at no great distance across a ploughed field. Thither the barmy trio betook themselves, the humans soon footheavy with loam, the dog at a quick advantage. In the wood's centre there was a silence. They were overcome with shyness, as though it were their intention to lie together in a church. Had he ever looked at Jo in the world before? Not that a sacred wood could be called the world, but suddenly, at the end of the first little chapter of their running away, they saw themselves undefined by any walls and whitecoats: in fact alone. How would their love be when it had no oppressive strata of discipline to bubble through, no regulation? The pure air made them dizzy, and embracing in their bulky coats they swayed on their feet under the still treetops. Best get some sleep, said Nelson, so we can walk in the night. They lay down side by side, and the dog, whose name on that occasion was Fix, lay down also, at their feet.

Though they closed their eyes, Jo and Nelson at least, neither wanted to sleep. They were like children, only doing as they were told. Before long the silence itself was difficult to bear and they opened their eyes, to defend themselves; but saw an utter stillness in the trees above them. Used to agitation, they found it hard to lie still in a wood. The silence seemed to be throbbing or thumping. For Nelson it was worse, since he was bound to remember the wood he had hidden in after his daring escape in Lincolnshire, and he imagined he could feel the pains again, especially in his foot. But this wood was entirely kind, and perhaps what he was frightened of was too much happiness coming up out of the ground and descending through the leaves out of the sky and over-whelming him. Then he supposed that Jo, being the girl, might be expecting him to start trying to make happiness out of their two bodies, and the onus of this greatly increased his trouble. They were side by side, touching all the way down, most inti-mately at the backs of their hands. To go to sleep would indeed have been best, but neither could. The silence or the potency of the place began to work on Nelson like a pressure in his head and around his heart. He foresaw no release from it except in a flood of tears. When he felt against his index finger Jo gently rubbing hers, he sat up. Best go on a bit, he said. They'll mebbe come looking for us in here with an alsatian or something.

Once they were out it was better. The mongrel showed them the way. They found they had come right through and that the wood had been a sort of island in a vast ploughed field. They trekked on over the turgid waves, getting fatigued but in their former hilarity. At last they struck upon a disused railway track and just beyond it a stream; got across both and proceeded among some sheep on a sedgy grass. Fix was excited and they kept his lead pretty tight. Soon, still at a distance, they made out a roaring noise which they could not put a name to. They closed up and went more cautiously. There was a farm to the north and a low village, but they kept on westwards. Cross-country, said Nelson, and he liked the phrase. The roaring was traffic. They were a long time thinking of anything so obvious and actually came right to it, over a rise, before they knew. There were six lanes, dense, rapid, all shapes and sizes of things heading north and south with a steady noise. Jo said there was nothing for it but to cross. Nelson agreed. Any bridge, not that they could see one, might already be guarded. Nelson took the dog in his arms and rolled the string up small. They came down the bank, where a few trees had been started, and stood by a phone box among the shreds of massive tyres. For a lark Jo lifted the phone and a voice asked her where she was. She left it hanging. Nelson was looking if there might ever be a gap. Stick close, he said. Jo read out the names and origins of the giant trucks. Mebbe get a lift, she said. If they stood there long enough they would be sure to see one with Mexico on its side. Good job you've got me, she said, to read. Nelson nodded. He was glad of her powers. Best wait a day or two before we hitch a ride, he said. Till the hunt's quietened down. Then he took her arm in his, hugged the dog close, and stepped through a moment's interlude in the slow lane. Do it in stages, he said, but his voice was lost.

Close and often three or four times their height the traffic parted around them south. They stepped again. The iron brushed by. And again. They were delighted by their safety in the central reservation. The noise each way now buffeted their heads. The north was just as thick, fast, middle and slow, but they stepped through like dancers, in a strange exhilarated faith. They even saw faces, and laughed to see the amazement they were causing. Nelson was proud, and so full of love for Jo that he shook his head, there amid the din, in wonderment. And how the dog trusted him! Between the middle lane and the slow he stood a while longer than was necessary, letting an opening or two go by. He and Jo were athwart the usual world, and he felt invulnerable.

There was no other ordeal after the motorway. They did a mile cross-country, easy going, they let Fix have a run. Then came the railway, the great line north and south. Nelson and Jo, holding the dog, stood and watched an express go by. People, clearly at ease, were thrown across their vision at an unbelievable speed. There must have been a couple of hundred different lives flung past them while they stood. They stepped with reverence on to the still quivering track and watched the carriages show on a curve, then straighten and at once diminish.

Only now, standing in the track, did Jo realize that they had arrived, so to speak by the back door, into the village where she had often come as a child to visit her Aunty Honor and Uncle Frank. Their house was one in the nearest terrace, whose yards reached almost to the line. Nelson was anxious they would be betrayed, but Jo said Aunty Honor was her favourite aunty and would never do her wrong. In fact the good lady was at a lunch-time meeting of the Rechabites and Uncle Frank was at the club, so that when Jo and Nelson came through the yard and let themselves in, Jo loudly and cheerily calling out her favourite aunty's name, there was no answer. Jo said nobody would mind if they took off their coats and ate something. They ate a tray of lardy cake still warm and drank a pint of milk between them from the bottle. Then Jo led Nelson and Fix upstairs.

Aunty Honor's bedroom looked over the railway line, but Jo only glanced that way and turned at once to the great marriage bed. Tell us again, she said. And standing together at the bed-end, holding the iron rail as though drawing power from it, Nelson did as he was bidden and told her, who had heard them countless times already, the things he had been forced to do when he was very young in order to escape from a terrible captivity. When he had finished she licked her lips, seeming out of breath, and asked him would he show her the holes again, and said, when he stooped to unfasten his boot, that Aunty Honor wouldn't mind if he sat up on the bed, and when he had sat up there and she had taken off the boot and sock and felt at the little cavities under the ankle bone, she looked up at him with a different sort of mischief, her lips in a dry smile so that her tongue was for ever flicking out, and asking permission with her eyes, never shifting her eyes off his, unzipped his jeans and dug in with her fingers to get his thing out which she had never seen before, and only when it was in her little fist and grown and beginning to be slippy did they look at it. Out of its slit, every time her hand went down, the clearest fluid was rising bead by bead. Nelson, said Jo, and her thumb against the rim of the head made an audible slip-slip, my knickers are wet. They were what the Institution had provided her with, not pretty in the least, her skirt was somebody's cast-off, shapeless and dark, and she wore a shirt that might once have been a police-man's. When she was naked and Nelson was staring at her she took his hand and put it between her legs. See what I mean, she said. Get up, she said. Undress. The silk counterpane slid off with him, making a sigh. Aunty won't mind, she said, opening the bed for Nelson and herself. Now and then a train went by, shaking the sash, the bed and the little ornaments on Aunty Honor's dressing-table, but eventually Jo and Nelson fell asleep and what woke them was not a train but Fix's barking and Aunty Honor's screams.

Jo was wrong. When Uncle Frank came in he was all for leniency but Honor was adamant. She had no time for Jo, who was turning out like her mother, so it seemed, and vice wanted rooting out wherever it reared its head. She sent Frank for the police, but Frank, who had had a few and was feeling brave, phoned the nut-house instead. When Jo and Nelson had got dressed again and, with Fix, were being driven away, Honor went and saw the state of her carpet and her sheets. She warned Frank solemnly, standing at the top of the stairs, that sure as fate she felt one of her turns coming on.

Now the cover of the unhappy couple was blown. Rule number one in a place like that being: attract no undue attention, now they could not prosper. At some of the teasing and innuendo they blushed with pride. Eh, Jo? he grinned. Didn't we? Weren't we? But what they had been and what they had done attracted inter-ference as a rose does cankers. Lovers in a corner playing with each other's hands, lovers eye to eye across the common table, lovers silently smiling in the usual hubbub, this is asking for it. Besides, they were more demanding, having lain together in a double bed. The ordinary discipline irked them worse, they could see no sense in it. Rota is a fine thing for an empty man, but if the miraculous happens and he is filled with a passion, the day's official timetable goes over him like a harrow. When set to tasks apart how they must have chafed and fretted. Their reunions then at playtime were headlong, and a source of entertainment for everybody present. The controlling gods in white and their sidekicks in green shook their heads more in sorrow than in anger and forbore a little longer to intervene.

It entered Nelson's head as he lay there one night listening to the owls that she, his true love, was betraying him with a charge nurse by the name of Henry. Innumerable proofs avalanched upon him at once. At breakfast time, red with sleeplessness and weeping, his eyes implored her to come quickly through the door alone and looking for him; but she chose that morning to dawdle in chatting with a fellow patient by the name of William. The worst he had proved to his heart with respect to Henry he transferred there and then to William, a former explorer and a man whose power with words was greater than Nelson's by a factor of at least ten thousand. There was a scene. Mischievous Jo laughed and eluded him among the tables. The feasting company roared encouragements and banged with their special cutlery. Nelson groaned, called on Jesus and beat his own head with his fists. Jo ran down the corridor and hid herself in a female lavatory. Beseeching her with kicks and thumps on the insubstantial door he was taken at a run by the institution's Immediate Response and Intervention Squad (IRIS) and confined for twenty-four hours in the locked ward with the wild men.

Ben asked was Bedlam as it used to be in the old Queen's day: roarings, cakes of shit? Nelson answered no. They sit slumped around the walls for the most part silent, or muttering perhaps. They eyed the new boy apathetically. And if ever they fall in a rage and roll on the floor in the old style or bounce from wall to wall like bluebottles, it is not for long. When Nelson woke it was dark. Nightmares were going the rounds, the visited sleepers sobbed and groaned. He believed that Jo would buy her freedom with the oblation of her body to Doctor Macnamara, a young and powerful consultant, and that he, Nelson, would be kept in confinement until he was geriatric. Ben smiled at these foolish fears, showed him the vista through the insubstantial fence, and reminded him that he was still only a boy. Asked how and when was he enlarged from Ward 18. Next morning, Nelson replied, in the quietest manner. But after breakfast, during which he wept and trembled, he ran away into the farthest corner of the grounds and, close to the wall, on autumns of leaves, lay down, missing his dog. There Jo found him, and put her bitten fingers on his burning eyes. Had they known the whereabouts of Fix they would have scaled the wall at once and made another dash for the western seaboard. Instead they lay on the leaves kissing. When they awoke it was under ironic eyes. That afternoon Nelson was transferred to the hospital in the city.

It was now, if ever, that his career as a penman might have got under way. He took some instruction in the art from a sister of mercy who had seen his plight. JO, he wrote, biting his tongue. At table in the margins of their bloody news if Ben encouraged him he would form the letters of her simplest name. And of his own? NELSON. There he ran into trouble, since it was longer, and Ben had to guide his hand. DEAR was another word he had all but mastered, and the little word that joined his name and hers, the little active doing word beginning with L, he remembered that too under Ben's tuition, and did it leaning queerly. Now Nelson recalled the delight his first four words had given him. It shone in his face again. Ben felt as the sister must have done, rewarded. Once she had taught him how to make the words come out of a pen — any pen, Nelson, any cheap old biro with a rod of ink in it, any stub of black lead, any chalk or crayon — there was no stopping him. He wrote them on his jacket, of hussar blue, down his bare left arm from the elbow to the wrist, and down his trouser leg and once on his own forehead, boldly and blindly. This last inscription, when he ran to a mirror, appeared to him most strange. Ben took him by the hair, smoothed out his brows, as he might have a beloved son, but regulation soap and water or the winds and rains of heaven or his sweat or a back of the hand wetted with snot and tears had obliterated his statement to the world.

But having practised for some time on his proper person Nelson appealed to the authorities for a sheet of paper and watched by half the laughing ward he composed a short communication to his sweetheart in the country. DEAR JO, it read, LOVE NELSON. The envelope was buff, he sealed it with a loving kiss. JO, he wrote. But what came after he had no idea, it never having emerged between them in their laughing and giggling conversations, nor ever having passed from mouth to mouth. It was the sister of mercy finally who wrote in a lovely copperplate under his two big letters the name of the hospital of her whereabouts and bade him not lose heart, it would find her, there was only one, or if there were more than one only one could expect a communication coming from where his came from with the name of his darling in such simplicity. Ben asked what of that gentle woman most stuck in his mind. Her finger, he replied, going along the helpfully large letters in a primer for five-year-olds, its perfect shell-like nail unbitten and unbleeding, the whole hand (turning a page and flattening it for his laborious perusal) of a consistent beauty, not a finger on it nor on its pair any less than perfect.

Those were anxious days, said Ben, once the letter had gone and you remained in the wards and waited for an answer. Did you lose your appetite or did you, as some do, nervously eat far more than usual? Both, said Nelson. He found a male lavatory through the barred window of which, standing on the toilet seat, he could observe the drive up which every morning, regular as clockwork, whistling a traditional air, the postman pedalled. Poor child, did you imagine he would carry yours separately, tucked in the band of his cap perhaps, or that by some other means, a grin on his kindly face, he would signal to you, whitely staring through the window, that he had spotted her infant writing on a grubby envelope? It all went to the office. At length he became persuaded that they had intercepted her letter, or more than one perhaps, for being a good writer she must have written repeatedly, and out of spite they had decided to cut the connecting threads of love with official shears. Prowlings outside the office door; an attempt, hopelessly bungled, to burgle the place at dead of night; his constant refusal to listen to reason.

3

That sister in there, her laundered whiteness, the clean scent of her person, but most of all her hands, Ben often thought of her, often in the dip or under the fierce shower and when he was issuing the regulation underwear to somebody fetched in soiled and stupid off the roads. Black Jock was in (his cakey hands), Bengali Joe, and Leg and Crump the Nutter. Carl went out, swearing vengeance, and Gob after the Lord appeared to him in a vision and said he was needed overseas. McGrury's feet were gone all soft, like mushrooms, crumbling and slimy, but he left, he crept out of sight. Fergus went with him, said Ben Gunn. Fergus! said the Captain. But he's only just come! I spent my coffee break writing down his details. I started a new card. He told me the old one was full of lies. Seen this? said Pat. It was in the Echo. It was the story of a man from Hartlepool who would eat nothing but carrots and drink nothing but carrot-juice and when he died, which was soon, he was entirely yellow. A health fiend, said Slim. But Fergus, said the Captain, whatever did he want to go running off again for? He told me he felt he belonged here after all. He said he believed he had a mother still alive in Witton-le-Wear and as soon as he'd got himself cleaned up he would move in with her and brighten her dying days as any son would. What a waste of time it all is. Where's he gone? Glasgow, said Ben, or Walkden. But he's just come from Walkden, the Captain cried. He said he'd never go back there, not if they paid him. He said the man down there was a homicidal maniac. Then Glasgow maybe. But he set off south.

Once it was obvious to Nelson that his mail was being intercepted he took a fellow inmate into his confidence, one who had the advantage of literacy over him, a youth called Claude, and dictated into his pen the poor seeds of a desperate love-letter which Claude, a wizard, caused to flower. Heart's Darling, he wrote, my waif, my lostling, my wandering in the mind girl, this comes to you in tears from your wordless and confined lover via a FRIEND in the hopes of going behind the backs of our gaolers and entering again into the paradise which is rightfully ours. They have been burning your letters by the sackful, Jo darling. The postman labours up the hill in vain, for of the millions you have written I have received not a word. Remember the wood, my sweetheart, your Aunty Honor's place, and when you came and found me on the leaves. Since then the days have been interminable and the nights even longer. There is no way those bastards in the office are going to let me get at you or you at me with the written word through the normal channels. So: DO OR DIE. Go over the wall after breakfast next Thursday and come into town on the 67 bus. I will be waiting under the HORSE at midday and will stay there until 4 or until I am caught or until you come, which ever happens first. If you do not come I will know they are bugging my every move and have probably got tabs on you too. In that case: WATCH FOR NEWS. I miss you and the dog. Where is the dog? They said they would look after him, the liars. Here I am making coat hangers. What are you making? I am getting on with the reading and writing, but must still employ an amanuensis, as you see. It is not to be hoped that I shall ever be fluent enough to keep pace with the way you run and skip and who once has heard you singing under your breath would anyway throw his paper and pencil to the winds. Dearest, when I sleep I am mithered by bad dreams, it is all roaring and noise here or a deadly hush, we do not have the trees and the big heavy leaves blowing, though even where you are the leaves will all be down by now, but what I dream is of my head being clamped about the jaws and of my eyes popping and I am in that agitation you have often seen me in. I kiss your bitten fingers. NELSON.

Nelson was beside himself with love and pride. He never knew he had it in him, he said, but now he knew he had. He admired his own bloody fingers, and thought better of his heart and brain. Claude swore by everything holy that he would get this letter stealthily into the honest mouth of a public postbox. I too have loved, he said, and it is no fun.

Young Nelson sat under the equestrian statue, chin in hand, waiting for his love. It was a normal day, the drunks were rolling and bawling and the Law, wearied to death, passed by on the other side. Patient Nelson sat under the monument raised by a grateful populace to their local abuser of power, a fine figure of a man in a busby, wielding a cutlass as at Peterloo, on a neighing charger. Chip papers from the night before waltzed to and fro in the usual gritty wind. Nelson sat facing north-north-west down the cobbled street up which she must come if she came. The church clock according to its mechanism bonged the quarter hours.

Between twelve and one there was a toing and froing of more or less normal citizens. Mothers, for example, rode the narrow pavements behind enormous perambulators. There were the near misses, the glancing blows and the head-on collisions of which life in society is composed. Words remonstrative, words apologetic, words insulting jostled for air-space. During this hour Nelson was bright and hopeful. He shielded his eyes against the radiance of his at any minute arriving love. Between one and two there was a lull, several shops stopped trading and men, women and children who had food to eat ate it, whereupon the men and women at least were oppressed with a languor and sadness which they combated as best they could. Nelson, though he fasted, himself suffered towards the end of the hour a lowering of spirits, a diminution of hope. He unshielded his eyes, there having been as yet no radiance, and rubbed them, they were tired. Worse was what accompanied, between two and three, the evacuation of the public houses. To see the brief merriment of the drunks wither in the wind would have moved the bowels of your compassion. How hearty their faces and loud with rage, the highspots on their cheeks empurpled with broken veins. See them setting their caps and trilbies more or less to rights. Farewell, shout the lucky ones with dinners at home to backfire and wives to thump. The houseless left in the long cold afternoon. The drink goes off them like a blanket graspingly reclaimed by a warden in the Sally. Some fight a little to keep warm, some bring it all up there and then and wipe their mouths and make a sad exit from the market place. Disconsolate, the Polis heave the loudest into vans. Nelson sat, and was angered by this carry-on. He blamed it for his sweetheart's non-appearance. Be quiet, he muttered, stop the noise. How can she come in all this pandemonium?

The fourth hour was the quietest. Before it ended a few dim lamps had been lit. When Nelson rested from gazing by declining his head he saw below him, set into the cobbles, the skylights of an underground gentlemen's convenience. Out of that tomb, seeming very distant, came the occasional slam of a door, the sluicing of water and the voice of the attendant singing an old song at his work. Nelson could not keep still now but began to circle the prancing horse in a spiralling fashion, descending as he went from the top step to the cobblestones and on the next circuit rising again. The street up which she would not come debouched steeply into the little square between a canyon of shops. He looked down it into a a shadowy pit. Come on, come on, come on, he said. Outside the bank a cripple shouted Echo through a cleft palate. His rival opposite, outside a surgical stores, over a hare lip shouted Chron. Two ragged crows, twa corbies. It was the time of the gathering of starlings. They came over the red sky in a pall, and jostled for perches on every ledge. Panic of cicadas at vertical noon is nothing beside the squeaking, creaking, phthisic gasping of the starlings when the cold settles down on a loveless town at dusk. He had not seen climbing into the square throughout his vigil one female in the least resembling her. He had seen nothing to be grateful for. That late afternoon the wells of his unhappiness, his childhood fonts of grief, were broached in him, and he sat uncomforted, sweating and trembling, whilst between his fingers a weeping flowed and flowed. The starling noise went to and fro across his nerves. Echo and Chron croaked louder.

At four o'clock, the last stroke passing away, Nelson wiped his eyes on his sleeve, blew his nose on a red bandana such as cowboys wear, and drew out of its furry sheath a six-inch knife, bone-handled and blunt. This in hand, he stood up with a cry and ran at full tilt to the City Housing Office where, after a dull day, they were shutting up shop. Steady on, old chap, they said, as he rushed in. He waved the knife and in an odd voice demanded to see the fucking Manager. Steady on, old chap, they said. The Manager had slipped off five minutes early to buy his wife a rose. He was beginning to be infatuated with one of the office girls and that very morning had made some trifling advance. Elated at once and bloody in the heart with stabs of guilt he had thought that buying roses might make him feel better. Not mincing his words however, Nelson let them all know there and then in the dull little office that he had had about enough of waiting around and being pushed from pillar to post and what he wanted – waving the knife – was accommodation for himself and Jo, he didn't care where and he didn't care what so long as it was clean and they could have the dog with them, and he wanted it now, nor was he going until he got it. There was some screaming, but almost mechanically, and a sensible man by the name of Mr Small assured him that they sympathised and were doing all they could. Was he registered with them and would he not, please, put his knife away? In a speech addressed to the whole world and delivered at the top of his voice Nelson summarised, in all its wretchedness, his life to date and laid the blame fairly and squarely where it belonged: at the feet of God, the family and local and central government. He was a rebel, he said, and a fighter for justice, which was why they had interned him against his will – he had signed none of the necessary papers – and separated him from his helpmeet, a girl with close-cropped black hair, a pale face, shadowy dark eyes, bitten fingers and small breasts, who answered to the name of Jo. Where she was now and what was being done to her in his absence he dreaded to think, what was being done to him was bad enough and he was a man, and a tough one at that, and could stand it, but she could not bear pain, she wept at the very thought of its infliction upon any dumb creature male or female. In short, he begged them to see reason and to house him and his young wife together, preferably in the country with a bit of ground and a few chickens, which being done they would be no further trouble to anybody, all they asked was a quiet life. Mr Small nodded, like the sensible fellow he was, and held out his hand, with more than a little hope of success, for Nelson's wildly gesticulating dagger. But a colleague meanwhile, wishing to be helpful, had slipped out the back way and fetched the Force. They arrived now at the double with a roar and a crash. Nelson, quick as a cat, leapt upon the counter, kicked the outgoing post to left and right, and, up aloft, his face a shade yellow and spittle of an old man's white flecking his lips, to show them he meant business drew the knife, the blade of which was blunt, across the emergent wrist of his left arm and beginning then, after two or three attempts, seriously to bleed, he stood there in the absolute silence, frightened.

Yes, said the Captain, Bassett had a note from Housing the following day, his usual refusal but with blood on it, that would be Nelson's blood, and there was a line or two in the Echo and half a little paragraph in the Chron, but no picture in either.

4

Then the Ape came back. They were returning from an occupation in the disused morgue, Nelson and the one they call Ben Gunn bringing up the rear, when they heard him shout. He was at the wire, thrusting his nose through a rusty diamond. He wore a hideous coat down to his ankles, a sort of astrakhan, and behind him the bloodiest sky you ever saw was reared up over the miles of cabbage fields. I got the dog, he cried. Ben followed Nelson to the wire. Not drowned then, Ape? he said. Or perhaps you're resurrected? Me and the boy are starting again, said Ape. I've fixed us both a job in Alice Springs. Let's see the dog, said Nelson. Ape undid a couple of buttons towards the middle of his coat: the dog's head poked out. That's not the one, said Ben. That's him alright, said Nelson. The dog began to make little cries, perhaps of joy. I'm coming, said Nelson. He ran – how he could run – and was back in no time with his sheepskin and a ministry blanket. I got his string, he said. On hands and knees he crawled through the hole behind the Captain's old privy.

Their reunion was very affecting. The dog came out of the Ape's belly like a kangaroo and drenched his young master's face with kisses. The Ape beamed. Yes, he said, it's a new life starting for me and the lad. Ben spoke to Nelson. Think of the cold, he said, think of the terrors every late afternoon when the dark is coming on and you have nowhere to go. The Law, the alsatians, the rats, the gangs, the numberless casual accidents. Worst, the cold. Your shaggy friend here will not keep you warm. Look at the sky. There's frost on his moustache. But Ape took out a hip-flask and began to jeer at him: Who's sorry now? he sang. Whose heart is aching? Not fucking mine. You stick around in Stalag 90 with the dossers. Me and Nelson are off to Alice Springs. Think we care about a bit of cold and wet? We don't. Get back in by the fire, grandad, and ask the Boss for another hotwater bottle. Nelson, said Ben, there's nothing for you in Alice Springs. I've a sister in Barmouth will give you bed and board. I'll write tonight. Or wait till spring and we'll set off there together. She's always begging me to pay her a visit. Ape danced a

jig. Listen to Whiskers, he roared, listen to Benny Gunn! Him
and his sister! Nelson, said Ben, the roads are unsafe, there's not
an ounce of charity going begging between here and Liverpool,
you'll fall among thieves, the Law will club you to death, you'll
get fifty years if you're caught with this fat dick. The Ape
laughed, and laid his arm around the waif's thin shoulders.
Nelson, said Ben, there's a war on, don't forget. Men even less
fit than you have been disappearing into the bully-beef factories.
You'll be pressed. And what will you eat? Whatever else, we
never starve in here. Bloater has done us dumplings for tonight,
and jamroly pudding as an afters. And think of the company:
there's Dougie on the spoons, and Pat with another story about
his time in Rochdale. And weren't we making progress with
your letters? Wait till the spring at least. Come back in now and
finish your education. But Ape had begun another song. Home
on the range, he sang, where the deer and the antelope play.
That'll be us, he smirked. And you'll be in here warming your
chestnuts. Nelson, said Ben, what if a message comes? What if she
writes? How will her letter find you? She's dead, he said. I told
you they killed her in the hospital. In bed with the Big White
Chief more like, said Ape. Ben got a hand through the wire
to touch the boy's cheek. Then Nelson swung away. See you, he
said. Ape jingled a pocketful of coins. Ben watched them go.
Due west they went, across the cabbage fields, breached a hedge,
breasted a slight rise, he saw them silhouetted on a sky becoming
shark-white as the blood drained out of it.

Was Jo dead? Nelson had said so, but he was very low in spirits
at the time, and it was as much as Ben could do to sustain him
with any other possibility.

The doctors were cross with Nelson after his escapade, their
motto being: the less we're in the Chron the better; but they hardly
needed to supervise him more closely since he was very listless.
Then a letter came. He had given up watching for the postman
from his vantage point in an upstairs lavatory and when the sister
of mercy, she of the perfect hands, brought him his letter with a
smile he was seized simultaneously by joy and fear. So mistrustful
had he become of any in authority over him that he refused the

kindly sister's offer to disclose its contents there and then by read-ing aloud, and ran instead to his confidant and writer Claude. There was nothing on the back of the envelope, neither SWALK nor POSTMAN POSTMAN DON'T BE SLOW BE LIKE ELVIS AND GO MAN GO. Claude felt some misgivings. Effect-ing an entry with the handle of a plastic spoon he read not the child of nature's own jumpy scribble but a typed communication, as follows: Sir, They say it will be best for the both of us if we no longer try to communicate with one another by the written word, the word of the mouth or thoughts, and they know what they are talking about. There is no future in us. Yours sincerely, JO. Claude showed him the little signature. In Nelson's eyes it seemed to be trembling. She signed, he said, but only after they forced her, with drugs. Claude said she was surely whispering something different under her breath. Love such as hers, he said, cannot be eradicated by mere electrodes, needles and torpedoes.

The certainty that his sweetheart had died of a brain tumour brought on by excessive doses of ECT visited Nelson one night in his sleep and he woke in the ward sweating and screaming. But before we come to that we should mention another of his certainties, namely this: that the child was with child by him as a result of their lying together inexpertly in her Aunty Honor's bed. This came to him one late afternoon in an hour of deepest apathy whilst his sore fingers were occupied with some regulation basketwork. The blood went from him as though there were a hole in his veins again. Between horror, love and pride he stumbled in his thinking to and fro. In his heart of hearts, he said, he must have known it all along, or why else would he have made such a desperate demonstration in the Housing Office? With a kiddy on the way he and his young missus were of course priority. He must get back there at once and put his case to the considerate gentleman called Mr Small. Nurse, he cried, Joanna's going to have a baby. What's the good of me sitting here making baskets? Patience, Nelson, she replied.

No gynaecologist, he imagined her big already; but Claude, a more experienced man, doubted whether there would be much visible swelling of the belly before the third month, and she shrank again. On the whole Nelson preferred to think of her as both pregnant and unswollen and lying awake at nights, hearing the trains, he easily did so. Fetched her through the air, across the cold intervening distances, in flat disobedience of official prohibition, and hugged her in his arms, whispering plans into her subtle ear. DEAR, JO, NELSON and LOVE he printed in defiant capitals on scraps of paper, on the oilskin tablecloth and on his person. Claude, irrepressible, composed another love-letter off his own bat and read it aloud to Nelson as they stood together at the sink. Proudly Nelson put his name to it, and a male orderly by the name of Jock, who, for reasons of administration, visited the asylum in the country once a week, agreed to be his postman. Some days later, pushing a trolley through the recreation room, Jock gave Nelson the thumbs-up. Nelson rejoiced, and passed the day singing; but that night in a dream he saw her white face staring stonily at him, her lips were thin and black, he said, her eyes were coal-holes, her hair was cropped almost to the skull. Worst was the stony coldness of her expression and the marks of burning fangs at either temple. He became convinced that they were seeking to erase her love by treatment. Where was love, where did it have its residence? They were beginning in the head. They were cauterizing love with electric adders' tongues. And when she had been knocked out by the needle and her protecting hands had been removed from off her womb what hope did their baby have then crouched in its sanctuary shutting its ears against the institution screams? He tried other ways of thinking about her but the same face always reappeared.

There was another break-out, another flouting of all the rules of the institution and of common sense, in a last desperate bid to see the beloved face to face. For nothing had come of Jock's initiative. Nelson raised some cash, perhaps by theft, perhaps by offering his services as a fellator to a charge nurse called Donald, and broke out early through a gap in the railings under the viaduct. From there it was only a step to the bus station where he merged with the coughing, rheumy, bag-eyed multitude and boarded the 67. That road! Its villages hang upon it like boils on a tapeworm. Though a sort of life continues in the public houses,

in the Kicking Cuddy, the Boyne, the Spread, the Loves, the
colossal co-ops and the picture palaces are all boarded up and in
them the only life is rats, trapped pigeons and a drunk or two.
Little by little the floors are burned for warmth, and water runs to
waste from countless bursts and freezes down the flights of stairs
during the long winters. The draughts on such street corners,
the back-end icy winds! The lumpy women in their jumble sales,
the shuffling ruptured men, the blobs of phlegm. Shopwindows
full of articles at a discount. The back-to-backs, their alleys and
their privies, the women's courageous washing and their brown-
stone finger-boning steps. Pits at a little distance, stink-heaps,
rusting winding-gear. And when it shakes these habitations off,
sloughs them behind, why is it black, that road, why are its grassy
verges as black as soot? The flat fields laid out hopelessly on either
side, a stink of rotting cabbages, the heads of swedes gnawed at
by sheep as black and matted as the verges.

In the steamy bus, his cheek on the wet pane, what did Nelson
see of all this? Nothing, he said. But he sat hunched in his smelly
sheepskin clutching his ticket and his change, his knees raised
against the next seat-back, her name in fading capitals there for all
to see. He was scared, he was rank with fear. Then he alighted as
the only one under the suspicious eyes of the driver and conduc-
tor in their uniforms and stood by the roadside twisting his ticket
until the bus moved off and splashed his legs with dirt. The walls,
the iron gates. The trees inside were nearly bare, what leaves were
left even in a sudden fierce gust would not have made much of a
show, no storms such as he had enjoyed with her, no red and gold
in abundance, spinning, sailing, cartwheeling and falling, when
he was catching leaves with her in the time of wishes when his
wrists had not been hurt. He had the good sense not to present
himself as an o.k. visitor at the porter's lodge and struck off
instead north-north-east as it were indifferently, following a lane
in the general direction of a village smoking like Gomorrha but
called Mount Pleasant.

Silence, nobody in sight, but Nelson was fearful nevertheless.
As soon as he dared, having got clear of the highway, he stepped
off through a wayside litter of cans and photographs, found the

wall and felt along it for a place to climb. Climbed, bestrode the
coping stones, dangled and dropped. His noise frightened up a
pheasant from the tangled undergrowth. And who can move
silently through brittle twigs in knee-depths of dead leaves? Even
for a Romany it is impossible. He was full of thorns, his sheepskin
horrendous with twigs and burrs, he was like a beast in pastoral or
like a baffled scapegoat when he emerged at last, butting with his
desperate head, on all fours into the vegetable garden where a
trusty imbecile, an old-timer by the name of Pilkington, stood
with a wheelbarrow, alarmed. Nelson wet himself. Like a sheep,
pissing with fear, he did the daftest thing: broke cover immediately and bolted over Pilkington's compost heap and through
his frosted dahlias. Pilkington gave a shout. But had Nelson had
his wits about him still he might have saved the situation – might
have engaged the old fellow in conversation, slipped him half a
crown, explained himself. Instead he ran for it, across a lawn, across
a yard, through the dustbins headlong into a kitchen and before
he knew where he was he was in the wards. And there he should
have sauntered, quietened his breathing, assumed a nonchalant
and familiar manner, as though he had never left, and perhaps
hardly an inmate would have noticed him, for if he was strange
they were just as strange, and doctors and nurses hardly ever knew
who among their charges was in and who was out and who was
in again. But Nelson ran, hearing behind him (though it was in
his head) a terrible hullaballoo, he tasted his own tears and
smelled his stink. He told the one they call Ben Gunn that it must
have been by instinct that he found his way down all those
corridors and through so many wards and among such numbers
of inhabitants to where Jo sat and pitched up sliding on his knees
across a polished floor as far as her knees, which he embraced.

She was sitting on a chair in the corner doing nothing. She had
a funny overall on and flat shoes, no stockings. Her hands were in
her lap, very quiet. Her nails still bitten? Worse than ever, bloody.
Her face was as he had seen it in his dream: very white, her eyes
larger than ever and darker, the pupils reduced almost to nothing,
to pinpricks. Her hair? Ben asked. You would have said her head
had been shaved bald and the hair had only been growing again

for two or three weeks. And her expression? Dull through and through. And seemed not to know you, Nelson? Not a sign, not a flicker. She did turn her head to look at him, that was when he saw how tiny her pupils were, but he might have been anyone or no-one. Ben asked did Nelson not seek to rouse her by speaking her name or by touching her. Nelson replied that he had taken her hands and that they were cold though they never used to be cold, and that he squeezed them tight and that he kissed her fingertips where there were no nails. She let him, she was lifeless.

Ape said, whenever the subject came up at table whether Nelson was there or not, that lifelessness like that was because of the treatment. I've been like that myself, he would say, and look at me now. He said a few cups of coffee would do the trick. But Nelson when he was there, if he heard that said, he answered that it would take much more than coffee in her case, she was dying. She was nearly dead. He saw the holes in the sides of her head where they put the wires in. By now the greencoats and the bully boys were closing in on him from behind. Turning, pointing at Jo, he made a speech full of grief and rage, but nobody would listen nor did they give him the chance to come quietly. He resisted arrest, fighting as hard as he could. The odds were overwhelming. As the battle ended he ran for a window, to throw himself through it, but the squad were on top of him before he got there. They applied minimum force. Passing out, he saw the lost daughter of the Queen of Spades look his way with perhaps the beginnings of an expression.

Claude said, when Nelson was brought back in, that the enlargement of her eyes and the mask of vagueness over her face and the stillness of her hands in her quiet lap were perhaps to be understood as signs of pregnancy, and the one they call Ben Gunn said he agreed with Claude. But Nelson left with the Ape for Alice Springs.

5

Terrible things were behind him when he first came to the Spike and stood in the rain asking for admission. That evening when he knocked at the gate it was not opened unto him but Little Hitler, the Night Porter, told him to fuck off, please, and drown the dog and then we would see about it. He had come from wandering the streets with his dog and before that from wandering them with his dog and Ape and before that from incarceration in one or two mental hospitals but the very worst things were behind him even then, for he had, he said, escaped from an earlier imprisonment by murdering his captors and was on the run with blood on his hands. He told his story frankly to the doctors, who must have taken it into account when they were healing him, and of course to the Captain, who entered his particulars and filed him under N, and in bits and pieces he told it to the one they call Ben Gunn and during the nights a man above him or a man below him could always pick up the gist by listening to him babbling in his dreams.

It was in the past, but his past did not go back far enough, the past in his life was not abyss enough to engulf the innumerable wicked things. When he was in and had left the murderous world outside the wire the Captain patted him on the arm and said forget it, child, and advised him to draw a line under it and make a new beginning, and the roughest men, clapping him on the back, advised the same: forget it, son, they said, themselves remembering something when he came in trailing a length of string and clouds of buggered innocence. But his past wasn't deep enough, he was burying his corpses in very shallow ground and after the natural tendency of things in the ground to work themselves to the surface there were bumps and bulges wherever he looked, and at nights and in the early mornings and even at quite harmless times during the day a fist would erupt into the light, a knee, a boot, his father's face, his mother's merciless smile. Oh, had those men, his rough companions, been the very bandages and lint and cotton wool of human kindness and had they swaddled him around with their goodwill, there would have been some seepage nevertheless, a considerable leaking. He was not deep enough, he wanted a mine shaft in him down which to drop his mam and dad. Or another life, quite simply. Had God been more accessible Nelson might have asked to be allowed to start again.

His inordinate love of friendly little dogs derived perhaps from his having been confined for many nights of the year, summer and winter but especially winter, in the kennel, which stood outside in the yard, of the household's Jack Russell terrier called William. This being confined in a small wooden house, locked in supperless, had begun as a punishment, but he had become used to it, as to many others of his parents' devising, so that to punish him they had been obliged to think of something else, after which other punishments he had crept very willingly, very gratefully, into the kennel and had soon fallen asleep, hugging the dog.

It was not the job of the Jack Russell terrier to guard the property at nights. Ben Gunn wondered why they kept such a little dog at all and Nelson could not tell him. An odd throwback perhaps. The property was guarded by an alsatian called the Ripper. It was for the Jack Russell's safety that Mister locked him in and little Nelson with him, or he, the dog, and he, the child, would have been in danger of being mauled or even, since Mister kept him hungry, eaten by the Ripper. As it was, the Ripper came snuffling at the kennel door during the night and felt with his paws and nose at the bolt, which woke William and Nelson.

The dog Little Hitler, only obeying orders, took such exception to was certainly not William. That creature on the end of Nelson's piece of string was a mongrel in which the Jack Russell was scarcely, if at all, represented. A Romany never leaves his dog, he used to say; but this, like much of what he used to say, was less a fact than wishful thinking or a received opinion he liked the sound of and applied to himself without much justification. For when Little Hitler told him no way, son, do you get in here with your four-legged friend he, Nelson, went and put the mutt in care, so great was his fear of spending another night outside. But any true Romany would have stood up to the gateman and replied: love me, love my dog, man and dog are one flesh etc. But perhaps he wasn't a completely pedigree Romany and so in an emergency, which that late afternoon most certainly was, he could bend the rules a bit to suit himself.

His father and mother kept a smallholding in a remote part of Lincolnshire and if they had once been travellers they had given up travelling, for a time at least, and had decided to infect one particular spot instead. Their habitation was littered with broken glass, old iron and a good deal of carrion that even the Ripper, ravenous though he was, turned his nose up at. When the sun shone the place stank more than a little, but a merciful fogginess was the usual climate and in the damp and cold they, the tenants, stamped, swore and laid about them with a horsewhip.

There were few callers. The postman cycled out to them occasionally with a summons or a final demand. One morning he witnessed the opening of the kennel door and the releasing of young Nelson into the daylight. Wet his pants, said Mother, so we give him a night in there to teach him a lesson. Well quite right, lady, said the postman, I'd do the same myself. But this was not his true opinion and he reported what he had seen, with indignation, at all his ports of call. Yes, it was more than suspected in the scattered neighbourhood that the boy at Boggart Sink was ill-used by his parents. One or two nosy-parkers took the trouble to call, on some pretext, to see what they could see; and although they saw nothing particular they saw the kennel in which, according to the postman, Nelson had been confined, and they got, so they said, the feel of the place – its crows, its rust, its hen-scraped scabby earth – and shivered to think of the wicked goings-on. Nobody interfered, partly because Mister was a big man but chiefly out of respect for the sanctity of the family and on the general principle of minding one's own business and keeping one's own house in order.

When the Captain was asked by female visitors how his inmates got like that he would sometimes answer: want of family life; but he might in many cases with equal truth have answered: excess of it. For Mister and Mother and little Nelson were a tight-knit family, and no mistake. They thought of one another constantly in all their waking hours, and when they slept they visited one another in their nightmares. Nelson believed that a brother or sister had gone on ahead of him, but had not lasted the course. Certainly, the household needed at least one child. Mother and Father wanted something between them, something more capable of suffering than a dumb dog, something shaped like them, over which they could fall out and make it up again. They must have been glad that Nelson did not die in infancy. For what, after all, can a toddler stand? Not much. But a growing child, three foot or four foot in his shitty sockless shoes, is a better and better thing; and a near five footer, a lad getting into his teens, what can one not inflict on him without much risk that he will let one down and die? Always to have the little chap around the house or within bawling distance in the yard or not beyond easy hunting distance (the Ripper on a taut lead) in a hedged-in field, this gives every day its point, its recreation, its relief in any period of ennui. No inconvenient accident occurs but there is somebody to take it out on, and every little pleasure is enhanced when there is somebody to keep it from.

There was not the least grey in Mister's hair, nor any thinning or receding on the crown or forehead, but his hair was black, dense, bristly and came down in sideburns below his ears. Tufts, jet-black, sprang from his nostrils and from his ear-holes too. He wore an immense gold ring, of gypsy gold, he said, and a silver crucifix on his hairy throat left him by his dear mother. At the mention of his mother's name tears would well into his manly eyes and he would cross himself. No finer woman ever walked this earth, he roared, and twisting his wife's hair with his left hand he would pull back her head until the tears were in her eyes also and demand that she swear on the body of God that no finer woman than his mother had ever walked this earth and that she, his wife, was pig-shit by comparison. She swore it. What the fuck else, he wondered, could even he father on tripe like her but a crud like that, their Nelson.

Nelson was the witness of much violence between man and wife, and not just on Fridays and Saturdays as you might expect, the male having had a few, but every night of the week and during the day as well. He soon became inured to the sufferings of his mother at the hands and feet of his father; for, he said, kicking her, his wife, Mister was not thumping him, his son. Nelson, watching from under the table or through a slit in the door of the cupboard under the stairs, prayed they would deal each other a death blow; but they never did. Worst of all, he said, and the thing it upset him most to remember, was the moment when, say as she bit her husband's smothering hand, their passion suddenly veered towards the connubial and on the floor, among the wreckage, they began kissing with bloody mouths. Of his father's paw snuffling between his mother's nylons, of his mother's whiter hands urging on his father's bum, Nelson could not bring himself to speak. He hid his face. Soon, as an ingredient in their tenderness, they remembered the little one. Infallibly at the first bellowing of his christian name he wet himself. Wherever he was, he stayed, but not in the hope of evading discovery, merely because he was incapable of making any move. Best, he knew, was to be winkled out immediately, for the longer they searched the greater was the head of feeling that they must discharge; but a paralysis prevented him even from whimpering and often they found it necessary to bring in the Ripper.

Smiles. His mother's dress ripped, blood in a trickle at the corner of her mouth, her lashes stuck with tears. Smiles between husband and wife. Father and Mother standing over him, tall Father's hairy arm on Mother's shoulder. A hug. Diminutive Nelson smelling like a puppy. No wonder he never got on with Little Hitler and others of the gatemen who wear boots and belts and in the latter, nodding thoughtfully, grinning at an audience, stick their thumbs. No wonder he never lay abed until the knocker-up did the rounds to flush out sluggards with his German dog. He remembered above all else, behind his father's rising and falling arm, his mother's face, her shining eyes, her parted lips, the growling or moaning in her throat, and her standing close, entranced by the rising and falling unwearying right arm, and pressing her married hands upon her womb. He believed it was never out of mercy that she bade Mister desist, always only because she wanted his attentions upon herself.

The Grampus, for one, refused absolutely to give any credence to this. After a good hiding, he said, when Father had gone out again, Mother would be sure to bring him in a sugar butty or a bacon bone and tell him not to mind, it was the drink, he'd do the same himself one day, there, there. It stood to reason, it was in the nature of things, that what the man did wrong the woman put right again, and the Grampus, even while being kicked, would look forward with a little inner smile to falling asleep at last with sugar on his lips or sucking the fainter and fainter savour off a bacon rib.

But the Grampus was one of the lucky ones and tended to look on the bright side.

Was there no light at all in Nelson's early history? None, or almost none. He remembered with less revulsion those days on which he accompanied his father tatting. They owned a pony and a cart – a fleabitten, underfed pony and a flat and rickety cart – and would go out for three or four days at a time among the surrounding villages and even to the coast in search of rags, bones and old iron. The Jack Russell went with them, trotting along beside or behind or leaping, with a marvellous agility, on to the tailboard and there riding high. Nelson, for his part, sat, legs dangling, facing the way they had come and saw the villages receding and the long roads dwindling; his father, of course, sat up front, facing the nag's sore arse and flicking idly at it with the reins. Between father and son, thus back to back, lay verminous old clothing and rusty objects in a growing pile.

There was doubtless something in these excursions which reminded Mister of his earlier life as a bona fide traveller, and a certain softening of his mood, a nostalgia for the past or even an innocent enjoyment of his present liberty, was sometimes evident. Nelson remembered, with a mixture of terror and bewilderment, that sitting facing away in a doze he had suddenly heard his father singing an old gypsy song, one having to do with lost love, homelessness and wandering. Later – it was towards the evening of a long summer afternoon – Father had bidden him come and sit up front and had ridden for perhaps a mile, towards the sea, resting a gentle arm upon his shoulders. The fear of a sudden reversal or of retribution for this charity was so intense in Nelson that he sat as tight as a rusted nut and bolt and wet himself with relief when they halted for the night and made camp.

And it was at the seaside, though almost certainly on another occasion, that Nelson entered again, though not for long, into his father's grace and favour. He had been sent to get driftwood for the evening fire, and a little below high water, the tide being in retreat, he had spotted something unusual. He had seen it rolling in the water two hundred yards ahead of him and had taken it for a log which he would come to in due course and perhaps retrieve; but since he soon had more than he could carry of bone-dry and bone-white fuel he was about to turn back, and had he done so he would not have made his marvellous find. William had run ahead. It was sunset, the sea had withdrawn, and in a mild light the stranded object lay exposed. The canny little terrier was sniffing at it. Nelson could see that it was not a log, it was more than a log. He put down his firewood and ran the intervening distance over the shingle and the wet sand. The thing from the sea was a wooden statue. It lay face down, tasselled with barnacles and beginning to be honeycombed by shipworms. Nelson knelt and rolled the statue over. It was a man in his middle age, bearded, wearing a stove-pipe hat. His two hands were holding a bird – perhaps a dove or a cockerel – close to his chest with the greatest gentleness. He wore a smock, breeches, and his feet were bare. Let's stand him up, said Nelson. It took all his strength, but he managed it, making the feet firm in the sand. This man from the sea was a head and shoulders taller than Nelson and looked down at him sadly and kindly.

Nelson backed away. Then ran, retrieved his firewood, ran to his father in fear of a hiding for having delayed. But Mister was sitting on the hard ground, leaning against a wheel of the cart. His hands were in his lap and his face, lit up by the last of the sun, wore an expression of terrible sadness, almost absentmindedly as it seemed. The boy stood with his arms full of driftwood, frightened. Drop it down, lad, said Father, drop it down, wilt tha? Nelson dropped down his wood where he judged the fire might be made. Our dad, he said in a whisper, I say, our dad. Aye, what is it, son? The man spoke gently. Our dad, said Nelson, I've found summat, summat funny, on't beach. The big man looked amazed. Show us then, wilt tha? Show us what tha's found. And Nelson related, and swore it was true, that they went then, father and son, hand in hand through the samphire and the sea-holly to the banks of pebbles and through the strata of bone-hard seaweed stalks and whited cuttlefish to the beach, the sea yet more distant and the light from the now vanished sun cascading slowly out of the sky. Clear as a ninepin, there stood Nelson's find.

Mister and the statue were about the same size. Nelson and William looked from one to the other in wonderment. The man of wood was kinder than the man of flesh and blood. He looked the father sadly in the eye. Father looked back. He's the worse for wear, he said. There's worm things on him. Still, he'll mebbe fetch a bob or two. And that was that. The big man shouldered Nelson's wooden statue and carried him away, face down. The boy followed, walking between his father's deep prints and breathing in the sea-smell off the wooden limbs and clothes. With Nelson ran the dog, sniffing at every drop of falling water. Back at the camp they set the figure upright against the cart and he observed them as they lit the fire, grilled their bacon and brewed their murky char. Father christened him Old Nick, and frequently glanced his way. All evening and all through the night nothing unpleasant happened to Nelson. Mister drank quietly from a hip-flask and took himself off to sleep without an unkind word. Nelson and William slept curled together at Old Nick's feet.

Next morning, without being asked, Nelson began to clean him as best he could. Though the barnacles and, worse, the emergent shipworms were disgusting to his touch, he persevered and with a rag from the pile and the blade of an old knife he worked particularly hard at the features of the face, at the fingers and at the bare feet. He had never seen such charity in any face, nor such protective gentleness in any other hands, nor such patience in any feet. Father loaded Old Nick on to the cart and Nelson continued his work as they turned from the coast inland again. During a heavy shower he covered him with rags, though of course the wood was still sea-sodden inside and might take months to dry. Father was morose and nervous, and kept glaring back. Leave that thing be, he said. But it was more than Nelson could do to obey him and surreptitiously his hands resumed their work.

That evening, camped by the roadside miles from anywhere, Nelson's father beat him severely. There was no cause, and when he had done it he turned aside with a groan. Nelson lay in the rags all night with his arms around the sea-smelling statue and the dog

at his feet. Next morning Mister was late rising. Nelson cleaned
the bird that lay so safely in Old Nick's hands. He seemed to be a
poor man: his smock was ragged at the sleeve-ends, a cord held
his breeches up. The hat was an odd one, not quite a stove-pipe,
having a broader brim and a wider, less steeply sloping but still
unusually tall crown.

Towards noon, within sight of a tall and beautiful spire, they
met a poor scholar coming towards them down the dead straight
road. Coarsely Mister offered him the statue for half a crown.
Nelson sat still, his hand on the bird. Shift, said Father, let the
gentleman see. The scholar, whose name was Hugo and who
depended for his subsistence and for the books necessary to his
studies on a benefaction left, three centuries previously, by the
devout Widow Scattergood, took from his wallet a shining half
crown and said: This is all I've got until a week on Friday. But you
can have it if I can have that man. Mister rubbed his hands. You've
got yourself a bargain, sir, he said. Nelson made no protest, only
touched the hands, the lips and the bare feet of the statue, to
say good-bye. Father unloaded the heavy wood with a heave,
as though it were nothing, and pocketed the scholar's half crown.
Then drove off quickly.

Nelson took up his accustomed position, dangling his feet over
the tailboard, and William sat by him. The scholar was standing
with his purchase in the middle of the road. What had been light
work for Father exceeded the strength of the poor scholar, who
would buy a book if ever it was a toss-up between a book and a
hot dinner. He had clasped his arms around Old Nick's waist and
was endeavouring, but without success, to hoist him on to his
shoulder. The statue tilted after Nelson in a stiff bow and Hugo,
through want of funds an absolute teetotaller, staggered like a
drunk and did well not to fall with Old Nick on top of him. So
they were left in the flat landscape, the man of wood and the man
of letters, in the middle of the empty highway, occasional stately
churches and one extraordinary spire visible in the distances around
them. The sun shone, and many larks were rising and singing. As
they lessened in size Nelson saw Hugo gently recline the statue
into his arms and, walking backwards, begin slowly to drag it

towards nowhere in particular. He would have liked to run down
the long road with some rags in which to wrap Old Nick's bare
feet. His heels'll be rubbed raw else, he thought. The road was
straight and level, hedgeless, raised above fen fields rich in snipe
and quail, and it was some time before Nelson, proceeding backwards at a guilty lick, and Hugo, proceeding backwards at the
speed of a tortoise, had gone for ever out of each other's sight.

6

He was woken, after the buggering, or returned to consciousness
by William licking his salty cheeks. His first feeling, sooner even
than pain and shame, was of the strangeness of his surroundings.
For he and William were not confined in the kennel but lay on
the rag hearthrug in the back kitchen. He saw coals still faintly
glowing and realized, with more anxiety than relief, that for once
he was not cold. Then he began to tremble, he began to shake
from head to foot like a lad on a thresher. He shook like riddling
ice, he sweated and the dog nuzzled him and whined.

It was some time, so great was the power of his father's will,
even the power of what he imagined to be his father's will, it was
an hour at least and the coals were already fainter, before Nelson
thought of himself as having any choice. He lay where he was. He
supposed his father must want him there, to do something to him
again. But slowly and irresistibly his choice came up in him, it
broke and he got to his knees in time to vomit. Choice? More a
fact: that he could not bear the same again and must prevent it.
All his choice was how. At once he begged the thought to go
away, since even the thought must be against his father's will and
he believed absolutely that even absent, drunk and sleeping his
father had the power to sense the very faintest contradiction of
his will. But Nelson had had the thought, the thought was in the
house, he believed his father would come and sniff it out. That
terror drove him to choose how.

He had only a shirt and jacket on, and his shoes. His trousers
lay where they had been thrown. William went with him as he
crawled across to them. It was whilst he was pulling his trousers

on that outrage entered Nelson's motivation. But the terror which
had driven him first was still the stronger. Hence his haste. He was
contradicting, he was answering back, and it would bring him
inevitably into retribution, unless he pushed it quickly to the
unheard-of limit. There was only one escape: a death. He believed
that Mister would never die naturally, nor ever age; his hair would
always be black and bristly, his hands implacable. And wherever
Nelson ran Mister would easily find him and fetch him home.
So there had to be a death, to finish it.

Once he had thought of the guns, two double-barrelled shot-
guns leaning for Father to seize by the back kitchen door, Nelson
did not delay. Once had, the thought of the guns, so it seemed to
him, ran clattering up the stairs to wake his father, the Ripper
outside barked with the news of it and the whole house shuddered with horror. When Nelson stood up in his trousers too big
for him and in his collarless shirt and smirched black jacket that
had been perhaps, before it reached the rag pile, a lawyer's son's,
William whined. It was perhaps a thought of the dog, the wish
not to leave him, revulsion at the idea of killing him first, that
decided Nelson between suicide and murder. That and the pains
he had not had before. Clownish, woeful, all but deranged with
fear, there on the foul rug he quaked and swayed. Upright, he
heaved; doubled up, he threatened to roll down in a ball. He blundered then to the back door for the guns.

They were bigger than he had bargained for, and heavier; or he
was smaller, weaker, more trembling and fumbling. He dropped
one in the doorway reaching for the other and was lucky it didn't
go off. Then kicked over a stick with a lead end, all in all a good
deal of racket, and the Jack Russell snuffling and whining. But
the more the noise the greater his hurry. He'll crucify me, he'll
crucify me, he whimpered. He leaked and stank. Everything
bumped into him. The silly dark. Outside the Ripper barked once.
Nelson climbed the stairs, dragging the guns, bump, bump, encum-
bered with baggy trousers and the dog under his feet. Fifteen
stairs and a threadbare carpet. Somebody'll break his neck here
one of these days, Father used to say, neck like a bull's, head like
a gorilla's, hide like an elephant's, take more than a fall downstairs

to damage him. Such a noise. What had they drunk or what
stupor had they administered to one another that they did not
wake in alarm and stand in their night-clothes or, worse, naked,
at the head of the stairs, switching on the lights and shouting out
who's there? Nelson in the light, blinking, trailing his guns.
Though the way seemed barred by his reared-up father and
Nelson could hear the roar he would emit, by very terror Nelson
was driven on and reached the landing and their open door. He
could not pause, there was no plan to be made, but in the hurry
of a desperate fear – snivelling with fear, saying aloud like a Hail
Mary again and again our dad, he'll rip me up, our dad, our dad
– he blundered in, into their lair, a place they lay together in and
beat at one another with their flesh. If it was quiet he filled the
silence with his banging heart and strange little whimpered prayers,
and if it was dark no darkness on the earth or under the earth was
black enough, then or ever again, to cover the image of his
father's dreadful head. He saw him right enough and the woman
by him, her head next to his head on a whiteness in the darkness,
pillowed. He knew their bed. He had often been called to it and
had answered them through the end. He had been spoken to
down the double length of them through their yellow feet. He
had seen them naked from a strange perspective. He knew their
hair, their smell, their redder parts. And now they had rammed
their essence into him. Nelson took up the first gun, of two
barrels, and laid it with a clatter over the iron bed-end. Then its
weight was off him, though his shoulder was too low and he held
the great thing feebly, vaguely, his shivering knocking iron against
iron and all the brass knobs on the bed-rail in a fright.

He fired at once. The recoil wrenched the shotgun from his
hands, clattering it backwards over his shoulder. The room explod-
ed with noise, noise hurtled off the windows and the looking-
glass, seized and rattled the bed. And there was a human noise:
Nelson's frightened shout. He took up the second gun, for he
was certain that his father was nearly bullet-proof and although
bloody and full of shot could rise up nevertheless and nail him to
the beams. He fired before the perturbation from the first had
ceased, one trigger – save one for the Ripper, his guardian angel

whispered – but then immediately the other since he feared his father more than any dog. The crashes, following so close, jostled and buffeted one another in a panic, the din itself seemed desperate to find an exit from the room. Then only smell, and silence collecting itself, the gun with its brother empty on the floor, the Jack Russell stunned with terror against Nelson's feet. And slowly the brass bed quietened too, little by little it ceased rattling and shivering. Nelson did not wait to hear it begin to drip.

The Ripper was loose outside somewhere in the dark. From the front door or the back door it was fifty yards or so to the nearest gate. Nelson took the stick weighted with lead that his father used to finish off half-dead creatures and went from the back door to the front and to the back again clutching it. William followed in bewilderment. Nelson could see through the storm windows in either porch out into the wasteland of the family's property. There was not much moon; where the Ripper was amid the old iron, the empty crates and the broken carts, he could not see. To make matters worse, the brute had fallen silent.

There was a sort of lull in Nelson's terror. He made quite cool preparations to escape. He felt in the pockets of his father's evil-smelling topcoat which hung by the door where the guns had been, as heavy a presence almost as the man himself, and found some small change. He looked for his mother's handbag, which was usually on the sideboard, but could not find it. From the larder he took bread and cheese and a knuckle of ham, cramming his pockets with them. Then he could not postpone his attempt any longer. He feared the upstairs of the house, his fear was coming over him, wave upon wave.

Where was the Ripper? Nelson listened at both doors but could not hear the least sound of the dog he knew to be loose in the yard. He dared not go upstairs to spy from a bedroom window. He must leave, before it was light he must put miles between himself and the house. He wished the chance had never been given him. He wished he were in the kennel with William and the Ripper snuffling and pawing at the bolt but unable to get in. He went irresolutely to and fro, muttering to himself and gripping hard on the heavy stick. William trotted after him, always

enquiring upwards for an explanation. The dark house was horrible, he must leave; but outside, silent and invisible, the guard-dog
was listening and watching. Beyond the fence there were the flat
straight roads, leading to freedom in every direction. How he would
run, he and the little terrier, away, too far away ever to be caught
by man or dog. Before it was light he would be somewhere safe.

Nelson began to hear noises in the house, only the rats no
doubt or a breath of wind in the chimney. Was there any wind?
He looked out again, craning his neck for a sight of the sky. The
yellow and shapeless moon lay in the path of a travelling cloud.
Nelson swore a solemn oath to himself that that he would go
when the cloud had swallowed the moon. It was elongated,
shark-shaped. Up there at least there was a breeze and the cloud,
the moon's devourer, was moving rapidly. The moon looked
yellow, lolling to one side, peaked in its features, feeble in light.
Nelson felt sick, his chances were poor, best to lie down on the
hearthrug before the dead fire and hope to die. Then the terrier,
always under his feet, left him. Nelson continued staring at the
purposeful cloud: a few more yards, miles of sky perhaps, but
yards, seconds. Fifty yards from the door to the fence.

William had left him. Nelson heard him in the dark at the back
door. He was growling; but the undertone of that would-be
menacing sound was a whine of the purest terror. The growl was
deep in the throat but continually a whine and a whimper broke
through into the higher reaches. Then the cloud leapt upon the
stricken moon, there was a last moment of feeble radiance, so that
Nelson saw the long black body of the cloud, and saw it vanish in
undifferentiated darkness. William began to howl, howl like a child,
and Nelson acted: reached to unbolt the door but found it already
unbolted, opened it wide, screamed to William and ran, ran full
pelt down the cluttered filthy path to the high gate and got his
fingers, still grasping the weighted stick, into the mesh and heaved
and set his foot on a cross midway and was stepping higher.

The Ripper, a shadow, utterly silent, took off from an arc of
speed and seized his foot. Nelson screamed, tugged. Sockless, too
small for the boot, his foot, which was only beginning to be
rivetted, came free. He swung over the gate, he turned. How had

he imagined things would be? That he would be able to lift the
terrier over the gate he himself was obliged to climb? That there
might be a place in the fence through which a Jack Russell could
squeeze but not an alsatian? That there would be time?

William, starting a house-width behind, had made up the
difference and was following pretty close. He had his one poor
chance in the moment when the Ripper was fastening his teeth
into Nelson's foot. In that moment he leapt as high as he could at
the wire of the gate, but fell back. There was time for one more
leap as the Ripper shook the pierced boot from his jaws. Nelson,
aloft, leaned down; but without the impetus of a run William did
much less well. Still Nelson, with outstretched fingers, touched
his head. Then there was no more time. Nelson leaned down,
flailing with the heavy stick, and struck the alsatian across the
spine; but this was not enough. The Ripper merely dragged the
terrier to a safe distance. Nelson hurled the stick, but it fell use-
lessly. He could not see what was happening. He sat on the top of
the gate, swearing and weeping. He began to lower himself back
into the compound, thinking to take up the heavy stick and fight
the Ripper; but at that moment he heard, with a terrible distinct-
ness, the alsatian's jaws breaking William's neck. Nelson climbed
down on the safe side, finding a foothold on a padlock; then fell
the rest of the way, and vomited.

Dragging his bare foot, once he could stand without retching,
Nelson set off into the night. There was no sound from the alsatian.
When Nelson looked back he saw only the outline of the house
in darkness. Then the moon escaped the cloud and illumined
greyly the dead straight road. It was a road north, but he soon left
it, obscurely fearing some form or other of pursuit, and bore
away westwards on tracks that even in daylight he would not have
been familiar with. When for fatigue and pain he could not go
any further he pushed through a hedge and entered a wood,
going in deeper and deeper, and on dry pine needles, on a cush-
ioned bed, lay down.

More than ever now, more than at any time in his life, Nelson
wished himself dead. His foot throbbed and burned, the pain of
it ran in stiff callipers up his leg, and when he closed his eyes he

saw the Ripper, the shadow, launch through the air and he felt again the man-trap jaws snapping on his boot. He grieved over the death of William and blamed himself. Soon he slept, and in a cold dreaming delirium he heard time and time again the sounds of the death of the terrier he had slept with summer and winter night after night and woken with and hugged when they heard outside their prison and ark their enemy, the Ripper, the frustrated assassin.

So he came out of the wood after two days and two more nights, having eaten all his few provisions and with his foot turned septic. Sat in the square in Withern or some such place, before anyone else was up, sat on a bench, nursing his foot, head bowed, his lawyer's son's jacket and trousers ripped and muddy, leaves in his hair, his mouth unable to stop whimpering and muttering. He had found a new pain, it was in his fingers, the fingers of his right hand were blue and swollen. He had thought this might be in some way due to his having tugged so hard on the triggers of the guns, but it came to him sitting there at last what the reason was. His mother had trodden with her heels on them when he dropped from his father and was crouched.

It was a Sunday and the parson found him, crossing the square to his church. Asked no questions but heard from Nelson, unasked, that he had blood on his hands and wasn't sorry and didn't mind if they hanged him. Still the man asked no questions, but took him home and sent a message by his housekeeper to those few waiting for first communion that there wouldn't be one and to come back for the second. And bathed the boy himself, heaping the manky clothes for incineration, careless of lice, tender towards the sores, applied a painful iodine to the suppurating foot and bade him again and again be silent about the blood. Gave him porridge and tea.

7

That parson was the first to doubt whether Nelson really was on the run with the blood of his mother and father on his hands. He meant well, of course, but it is not certain that he was on the right lines. It was not guilt that Nelson wanted removing from his mind, but fear. He felt no guilt at what he had done, but feared that even that act, the most he could ever hope to do, might not be final enough. The parson had bathed him and knew the nature of his wounds. Feeding, clothing and soothing the boy as best he could, gently he began to try to get at the truth. But Nelson left him, before he called the police.

Nelson did feel guilt, but on account of William. He told Ben Gunn an atrocious story: that he had run for the gate carrying the terrier in his arms and that, seeing the Ripper coming round the house, he had thrown his burden down, as a lure or sop, and had climbed the gate whilst William was being killed. Dog had no chance anyway, he said. And whenever he said a Romany never leaves his dog his eyes were pitiable in their depth of grief and guilt. He told the Captain, when the Captain took him aside one day, saying he seemed a bit down in the dumps, that he should have run with the little dog in his arms and flung him over first and made the best of it himself, using his father's stick with the lead on the end. Jo said it was obvious to her that William had sacrificed himself so that his master could get away. His howling at the back door, she said, was done deliberately to keep the Ripper there while Nelson made a dash for it from the front.

He was best off telling his stories to Jo. Though she was not so interested in his earliest life – except for the trip to the seaside and the finding of Old Nick – she made him tell her again and again how he had taken the law into his own hands and blasted his wicked father and mother to kingdom come. She had a thousand questions. The Captain might ask why the door was unbolted already when Nelson reached to unbolt it before he made his run, or why the gate was padlocked on the outside and not on the in; but Jo asked was he sure there were no screams and did nothing seep through the ceiling or trickle down the stairs before he left? Nelson thought harder when he had been questioned by her, and often another detail did occur to him. Often he thought of something while they were separated, and told it her at once when they met. Then her eyes shone, and she attracted the attention of the regular inmates, who asked: What's so funny? What's got into you?

Nelson showed her the holes that the Ripper had made in his ankle. Of course, they were not holes by then but the marks of puncture, on either side, under the bone. Ben Gunn noticed them when Nelson first came in and had his shower and was sitting on the bench in the grey wash-house lifting up that foot, his left foot, and resting it on his other knee. When the Ripper did them there were also lacerations, though not deep, where the teeth tore the skin as the boot came off; but these had healed away, leaving the holes, or the marks of holes, very distinctly.

When Jo first saw them that was before she and Nelson tried to escape from the hospital. He took off his boot in the tea-room where they went some afternoons to look at the visitors. Touching the little depressions with her fingertips made her laugh. The next time was at her Aunty Honor's house in Chilton, upstairs, in the bedroom, on the bed. When they went through the story of the murder that afternoon they did it better than they had ever done it before or ever would again.

Aunty Honor's marriage bed was a high and wide one, draped to the floor with a silken spread that concealed a jerry and two pairs of slippers. Its end was of black iron bars and uprights florally decorated in gold and knobbed with resplendent orbs, two large and a dozen small, of brass. Nelson said his mother and father's was much the same, only dirty. He pointed out to Jo how short a distance the shot had to travel, from the bed-end to the pillows, such close range, much closer than at the funfair. You were over their feet, Jo said. He admitted that the darkness (only a faint whiteness where the pillows were) had made it easier to do. He had closed his eyes as well, since he was certain that even so he could not possibly miss. She asked did he never think of trying to spare his mother at least (the Grampus, through Ben Gunn, asked the same), but he answered there was nothing to choose between them really, and mentioned how and when her heels had bruised his fingers. Besides, there was no way of hitting one and not the other in the dark. He and Jo were standing side by side at the end of the bed with their hands in a row. When they crossed them for a game, his hers his hers, the bed made a music of tinkling brass, a shivering of knobs, the little ones were solid but loose on their screws, the large were hollow and resonated nicely when agitated. Tell us, she begged him, tell us again and again. Her knuckles were white. God's truth? God's only truth. Cross your heart? He crossed his heart. She took his finger, licked it, wiped it, said say after me: My finger's wet, my finger's dry, cut my throat if I tell a lie. He said it. Fix was with them, in the place of William, at Nelson's feet, in the cheerfullest frame of mind. He stood his ground even when an express train began to rattle the bedknobs and all the little ornaments and pots on Aunty Honor's dressing table and then the sash and then the whole house. Jo and Nelson laughed aloud but under the train they could only see that they were laughing and not hear it until the din outside was trailed away and the house, the room and the marriage bed went quiet.

Jo put words into his mouth – really so, into the warm cave, sometimes one or two, sometimes a stream of words. Then stood back and asked him how many he had got. It was a game, but she also said she was teaching him. She never showed much interest in teaching him to read, though Ben Gunn said she would surely have made a fine teacher. Instead, she wagged her tongue inside his mouth.

Of course, that was the reason, or one reason, why on the occasion in Aunty Honor's bedroom they went from committing murder (in a story, at least) to committing what Aunty Honor called fornication. Their heads were so close together at the bed-end and only now and again did they glance towards the pillow to get some idea of how the wicked parents must have looked, in the dark, before Nelson let them have it with all four barrels in revenge; their heads were close, their whispering, the rapid questions and answers going to and fro at closest possible range, their lips, their tongues, even their teeth were for ever touching, and so it is no wonder they were in the state they were in by the time they had finished, any boy and girl would have been, especially on a day out from a place where they were minded and often kept apart.

When Nelson had done as he was told and they were both undressed and had climbed into Aunty Honor's double bed, Jo was in such a hurry to get on to the last thing that she only –

so to speak – *visited* all the others first, and put them off properly till afterwards. She was in a murmur of excitement over Nelson's body, and wouldn't let him cover himself with the sheet. Since running away from home and getting a better diet (perhaps) he had grown quite long and she went the length of him with her busy little tongue, continually exclaiming and laughing to herself. His skin was clean and white. He lay on his back and shut his eyes in bashfulness. But Jo was very open-eyed, and her fingers got quicker and quicker. She tried to scratch him, and for the first time in her life regretted not having any nails. She dwelled with her lips on the dove-shaped birthmark below his heart, but constantly came back to the thing sticking out near the middle of him, that was so funny, helpless and big. She began nuzzling and murmuring over this as though it were another friend, whom she must induce to fall in love with her as she had easily Nelson. Then abruptly she lay back, bossed him into position on top of her and looking away, looking very thoughtfully in a real concentration, with her right hand began to fit him in. Nelson was fearful of hurting her and his gasp, when the little skin at her opening gave, was louder than hers and much more alarmed. He would have come out again at once, but now she was delighted, she was full of glee and triumph to have got him in there tight, and freeing both hands she used them to urge him, with a childish vehemence, to push all he could, and let him slip, and urged him to push again.

8

Then Ape came back. It was around Christmas and they were coming from burying one of their number, Stanley perhaps or French, the year was turning merciless, when they heard him shouting will some fucker kindly open this fucking gate. Little Hitler let him in and the Ripper sniffed him for illegal substances. The Captain, distressed by the death of French or Stanley, gave the Ape only a very cursory interview and told Ben Gunn to see him bathed.

You can backfire them, grandad, said Ape, stepping out of his bell-bottoms and his flannel drawers. I want my regulation issue

and no arguing. Where's the boy? Ben asked, forking the cast-offs
into the incinerator sack. Ape grinned, he had lost another tooth,
thought you'd be asking that. He paddled in the cloudy trough.
His rump, his pot, his fat retracted dick. There was not enough
steam to hide him. Ben watched him soap the left armpit then
the right. His hairy black chest. He thrust his big head forward, the
hair flattened over his baldness, his doleful moustaches dripping.
Then, perhaps only to give offence, he stepped clear and soaped
his privates into a grey froth. Where is he? Ben asked. Ape took
his time, and became aware of an injustice. Dunno, he said, don't
fucking know. And I'll tell you something else: I don't fucking
care either. Who cares about me? Nobody. It's always him. Nobody
asks where I am. We can see where you are, said Ben. But you don't
care how I got here, do you? Don't want to know. Wouldn't bother
you if I was dead. You're not. I'm not!? That's all you know about
it, Benny Gunn. You stand there saying I'm not dead and couldn't
give a monkey's whether I am or not. The soap, under the playful
shower, had melted off his unmentionables and they emerged,
like newborn rats, out of the foam. Ben asked: Well are you dead
or aren't you? Ape replied: No, I'm not, but it's no thanks to you
I'm not, and I fucking soon will be, and then we'll see who's right.

Ben handed him the towel. Thought you'd gone to Alice
Springs, he said. Well you thought wrong, said Ape. Me out there
with the coyotes would've suited you very nicely, I daresay.
Dingoes, said Ben. Me being eaten alive by dingdongs would've
suited you just right. Well too bad, Mister Whiskers, I'm back
and I want my hand-out. Here it is, said Ben, a vicar left 'em.
Where's Nelson? Look at this, said Ape, extending his right arm.
New cicatrices. Lefthanded, eh? said Ben admiringly. The other
side's full, said Ape. Then added: And that's only the slashes. The
rest's in here. He slapped his gut. Pills? Mainly. Lanry once or
twice. And hangings? Ben asked. Sudden rushes into the traffic?
Rivers, window-ledges, gas-ovens? I want some human sympathy,
said Ape, I don't want always laughing at.

He sat on the bench, a pair of briefs, decorated with the story
of the King of Hearts, raised as far as his knees. Nelson's in Stoke,
said Ape. Or was last time I saw him. Doing what? But Ape had

begun to speak with wonder and admiration of the readiness of
the authorities in those parts and of the voluntary bodies and even
of private individuals among the general public to pay him some
compassionate attention. Half a dozen hospitals had been more
than willing to have him in and pump him out. Nowhere, not
even at the Police Station, had he been told to run along and try
it somewhere else; no one, not even the Samaritans, finding him
on their doorstep bleeding or dilated, had cried oh Jesus Christ
not you again; but he was received everywhere with the expres-
sions of horror and pity a man doing away with himself in a welfare
state ought to be able to count on. Different class of person altogether down there, he said, at last covering his pudenda under the
King of Hearts. Not so brutalized by poverty perhaps, said Ben,
or more likely they hadn't got used to you. That vest's a funny
shape. It was a string vest, khaki-coloured. Bloody queer vicar,
the Ape remarked. If you'd stayed another week or so they'd have
tret you like they do round here, said Ben. Like a dog, said Ape.

Where's he lodging? Ben asked. In the Sally, Ape replied. Is it
rough? There's worse. Then the one they call Ben Gunn began to
mutter, more to himself than to Ape, though they were questions
he was muttering, but Ape in the vicar's underwear had sunk into
a mournful trance, his hands were on his knees, his intelligence
was absent. Ben Gunn was walking in a small circle, like a bad
actor learning a soliloquy. Who looks after him, he muttered,
makes his bed, cleans his shoes, sees to his meals, keeps him
amused in the long afternoons, turns his mind from unhappy and
violent thoughts in the long evenings, asks him his dreams? Is he
further on in his letters? Does anyone sit down with him daily, as
it must be, for discipline is what he needs, sit down with him
daily, two at a simple table side by side, indicating with a forefinger the mystery of the letters joining in words and of the words
consorting in sentences? Who does? Does anyone? Does anyone
hear him read, letter by letter laboriously uttered, word by
stubborn word and each being forgotten behind him as he goes,
like the wake of a very small boat on an ocean of ignorance? Can
he still spell JO? Can he write her name? Can he write LOVE?
Can he write I LOVE? Who listened all this time to the noises in

his head, the terrible rushing noises, who listens now? Does anyone? Who helped him with the pictures, the frightening pictures in his poorly mind, who sorted them out, who put them into words? And what has happened to him since, what has been done to him and what things has he done that it might help him to confess? Ben stopped. Where's the dog? he asked. Got kicked to death, said Ape. Well, here is the vicar's jacket, said Ben, and here are the trousers. Perhaps you will find some crumbs of love divine all loves excelling in the turn-ups or in an inside pocket or gone through into the lining. I'll have a look, said Ape.

9

They stood at the wire during the first piss-break. A little snow had fallen but the frozen wrinkles of the earth still showed and a few gangrenous stumps. I love him, Benny, said Ape. What can you do? He pushed his red nose through the wire and sniffed, as though starting again.

It had been Ape's plan to have the sun behind them when it rose and in their faces when it set. That way they would be sure of hitting the coast, where they would jump a ship for Alice. And he reckoned that on clear nights they might make some headway steering by the stars. Night came early, day came late. At noon they took a break. So long as the money lasted Ape was lavish with it. In saloon bars they sat either side the fire, their strange coats giving off a fug and the dog between them a lesser smelly vapour. They fed him crisps and little silverskins, wiped the froth from their moustaches (the Ape's a black draggle, Nelson's soft and fair). This is the life, eh kid? he would often say. Better than back there with the no-hopers. He viewed his own past life with pity. I'm shut of all that, he said, shaking his heavy head. For days on end he never threatened suicide. He was putting the past behind him, making a fresh start, and he urged Nelson to do likewise. No use crying over spilt milk, he said. She's dead, isn't she? And besides, I never met a tart that's worth the trouble.

But Nelson was not certain Jo was dead. He had no news either way. All he had was his feelings, which were up and down.

He thought no one could survive the kind of treatment she was getting; or if she did she'd be as good as dead and more like an alien than a human being. Ape agreed. They done it to me, he said. That's why I got out. That's why I'm heading west. Of course, he hoped Nelson would forget all about the girl and come round to him in time. But you never knew where you were with Nelson. One minute he'd be striding off, the dog and even more so the Ape having a hard time keeping up with him; the next he'd be sitting on someone's doorstep with his head in his hands and neither Ape nor the mongrel could move him. It's like I'm running out on her, he said. If he didn't stand by her, who would? Ape had an argument which, for a while, seemed to have some virtue in it. First you make a pile, he said. Then you go back and set her up in a decent place. Or he sends her a ticket and she joins him with the kiddy overseas. This country's finished, Ape said. Nelson had to admit that he liked the idea. Might get a car, he said, and call for her in it. Be a nice surprise. His tears ceased, his face was radiant. That's more like it, said Ape.

In the saloon bars, after some quantity of drink, Ape became affectionate and lascivious. He stretched himself and opened all the buttons of his astrakhan. Nelson drank up hurriedly when he saw these signs. He never lost his fear of the local men who sat in silence at the bar or in the far corner. They were always watching. Nelson drank with the Ape, but his gaiety was fragile. Though his mouth might smile and even laugh his eyes were on the look-out nevertheless. So when Ape began to giggle and smack his lips Nelson stood up and left with the mongrel Billy at the double-quick. These departures themselves, so abrupt and fearful, must have concentrated the attention of any men watching. Then Ape in drink was given to complaining aloud, and being suddenly abandoned when all the buttons of his long coat were still undone, his face flushed, the dome of his head, if his skull-cap were off, moist and perhaps fuming, he must have been a spectacle likely to bring out the worst in people.

Nelson was waiting for him where the street went into the country, at the sign which lifts the speed limit on motorists; and his greeting, when the puffing Ape came up, was always a harsh one. You'll get us fucking killed, he said. Or: Thank you very much.

It is certain that Nelson and the Ape attracted attention. Mothers shopping or fetching their children from school and men out of work must have watched them curiously and might remember in considerable detail what they looked like, if anyone went and asked. And soon, as the afternoon declined, it would occur to any householder to wonder where these two would be bedding down that night. Dusk is a bad time to be observed by farmers who own barns and outhouses. So Nelson's uneasiness was always greater in the afternoons, and he cursed the Ape for fretting his nerves mile after mile with propositions in an injured tone. Did Ape have none of Nelson's fears? It was as though he had no room for them in his large head and his large heart, being taken up by the immediate moment and how it was treating him. Or was he too dumb? Whenever he was easy in his present moment, in drink and when his affections were coming on him strongly, he would stand with his arm around the boy's shoulders, cluck at the dog and beam his own rays back at the setting sun, as though the night would surely be mild and they would be lying in clover. The night was cold, needless to say, and the ground hard; his moans then were always louder than Nelson's.

The money was running out. They were west of Crook, west even of Tow Law and making for the old Roman road where, Ape said, they would be sure to hitch a lift in a stone wagon. They had a bit of bread left and some tobacco. At mid-day they ate all they could of the little free appetizers along the bar, and took a glass of stout. More warmth in stout, said Ape, and it feeds the stomach. They took a few bottles for later with their last shillings and pence. When they came out into quite a painful sunlight Ape began to grumble. I've done my bit, he said, and nobody can say I haven't. Time somebody else started doing his. Nelson ignored him. Ape continued: Fine fucking Romany you are. I never heard of a Romany starving to death. If you was half a proper Romany you'd find us something to eat. And he went on to insult the mongrel Billy, calling him useless, a burden, a scrounger. Thought you said he'd mebbe get us a rabbit when we wanted. They go for rats, said Nelson. Besides, I haven't trained him yet. Well time you fucking did, said Ape. He's young, said Nelson. His brain's not ready yet for taking commands. Never will be if you ask me, said Ape. And I'll tell you why: because he's fucking stupid. Billy moved closer to Nelson, who stooped and patted him. He'll be alright, said Nelson, when his brain's ready.

They walked on. The sky was becoming green. Nelson often gripped the bone handle of his knife. It riled him when Ape made fun of his Romany origins, and he felt a rush of shame. If I could get a pigeon, he said to himself, or a salmon or something. They were passing through a farm, its buildings lay on both sides of the road which went down in a very open way to a silver river and a copse of trees before climbing again through large and empty fields to the skyline. The openness and the emptiness were beginning to frighten Nelson. Ape's spirits were sinking too. If you was any good, he said bitterly, you and that dog, you'd lift us a turkey or a baby pig. But I'll be dead of hunger for all you care. When they were through the farm and the road was beginning to descend, Nelson halted. Mind the dog, he said, and wish me luck. Ape fastened Billy to his leg and slumped against a drystone wall.

Ape fell asleep. The next he knew Nelson was tugging at his boot, to release Billy, and telling him to run for it. Dogs were barking. Nelson had his sheepskin bundled up in his arms. He ran, and Billy with him, trailing the string. Then Ape, the left boot in his hand. To God watching or to any farmer with glasses on any vantage point around the rim of that great bowl in the hills they were very obvious as they scuttled down the unfenced road to the middle landmark, the copse by the river. Only Billy was gleeful. Ape cursed and cried. Nelson, however, was in a sweat of fear. The wood was distant, they could not keep up the pace. Go slow, Ape gasped, that way we don't arouse suspicion. But Nelson hurried, though his breath was coming in sobs. Stars had appeared before they made it into hiding, and the sky was slipping out of green and pale blue and pink into the darkness. Nelson would not stop until he had reached what he reckoned to be the very heart of the little wood. Often they fell, their noise was dreadful.

Then Nelson lay on his back, struggling to breathe quietly.
When Ape lay down beside him and began to moan that he had
hurt his foot Nelson lashed out hard and hit Ape in the eye with
the back of his hand. Then the wood recovered its silence. There
were no sounds of pursuit, only of Ape in pain. It was pretty well
dark by now and darker still by the time Nelson, who had begun
to shiver, decided they could risk the rest of the business. What'd
you get? Ape asked. Chicken, Nelson replied. But I still gotta kill
it. He had cornered the bird on a patch of stinking mayweed and
smothered it with his heavy sheepskin. Let's have a look, said Ape,
flicking a bluish flame from his lighter. The bird was in there
alright, as still as a stone. You wring their necks, said Nelson, so
I believe. Or chop 'em, said the Ape. I'll do its neck, said Nelson.
The hen had a poor appearance around the neck. It had been
pecked by its fellows perhaps, or had moulted, or had rubbed itself
bare by pushing its hungry head through a wire. When Nelson's
hands came down for it, it squawked, and the noise seemed to
Nelson to alarm not only all the wood but all the vast bowl of
land they were at the centre of in hiding, and in terror he tugged
and twisted and sought by every conceivable action of his hands
to end the creature's life, but could not, and could only cause
its mouth to gape and its eyes to bulge and could not even stop its
unbearable noise. Don't seem to have the knack, he said, leaving
go. Give it here, said Ape. But his gross hands were less use still,
nowhere could he get the purchase for a wringing action and if
his tugging stretched the neck whatever kept the bird alive in
there, though doubtless impaired, continued well enough. You'll
pull it off, said Nelson. You'll have to chop it, said Ape. The hen
shook itself, cackled, and would have escaped if Billy had not
pounced. Good boy, said Nelson. Ape knelt, Nelson fitted the
body between Ape's knees, took hold of the small and angry
head, stretched the neck and sawed with the blunt blade of his
knife until he was through.

Ape was not prepared for the kick, the shuddering, the con-
vulsions between his legs, for how long they lasted, for their
gradual diminishing, for their late surprise revivals; nor Nelson
for the terrific jet of blood. The blue light went out. I got a match,

said Ape. Save it, said Nelson. We gotta cook him yet. Stand up and hold him by the legs. Nelson began to pull the feathers out. Still there were shudders in the carcase from time to time, and blood continued to empty copiously, then drop by drop. The softest feathers would not land, but hung in the air. That'll do, said Ape, a few still on won't hurt. The cadaver became more visible as its plumage went. And it never entirely cooled. Nelson was kneeling, Ape rose above him into the darkness. When Nelson was sick of plucking he turned away and put on his soiled coat. You clean him out, he said. Ape sat down with the bare flesh in his lap. Which end's best? he asked. The bum, said Nelson. Give us the matches.

It was easy to make a flame in the dry leaves and twigs. The light they gave illuminated Ape. He was wearing the chicken on his fist like a giant glove, or as though his arm, hidden in the astrakhan, came forth into deformity. His good hand, by the empty neck and with a vomiting noise, then tugged it off. That'll do, he said. A bit left in won't hurt. He threw the insides to Billy, who swallowed them. Nelson mended the fire. Stick a stick through him, he said. Ape did. Bigger than that, said Nelson.

Then they were settled either side the fire, holding their meal over the heat. The wings, largely unplucked, flared up; and when Ape allowed his end of the stick to burn it broke and everything fell. Nelson reviled him as they fitted another spit. But Ape, his right eye streaming from Nelson's blow, his left foot still without its boot and his hands all over blood and offal, only grinned and beamed. This is the life, he said several times. And he took from the deep pocket of his moulting coat one of their bottles of black stout. The bird singed and scorched, its drops of fat soared up again as flame, but through it all, increasingly, came the smell that made the water fill their mouths. Nelson swigged, his nerves began to be stilled, he grinned. The fire, now mostly of fircones, glowed as it was meant to and the heat was fierce. They turned the stick whenever Nelson said the word. Ape was generous in his sharing of the drink. The bird crisped, blackened, gave off a true scent. That'll do, said Ape, a bit underdone won't hurt. Out of his pocket he took a hunk of bread, handed it over with the bloodier of his hands. Nelson bit, swigged, had the stout and the bread in his mouth. I got him, he said, I did him. He fished the chicken his way over the fire which now they could feed, so that it flamed, lit them up, warmed them through, and in the safe heart of the wood they crouched close with the hearth between them and Nelson with his hands broke the bird roughly fairly and squatting back they feasted, quickly getting their teeth through the charcoal crust into a white and sweet flesh, and on, tossing the wreckage to Billy, who cracked and mashed it. With the bread and the stout they had enough. They belched, they wiped their glistening lips, the Ape had greased his beard as much as it would hold. His eye had closed. To wink he used the other. Give us the proper stuff, said Nelson, then we'll see. Ape dug for the hip-flask and Nelson drained it. Now his nerves were placid. The wood was safe. Ape winked again and opened his lower coat. Dirty bugger, Nelson said, but not harshly. He moved where he was wanted and Ape took in his hand. The hand being greasy the act did not take long. The shock through Ape seemed it might break him up. His cry frightened the wood. His face, when Nelson bent to look, was red, smiling, and drenched off either rosy cheek into his hair with tears.

So they slept, Nelson nearest the fire and the Ape enclosing him, his own back into the cold. Each woke, but separately or if together then without a word between them. When Nelson woke the drink had left him and he was exposed wholly to strangeness, not comprehending who he was or where or why. He reached for the fire and played with it as though it were a pet, and through the flames saw Billy among the bones. Ape's massive arm was around him, Ape's snores beat at the back of his head. The wood was full of owls. He remembered himself in the asylum, the owls in the trees near his window, Jo in her ward elsewhere who was also listening, he saw his own wrist emerged enough out of the sheepskin to show the cuts, he seemed in pieces, his life scattered here and there, his head only a camp through which the bad thoughts passed. He was on the verge of terror when sleep came out of the fire into his midriff and overwhelmed his head. When Ape woke it was different. He heard Nelson whimpering. With his right hand, when he had raised himself a little, he could feed the fire. There was no remedy for his own cold back, but what he wanted when he woke in the wood in the middle of that night was to keep the boy warm between himself and the fire and to soothe away, if possible, whatever was distressing him. He had only the fire and his own heavy body in its soiled clothes. From head to toe he laid himself yet more closely around Nelson and tried as best he could to make himself of use as a comfort. When the whimpering ceased, when Nelson began to breathe as though his sleep were a place of blessing and not of torment, Ape was glad.

Later the cold grew very sharp. They woke as the wood began to lighten. They were stiff, their bellies weighed like lead, Ape's eye would not come open, his foot hurt. When he stood up to piss he tottered and cried out in pain. Nelson was in a fret to be away. He saw the bones of the bird's wings, how bloody they were. Not even cooked, he said. The ash was soft, neatly circled with stubs. Ape farted non-stop, and moaned that he was finished. You done my eye in, he said, you done my foot. He couldn't walk. Nelson handed him the empty silver flask. If you think I'm carrying you, he said, you're wrong. Billy was alert, Nelson took up his string. Ape was collecting the empties. Billy leading, they trod and battered a way out of the wood. Outside they met with space, an immense room, the great slopes empty and their little road doing bravely to the horizon. Half the sky was a furious mottled red, the other was blue. We'll live off the land, said Ape, we'll lift a few taties, you'll get us another bird, we'll hitch a milk lorry. But his voice was weak. Nelson with a shout of rage and fear set off at a pace the Ape would never manage.

10

We were on the prom, said Ape, handing out leaflets for the Illuminations, when he saw a tart behind a candy floss who reminded him of his one and only. That night, hearing him sobbing on the bunk below, Ape leaned down and spoke to him out of an inverted head. He said: What's up, kid? Tell us what's up. Nelson replied that he was certain she had borne him a child, a son most likely, to whom, in due course, he would teach the Romany arts of tracking and trapping, and that, incarcerated at her gran's in Darlington, she was pining for him and lamenting his infidelity. Ladders had come to his mind, he said, ropes, and a motorbike and sidecar for the escape. Thereafter a place in the country some-where, a smallholding, a garden swing for the infant, Jo soon carrying their second. A bit young aren't you, kid? said Ape. You want to see the world first. Once we've cleared a few quid here we'll jump a ship for Alice. But Nelson was sick of that idea, and Ape for ever yapping at him he was sick of that too. Ape wept a little, upside down; sadly then withdrew his wellmeaning head.

An atrocious dawn. There was a scene: Nelson strapping up his bedroll and packing into a rucksack the couple of shirts, the biro and the unread infants' reader that made up his possessions; Ape squeezing his bum and morning glory into a pair of tight bell-bottoms and pleading with Nelson to think again; the other inmates crying out for Christ's sake shut your faces. Ape with a broken hold-all clattered after Nelson down the fire-escape. Tied to this was the dog, wagging his tail. Drizzle. Smell of garbage. They kicked old cans and sent a bottle rolling. Ape's remon-strations continued along the prom: I set you up, I seen you right, that's all the thanks I get. Tret like shit. Etc. Sodden chips, vomit, a man or two recumbent. Nelson's loping walk, his beautiful silly face determined; and Ape came after, whining and hugging his hold-all which, like his hello-sailor trousers, showed its contents through a grinning zip. Nelson swung away, he was tireless in his seven-league baseball boots, his eyes were on Darlington. I was all puffed out, said Ape, and he wouldn't wait for me, the miserable little dick.

On the dogshitten verge, on the posh outskirts of Blackpool, when a wagon drew up it was only Nelson and the mongrel who got taken, for Nelson, jerking with his thumb, said: This funny fat fucker here is heading south. Ape wept and followed in a lorry from the abattoir. It was carrying hides, bones, inedibles, and in that stink, advancing after Nelson at never more than fifteen miles an hour, for most of the day he afflicted the driver, a man too kind or too dim-witted to devise a means of dumping him, with the interminable account of his unhappy love. By four o'clock, the day already ending, he had got no further than Lancaster and there, hard by the jail, lay the driver's destination, the premises of a maker of bone meal and dubious animal foodstuffs. Ape ran off without so much as a thank-you and stood with a pork-pie under a lamp-post on what he took to be the road eastwards and northerly, the rain setting in for the night and traffic very sparse. Pat said how anyone could eat a pork pie after riding all day in a wagon full of offal beat him. Slim said the thought of the jelly in a pork pie made him heave. Norman sucked on his peppermint. Walter said some people, Fatty included, would eat anything. Cack was different, he had a worm. The Grampus said one thing he couldn't eat was black puddings owing to a mix-up when he was a kiddy. Ape waited under the lamp-post, hours, in vain, thumbed, v-signed, stamped and foul-mouthed at the universe, all in vain. It was gone midnight before the Law came by and took him, sobbing, out of the gutter for his own safety and did him the kindness of locking him up and kneeing him in the ginger nuts, in Preston.

Ape wept. The sum total of wrong done him was, whenever he reflected upon it, overwhelming. He wept, wished he was dead, called for a blade, five hundred paracetamol, a gallon of paraquat, a noose, a London express, but Slim handed him the digestives and he was able to continue. Next morning given a hearty breakfast of a cup of tea and a kick up the bum he made all possible speed from the cells to a likely road and there, being the early worm, was snapped up by a hood from the Smoke driving a Chevrolet who told him tales to make your toe-nails curl. His suit, the Ape recalled, cost fifteen hundred pounds, his cigars were a foot long and his natty tie was held in place with a pin with a head (of emerald) the size of one of the Grampus' boils. Jesus, that man's lies, said Pat. But Ape hit Darlington in time for elevenses and smirking his thanks to the man sent up from London to write finis on a man in Gateshead (first visiting his mam in Manchester), he began enquiring of all and sundry where Hummersnot Gardens were. Walter said he'd lived thirty years in Darlington and there was no such place.

It rained. Ape sucked his wet moustache, squelched hither and
thither on stolen shoes a size too small, and finding himself at last
on the street where she lived he was impressed by the bay windows,
privet hedges and fancy brickwork of its comfy semis, and
marvelled that his Nelson, an illiterate Romany, should have
made it to have dealings with a female of so high a social class.
Ben Gunn reminded him that appearances are deceptive. And
besides, the daft are classless.

Number 13, unlucky for some, stood with its partner near a
nice lamp-post against which, at that very moment, a dog not
unlike Billy or Fix was pissing. Ape himself felt the need to answer
nature, but thought he must not, being human. Instead, he
looked head and shoulders over the black privets through a
laburnum rattling with poisonous pods, and wondered how best
to pursue his enquiries. He decided it would be foolish to march
in boldly and ring the chimes and ask has anyone seen our Nelson;
but best present himself at the door as a scrap-metal dealer and
seek then to turn the conversation, if one ensued, in the general
direction of waifs and lunatics. So he rang with his hairy forefinger, ding dong, dingdongdingdong, and stood through a long
pause, dripping. Then the door was opened by a blonde in
curlers. Come for the club, have you? she asked. No, said Ape,
hugging his bag. The slattern stooped for the milk. He saw her
tits, still warm and sleepy in her dressing gown, though it was past
midday. Keeps happening that, said Pat. I knew a man in Watford
spent his life knocking on doors and hoping it would happen. But
Ape was not interested in tits. He said in a forthright way – but
his voice after a silence and especially in wet weather was apt to
break – No, missus, have you any scrap? Alf, she yelled, chinking
the cold milk, man here after scrap. Give 'im that fucking waste-
pipe, Alf yelled back, in bed. Go round, said the slut, he says you
can have the waste-pipe. It nearly did for him yesterday. Fell on
his head. Ape waited till the side gate clicked. It's there, she said.
It was lying on the lawn, cast iron, seventeen feet of it. You'll
manage alright? Oh aye, said Ape, I've a mate further on. Seen
him have you by any chance? Young lad, wears a sheepskin. No,
she said, her eyes were cloudy with the need for tea. I'll let you

out. How's Jo? Ape asked. The kettle whistled, Alf's teasmade
yawned. Manage alright, will you? No problem, said the Ape.
But the weight of the waste-pipe when he shouldered it crushed
him to his knees and forced his tongue out. My hold-all's bust, he
gasped. That's the trouble. Mind Alf's bird-table, she said. He'll
kill you if you touch his bird-table. Jo like birds, does she? Ape
asked. I spect you've got a barrow, the blonde in curlers said.
After you. The gate, the click again. Hook your bag over the end
of it, she said. One handle looks alright. Ta-ta.

Ape down the road, but slowly, tilting his hollow caber hung
with a one-armed hold-all. Long road, the Hummersnot. There
at the corner of Acacia Avenue Nelson was sitting on a wall and
plucking dumbly at a laurel hedge, his rucksack and Billy the
mongrel at his feet. You again, he said. They won't tell me where
she is. She live here? Ape asked. Nelson began to run up and
down, tearing at the hedge and kicking at the garden gate. Billy
ran too, barking. Ape leaned his pipe against the gate-post and
said I'm sorry I'll have to have a piss. A correct voice from an
upstairs window said she'd give them one more minute then she'd
phone the police. Ape facing her way turned around in fright.
Nelson was shouting that he wanted Jo, he wanted his kiddy, he
had every right. He shook the gate, which fell to bits. Then next
door's window opened: She's gone to Stoke. Then the posher
voice at 113 again: You mind your own business. Then 111: They
sent her to her Aunty Betty's. Then 113 and 111 together: You
cow, this used to be a respectable area, you bloody busybody, we
never had no nutters here till you moved in, you bitch, and
another thing, your dog do its business on our lawn again you'll
get it through the letter box, so help me God. That the house?
Ape asked. I got it wrong. She's working in Boots, said 111. Run,
said Nelson. He and Billy were clear away, but Ape, taking up his
pipe, had only gone ten yards when the Law arrived on bicycles.

Ape was made to walk, carrying the scrap they swore he must
have stolen, between two officers comfortably mounted, the
couple of miles to the police station, where he was unable, for
want of breath, to protest his innocence. The pipe was labelled
and Ape was laid in a cell.

Funny how it takes people, said Pat. Love, he meant. Man I knew in Stockport when he was getting nowhere with the tart he went and stuck his how's your father through her letter-box and rang the bell. He was mad for the woman, daft. He measured it all up first, for days he was passing the gate and squinting in. He had to bring a chair with him to stand on. And did it advance his suit? Well, no, said Pat. She couldn't make head nor tail of it. When he shouted out: Alice, it's me, she hit it with a *Woman's Own*, and he fell off the chair. But tarts are just as bad, said Pat. When it takes them, he meant. Did I ever tell you why I can't eat tripe? All on account of a married tart in Rochdale. I'd rather hear why you can't eat tripe, said Stetson, than why this dickhead here – he meant the Grampus – can't eat a black pudding.

But the Captain had come in and joined them at the long table. Carry on, he said, for heaven's sake don't mind me. They paused nonetheless. His office set him apart; that and his sadness. Just hearing how young Nelson got to Stoke, said the one they call Ben Gunn. My mother came from Stoke, the Captain said. Warm-hearted people there, I always thought. Don't let it spoil your story, he went on, but I'm asked to ask you do you know this chap. He laid a picture out. I'll drink a cup of coffee with you while it circulates, and any man recognizing him, please raise your hand.

The man was naked on a mortuary slab, balding, in his forties, a bruiser's face much bruised, with glaring eyes. Reminds me of Percy, said Bassett, bit better looking perhaps. Percy's in Broadmoor, said the Captain, I had a Christmas card. No. it's certainly not Percy. What was the name of that Scots laddie? Slim asked. He used to come in here pushing a pram. Never spoke. I never heard him speak. He spoke to me once, the Grampus said. Oh, said Stetson, and what did he say to you – Good morning, sweetheart? He asked me was I saved. We were in the shed, counting out sheets of toilet paper, when he suddenly come up close and squeezed my elbow. Tell me, matey, he says… He called you matey? Stetson interrupted. Aye, matey. Sure it wasn't tatey? No, no, matey, I'm sure of that. Tell me, matey, he says, are you saved? And what did you answer, Grampus? the Captain asked. Well, Captain, the Grampus said, I didn't know what to say. It was getting dark and he was hurting my elbow gripping it. Besides, I've never liked that sort of talk. It makes me feel funny. But what did you tell him? Stetson asked. We want to know. We've a right to know where you're going so's we can make our own arrangements. I'm damned if I'm spending eternity with you, it's been long enough in this place. His name was Jock, said the one they call Ben Gunn, and he was sixty if he was a day when I last saw him, and that was ten years back.

Nelson meanwhile, shouting his unhappiness at innocent passers-by and dashing the tears from his eyes, ran out of town. He was heading for Stoke but, being unable to read the signs, he blundered for two or three hours in wrong directions, thumbing lifts with kind but puzzled people. One elderly gentleman gave him some chocolate. It was dark before he reached Catterick. He drank a cup of tea there, braving it among the soldiers, and tried to calm his heart; but he was muttering, his lips would not keep still, he attracted curious looks. When the girl came over to take his empty cup he started at her shadow. Left then, slinging on his rucksack and whistling for the dog, with a bravado it would distress anyone to imagine. Still the rain.

Ape lay in jail, accused of stealing a soil pipe, and Nelson made it overnight into the Potteries through the courtesy of two long-distance lorry drivers and a Professor of Moral Philosophy who was also a bassoonist and, as he soon confessed, a bigamist, who, on the pretence of attending an academic conference, had left the first of his wives and was travelling to rejoin the second. He could offer Nelson a lift back north again in three days time. But Nelson, arrived in Stoke, had no wish to leave that place, not without Jo at least. He asked an Inspector in the bus-station (in whose lavatories the Professor was changing his clothes, for he made it a rule never to appear before the second of his wives as he appeared before the first) whether he happened to know Jo's Aunty Betty, but the Inspector could not help Nelson. Can't help you, son, he said. Nelson, penniless, accepted breakfast of the emerged Professor and asked him also whether he knew Jo's aunty. The Professor shook his head, he was a poor one to ask, he said, he never went out but kept indoors, doing the little jobs that husbands ought to

do. Good luck in your search, young fellow, he said. Love is a
terrible thing. And gave him half a crown.

They found poor Slaggy in a ditch, said Leg, a level sadness
in his voice, his arms extended, resting on the soiled table, the
photograph between them. No trouble identifying Slag. Head
like Frankenstein. I hope I make it to the Spike, that's all. Leg had
a horror of dying out of doors, he was frightened of the sky.
Don't want to be in the open when it happens, he often said.
They tried to tell him he might make it to a bed, with sheets, to
a light and airy room, flowers by the bedside and the laundered
freshness of a nurse's bosom leaning over him, but he doubted it.
One in a million, he used to say. Can't think why any of you
leave, the Captain said. Isn't it cosy enough in here? Take Desperate Dan, he'd no need to go rushing off like that, and I told
him so. He could have been with us now, listening to the stories
and looking forward to his dinner. Pat set his crooked thumbs up
vertically at the bottom corners of the unlucky photograph.
There was Dicky Fadge, he said, creeped into one of they kilns
behind the railway line, for a warm night. Next thing he knows,
he's baked. And remember Ginger? He drowned, his slimy tonsured
head appeared among the empties in the old canal. Shouldn't like
to be out, said Leg, shouldn't like to be on my own. Alright if you
don't wake up, said Bassett. Aye, said Leg, but how many sleep
through? I was with Teddy when he went, said Slim. He never
woke, I never knew he'd gone. You mean you never woke, said
Ben. You'd had a few and you never woke and Teddy woke and
opened his eyes and died. Heard Slim here snoring, said Walter,
thought he was going, didn't want to be left. That's it, said Leg,
nobody wants to be left. That pipe, said Cack, be worth a bob or
two. Seventeen feet, you said? The Law kept it, said Ape. They
couldn't pin nothing on me but they kept my pipe.

Bluebeard had approached and with him his faithful alsatian
Hammer. They were looking for the Captain. Beg pardon, sir,
said Bluebeard, touching his cap, two men out there want in.
Familiar? the Captain asked. Very, was the reply. And have they
drink on them? A little, sir. Shall I send them walk-about? How
are they dressed? the Captain enquired. Two shoes between them,

sir, one sports jacket. Hats? One editor's green eye-shade. In this weather, the Captain said. Drink or no drink, let them in. Savage, I'll bet said Slim. Yes, said the one they call Ben Gunn, and the Cobbler with him.

The Cobbler had frostbite, since for the last three miles it was Savage's turn for the shoes. Both men, when Ben Gunn had hosed them down, tingled throughout with chilblains. Smudger's a gonner, Savage said, scouring his blotchy body with a grey towel. They left him torkelling in the fast lane on Chester Moor. His head was away, he was showing the world, in poor visibility however, his magnificently tattooed chest. Snow on his grey hair. You left him there? Ben asked. No option, bonny lad, he was away. Never leave your mate, said the Cobbler, raising a red and blue finger, except in an emergency. The Baron's gone, he swapped his bowler for a panama and a bottle of brown and the wind blew hard and took his panama, on the road north it was, and his baldness was grievously pelted with dobbers of hail. But the jake warmed him, he died before he was cold. Who made it south? Did any to Walkden where the rain is warmer? Any as far as Camberwell where the sun never sets? No word of any. But a man from Walkden was seen on broken knees in Spennymoor clutching a letter of introduction to the landlady of the Knicky Knack Guest House and complaining that conditions down there surpassed belief. And in Camberwell, he had heard a fugitive on his last legs croak, such a reign of terror had been instituted by a new incumbent fresh from training college, that even the rats were packing their bags and leaving. There you are, said the Captain, perking up a little, why leave? Why ever do you chaps want to leave? Look at the frightful weather. Give me that photograph, it's too depressing. And Matron said the Cobbler will lose three toes. That all? said Stetson.

11

It was an evening in February, still brightening from the west, and the destitute inmates of Stalag 90, prefabricated city of the plain, having attended their Captain in the ceremony of the flag, were at a loose end till bedtime. Tell us a story, grandad, said the Ape, and the old gent thus addressed, the one they call Ben Gunn, the bearded one in rags and a multicoloured blanket, began.

It was a morning in November, dull, damp, and the forecast unpromising. The inmates of Camp Walkden, having breakfasted richly on porridge and fry, were sitting around in the sitting-room at a loose end till bedtime, when one of their number, Pinker by name, began to choke. Mr Pinker was afflicted with a respiratory complaint and drew breath, thanks to medical science, then in its infancy, not through his windpipe but through a plastic tube. Alas, his tube had become blocked with sputum, mucous, phlegm, snot, catarrh and breakfast. The physicians attending Mr Pinker, foreseeing the possibility of such an accident, had provided him with a small hand-pump, in the manipulation of which for the clearance of his vital conduit he had over the years grown very adept. But his pump on this occasion let him down. Aargh, he said, aaargh… which his companions, aided by his gestures, understood to mean that one among them should seize on the engine's bit of hose and suck him out. Not I, said the Rat, not I, said the Cat, not fucking likely, said one and all. They sat around, Pinker was on the carpet on his knees. Aargh, he said. Now they were not made of stone, these men; nobody, for example, had the heart to leave the room. It would have distressed Mr Pinker greatly had they all, as they were free to do, upped and left him on the sitting-room carpet croaking on his own. Instead, they sat and watched him wiggle his bit of pipe at them. They saw the colour he was turning and his bulging eyes. And nobody thought it was any fun, with worries enough of their own, to sit on the sofa or in the greasy armchairs watching Pinker choke. They looked at him, they looked away, they agreed, by looks, with one another that it wasn't up to them. Who was it up to? Somebody went to fetch the Commandant, who, entering, saw at a glance what it would be necessary to do, but would not do it. One of youse, he said, you've swallowed worse than that. Aaargh, said Pinker.

Did nobody? said the Captain, would no one there…? Yes, said the one they call Ben Gunn. Well, said the Captain, thank goodness for that. A man by the name of Dobbs, whose preferred drink was ale with dettol in it, said he would suck Mr Pinker out, and do it cheap at that. All he wanted was a pint from every man in the room and a bottle of dettol from the Commandant. The Commandant, a gentleman, agreed forthwith; but the others felt themselves blackmailed by Dobbs' demand and put up an angry resistance. If he was going to do it he should do it for nothing, only because he didn't want to see a fellow creature die. Ten pints, said Dobbs, I don't care where they come from but I want ten pints. Aargh…said Pinker faintly, and raised five fingers. But Dobbs was not so foolish as to enter into any bargain with a man made liable by circumstances to promise anything without due thought. I wouldn't take them off you, laddie, he said, I'd feel a swine. And facing the company he repeated his offer. It was not coming down, he said, and if they wanted time to think about it that was alright by him. And Dobbs resumed his seat.

Thereupon the Commandant offered two pints, in addition to the dettol (which he intended stealing from the first aid cupboard) and little by little general negotiations got under way. A spokesman rose then and promised Dobbs on the camp bible, speedily fetched, that if he sucked out Mr Pinker's tube he should have his full reward. Fine, said Dobbs, and knelt. But Mr Pinker had in the meantime died.

Well, that's a horrible story, the Grampus said. Smudger can vouch for it, said the one they call Ben Gunn, or could have if his friends hadn't left him staggering in the fast lane. I'm sick, the Cobbler said, don't look at me. And Savage is Savage. Well, said the Captain, at least it couldn't have happened here. That's not how we treat one another, whatever the custom might be elsewhere. There'd've been a mad stampede, said Stetson, to suck poor Pinker out. When Stanley died, said the Captain, I had a telephone call from his next of kin. Never knew he had any, said Pat. A wife, the Captain said, it's on his card. I had a phone call from his wife, I never told you chaps at the time, it upset me rather. She asked was it true he was dead and when I said it was she asked had he any money on him and when I said he hadn't she hung up.

They left that blind man on the Sally steps, said Pat, his own son and daughter. They left that baby on the counter at the NAB, said Slim, its own mam and dad. Cack found one on the tip once, didn't you, Cack? Him and Dougie, they put it in the barrow, it was dead. The family doesn't hold together the way it used to, Stetson said, and people do the dirty on their mates. But what can you expect? Nobody sets 'em an example anymore.

Just a minute, said Walter, tapping his nose, if that there Dobbs had done his best and the chappie in question had snuffed it nevertheless, would they still have paid him? They stuck out for half rate, said Ben, but Dobbs argued, quite rightly, don't you think? that if he did it he did it and that was that. They weren't paying him for saving Pinker's life but for sucking out Pinker's tube. It was neither here nor there what effect that had on Pinker. In the end they saw his point, but it took some time. So Dobbs got nothing then? No, nothing, though he argued he ought to have got three pints at least and a dash of dettol for being willing to. Of course, if they'd agreed to ignore the fact that Pinker was dead and to treat the whole thing as a sort of dare, then he'd have gone ahead and done it. But the pressure was off and Dobbs had no leverage.

12

So Nelson was sitting in the market place in Stoke on the look-out for his sweetheart when Ape arrived and said: We need more information, kid. And how? Simple, he smirked, you look her Aunty Betty up in the phone book. Well do it, said Nelson. But for want of a surname or two they got nowhere at all and Ape sat down next to Nelson with his thinker's head in his hands. The hours passed. Nelson sent Ape to buy a pie. Ta, he said. You watch this way, I'll watch that. But Ape had never met the girl and Nelson's description of her – she's thin – was less than adequate. Besides, how long ago was that? If she's had a kiddy she'll have filled out a bit. But Nelson insisted she was thin, thinner at the hips than most boys are, her breasts easily concealed under her two hands. The Ape guffawed, how long ago was that? And wearing jeans, with his name and hers and an arrow and a heart in biro on the knee. And flat shoes good for running in. So now we know what we're looking for, said Ape. But his heart wasn't in it.

When Ape arrived Nelson had already visited Boots, asking the way there, again and again, from passers-by until he stood outside it and still didn't know, and had to ask again, of a lady who looked at him strangely. No sooner in, he was evicted, because of Billy on his bit of string. A man in uniform went to the trouble of showing them both the notice. Can't you read? Or perhaps you're blind, he said, and this funny animal's a guide-dog? Nelson had never been in a Boots before, nor in any shop like it. He stood at the glass doors looking in. Whenever they opened a warm scent came out. He pressed his face against the glass, seeing if he could see her, but he couldn't. Ran off with Billy and tied him to a railing.

Inside he became aware of his rough appearance. Without the dog the smell must be all his own. The man in uniform followed him around. Nelson was grinning, scratching his downy cheek, the girls were all as clean as the sister of mercy who had helped him with his letters. He dared not look much at their faces, he looked at their hands, their hands were perfect, he was looking for bitten fingers and could see none. The girls were scented, all the air was scented. Nelson went from counter to counter, and to the tills, but nowhere did he see any hands like Jo's and when he looked from under his hair at a face, though beautiful it was stern. Yet he must ask. The man in uniform was always at his side, but really Nelson must do the rounds again, asking did they know her, was it her day off? He said some words, but the girl could not have heard them. He said some more, and the girl said: Sorry? And when at the third he seemed to be understood she shook her head. Next to him now, on his right, and the man in uniform was still there on his left, stood a tall and important woman with red nails. She had a cut-throat voice. Just asking, he mumbled. Everything itched. The floor was cleaner than his face. His boots had ripped. Going to the exit, accompanied, passing the thousands of products and instruments with which the girls cleansed and tended and beautified themselves, he felt all their delicately painted faces were on him like a dazzling light. He scratched at a place at the back of his skull. And don't come in here again, said the man in uniform.

Nelson stood at the back way in with Billy when the girls left work. He had taken a drink, and besides in their going home clothes they were not so frightening. He asked did they know Jo. Most thought he wanted money and hurried past. But of course they must have remembered him. You on the run? one asked. Another did listen and he told his story in a rush. Though she couldn't remember anybody who might be the person he was looking for she said she would ask the others if they could; but next day when he stood there again she only shook her head. So he gave up that idea and went and sat in the market place day after day.

He'd do far better to sit on Cyril Street, said the Captain, on the corner of Cyril Street and Regent Road. There's a bench outside the Ebenezer Chapel, or there used to be. That's going back a bit, of course. How long? Forty years maybe. Mother's been dead that long. Anyway, everyone passes that corner sooner or later. The boy would be bound to see her, her and her baby if she's got one. There's too much coming and going in the market place, you'd easily miss seeing her, I should think. No way for a lad his age to spend his time, said Bassett. I've had enough, said Ape. He can sit there till he croaks for all I care. Too many like him on the streets today, said Walter. Too many kids. Something wants doing about the number of kids. The world would be a better place, said Walter, if there was no one in it under forty-five. The Grampus said he didn't think it was such a bad life, sitting in a square all day, under a statue say or on a public bench, watching the people. He'd had a few years doing it himself. When the weather was decent he could think of worse ways of passing the time. Can of beer perhaps and the day went quickly enough. Sat on his bum and grinned and shook his wondering head and heard the clock strike all the quarters and thought maybe I'll have a jimmy riddle and went below and got it out and looked at it and gave it a shake and said that's better, that's much better, and glancing up he saw the soles of fellow citizens on the opaque glass above his nut and thought that's funny and climbed out again and heard it strike and before you knew it it was time for tea. Stetson was furious. Then bo-bos, he snarled, and another step nearer your grave, not that you'll notice in your case, not that it'll make a

ha'porth of difference, but there's men in here, one anyway, wants
more out of life than wondering whether you feel like another
piss or not. If he could read, said the Captain, that would be
something. I know he'll not want to read while he's on the look-
out for that girl of his, but in the long evenings if he could read a
book it would nourish his mind at least. We were coming on
nicely, him and me, said the one they call Ben Gunn, but Ape let
him fall back. Waste of time, said Ape. Fact is, he hasn't got it up
here. And he tapped his heavy conk. In my view, said Walter, that
kid is in the state he's in ninety-nine percent because of this fat
gent (the Ape) and what he needs is locking up until his head's
gone quiet and he can read the newspapers. No one, in Walter's
view, should be on the loose who can't read the Echo and the
Chron. Ape, speechless, tearful, pointed with a finger at his
wounded heart. No use blaming Ape, said Pat, he did his bit, I'm
sure, but what's gone wrong with the boy went wrong long since.
Never had a chance, said Savage, just like me. Father drank, just
like mine, mother on the game, father buggered him in infancy,
or was that the Grampus's? Hey, Grampus, was it your dad or was
it young Nelson's who brutalized his offspring in an unnatural
way? Ee, lads, said the Grampus, don't ask me, spect it was mine
alright, he was a devil in drink, I wouldn't put anything past him,
but a nice enough feller when he was sober all the same. Our
Nora's having another, Cack remarked, she never knew, that'll be
three she's had and never noticed till it come, her being so fat.
Shouldn't be allowed to breed, said Stetson. He'd said it before, he
said, those fit to breed should have a certificate saying so and
the rest should have an operation. That way three quarters of the
inmates of this fucking place would never have seen the light of
day. Cack asked the Grampus would he rather have not been
born. Ee, lads, said the Grampus, that's a tricky one. He said there
were things he'd be sorry to have missed: jamroly pudding, for
example, and seeing the Princess Royal when she opened the
new jail. And he might have thought of more but Stetson intervened: Who cares what little pleasures the likes of him can tot up
at the end of their miserable lives? The point of view's all wrong.
You don't ask this old nutter whether he'd rather not have been

born or not. In the first place anyone can see he hasn't got the
wit to answer. But even if he had it isn't him you ask. You ask
Society, them with a certificate, and if you ask me whether he
should or shouldn't of been born then without allowing myself
to be swayed by prejudice – though I hate his horrible guts – I'd
be honour bound to say of course he shouldn't. And I'll tell you
for why. Because it's not a question of what pleasure he's had but
of what pleasure he's ever given anyone else. And don't try telling
me the people the Grampus here has given any pleasure to would
fill the Albert Hall. You'd get 'em all in the privy where there's
only room for one. And that one's Number One, himself.

His mam perhaps? His dad who loved to knock him down the
stairs? Pleasure's a difficult matter, Stetson, Ben Gunn replied. It
gives some people pleasure to look at the Grampus and say poor
old feller how do they get like that? But anyway, Nelson was
sitting in the market place in hopes he'd spot a girl pushing a
push-chair who might be Jo and his small son or daughter. Well
there you are, said Walter, fancy letting a hilliterate breed. I see
they pulled that vicar in, said Pat. What vicar's that? Slim asked.
The cowboy man, said the one they call Ben Gunn. They've
lifted him. No harm in dressing up, I shouldn't have thought,
said Bassett. Me neither, said Slim. I shouldn't have thought. Fine
looking man, by all accounts, said Pat, with all his paraphernalia
on. I saw him once, said Dougie. He used to ride in every Thursday for his benefits. Ten gallon hat, silk neckerchief, silver spurs,
the lot. He hitched his horse to a a bus stop outside the Nash.
Fired his guns off to amuse the kiddies. That what they pulled
him in for? the Grampus asked. No, said Pat. What then? A gross
indecency, said Ben. The usual.

The Captain said good-night. Others began to doze and
mutter where they sat. Stetson took himself off to the farthest
privy, to think his sharp-edged thoughts alone. Bloater did cocoa
for those still conscious in the warm. He tret me worse and worse,
said Ape. As the days passed and the weeks Nelson's disappointment made him cruel. They were in a bedsit, let them by the
NAB. Night after night Nelson turned his face to the wall. Ape
gave himself his own relief, and in his sadness afterwards howled

like a coyote. Even asleep, though plagued by nightmares and surely needing to be comforted, if the Ape came tiptoeing across and said what's up, kid? tell us what's up, Nelson cursed at him and lashed out with a fist. Ape drank, on money paid him by the NAB, and complained to all and sundry how he had been put out of his friend's affections through no fault of his own; but it got him no sympathy, only ridicule and once or twice a beating. When he showed Nelson his bruises and said that's the thanks I get, the boy only shrugged and told him to keep his big mouth shut, Stoke was no place for pufters, and he didn't want any rough stuff coming his way, he'd finished with all that, what he wanted·was a proper family life.

It was then that the Ape began another run of suicides. But although the response he got from the general public and the authorities was good – best anywhere, he said – the response he got from Nelson was nil. When he stood there threatening death to his own person in a manner too horrible to mention all Nelson said, if he said anything, was: fucking do it then; and whilst Ape did he hid his head under the pillow.

But Ape came in one morning a changed person. Nelson was dressing, his mind on the market place, when Ape came in with a bottle of milk and a loaf of bread. He had drunk, he said, on the advice of the people at Casualty, thirty-seven cups of black coffee and was feeling fine, he had not even needed pumping out. He spoke with pity of his recent life, and said he was sorry if he had been a nuisance. He could understand Nelson wanting to settle down and he was going to make it nice for the three of them, and for the kiddy if there was one. Starting now. And he laid fresh sheets of news-paper on the table, and did some toast at the electric fire. There's a man down there at Casualty, he said, who says he'll set me up clean-ing windows. You look for Jo, he said, I'll see to everything else.

Nelson was sitting in the market place, looking for Jo, when Ape came through on a racing bike. Got this from the NAB, he said, Probation's giving me a bucket and a ladder. I'll make a few quid in the afternoons. He passed through later with a bucket on the handlebars. Ladder tomorrow, he cried. I'll get your tea. The bike was small, its back wheel hidden by his astrakhan.

Nelson came in from another fruitless day. The room smelled of vim. Two places were set on the local news. I've done us chips, said Ape. And he had cut out a picture from a magazine, of a woman and her baby at the seaside, and stuck it on the wall. I've made a start, he said. That'll do, said Nelson.

But Ape was in a fit of industry. He cleaned, he cut out pictures, he ran from the kitchen with different things and chips. Probation put him off a day or two. He rode past Nelson, clanking the empty bucket. When Nelson came in he was met with hopefulness.

She'll love this place, said Ape. You ask the Social for a double bed. He ran to the kitchen with the washing up. Nelson lay down, his face to the wall.

It ended. Ape's bike was stolen from outside Probation. He was inside, signing for the ladder at last, and when he came out the bike had gone and the bucket with it. Ape carried the ladder to Nelson in the market place. Nelson waved him aside. You're in my way, he said. When Nelson came home there was a note for him. It was on the table between his knife and fork. It said: Gone in the river. You can get your own fucking tea. But Nelson could not read it.

Nelson went out later with the little dog, as he sometimes did, on the off chance of seeing her crossing the market place, and met the Ape in drink. He had sold the ladder, he had drunk it. The pubs were coming out. That was the worst time to be on the streets, Ape being so loud. Every terror revived in Nelson, and with reason. It was like in his nightmares, having to run again. He split from Ape, the skins chose him, he would have outrun them but for carrying Billy. Not carrying Billy, he did. When Ape came home Nelson pulled the knife on him. Ape had to risk the streets. Next morning he got a warrant from the NAB, to visit his mother dying of cancer in Darlington. He can croak for all I care, he said.

But stood at the wire then with the one they call Ben Gunn, in the dark, pushing his cold nose through at the sparkling snow. Can't leave him, Benny, and that's that. On hands and knees he went through the opening behind the derelict privy. Set off again. Ben watched him do a ridiculous arc. He was bearing slowly south, he would hit the road, he would stand under the moon thumbing a lift.

13

She knocked. Can't you read? Little Hitler cried. No women in here. But she said she had come about the job of Matron which she had seen advertised in the Echo and the Chron and that her name was Miss Fortune but everyone called her Mo. In that case, said Hitler, you'll not need sniffing. She wore baggy trousers and a bright red beret, her lips were made up the same bright colour. She carried a battered suitcase on each side of which there was a sticker saying LIMA. Later the Captain marvelled at the power these yellow stickers must have had over his mind. He would almost say he had appointed her on the strength of them.

Yes, she had arrived, she said, only the week before from two years working among the down-and-outs in the slums of Lima. And she would have been there yet, she said, but for her getting hepatitis, which explained why she looked unhealthy, if she did. In Lima, she said, she had been confirmed in her aversion to strong drink by seeing so many helpless victims of it; by that and by her hepatitis. This may not be Lima, said the Captain, but our men are down and out and the drink does afflict them. He had to admit that he was impressed by her. Her earnestness was palpable; and he thought it a fact in her favour that she was wearing trousers. She named a judge and a bishop for her referees. We'll take a chance, said the Captain, trusting his instincts. And he asked Ben Gunn to show her to her room. She had a child's face, but aged.

The Captain did not write immediately to the bishop and the judge. He put it off a day and then another. By the third day there was no need. The end had come. There was a queue that morning to see the Matron. He ran his eye along them, sternly. They groaned, and pressed the parts they said were hurting; but he caught a snigger when he turned his back. Long after klaxon some were still missing from their tasks in the old morgue. Seeing matron was the answer when he enquired; and again the sniggers. The Captain gave up his piss-break to visit her himself.

The queue had gone, but where it had slouched there was a whiff of lawlessness. By now the Captain's instincts were all the other way. He knocked. The door opened. Out came Slim. Me and Mo, he said. Slim, said the Captain, you've drink on you. Mo and me, said Slim. Miss Fortune sat behind her desk. Oh, she looked odd! Her red beret, for a start. Her eyes: two coal-holes. Her mouth: plastered. In haste perhaps she had done up the buttons of her white coat out of true. She had three extra at the top, no holes for them, and by this mismatch all her childish person was thrown to one side. But she received the Captain bravely. Poor Slim, she said. He says nobody understands him the way I do.

The Captain had some notion of settling things discreetly. He closed the door. She offered him a tot from the last bottle, but without much hope; then her face collapsed, its colours ran. There was spillage everywhere, and the spirituous smell. Captain, she cried, and began to come at him round the desk; but her trousers seemed to have slipped and she fell on her knees. In a rush she got out something at least of her unhappy past – her overbearing father (a medical man), her catastrophic romance with a Peruvian apple-picker – and of how, having seen the worst and being herself one of the worst, she was curiously hopeful of working miracles among the wretched if only she could be allowed to go about it her way. Though ruined, her voice was cultured, and this, like the stickers and her wearing trousers, must have told in her favour with the Captain. My dear Miss Fortune, he cried. She had clasped his knees. Never, he admitted later in confidence to the one they call Ben Gunn, never before or since had he had his knees clasped by a member of the opposite sex. But he stood firm. It's more than my life's worth, he said. He gave her his clean white pocket handkerchief and at last she stood up, small and askew, under the portrait of the King. Now adjust your dress, he said, and I'll send the Porter for your suitcase.

A crowd had gathered in the nissen corridor. They were supporting or restraining Slim, who, in the rage of his love for Mo, was forgetting himself entirely in his language to the Captain. The Captain ordered them back to the morgue and to their duties in it. He was at fault, he knew, and his authority was slipping.

The Captain stood at the gate to see her off. He had rung for a taxi at his own expense. Then she appeared, ushered along by Little Hitler. He had her suitcase in one hand and the Ripper's lead in the other. This way, lady, he was saying. Stripped of her white coat she looked little and clownish. The sun shone at her mercilessly. She wept still, and coming to the Captain she begged him again to give her another chance. She said she understood things nobody understood who had not been where she had. But he led her to the taxi, which seemed longer, blacker, roomier than usual, and its driver more sombre. She turned before getting in and Slim, pressed with the others against the wire mesh, cried out in a loud voice that she was the only woman he had ever loved and that he was hers, if she would have him, until the Rockies crumbled and Hell froze. She made a little wave, her hand not moving from the region of her mouth.

If that was bad there was much worse to come. Discipline faltered as the Captain brooded on his mistake. He was tormented by doubts. Sometimes it seemed to him that he had let slip the possibility of a miracle. What if she were an angel after all? Siesta extended itself unconscionably, drink got in. He was woken out of a black reverie by Bluebeard and Little Hitler together at his door. Their dogs were grinning. Something to show you, sir, said Hitler. Begging your pardon, sir, said Bluebeard. The Captain feared the worst, but it was worse than that.

When he rounded the huts and peered across the old parade ground to the western fence the Captain was still wearing his reading and thinking glasses and supposed that to be the reason why he could not believe his eyes. He took in the fence and, on the sidelines, Ben Gunn in a many-coloured blanket, but the rest he could not rightly comprehend. He saw shirt tails and fallen trousers, from the back, and men against the fence as though flung or sucked there by a tremendous force, and seeming flattened. There were cries such as he had never heard before. Then out of the cover of one man, after the emission of his particular shout, came Mo in only the left leg of her trousers, and stumbled to the next man, into his cover, so that she disappeared. Strong bottles everywhere. The Captain saw her suitcase in the sun, open and its contents, bottles and women's things, all spilled. Then he approached, and began to distinguish everything. To enforce discipline he went to the wire itself and looked along it: the men were through wherever they could protrude, strangely, at all angles, at different heights, in every shape and size, all in their individual rusty diamonds, and Mo, like a bee or like a barmaid at closing time, was busily visiting them, still visiting when the Captain raised his voice and called a halt. She fell off backwards, fell off a cry that was like a donkey's, and lay in the dandelions, stramming with her legs and showing her milky bottom. Her mouth when she sat up and the Captain begged her to cover herself ran over at either side.

The men were coming away, hoisting and buttoning, some proud, some sheepish, and soon all were sheepish, except for Slim, plastered at the very centre, where he had filled with an unheard of courage. Slim began to roar, and to shake at the fence, he roared that he would marry his little Mo and that he would have the fucking fence down to clasp her in his arms. The fence heaved like the sea. Calm yourself, Slim, said the Captain, you'll do some damage, you'll open up your cuts. Slim roared that he would have the woman home, he'd see her right, she'd want for nothing in the place he was taking her. He gripped the wire with both hands at the level of his chest, he breathed in an elephant-fill of air, he troated once, and then he ripped. The fence tore slightly. Hit it, Slim, said Savage. Give me room, said Slim, I'll *destroy* that fucking fence. Your operation, Slim, the Captain pleaded. Slim came in sideways with a run-up. The rebound threw him back among his pals. Mo lay delighted in the dandelions. I'm coming, Mo, he cried, I'm coming for you, sweetheart. We don't have to live like this. Slim, said the Captain, it's government property you're assaulting, I'll have to make a report if there's any more damage. Shall I rip him, sir? Little Hitler asked. Oh, for heaven's sake no, said the Captain. Cheers and a roaring as Slim came in again. He hit the weak spot with his head. Good God, said the Captain, he's through. Bloody about the temples, the shirt ripped off his back, all his white scars displayed, he was. Oh Slim, said Mo, oh Slim, you silly man.

The Captain stood at the gaping fence. A bit of string for now, he said. I'll put in for a repair. What explanation shall I give? That poor Miss Fortune's personal things all over the ground. But she'll be back, and it's none of my business. Mo in his arms, Slim had got across the ploughlands. Soon he was on the skyline at a hole in the hawthorn hedge. Fainter and fainter his roars of love and rage. He'll be back, said the Captain, I'm sure we needn't worry. If only his cuts have not opened.

14

But who could forget the morning of Slim's departure to join his sister in a council flat in East Kilbride? It was little more than a month since he had hurled himself through the wire. Brought back in nearly dead, his shirt glued to his flesh with blood, when he could speak he said he had learned his lesson, from now on he would be thankful for small mercies – the salt and vinegar, the ketchup, the dopey fire – and not go looking for trouble, it wasn't worth it. But he was jumpy. When Gob, for a lark, crept up and farted in his sleeping lug poor Slim, done scarlet down one side by the roaring fire, clutched at his heart and opened his white eyes as wide as a squid's. He said very little. When he thought of their being discovered, him and Mo, asleep and badly soiled on a mattress in the outside lavatories in a derelict school in Pity Me, of the torch on them, he suffered grievously from love and shame. Alone then, always alone, she was found under the Horse; or with her head in the font of the church in the market place; and under the windows of Olive Daunt's Singing Academy, half undressed, she sang a love song with the little girls, until the Law arrived. It was in the Chron, a mention, and word of mouth gave details. Slim heard, though he pretended to be asleep. He covered the court case with his mug of tea. Not your fault, Slim, said the Captain kindly. But Ben Gunn said: He's afraid of repercussions. Slim said less and less.

He drank, he drank whatever he could. Cack found things on his travels and Dougie had a bottle from the Doctor for washing out his eye. Thanks, said Slim. Then worse he had a treble win at Doncaster. Loud with his luck he burst through the wire again. He suffered, like Leg, from a morbid fear of open spaces. He was most at home under the hoops of a nissen hut; the black tatie fields, the dripping sky and the unbending road filled him with dread.

So he took some company, to boost him, and hit town at a jog-trot. Though not a generous man he watered all and sundry copiously until he had momentum. In the bar there was like a blizzard of pound notes. Then, full of courage, he put all his little tug-boats off and took to the streets alone with money in his fists. Outside the Bridge he destroyed a new saloon car with his head and feet, outside the Gardener's he flattened a belisha beacon. But leaving the Elm Tree he ran out of control down the cobbled bank and hit the wall of the Fighting Cocks. This withstood him and he collapsed. The Law arrived.

The usual, with criminal damage, the Captain fetched him home. I'll put in a word for you, he said, when you come up. Say you've had emotional worries, that sort of thing. Only sit quiet now, there's a good chap. But it was then Slim remembered his sister's promise, given years ago, that there would always be a bed for him at her place. He appeared at breakfast. I'm leaving, he said.

His appearance was of an almost spectral dignity. He wore his left arm, that had borne the brunt of his charge against the wall, in a snow-white sling. His right hand gripped a valise. But his face! It glowed, it gave off heat. He had shaved too close and splashed his numerous cuts with an astringent male cologne. There was blood on his collar and on his white shirt front (the visible bib of which he had got one-eyed Dougie to iron). His tie, that of the Royal and Ancient Order of Buffalos, though oddly knotted, was speared with a bright pin. His shoes, though cracked, gleamed like broken coal.

Rising among the ruins of breakfast the company pleaded with him to think again. They advanced a score of reasons for staying put. Slim shook his head, he had been there long enough, it was time for a change, his insides were playing up and there was no doctor in England understood what their colleagues north of the border had been aiming at. Besides, he wanted to see his sister and all his little nieces and nephews to whom he had never yet given half a crown; and setting down his bag he took from his breast pocket a sepia photograph of the happy family under the Christmas tree. He passed it round. His hand was shaking, the blacking was beginning to trickle out of his hair. And where's she live? Pat asked. I used to know a tart from East Kilbride. Behind the dog track, said Slim. And spacious enough? the Captain asked. There'll always be room for me, she said, said Slim. And your court case, Slim? You don't want to come bringing trouble into your sister's home. But Slim said he'd never known 'em bother with a man gone away to Scotland. No, he said, it'll be a fresh start with my own kith and kin.

It was a fine day. Cack, eating a dandelion, had paused in his munching so that the yellow flower seemed sewn like a bright button in the hollow under his nose. Slim went so far as to wring the hands of the gatekeepers and to pat their dogs. Then, shaking his head, tempted perhaps to abandon the whole idea and see Matron instead, he picked up his case and set off down the dead straight highway into town.

15

Though it made Ben nervous when people left, especially when they did it on the spur of the moment, as they often did, without forethought, without proper provision, in the wrong clothes often, often for the wrong reasons, suddenly upped and left, though it made him nervous and, to be honest (he said) sad, sadder every time, a little bit sadder, thinking of himself and how he never had and never would, though it made him that little bit sadder every time until you'd think he must be nearly full by now, full to over-flowing, full to bursting, when the Ape left yet again though Ben was sad, nervous and sad, he was also glad because, to be honest, he wanted news of Nelson. Same as everyone else in there he read the newspapers, the Echo, the Chron, and the big letter nationals whenever one came in, he read them all under the mugs and plates and also on the kitchen floor with the wet coming through, but Nelson was never in them again, though some others were – Slugger for pissing at the Horse, Cack for a little theft of lead – but Nelson never, though by his own confession he might have been, any day, he used to say, when the Law caught up with him, for murder, but he never was, and Ben had to admit that in that sense no news was probably good news since he had never known and nobody else in there had ever known anyone in the papers for anything good. So news if it came would come by word of mouth.

To the Captain often and once, on a day of incessant rain when his spirits were very low, even to Little Hitler Ben Gunn said he was thinking of writing to his sister in Barmouth, about a room with her, and whether she could accommodate Nelson too and help him find a job in the holiday trade, outdoors if possible, fresh air being what he needed. He said the seaside would be better for him than Stoke, and the Captain agreed, despite being fond of Stoke for family reasons, and said he should certainly write the letter, but then he never did. He asked Dougie, who was always out and about, to ask the boys who said hello to him in town whether they'd lift him something from a bookshop that would be suitable for Nelson to learn from, if he came back. Dougie asked, the boys said they'd be glad to, and soon Ben had a few books given him by Dougie from the boys, in a plastic bag. Unfortunately, the books were too advanced. The stories were simple enough, being mostly about killing, but the words in them were too many, too long, too close together and too small. Pat said that was the trouble in Nelson's case. He wanted an adult sort of book, and the ones Dougie had got him were fine from that point of view, but in little children's language. But Walter said Nelson was an idiot and fairy stories was all his brain could take. There's easy words in the paper, said the Grampus with a smile, but what they say's grown-up. Dougie said Nelson would maybe get on to the books in time, and Ben, who was grateful to Dougie for going to the trouble, said maybe so, and he stowed them away in a pocket (he had scores of pockets) under the coloured blanket.

Then came a sunny day, Ben said, two or three in fact, at Easter, which was early that year, early and bitter cold, except for the two or three hot days which cheered people up. The Captain said he saw no reason why they shouldn't take their coffee out of doors, and they did, for the first time in that year. My word this is pleasant, said the Captain, hunkering down. Slim had offed with his shirt, so that they saw his tum, his folds and the long reach of his operation scars. He had always been cut open wherever he went, by doctors keen to discover why he had been opened the time before. He dozed at once, he reddened quickly, not quite instantly as prawns do in a pan, but quickly, his eyes began to puff and the blacking left his hair. The Grampus blinked, he fingered at his grizzle, his mouth had fallen open. Everyone looked much worse in the sun. Bassett, for example: his head seemed somehow enlarged. Mick took his teeth out. Can't eat with 'em in, he said. But Cack had eaten all the ginger nuts. Norman, in a collar and tie, sucked on another peppermint, his stomach was worse, much worse. They all had a wintered look. Well, said the Captain, this is just the job. Another five minutes, lads. I think I'll go and change into my blazer. N'er cast a clout, said Stetson as the Captain left them. I've seen this weather before.

They were waking, rising, beginning to trail towards their tasks in the old morgue, when Ben was called away to rinse a new arrival. Grub, he said, seeing the wheelbarrow. Grub, said Little Hitler. The Captain's not bothering with his particulars, but clean him up as best you can, and rather you than me.

Grub was a small man, smaller even than Cack, or perhaps he might have been about as big as Cack if anyone had unrolled him. It was hard to clean him as the regulations required, and Ben Gunn soon desisted. Grub would be gone again in a day or two, when somebody came to wheel him, so why bother, the Captain hadn't. The usual issue being useless in Grub's case Ben fitted him almost tenderly into a silver smock that had come, with other stranger things, by mistake to them instead of Barnardo's. Any news? he asked, for Grub had been most places, in a barrow and on public transport, and though old he was still mobile. Saw your friend Porky Pie, he said, lying on his side for greater comfort. Ape? Ape. In Stoke: a chap I know was wheeling me through the market place and there was Ape on a public bench looking very down in the mouth. He said I was lucky to see him alive, for he had just made up his mind to top himself. Ben asked after Nelson. And that was the reason, Grub replied. A tart from Boots, not one in white, you understand, but one employed after hours to clean the floors, had only five minutes since informed our friend that Nelson – with whom she remembered seeing him in the market place – had gone to Penzance after a tart she'd skivvied

with. That fits, said Ben. I went on my way, said Grub, I had a bus
to catch, but a man I met in Walkden – Jesus! what a fiend they've
got in charge down there! – told me he'd seen Ape (he was sure
it was Ape) in the traffic north of Stoke and couldn't for the life
of him decide whether the fat fucker was hitching north or south
or trying to get run over. But he never showed up in Walkden
before I pulled out. Ben said their conversation passed to other
matters then, though he could hardly pay attention for thinking
about Nelson in Penzance.

The Captain said – it was late afternoon, they were by the flagpole, the Captain in his blazer beginning to feel the chill – that if
Nelson was doing in Penzance what he had been doing in the
market place in Stoke, namely watching for his sweetheart, then
he was altogether better off and he, the Captain, felt altogether
more optimistic on his account. For though he was fond of Stoke,
having grown up there with his mother, he was in some ways
fonder still of Penzance, where he had spent a very happy holiday
with her, in a little boarding house quite near the harbour, and
as far as Nelson's personal needs were concerned, between the
two places there was no comparison: Penzance won hands down.
He must sit under the statue of Sir Humphry Davy, nowhere
else, outside the noble Market Hall, where Market Jew Street
rises into town. Everyone climbs that hill, the pavements split
either side the very handsome legs of Humphry Davy, a local boy
who made good in a multiplicity of ways. How hopeful Nelson's
future had become! The Captain remembered the statue vividly.
It had astonishingly handsome legs. He recalled that his mother
had pointed them out to him, and that she had commended the
man – a scientist, a philanthropist and a friend of the greatest men
of letters – as a model any youngster would do well to set himself.
In a matter of days, said the Captain with absolute conviction,
perhaps even in a matter of hours, if Nelson sat beneath that
statue his vantage point would guarantee success.

Left at the pole, snapping a pencil in one of his hidden pockets,
Ben Gunn, to be honest, did not know whether he wished Nelson
success or no. You Nelson? the little skivvy must have said. For
many days perhaps she had been eyeing him in the market place

as he sat there first with Ape and then alone, at last deciding he was the one – had Jo described him, his terrible coat, his ear-ring, his soft hair? – and at last plucking up the courage to deliver her message. Jo said to tell you she's gone to Penzance. Nelson's delight (the transformation of his face when he ever had anything to be glad about was like the visit of an angel), his wonder, his questions, were easy to imagine. He knew Penzance to be pretty far distant but in what direction he could not be sure, and nor could the little cleaning girl, whose name was Angie. Thanking her, whose own life badly wanted cheering up, crushing her – by now wide-eyed at her importance in this romance – against his soiled and woolly person, he hurried away, very likely in the wrong direction, to throw himself upon the charity of long-distance drivers. All this was easy to imagine. And Ben, stealing the Captain's childhood memories, seated himself under the famous statue and saw, so to speak, by staring east down Market Jew Street, Nelson come into town. Their reunion at Humphry Davy's feet brought tears to his eyes. Nelson's appearance being so odd and his face so brave, it would have been very easy to pick him out in that little Cornish town, especially so early in the year, before there were many visitors. And once they were reunited, once he no longer needed to keep to his post all day, what a fine place to idle about in the harbour would be. The harbour with its gulls and smells, in the spring sunshine.

Stetson was right about the weather. It reverted. Stetson was always right. The snow came back, the Captain resumed his fur. But he refused to be any less sanguine on Nelson's account. Nothing like this in the far south-west, he said, you can be sure of that. Coffee indoors. Says here, said Pat, milking his nose on to the page itself, says here you're twice as likely to have a heart attack doing it with a tart that's not your wife. Bad enough with her, said Bassett. I was a fortnight getting over it. In Saint Camilla's. Never again. The morgue was cold. The Captain wisely had them bat themselves before their work began. And men who had set off prematurely were brought in shivering and in one case (Bengali Joe's), stiff. Same every year, said the Captain, too impatient. He took down their particulars, card after card. All lies, he said, all lies, filing them away. When a man came in they didn't know, Pat asked him, looking askance, looking almost fearful, had he ever run the UCP on Cannon Street in Manchester? He had the complexion: soft, white, pocked. But the man said no, he'd never been near the place. Spitting image of my Uncle Billy, said Pat, and wouldn't see reason though Stetson proved that Uncle Billy, if still with us, must be over ninety and the stranger wasn't, he was a young man, only very poorly. He locked me in, said Pat. In the cold room, with the stomachs.

There was news of Ape, but very inconclusive. He had been seen in heavy traffic both north and south of Stoke, bare-headed but still wearing his astrakhan. Ben questioned the new arrivals closely as soon as they could speak. He improved the issue for exacter information. Crump, for example, got a decent pair of shoes (a magistrate's, Ben said) when he seemed to remember noticing that Ape was thinner in the face. Nobody had news of Nelson. Ben blushed to confess how deeply he would have dug into his private sack had any man gone to the trouble of spinning him a yarn. But nothing, not a word. He was forced to pin his hopes on Ape.

Ben woke and lay there. The coughs, the hawkings, the steady rattles and the murder going on in everybody else's nightmares worked him up. He rose and mooched along the western fence. The Ripper was loose, but never bothered Ben. The freakish snow had erased the fields again, under the moon there was a hard glitter. Won't last, he knew. And he forefelt with a terrible grief, a terrible disappointment in himself, the Camp's impatience, call it almost a hopefulness, when the bit of sun won through and the odd bird started singing. The roads would be crawling with deadbeats putting the best foot of their lousy two forward. No stopping them, every year. He was sure that Ape, dizzy in the traffic, bare-headed and by then perhaps in shirt-sleeves, when the sun got through would swing south with a curse; too late perhaps. For it seemed to Ben that the town down there where Nelson sat was more one to start from than to end in. The harbour troubled him. In the harbour if you hung around, if you looked willing, if you had an eager look, surely it would be easy to pick up work, on a boat, say, getting one ready for the new season and doing trips with the trippers, when they arrived. And being in work, earning a bit, to find a better place to stay, to get a decent room for a change would be an easy thing, once you had some money in your pocket a landlady would let you have a room and a bed with sheets. Lovely to wake then hearing the gulls, hearing a wind that wherever it came from had passed over the sea, how lovely to be in the little back streets that tipped down to the sea and brought you to it suddenly round any corner. Gulls hanging on the air with the clock chimes and perched, dazzlingly white and larger than imagined, on people's chimney pots, and crying. The harbour troubled him. Longing, longing to be off, off again, back again, back where it was better, off where it certainly will be better in some place not yet been to. The year every year coming up in you like the need to weep, it presses the heart, seizes the throat, prickles in the eyes, and rather than stand there weeping they don't know why, the dossers leave again on hands and knees.

It was getting light. Ben watched the queer moon losing its brilliance. A blackbird began to sing on the morgue roof. Before klaxon and flag-break there was an interlude. The bird got louder as the moon got fainter. There was maybe another on the old latrines, said Ben. Perhaps there was one on the summit of the hoop of every nissen door. There was a lot of birdsong as the moon faded. Ben put his whiskery mouth to the wire. His lips at a rusty hole, kissing nothing, were moving after the muttering in his head. Nelson had become as pale as a moon in daylight. Ben feared he would vanish like a cloud or a smudge of smoke or a bit of sail. Ben feared that the one they call Ben Gunn would be left with his mouth at the wire beginning again. So much, he said, nobody knows as much, nobody ever put it all together: Jo never did, nor the Captain, nor the Ape, nobody fitted it all together, not even him, not even Nelson, him least of all in some ways. Such a lot Ben had in his head that nobody else had in theirs. The sky by now was blue. He was keeping his eye on the bit of moon, the frail bit of moonshell, and listening to the singing, or better to say he was under the singing, better to say he was head and shoulders doused in it. The Ripper came and sniffed him curiously. Ben patted his head and the Ripper sat down by Ben.

Dog and old nutter looked at the ghost of a moon. It was an interlude. Ben licked his lips and felt for the broken pencil in his pocket. Then he said: When he came in here that day without the funny mongrel and the Captain having taken his particulars, when he came to me his rags were falling off him and I put them in a pile one by one and stood him to receive the shower. He seemed bewildered, he stood almost to attention, hands at his sides but a little lifted and a little turned my way, and smiled when the water hit his head, it flattened his hair, he was straight and tall, very white but for the weather at his throat, but for the lettering and the dove, all white but for the wrist, and that was red, twisted, raised, a nasty place, he showed it frankly, turned my way, still as a waxwork under the beating shower, firm on his feet, I scrubbed him clean, using the green soap and the regulation flannel, I washed the letters off without much heed, he didn't say don't, from head to foot I washed him clean, he was above my height, he let me, I was gentle, let me towel him with the regulation towel, when the shower was off he stood there being towelled, front and back, all over, head to toe, under, between, he never said don't, he let me, I was gentle, in our innocence he might have been my boy, he never moved, I saw the holes when I was on my hands and knees, the dimples under the ankle bone, and when he was sitting on the wooden bench I bent and touched them very gently. He let me, he began to talk.

For a complete list of Ryburn and Keele University Press titles in print, or to add your name to our mailing list, please write to Keele University Press, Keele, Staffordshire ST5 5BG, England